PRAISE FOR THOMAS ZIGAL'S
PREVIOUS KURT MULLER MYSTERY,
INTO THIN AIR

"THIS IS A FINE NOVEL. THE ACTION-PACKED
PLOT . . . NEVER SLOWS DOWN." —James Crumley

"ENGAGING AND OFTEN DARKLY FUNNY . . . .
[with] a cataclysmic climax that is both wrenching and
credible." —*The Atlanta Journal-Constitution*

"*INTO THIN AIR* IS TERRIFIC. THIS IS A BOOK TO
SAVOR AND TO ADMIRE." —Scott Turow

"A PROMISING DEBUT . . . Plot aside, what makes
Into Thin Air such a pleasure is its setting. Zigal nails
Aspen with the authority of a native."
—*The Times-Picayune* (New Orleans)

"ZIGAL HAS WRITTEN AN OUTSTANDING FIRST
NOVEL: he introduces a textured, fully developed
detective, places him in a rich environment ripe with
fictional possibilities, and surrounds him with a terrific
supporting cast." —*Booklist*

"THOMAS ZIGAL'S *INTO THIN AIR* IS A WONDERFUL MIX OF THINGS: a sleekly paced mystery, a wicked and knowing portrait of Aspen society, and a beautifully written story of a man trying to put his life back together. Zigal can be funny and he can be tender, but he also knows how to turn up the narrative heat. This is a series with a real chance to take flight!"
—Jim Magnuson, author of *Ghost Dancing*

"FAST-PACED . . . TWISTS AND TURNS ENOUGH TO KEEP THE PAGES TURNING . . . Thomas Zigal has done a fine turn in telling a gripping multiple-murder story . . . The mystery of the murders takes the novel to a high level of intrigue."
—*The Aspen Times* (Colo.)

"Somewhere between Jim Thompson's sordid Midwest and Raymond Chandler's decaying Los Angeles lies Thomas Zigal's Aspen . . . If the genre is about tough, sensitive good guys going up against venal, insensitive bad guys, *Into Thin Air* is a prime example."
—Marion Winik, NPR essayist and author of *Telling*

"SHERIFF KURT MULLER IS A RARE CREATION: a cop who feels. He loves his son, hurts for his busted-up marriage, yet navigates the murderous peaks and valleys of Aspen society like a crime-solving Tommy Moe. I loved the well-worn ex-hippie characters that populate this book, as well as Zigal's particularly skewed black humor." —April Smith, author of *North of Montana*

ALSO BY THOMAS ZIGAL

INTO THIN AIR

HARDROCK STIFF
A KURT MULLER MYSTERY

by

THOMAS ZIGAL

A Dell Book

Published by
Dell Publishing
a division of
Bantam Doubleday Dell Publishing Group, Inc.
1540 Broadway
New York, New York 10036

The trademark Dell® is registered in the U.S. Patent and Trademark
Office.

ISBN: 0-440-22452-7

Reprinted by arrangement with Delacorte Press

Printed in the United States of America

Published simultaneously in Canada

October 1997

10 9 8 7 6 5 4 3 2 1
WCD

To Annette and Danny

This is a work of fiction. I have taken occasional liberties with the history of Aspen and the geography of the Maroon Bells–Snowmass Wilderness. All characters and incidents are a product of my imagination. Any resemblance to actual events, or to persons living or dead, is coincidental.

THE EARLY MORNING chill carried a memory of winter. The air was crisp in his lungs and against his bare cheeks as he downshifted the '63 Willys, forcing the open Jeep up Summer Road, the dirt-packed service route that curled in lazy switchbacks to the summit of Aspen Mountain. Snow lingered in mottled brown patches beneath the fir groves high up the slope. The sky was icy blue, clear, flawless. On a day this tranquil it was hard to imagine how anyone, even Ned Carr, could wake up looking for trouble. But the old miner had telephoned Kurt in the middle of the night with trouble on his mind.

"Stepped knee deep in it this time, son. Cut a deal with the devil but the dirty bastard double-crossed me."

"Ned," he'd mumbled, "is that you?"

"My pride got the best of me and I tried to burn 'em at their own game. Now they're coming after me."

His speech was slurred. Kurt wondered if Ned had fallen off the wagon after all these years.

"Who, Ned?"

"I need to talk to you, son, but this ain't the time or

place. Likely there's a bug on my line. Come see me first thing after you drop your boy at school."

"Are you all right? Is Hunter okay?"

"If anything happens to me I want you to look after that little pistol."

Ned Carr's six-year-old grandson, Hunter, had lived with the old man for the past four years, ever since Ned's daughter was buried under an avalanche while cross-country skiing up Pearl Pass. Hunter was Lennon Muller's best friend.

"Ned, I have no idea what you're talking about. Are you in some kind of trouble?"

"Hunter's sleeping over at the Marcus boy's tonight. He'll be all right," Ned had said, coughing into the line, a phlegmy hack, fifty years of rolling his own smokes and breathing lead dust in abandoned shafts. "You come on by the Ajax first thing. Still wearing that badge, ain't you?"

"I'm on official leave. Six more weeks."

"I don't want to talk to anybody else. Just you, son."

Kurt wheeled the Jeep onto a rocky, tire-rut access road posted PRIVATE PROPERTY, DO NOT ENTER and drove another hundred yards up to the Ajax, the only mine still in operation in the ski area. In the 1880s, at the height of the silver boom, there were a half-dozen mines and their ramshackle headframes, a thousand promising claims, on this north slope. Sixty miles of shafts, forty levels deep, tunneling seven hundred feet below the town itself. When Kurt was a boy he had heard tall tales about the hardrock miners, their prodigious work lost to history, and he wondered if Aspen Mountain was now hollow inside, if someday it might collapse upon itself in a thunderous earthquake.

He parked next to Ned's flatbed truck, got out, and gazed down at the charming gingerbread and chimney-brick village his father had helped resuscitate after the long postmining depression. The view from here was so luminous he could see downvalley past Red Butte to the private planes rowed at the airport. The clarity of light created the illusion that he could reach out over the basin and touch his home on Red Mountain.

"Ned!" he called, walking up the hill to the shabby mine office that looked as if one good kick could dislodge the rickety platform legs and send a junkpile of rotting lumber clattering down the mountainside. Nearby, a weathered silver Airstream squatted on cinder blocks, the trailer where Ned stored his tools and dynamite.

"Hey, Ned, you home?"

He plodded up the sagging wood steps and knocked on the office door. When no one answered, he opened the door and poked his head inside. The place was empty, a white mug of coffee steaming on the scarred rolltop desk where Ned's ledgers were haphazardly stacked, his loose invoices heaped in messy mounds. Cedar branches crackled in the woodstove and the room held the aroma of coffee and a comforting warmth. Kurt sometimes brought Hunter up here to meet his grandpa after soccer practice. The office was small and rustic, the log walls as bare as a farmer's smokehouse. Scratched-up hard hats hung from the rafters by their straps. On makeshift board-shelves Ned had collected artifacts he'd discovered in the mine—rusted lanterns, pickax heads, broken shovel handles, battered boots, coins from another era.

"Ned, it's me!" he shouted up toward the shaft. "Where the hell are you?"

Nailed to the brace beam above the mine's dark adit was a worm-eaten sign from the old days: AJAX MINE, 1881. Ned Carr's last remaining stake on the ski side of the mountain.

Kurt could remember the first time Ned had walked into his life. A silent, snowy afternoon when Kurt was Lennon's age, six or seven. The grown-ups had finished skiing for the day and had decided on lunch at the Red Onion, an old miners' tavern on Cooper Street. The Mullers, the Pfeils, and Jacob Rumpf, the Chicago millionaire who had brought Otto Muller and Rudi Pfeil out to Colorado to help him transform this sleepy mining town into a modern tourist resort. The men were arguing amiably about who had won a race that morning when the tavern door banged open and Ned Carr strode into the long narrow entrance with a Siberian husky at the end of a tattered rope leash. Ned stopped and stared at their table, nine noisy flatlanders huddled over hamburgers and ranch-house stew. He was probably thirty years old at the time but looked to Kurt like a grizzled mountain man even then, his bristly face chapped from long winters, his hands venous and hard. He was wearing a red-and-black flannel hunting jacket, grease-stained dungarees, unlaced work boots with toes scuffed into mealy leather. A short, solid man, thick legs and neck, his teeth already going bad. It was the first time Kurt had ever seen someone wearing a knit toboggan cap underneath a Stetson. The strange wild sight of Ned Carr made the children shrink down in their chairs, duck their heads, and giggle.

Ned led the huge dog over to their table. A beautiful

animal with translucent blue eyes, a fluffy coat of black
and gray fur, its long pink tongue dripping friendly
slather. Kurt's brother fed it a scrap of gristle from his
plate.

"You that fella Rump from back East?" Ned asked.

Jacob Rumpf was a regal silver-haired gentleman
who had made his fortune in plastics. He was in excellent physical condition for a man of sixty. A fine skier
and fanatic fly fisherman, a trophy hunter with exotic
heads in the game room of his Michigan Avenue mansion. By that time he had purchased most of the dilapidated baby Victorians on the West End of Aspen, a
prominent hotel in disrepair, and an abandoned opera
house. Jacob Rumpf had noble dreams for his little
town.

"Mr. Carr," nodded the millionaire, dabbing his
mouth with a paper napkin, "I know who you are.
Would you and your friend care to join us for lunch?
I'm sure the children would be delighted."

"Thank you kindly, Mr. Rump, but I just stopped by
to show you something." He pulled a stiff document
from his hip pocket, unfolded the irregular creases, and
dropped the paper on Rumpf's smothered steak. "This
here's an official deed from the land office in the
county courthouse."

Rumpf glanced at the deed, then peered up at the
man standing over him.

"You folks have stuck a ski run right straight
through the middle of my mining property."

Rumpf's mouth parted in disbelief. He looked at his
two lieutenants, Kurt's father and Rudi Pfeil, for some
plausible explanation.

"You might take and buy out every dadburn clown

in this valley, Mr. Rump, but you ain't buying out Ned Carr. Go hack yourself another ski run somewheres else, partner. I got forty acres up there with my name on 'em," he said, jerking his thumb toward the shimmering white mountain visible through the tavern glass. "Your buddies with them silly-ass boards on their feet are trespassing on my private land."

Kurt could still remember the incredulous look on Mr. Rumpf's face. His staff had gone to great lengths to procure property on the mountain and establish valid leases. He retrieved a pair of spectacles from his shirt pocket, lifted the deed from the steak gravy, and read the text slowly and carefully.

"Yesterday?" The lines deepened in his face. "This indicates that the transaction took place yesterday." He lowered the paper and stared at the miner. "Mr. Carr, you must be quite a clever businessman. I salute your enterprising spirit." He smiled thinly and raised a cup of hot cocoa as a toast. "How is it you were able to come by that property?"

Even at six years old Kurt understood what was taking place. This rough-looking hick was trying to stop everyone from skiing on the mountain.

Ned Carr shrugged off the question. "A man would be making a sizable mistake," he said, yanking on the husky's leash, pulling the dog from the table, "if he took me for a fool like everybody else in this one-horse dive."

Jacob Rumpf regarded Kurt's father and Rudi Pfeil. "I can see you're nobody's fool, Mr. Carr," he said, his steel-gray eyes narrowed and gleaming. "I guess we understand each other, then."

Rumpf's organization made inquiries and discovered

that the man had simply gone to the county court-house, studied a claim-stake map dating back to the late nineteenth century, and purchased lapsed claims for five dollars an acre, his right under the Mining Law of 1872. For a mere two hundred dollars he had come to own forty acres of prime real estate in the middle of a burgeoning ski resort.

"Ned, are you in the main drift?" Kurt yelled, climbing the hill to the mine. A *nuisance claim*, that's what his father had called it. *He'll squeeze us for a pocketful of cash and then crawl back under his rock.* But forty years later the nuisance was still here, leasing out his land to the ski company for a tidy sum. Many of those winters Kurt himself had skied down Bear Paw Run, a black-diamond favorite only a stone's throw from where he was now treading.

A heavy ore car sat on a rusted, narrow-gauge track twenty yards outside the shaft. Kurt strode up to the entrance, a dark square cored into the rock outcropping, and stopped to call out Ned's name again. He couldn't bring himself to go inside. When he was a boy his friend Billy Nichols had fallen to his death down an old shaft like this one. Kurt and his brother, Bert, were with Billy that day, hiking up the mountain with rucksack lunches and canteens on their backs, playing hide-and-seek along the way. Their parents had warned them never to enter an abandoned mine but Billy was showing off, trying to impress the Muller boys. The Mountain Rescue team searched the murky ore stopes for two days before finding his body at the bottom of a seventy-foot drop.

"Come on, Ned, your coffee's getting cold!" Kurt

shouted at the tunnel. "I don't have all day. Who have you pissed off—?"

The explosion knocked him backward into the ore car. When he came to, he was jammed against the iron side of the car, blood spattered on his shirt and face. He could taste a bitter grit in his mouth. His head was throbbing and his chest hurt where something had struck him, a rock or chunk of timber beam. He blinked his eyes and looked up at the mine shaft. Oily black smoke was gushing from the hole, roiling into the clear blue sky.

"Ned," he muttered feebly. He tried to stand but his legs were rubber. There was a goose egg on the back of his skull. He wiped at the blood on his shirt, brushed a fine layer of ash from his jeans. Whatever had hit him squarely in the chest was lying on the ground beside him, smoldering like a charcoal ember. He picked it up by a dangling string but the smell of burnt flesh made him gag and he dropped the thing in the dirt. Inside the scorched work boot was a man's bloody foot and half a charred shinbone.

2

AN HOUR LATER the smoke had cleared enough for volunteer firemen and a team of EMS paramedics to enter the mine shaft wearing respirators, hard hats, and yellow asbestos suits. Holding an ice pack to the back of his head, Kurt sat in the rear of an ambulance and watched the men bring out Ned Carr one small bag at a time. The blood on Kurt's shirt was from the boot. Considering that the shaft had discharged like a gun barrel when the dynamite went off, he was lucky that a stone sliver hadn't impaled him to a tree.

"Jesus, what an ugly mess," said Muffin Brown, the young deputy who had taken over as acting sheriff during Kurt's leave. She was standing outside the ambulance, hands in the pockets of her sleeveless down vest, a department baseball cap pulled low on her forehead. Kurt hadn't seen her in two weeks. He was glad she was here.

"You had to figure that one day the law of averages was going to catch up with old Ned," Muffin said. "Anybody who fools around with dynamite that much. I'm surprised he didn't blow himself up twenty years ago."

"I'm not so sure it was an accident," Kurt said.

She turned and stared at him. "You all right?" she said. "That's a pretty big knot you got back there. Maybe a doctor should look at it."

"He called me about three this morning," he said, tossing the ice pack on the floor. "That's why I came up here. He said somebody was after him."

Muffin propped a cowboy boot on the ambulance bumper and leaned forward, resting both forearms across her knee. Kurt recognized the skepticism in those deep brown eyes. "He didn't say who?" she asked, raising a dark eyebrow.

Kurt shook his head.

"Well, that limits his enemies to about ten thousand people in the Roaring Fork Valley," she said. "Maybe we should get out the phone book and run our fingers down a page."

Kurt rose stiffly from the bench and stepped down out of the vehicle. A scarf of smoke coiled upward from the dark cavity in the mountain. Ned was just born in the wrong century, he thought. He didn't trust the modern world, and he forced everybody around him to march to his drum.

"There's a cup of fresh coffee sitting on his desk," Kurt said. "You couldn't drag Ned away from his morning coffee. He must've seen or heard something up at the shaft and went to check it out."

"He was getting old, Kurt. His mind was turning to Silly Putty. Maybe he just forgot about the coffee."

"He didn't make mistakes with dynamite," Kurt said. "He might've been a crazy son of a bitch, but he didn't take chances in the hardrock. Fifty years crawling in and out of every hole in the ground this side of Leadville, the man never had an accident."

Muffin toed the dirt with her boot. "I don't know, Kurt. The old fart was acting stranger by the day," she said. "A couple of weeks ago I had to cite him for shooting bottle rockets off the roof of that shack over there. He damn near set a spruce stand on fire."

"It was his *birthday*, for Chrissake. I hope I'm still shooting rockets off a roof when I'm seventy years old."

An older deputy named Bill Gillespie walked over to give them a report. "It's going to take a good while longer," he said, detaching the respirator from his neck. He was a tall, lanky man with sharp features and graying temples. "Must've been a dozen sticks in that charge. I don't know why the old man was working with so much pop. A whole section collapsed back in there about two hundred feet." Soot grimed the parts of his face that hadn't been covered by goggles and the mouthpiece. He looked as if he might lose his breakfast. "The EMS boys are still picking up spare parts."

"Go back in there and tell those guys to leave the detonator where they find it," Kurt said. "We need to get somebody here from Denver to take a look at the situation and tell us how it happened."

Gillespie lit a cigarette and squinted at Kurt. "The detonator," he said with annoyance, "is probably ten inches up Ned Carr's rectum. The question is, where do we find an asshole." He glanced at Muffin, blew smoke. "But that shouldn't be too hard to come by around here."

Kurt had never liked Gillespie. He was a retired career cop from Albuquerque who pined for a quaint snowcapped world without gangs or crack. Kurt shouldn't have hired him in the first place. Dick-swinging career cops never worked out in Aspen.

"You heard the man," Muffin said to the deputy. She was in no better mood to take shit than Kurt was. "We might have a crime scene here. Go tell the guys to watch their step."

Gillespie took another drag from his cigarette and flicked it away. "Yes, ma'am," he said. "I guess I'm just having a little trouble figuring out who my boss is today."

The deputy walked back up the hill and Kurt filled a paper cup at an igloo cooler, washed out his mouth, and spit. He could still taste the oily grit. "There's a cop with the Denver PD," he said. "Lorenzo Banks, best demo man in the state. He was with my brother in Nam. See if you can get him up here. He'll be able to tell us if the charge was rigged."

"My, my," Muffin said. "You're starting to sound like a cop again, Kurt. Better be careful. You might get your old job back."

Six more weeks to make up his mind, then the leave of absence was officially over. No more paychecks from the county. Fish or cut bait.

"How's your chest?" she asked.

"Sore," he said, touching the spot, coughing.

"Let me see."

He looked at her, flung the cup away.

"Let me *see*," she repeated, unbuttoning his bloody shirt. There was a purple bruise the size of a baseball on his sternum. "Ouch," she said, touching his skin gently with her index finger. "That must've hurt."

He clenched his jaw and tried not to think about the

way she had touched him one night, three years ago, in the darkness of her trailer.

"There's not much we can do here till the boys get finished with their jigsaw," she said, watching two paramedics haul out a dripping zipper bag. "Why don't you let me run you to the hospital for a quick scan?"

"I'm okay," Kurt said, buttoning his shirt. "I want to check out a few things this morning before I pick up Lennon and Hunter."

Her face lost its outdoor color. *Hunter.* An only child whose guardian grandpa they were scraping off the walls of a mine shaft. The first question that had shaken Kurt when he'd dropped the charred foot, the first real thing that had scared him: *What's going to happen to the boy?*

"Hunter can stay with Lennon and me till we get everything straightened out," he said. "Those two are real tight. He spends a lot of time at our house anyway."

Muffin was clearly disturbed. Until this moment the loss had been negligible: a cranky old man who had long ago outlived his welcome in the valley, the careless victim of a mining accident. But now there was a child to consider. Flesh and bone, orphaned and homeless at six years old.

"It's good you guys are there for him," she said.

Kurt stretched his neck. "I'll ask Dr. Hales to handle this one." The school shrink had worked with Lennon for seven months, helping him get over his fear of losing his father after Kurt was beaten and kidnapped by hired thugs last summer. "Let's go check that trailer where Ned keeps his dynamite."

The sleek Airstream hadn't passed a white stripe in

the road since Ike was president. Forty winters on this exposed slope had worn off the silver sheen, leaving the old rig the dull gray color of sheet metal. The windows were boarded up with cheap plywood. A heavy combination lock hung loose through the rusty hasp above the doorknob. "It's open," Kurt said.

The cluttered interior was dim and spooky and smelled like a marmot burrow. Animal droppings speckled the floor and the stacked, dusty cases of Du-Pont dynamite. Something small and ratlike was scurrying around in a dark corner behind the barrels of diesel fuel. Kurt didn't want to wander too far into the enclosure, where Ned had no doubt set his homemade booby traps to stop intruders. Steel-clawed devices that would snap your ankle in half, trip-wire pungi sticks. Kurt took two or three cautious steps, his boot soles gritting against the filthy floor.

"My god, what a pit!" Muffin said behind him. "Whatever we're looking for, we're not going to find it in here."

"Where is Tyler Rutledge this morning? He probably knows the inventory. Let's get him up here and see if any dynamite is missing."

Tyler Rutledge was Ned's sole mining partner, another irascible misanthrope, barely thirty years old, whose disposition improved with the solitude under a thousand tons of mountain. Ned had often complained that if Tyler had spent as much time working their two mines as he did lying on a cot in the county lockup, they would be Fortune 500.

"Tell you what," Muffin said, her eyes slowly panning the junk-heaped trailer. "Why don't you be the point man on Tyler. Him and me don't exchange many Christmas cards."

Two years ago Tyler had punched her in the jaw during a barroom brawl at Shooter's. In retaliation she'd nearly crushed his windpipe with a choke hold outlawed by law enforcement in thirty-six states. The attorneys on both sides called it even, and all charges and countercharges were eventually dropped.

"Warn the boys not to come in here," Kurt told her. "I don't want anybody getting hurt. There's enough dynamite in this place to blow up half the valley."

She backed out of the trailer into fresh air. "Did I hear the ring of authority in that command?" she said. "Sounds like you want in on this one."

He hadn't thought like a cop for nearly a year and that channel of his brain felt as sluggish and rusty as a clogged rain gutter. "I don't know, Muffin," he said. "I still haven't made up my mind about the job. If it wasn't for Ned I'd be at home right now drinking coffee and tying flies."

Ten years in office, most of them manageable years, until that business last summer. Kurt didn't want to put his son through something like that again. For months after the kidnapping Lennon had followed him around the house, sleeping in the same bed with Kurt, worried that strange men would break in again and drag his father away. So Kurt had spent his "recuperative leave" rebuilding the child's confidence, taking him on camping trips, teaching him to cross-country ski, toughening him for a world full of thorns. And now their long vacation together was drawing to a close. The department's leave extensions had been exhausted. In six

weeks Kurt would have to become a workingman again.
Somewhere.

"If you're concerned about stepping on my ambi-
tions, forget it," Muffin said as they walked down the
hill toward his Jeep. "I'm not cut out for political office.
I can't wait to get back on the beat. You neglected to tell
me how much fucking paperwork was involved in this
job. And how many Elks Club luncheons."

Kurt stopped suddenly to catch his breath, a spasm
gripping his chest.

"Don't be stubborn," she said, running her hand
through the thick hair on the back of his head, probing
the tender knot. "Go get yourself checked out. Do you
want me to come with you?"

"I'll be all right."

He sat in the Jeep and waited for the dizziness to
pass. "Get in touch with that demo guy in Denver," he
said, watching three firemen emerge from the smoky
mine shaft and tear off their respirators, gasping for air.
Poor Ned, he thought. Poor Hunter. "Lorenzo's the
best. It might take him a while, but he'll tell us what
happened."

Muffin turned her attention to the paramedics loading neatly wrapped black bags into their vehicle, stacking them like freezer meat. "I'm not convinced this was
anything but an old man getting careless, Kurt. But we
sure as hell agree on one thing," she said, a shiver racing through her small body. "Ned had his enemies."

3

HE STOPPED AT Clark's Market to buy three thick porterhouse steaks, then crossed the bridge west of town and turned off at the public schools, following the two-lane county road past the Highlands Ski Area and up the long narrow Castle Creek Valley toward the dilapidated remains of a mining settlement called Ashcroft. Miles Cunningham's cabin was hidden among the aspen groves near the confluence of two creeks. The reclusive photographer had installed a large plastic Jack-in-the-Box drive-thru intercom head at his front gate to question intruders and turn them away. Kurt stopped the Jeep several yards before the intercom's hose sensor, retrieved the .45 from under the seat, and stuck it in his belt. He was prepared to shoot the Dobermans if he had to. Or Miles.

He got out of the Jeep with the package of steaks under his arm and trotted down the barbed-wire fence line toward the shishing stream. The dogs spotted Kurt quickly and sprinted after him, barking, flaring their ears, baring yellow teeth. They looked lean and hungry, neglected, perhaps hung over from lapping bourbon out of the broken Wild Turkey bottles that littered

Miles's yard. Surly drunks, protein deficient, ignored by their master. Who could blame them for being in a nasty mood?

He ripped open the butcher paper and flung the three hefty steaks far into the brush, one for each dog. Lowering their sleek bony backs, the animals slowed down and growled at him through the fence, caught scent of the meat, and raced off to fight over it. Kurt heaved a sigh of relief and walked back to the aluminum ranch gate. He knew it was locked electronically, controlled from within the cabin, so he hoisted himself over the top and strode across the minefield of shattered glass to see if Miles was conscious this time of the morning. His surveillance cameras were no doubt tracking Kurt's every step.

When no one answered the loud knocks, he circled around to the back of the cabin and saw that Miles had finally completed his cinder-block bunker down near the creek, a project he'd begun during the Nixon years. In the early '80s, when they were on better terms, Kurt had helped him backhoe through six feet of soil to lay a cement foundation for this structure, which now resembled one of those stark concrete radio stations off a lonely prairie highway. As he approached the squat gray cube, the tangible manifestation of Miles's long slippery descent, cubit by cubit, into clinical paranoia, Kurt noticed that the reinforced steel door was open slightly, a light on inside.

"Miles!" he said, forcing back the meat-locker door. "You in here?"

A *shing* of metal, and a sudden *whish* of blade parted the air in a cold whisper near his ear. He yanked the gun from his belt, cocked the hammer.

"Jesus, Muller!" Miles said, the long gleaming blade of a Japanese sword drawn back over his shoulder. "You could've lost a fucking ear, man. What're you doing on my property?"

"Was in the neighborhood," Kurt said, trying to control the tremble in his hand. "Dropped by to say hello."

He wouldn't put down his weapon until Miles lowered his.

"How did you get past security?"

Kurt shrugged. "Red meat."

Miles glanced up at a TV monitor suspended in a corner of the room. The view from the Jack-in-the-Box head showed the grille of the Jeep visible on the edge of the screen.

"Spineless brutes," Miles mumbled, the sword resting on his shoulder. "Training them on a low-fat diet to steel their nerves. Heighten their senses. First lame temptation, they go soft on me. Tomorrow morning it's back to forced marches at 0500 hours."

The cinder walls of the bunker were lined with gunmetal-gray file cabinets, Miles's extensive photo morgue. A drawer was pulled open next to a buzzing light-table on which a dozen sheets of color slides were spread. The air was so thick from cigarette smoke that Kurt wondered if Miles had forgotten to install a ventilation system.

"Before I gut you from trachea to spleen," Miles said, "tell me why you're trespassing on sacred ground, hombre."

They were five feet apart, within swift range of the long Japanese sword. Miles wasn't backing down.

"Ned Carr is dead," Kurt said. "Blown into confetti

a couple of hours ago in the Ajax shaft. I don't think it was an accident."

Sweat glistened on Miles's high forehead, speckled his top lip, ringed the underarms of his khaki shirt. His small predatory eyes darted to the tumbler of Wild Turkey resting on top of a cabinet. The man needed a drink.

"Can't say as I'm surprised," he said, reaching his free hand for the whiskey tumbler. "The old bastard was long overdue."

Miles had been waging war against Ned Carr since the late '60s, when *National Geographic* had sent the photographer on a Colorado wilderness shoot and Ned had unloaded three rounds from a pump shotgun at Miles for trespassing on Carr mining property. Miles retaliated the next day by tossing a stink grenade full of repulsive butyl mercaptan into the shaft where Ned was working. Since those days the old miner had accused Miles of monkey-wrenching him a hundred times—pulling up survey stakes, clipping his fences, jamming gate locks, slashing the tires on his vehicles, spray-painting dire warnings across the Airstream trailer. Lightweight sabotage, most of it. Misdemeanors. Even Miles was reluctant to take credit for every suspicious offense reported in the newspaper. But Kurt had experienced the mischief firsthand. At a bachelor-party camp-out on the eve of Miles's second marriage, sometime in the mid-'70s, Kurt and his brother, Bert, had smoked too much herb around the campfire and let Miles talk them into creeping up on Ned's bulldozer and pouring sand in the gas tank. In those days half the freaks in the valley were devising dark plans to trash Ned Carr's nature-gouging enterprise. It wasn't something Kurt was proud of now, but he himself had mon-key-wrenched the old man. An adolescent prank that had cost the miner a week's income.

"If I was going to make a list of people most likely to celebrate Ned's demise," Kurt said, sliding the Smith & Wesson back in his belt, "you would be right at the top, my friend."

Miles took a long drink of whiskey and closed his eyes in pleasure, a dying man who'd found a canteen in the desert. "Haven't given Ned Carr a minute's thought in godknowshowlong," he mumbled.

"That's not what I read in the paper," Kurt said.

For the past year Ned and Tyler Rutledge had been stirring up controversy over a new access road they were bulldozing through national forest to service their second mine. The district court had determined that the road was legal under the Mining Law of 1872, and attorneys for the Sierra Club and the U.S. Forest Service were unable to block the miners from clear-cutting a half-mile swath through Engelmann spruce trees and Douglas firs.

A month ago the local newspaper had reported that the two miners had caught Miles Cunningham and an "unidentified female companion" approaching their road grader at midnight with an acetylene torch. Gun-fire was exchanged, the newspaper stated, and the two saboteurs had fled into the night. Yet no charges were filed and both Ned and Tyler Rutledge refused to elaborate on the incident.

"You know what your problem is, Muller? You believe everything you read in the rags."

Kurt noticed a camouflage tarp covering something

in an unlit corner of the bunker. "Who was the woman?" he asked, wandering over to inspect.

"I don't know what you're talking about, man. Where are you going? Hey, you toad, you're on delicate ground here. This is a U.S. citizen's private property. His inner sanctum. Take another step and I'll cleave out your liver."

Kurt jerked back the tarp. He was not surprised by what he found. Eighteen-inch bolt cutters, various wrenches, a mallet hammer, a chainsaw, three cans of WD-40, a slew of leaking spray paints, an acetylene torch.

"This constitutes an illegal search, you fascist dog! My attorney will serve your balls on an hors d'oeuvres tray for this!"

"You don't have an attorney anymore, Miles," Kurt said, bending over to dig through the boxes. "You owed him too much money and then you set fire to his lawn."

Sixty-penny helix nails, eleven-inch bridge timber spikes, number-four rebars sharpened as road spikes, military-issue caltrops for puncturing tires, three pairs of soiled work gloves, a case of DuPont dynamite. Kurt unscrewed the cap on a plastic milk jug and smelled the contents. Airplane fuel. The perfect party mixer for a Molotov cocktail.

"Miles, you've got enough monkey-wrenching shit here to send you away for ten years."

When he turned around, Miles was coming toward him slowly, a deliberate measuring stalk, the sword point jabbing the concrete floor in an ominous *tic tic tic*. Kurt stood up, his irritation stopping Miles in his tracks.

"Not mine," the photographer muttered, sipping his drink. "Holding it for someone."

In spite of the corpulent belly hanging over his silver NEVADA belt-buckle, Miles looked healthier than the last time they'd seen each other, nearly a year ago. His jowled face was ruddy from a fresh shave, his bushy sideburns trimmed, the gray fringe of hair barbered neatly around his huge ears, exposing the scar from a police truncheon in Santiago, 1973. He was wearing pressed slacks, a shiny new pair of snakeskin boots. This could mean only one thing, Kurt thought. There was definitely a woman somewhere in the picture.

"I've still got a badge, Miles. I'm thinking about dragging your crazy butt down to the courthouse and booking you for murder one. You've got about thirty seconds to give me a reason why I shouldn't."

Miles glanced down at the cache of ecotage devices. "I didn't kill Ned Carr," he said solemnly. "I didn't like the asshole, but I wouldn't do anything to hurt him physically." He stared at Kurt, as serious as Kurt had ever seen him. "There's a line I never cross, Muller."

Kurt knew where the line was drawn. Property, machines, equipment—the instruments of Ned's dirty trade. He couldn't imagine Miles setting out to *kill* the old miner. But mischief did sometimes go awry.

"How about the woman?" Kurt asked. "Maybe she tried something on her own and got reckless. How well do you know her?"

Miles drank, his perspiring face empty of expression. "No idea what you're talking about, man," he said.

Kurt slid the top off the dynamite case. Two tidy rows of DuPont Straights, long menacing tubes coated with red paraffin. A perfect set, none of them missing from the pack.

"I know this is an unpopular view around these parts, but I admired the old codger," Kurt said, lifting a stick to feel its smooth waxy texture, his fingers tingling. "Right from the start he let everybody know he was here first. These mountains were his stomping ground and he didn't back down from the greedheads who thought they could steal everything cheap."

"Like your old man?" Miles raised an eyebrow.

"My old man and everybody since."

Kurt gingerly replaced the dynamite stick in its proper slot alongside the others. "I got to know Ned pretty well after Marie was killed." Ned's daughter, her body not found until the spring melt that year. "He didn't know what to do with his grandson so he asked me to help him out."

Miles leaned a shoulder against a file cabinet for support. "Good gal, Marie," he said. "No beef with her."

"He's been raising a six-year-old boy, Miles. Now somebody has to tell the kid what happened to his grandpa. It fucking breaks my heart."

Miles sipped bourbon and gazed implacably at Kurt.

"If you had anything to do with this, I don't care how far back we go, man, I'm going to nail your ass."

Miles set the empty tumbler aside and shuffled over to examine the dynamite in the case. "Go hassle somebody else, Muller," he said, extracting the same stick Kurt had fondled. "Wouldn't put it past that weasel Tyler Rutledge. Two of 'em fought like cats and dogs. Transferred father-son animosity." He squeezed the long red stick, waved it casually like a baton. "Little prick probably did Ned in for the claim deeds."

Kurt wished this crazy man wouldn't toy with dynamite. "I'm going to back my Jeep up to the door, Miles, and we're going to load all this crap into the boot. Everything but the chainsaw and the WD-40."

"Can't let you do that, hombre. As appointed custodian I have taken a blood oath."

"Listen to me, Miles," Kurt said. "If the demolitions man tells us Ned's blasting charge was monkey-wrenched, you're the first person Muffin Brown and her boys are coming after, I can guarantee it. They've got twenty-five years of probable cause. If the Sheriff's Department finds this stuff, your butt's in the slammer looking at hard time."

Kurt watched Miles draw back his arm but didn't for a moment believe he would actually throw the stick. Suddenly it was arcing through the air, hurling end over end like a flung newspaper toward the reinforced steel door. Kurt dropped to the floor, covered his head, and waited for his brains to pour out his ears. But there was only a weak thud, then a bouncing sound like a toilet-paper roll on the loose.

"The Straights are mine," he heard Miles murmur. "Had them since Kent State. Waste of damn good money. Should've used them when the pope was here. Now they're dead as Reagan's dick. Fucking duds."

Kurt slowly lifted his face from the grimy cement floor. An old gum wrapper clung to his jaw.

"Christ, Muller. At least have the decency to leave a man his expired dynamite."

"Miles," Kurt said, rising to his knees, his entire body shuddering, "I'm leaving now to get the Jeep. If your dogs get in my way, I'm going to shoot them." He let out a deep breath. "When I get back here, if any of this stuff is missing, I'm going to cuff you and take you downtown. Do we understand each other?"

4

Kurt parked in the lot across from the elementary school and stepped to the rear of the Jeep to check the camouflage tarp secured over the load from the bunker. He had decided to store the stuff in his toolshed at home. If Miles was indicted, he would turn everything over to Muffin Brown immediately. If not, he would find a deep hole, maybe an old mine shaft, and bury this shit halfway to China.

"What's under there, Kurt, a dead body?"

Muffin had been waiting for him in a county squad car parked on the other side of an Econoline van.

"Some camping gear I don't want ripped off," Kurt said, rehooking a loose bungee cord.

"I got in touch with that guy Banks in Denver. He'll be in tonight."

"Good."

Schoolchildren were beginning to swarm out of the building, racing for the queue of idling Range Rovers where their mothers sat reading Patagonia catalogs, opening mail. Muffin watched the rowdy free-for-all under the covered walkway, the safety patrol trying to slow everyone down. "Dr. Hales said to meet her in the principal's office," she told him. "If you don't mind, I won't stay long."

Children were her only weakness as a cop. Gunshot wounds and compound fractures she handled like a war nurse, but the only time Kurt had seen her knees buckle was after they'd dug a mangled toddler out of an icy auto wreck.

Hunter and Lennon were waiting for them in the school office, sitting in the chairs reserved for behavior problems and angry parents. The principal and Mrs. Sears, the boys' kindergarten teacher, were conferring in solemn whispers near the copy machine. Dr. Sharon Hales, an attractive middle-aged psychologist with thick gray-streaked hair and penetrating blue eyes, was engaged in an animated conversation with the boys, curious about the glittery rock Hunter had produced from his army field pack.

"It's fool's gold," Hunter informed her, letting the psychologist hold it in her own hand. "I brought it for show-and-tell."

Lennon saw his father and said, "Hi Dad, hi Muffie," and jumped up to give them both a hug. He was still an affectionate child, soft and daydreamy, a strawberry blond with the same peachlike coloring as his mother. "Why are we here in the office?" he asked. "We didn't punch anybody."

"The office isn't just for punishment." Kurt smiled at his son. "Sometimes people have friendly meetings here."

"Dad, what planet are *you* living on?"

Lennon and Hunter were bright six-year-olds, outgoing, quick to laugh. Best friends, yet very different. Hunter was being raised in a remote cabin on the backside of Aspen Mountain and appeared tough, independent, almost feral; a short, thickset boy with dark features and skin bronzed from the sun. Lennon was tall and lean, awkward on his feet, his sensitive complexion easily blistered at this altitude. He preferred television to the outdoors and had somehow acquired the moody temperament of a French poet.

"It's really called iron pyrite," Hunter was telling Dr. Hales. "My grandpa gave it to me. He knows a lot about rocks."

The psychologist offered Kurt and Muffin a cautious smile and shook their hands. A somber moment passed between them. Kurt could see that this wasn't any easier on the professionals. But he trusted Dr. Hales and was enormously grateful for the way she had reassured Lennon after the kidnapping.

"Boys," she said, touching Hunter's shoulder, "let's go somewhere special to talk." She gave a confident nod to the principal and the kindergarten teacher. "Hunter, what's your very favorite place in all of Aspen?"

Hunter thought it over for a long time, his young face vexed by decision. Kurt knew what Dr. Hales had in mind. Somewhere pastoral, serene, beautiful. A babbling creek, a mountain vista, a buttercup meadow. Somewhere to help tranquilize the shattering news. He also knew exactly what Hunter was going to choose.

"My very favorite place?" the boy asked suspiciously.

WHILE DR. HALES rummaged through her handbag for more change, the two boys dug into their Happy Meal sacks, searching frantically for the plastic-wrapped prizes. Their second lunch today.

"I hope it's not the Magic School Bus solar system ruler," Lennon said. "I got that last week."

Kurt had brought Hunter to the Aspen McDonald's to celebrate their soccer victories with the team. The only occasions the child had ever eaten in a restaurant of any kind.

"I guess I should have known better," said Dr. Hales, observing Kurt at work grabbing napkins, straws, salt packets.

"Don't forget the ketchup," he told her. "It's mandatory." She looked out of place here, a nervous missionary whose plane had gone down in a primitive rain forest.

Kurt and Lennon walked outside to sit on a bench and watch the Aspen rugby team practice in soggy Wagner Park.

"Why can't we eat with Hunter?" Lennon asked.

"Dr. Hales wants to talk with him alone," Kurt said, glancing over his shoulder. The boy and the shrink had settled down at a table next to the window. Hunter was boring into his hamburger; Dr. Hales looked confused by the chaos of bags and wrappers and cup lids.

"How come alone?" Lennon asked, sipping his drink through the empty gap that had once been a front tooth.

"A terrible thing has happened, sweetie," Kurt said.

He was right, this wasn't going to be easy. Lennon had spent many afternoons with Ned and Hunter at their cabin, roaming the surrounding spruce forest, eating the old man's chuck-wagon cooking, listening to his ghost stories about Indians and fur trappers and lost treasure. Not long ago Lennon had come home elated because Ned had shown the boys how to tunnel for ore in the Lone Ute Mine.

"Hunter's grandpa was killed this morning in a mine explosion."

Lennon looked at him as though he didn't understand what his father was saying. The boy remained silent for several minutes, dragging fries through a pool of ketchup, humming as he ate. Kurt peered at the window again and saw that Hunter was still bent over his burger, eating ravenously, his small eyes fixed with a fierce intensity on the woman who was speaking to him. Kurt realized that if he'd walked into the mine shaft, Lennon would be sitting next to his friend right now, listening to the psychologist's same consoling words.

"Is Grandpa Carr dead, Dad?" Lennon asked matter-of-factly.

"Yes, he is, sweetheart. Dr. Hales is telling Hunter about it now."

Lennon turned to stare at the McDonald's window. "Then we need to get him a present," he said.

"That's an excellent idea."

"He already has a snake. And a rock collection." The boy thought it over. "Maybe we should get him a cockatoo."

"Hmm. What made you think of that?"

"They're from Australia and New Guinea. We learned about them in school. Or maybe we should get him a television. He doesn't have one."

"I like the cockatoo idea better."

Lennon watched his friend. "I don't think he's old enough to live by himself," he said.

"No, he's not. What would you think if he came to live with us for a while?"

"Great!" Lennon said, beaming at his father. "He likes to sleep on the top bunk."

"Then that's what we'll do. We'll invite him to stay with us."

Kurt glanced at his watch. He had phoned Lennon's mother from the school and asked her to meet them here. Meg had returned to the valley last August, in time to walk Lennon to his first day of kindergarten. She lived fifteen miles downvalley in an old farmhouse with a Zen master and four friends.

"How long can he live with us, Dad?"

"As long as he wants."

Lennon chewed his fries, lost in consideration. "Until Mom has another baby?" he asked.

He had wanted a brother or sister for some time now. Kurt didn't have the heart to tell him the truth. "Whatever works out," he said.

When Kurt looked again at the window, he saw that Dr. Hales was holding Hunter in her arms.

5

MEG RUSHED TOWARD them across the cobblestone terrace, breathless and visibly upset by what had happened. She gathered Lennon to her body in a smothering embrace, then opened her eyes and stared dolefully at Kurt. "Where's Hunter?" she asked, on the verge of tears.

"With Dr. Hales." He nodded at the McDonald's.

He watched her eyes roam toward the window and understood what was constricting her heart. Only six years old, his mother dead, now his grandfather. Alone in the world. Lennon was a lucky, lucky boy.

"I'm really glad you can be with us today, Peaches," he said.

"Yeah, Mom!" Lennon added. "Let's all go feed the ducks at Hallam Lake."

"Sure, baby," she said, squeezing him again. They shared the same light pattern of freckles across the nose.

"I would join you guys," Kurt said, "but I've got some follow-up to do."

Meg stood up and pressed Lennon against her jeans. "Are you working this as a case?" she asked, a mild reproach in her voice.

She had never taken seriously Kurt's career in law enforcement. Better than anyone else she knew he'd run for sheriff as a lark. But now, eleven years later, the humor had worn thin, the joke was old and stale. He studied the disapproval in her blue-green eyes and realized she would always think of him as the bare-chested hippie she'd met at Crater Lake in the early '70s, the carefree spirit whose only ambition was to ski hard and leave a well-tanned corpse.

"Muffin thinks it was an accident," he said. In their phone conversation he had mentioned Ned's call. "I'm the only one with a wild hair."

"I thought you were giving up the cop business, Kurt." Her eyes narrowed, her head tilted in a familiar wary angle, the same old passive rebuke. One of the many reasons for their breakup. "What are you doing this for?"

Hunter and Dr. Hales were emerging from the McDonald's hand in hand, ambling toward them in a slow mournful procession. Hunter was carrying the Happy Meal toy like a dead bird in his upturned palm. His face was lined and drawn, hard as an ax blade, his eyes so puffy he could've been in a fistfight. He looked older, too old to inhabit that small body.

"For him," Kurt said.

6

TYLER RUTLEDGE HAD not shown up at the Ajax site this morning, and that had caused Kurt some concern. He was still thinking about what Miles had said. Maybe this was a partners' feud.

He knew that Tyler usually came down from the mine at three in the afternoon to begin his drinking, a ritual that dispatched him round to round through the few Aspen bars still hospitable to Skoal-dipping ranch hands and dusty construction crews. Kurt tried Little Annie's first. No one had seen the miner, so he walked around the corner to Shooter's Saloon. The place was empty except for a gangly, slick-haired bartender sweeping cigarette butts off the dance floor. The man told him he'd eighty-sixed Tyler a week ago after a scuffle during the Cotton-Eyed Joe and wouldn't allow him on the premises. A stool fly at Cooper Street Pier complained that Tyler still owed him fifty bucks over a Super Bowl bet. A waitress at O'Leary's Pub said she intended to kick Tyler's skinny butt for stealing her tips. Three migrant workers shooting eight ball in Thurman Fisher's pool hall called Tyler a *pendejo*, a *cabrón*, and a poor loser. There was no sign of him at the Jerome Bar or the Flying Dog Brew Pub, and not a single kind utterance from the querulous regulars who, to a man, wished Tyler Rutledge would go fuck himself, a toast guaranteed to raise every glass in the house. Kurt eventually grew tired of the smoke and wisecracks and the treacly smell of booze and wandered over to the pedestrian mall to sit on a bench under the cottonwoods and breathe the clean, warming air. His chest was stiffening up on him and the knot on his head was beginning to throb. Muffin was probably right, he should see a doctor, take something for the swelling. He was pondering how to get his hands on a Darvocet scrip when a pair of hardy European backpackers tromped past him dragging their huge Siberian husky by a rope leash. And then Kurt remembered the most likely place of all.

The Red Onion was still there on Cooper Street, a narrow, redbrick tavern known as Gallagher's Saloon during the mining era. Modern glassy boutiques and Nordic sport shops now wedged the vertical façade into a seamless wall of mercantilism and the old building no longer maintained its conspicuous presence, tall and dominant, in a sleepy mountain village buried under snow. Kurt considered the Red Onion a lost relic, easily misplaced among the many perishing keepsakes from his youth.

Walking under the canopy entrance and into the bar he felt a momentary rush, the past searing through him like heat trapped behind an attic door. It was as if he had never left that day in his childhood when Ned Carr and his dog appeared at their table. Everything was the same—the cracked tile floor, the long Western bar with its buckled mirror and imperial rows of liquor, the cramped wooden booths off to the side, the greasy aroma of ranch-house stew. Kurt gathered his wits and had a quick look around. Tyler wasn't here either.

"How's it hanging, Kurt," nodded the bartender, a stout bearded man with the shoulders and chest of a stevedore. Frank Jaworski was considered the best mountaineer in the valley. Every winter he left his bartending job to spend a month as a climbers' guide in the French Alps.

"I heard about Ned. What a shame." Jaworski was the first person who sounded as if he meant it. "What the hell happened?"

"Not sure yet, Frank. Have you seen Tyler today?"

Before Jaworski could respond, a gummy, drawling voice said, "That boy's done shit in his chili. Won't find him around these parts anymore."

An old-timer named Tink Tarver was sitting under a wagon-wheel chandelier at the far end of the bar, making use of the light to fool with an oily motor he had disassembled on a spread of newspaper. His hands were black with grime, and there was a long smear of grease across his beaklike nose. Kurt had never seen Tink Tarver in any other condition. Soiled khaki pants, muddy work boots, holes in the elbows of his flannel shirt, his chin shiny from tobacco juice. The town eccentric, a junk man and inventor by trade, opinionated, surly, at odds with everyone who crossed his junk-digging path. Once a week for the past thirty years the local newspaper had printed his belligerent letters to the editor—amusing, erudite missives attacking everything in modern civilization from fluoride to microwaves. He had been Ned Carr's only friend by virtue of age and elimination. No one else could tolerate the two men, and they in turn often quarreled over the petty grievances that occupy cranky minds, more than once coming to blows.

Kurt walked back toward the old junk man. "I'm sorry about Ned," he said.

"What're you sorry about?" Tink said in his usual irascible manner. "You didn't do it, did you?"

Peering through jeweler's glasses, Tink employed a long-handled screwdriver to probe at the motor—something from a refrigerator, a lawn mower—his attention riveted on the dangling wires. He wasn't wearing his false teeth today and his mouth had caved in so deeply his nose almost touched his chin. Wide ears protruded under a rakish navy-blue beret, his peculiar trademark, and decades of bad weather had carved enough troughs and crevices in his face to qualify those features for a farm subsidy.

"When was the last time you talked to Ned?" Kurt asked, sitting uninvited on the stool next to him.

"I don't keep a calendar, son," Tink said, prying open the motor's casing with his screwdriver. "Couple weeks ago, maybe."

Near his legs rested an old Radio Flyer wagon, its faded red finish pocked with rust bubbles. He dragged that wagon around town wherever he rambled, searching through trash barrels and Dumpsters for rubbish to tote back to his fix-it shop near City Hall. Today the wagon was loaded with a toaster, a digital alarm clock, a rolled-up bamboo curtain, three crusty paintbrushes, and several scraps of baseboard.

"Did he seemed worried about anything?" Kurt asked.

"Yeah. His hemorrhoids was acting up."

What was it Ned had said on the phone? He'd cut a deal with the devil.

"Like maybe about—" Kurt was groping for something. He didn't know what. "About a business arrangement?"

"A *business* arrangement?" The absurdity of the idea prompted Tink to raise his glasses and look directly at Kurt. "Oh, yeah, the old sombitch had backers lined up all the way to Timbuktu. One time him and Prince Charles of England was going fifty-fifty on the Ajax. Another time he told me Liz Taylor come up to look things over, write out a check. To hear him talk, he was always just two shovels shy of the Comstock Lode. I guess that's why he lived so high on the hog."

Kurt smiled. "Was he getting along okay with Tyler?"

"Hell, I don't know. Ask the little shitass hisself, if you can find him."

This was going nowhere. Kurt should have known better than to even try. He stood up and nodded goodbye to Frank Jaworski, who was pouring the old man another draft from the tap.

"See ya, Tink," Kurt said. "Enjoyed the genial conversation."

He was halfway to the door when the old man called out something. "Bonedale," Kurt heard him say.

He stopped and turned around. These old-timers were strange men. Ned's friend for forty years, not one hint of emotion over his death.

"The Black Diamond in Bonedale," Tink Tarver said. He was hunched over the motor again, tapping and prying. "Only beer joint in the valley that'll still put up with that pissant."

7

CARBONDALE. THE NAME alone described how the place might have looked a hundred years ago, a layer of fine black soot settling over every leaf and pasture when coal was mined in the nearby hills, fired in beehive coke ovens, hauled by wagon to this small railroad spur on the Denver and Rio Grande Western line. The short strip of redbrick buildings remained intact, thirty miles north of Aspen, now mostly gentrified bean-sprout cafés and antiques shops for the meandering tourist. The real commerce had moved out to the highway, supermarkets and video stores, and the industrial yards that serviced local hay farmers who drove their pickups into town on Saturday mornings for butane and cattle feed.

Kurt parked his Jeep in front of the Black Diamond, a corner saloon whose upstairs boarding rooms had offered women for sale in the old days, a few convenient steps from the D & RGW depot. Now the Black Diamond was a no-nonsense shitkicker bar without the usual bubbling beer signs and animal heads. The stark concrete floor and cracked plaster walls gave the place the feel of a warehouse for damaged spirits.

Tyler Rutledge was arched over a warped shuffle-board table, sliding his puck back and forth in the saw-dust, working up a rhythm before letting it fly. Three young Latino men stood nearby, studying his moves, teasing him in Spanish. Nine thousand migrants had appeared in the Roaring Fork Valley over the past four years, and though most of them worked in Aspen as waiters and maids, they lived downvalley in affordable trailer parks and old rental houses.

"You going to take all day, *carnal*?" one of his oppo-nents goaded Tyler.

Tyler's arm stretched in a smooth release and his red puck sailed down the long, blond-wood lane, splitting two blues, cracking them both into the gutter. A roar of disbelief went up from the Latinos. Grinning slyly, twirling one end of his waxed handlebar mustache, Tyler fetched a Moosehead bottle and tilted back his head for a guzzling victory drink.

"Nice shot, Tyler," Kurt said, walking slowly toward him.

When he saw Kurt, the young miner spilled a little down his chin, wiped himself with a shirtsleeve.

"How about I buy you another round at the bar?"

"Middle of a game here, Muller," Tyler said, his eyes dancing about, searching for the nearest exit. "Got some serious business going."

Kurt noticed the dollar bills wadded in two piles on a nearby table.

"I've got some serious business of my own," Kurt said, grabbing Tyler by the collar of his denim work shirt. "Let's have a drink together."

Tyler put up no measurable resistance. Kurt was eight inches taller, seventy pounds heavier, sixteen years smarter. He escorted the young man to the initial-carved bar and found the only two adjoining stools with functional seats.

"If you try and run on me, Tyler, I'm going to chase you down and kick your scrawny ass."

Tyler caught the bartender's eye and pointed to his Moosehead. "I never run on a sport that's buying," he said.

He was a small-framed man whose exceptional strength and agility were well suited to the narrow stope-work of the mines. Ned Carr had often bragged that Tyler could handle a pickax, a pneumatic drill, and an ore car better than any hardrock stiff twice his size.

"I think you know what happened to Ned this morning," Kurt said, sipping dark ale from a glass that tasted like cigarette butts.

"Yeah, I know," Tyler said, biting at his bottom lip. He removed his stained John Deere cap and placed it on the bar, expelling a deep breath. "I was on my way up the mountain when I saw the smoke and all the emergency rigs. I couldn't handle it, man."

"He's dead, Tyler. Dynamite. How did that happen?"

Tyler scratched his scalp. Stiff, sweaty hair curled on his collar. He looked as if he hadn't had a shampoo since the last time his mother held him over a sink.

"The old bird was getting sloppy. His eyesight was poor but he wouldn't wear his glasses in the mines. I told him not to set any more charges unless I was there to check 'em. Stubborn fool thought he could do everything by his own self."

Tyler had grown up in the back rooms of a trading post near Old Snowmass. His parents sold thermal clothing and outdoor gear, taught cross-country skiing, raised sled dogs. When Tyler was eleven years old, Ned Carr came into their store for his winter supplies and the boy told him he intended to become a prospector when he grew up. Tyler had read Jack London and two dozen books about the history of silver mining in Colorado, the Forty-Niners and Sutter's Mill, the Comstock Lode. Ned was amused by the boy's enthusiasm and gave him one of the silver nuggets he carried in his leather pouch. He invited him to tour the Ajax Mine, and the following weekend Tyler showed up with a tent and a bedroll. For the next seven years he shadowed Ned's every footstep through the dark shafts. The day after Tyler graduated from Aspen High, he went to work for Ned breaking rock.

"Ned called me in the middle of the night," Kurt said, "worried that somebody was after him. Four hours later he was fried." He crooked his finger at the bartender, a graying, ponytailed dirt-biker named Skank, and asked for a clean glass. One that hadn't been soaking in mop water. "You know anything about that? Was somebody down his neck?"

Tyler shook his head, his lean hard face showing fatigue. "He was always in some kind of shit, man. Bill collectors, the Infernal Ripoff Service, the fucking Freddies." The U.S. Forest Service. "Every time he turned around, the pimps at the Skicorp were siccing their lawyers on him, ragging him over the ski lease and doing their best to weasel out of the money they owed. The goddamned tree huggers have been trying to shut us down since Christ was a cadet. Somebody down his neck?" He laughed bitterly. "Take your fucking pick, man."

Skank brought Kurt another ale and waited for approval. This one tasted like barfly lipstick but Kurt gave up and waved him off.

"He said he'd been double-crossed. Any idea what he was talking about?"

Tyler drained two inches from the beer bottle. "I'd like to meet the man who could put one over on Ned Carr."

Kurt stared at the cuneiform of initials etched into the oak surface near his coaster. "It looks like someone did," he said. "Now I want you to tell me everything you know, Tyler. Front to back. Let's do this the easy way, shall we? I would rather not have to drag your butt back to Aspen hog-tied to the hood of my Jeep."

"This ain't Pitkin County, Muller. It's Garfield."

"I guess you don't know me very well, son. I have been known to bend the rules."

Tyler gazed for a long time at the Moosehead bottle sweating in front of him on the bar, then finally shifted his upper body to look at Kurt. His red-rimmed eyes were angry and resolute. "I loved that old man like a daddy," he said, a sudden huskiness creeping into his voice. "Somebody messed with him, I'm going to cut their throat. It's that fucking simple."

Kurt hoped Tyler wasn't foolish enough to try and settle this on his own. He didn't cherish the idea of trailing after the little hothead while the assault charges started piling up.

"Who was the woman with Miles Cunningham?"

Tyler's attention was diverted to the tavern door, where a half-dozen men wearing identical cammo flak jackets had just entered. "I don't know. Some gimpy chick," he said, reaching for his cap. "Gotta go take a whiz."

He slid off the stool but Kurt caught his arm and sat him back down. "In a minute," he said. "Right now I want you to tell me what was going on up there on your access road. The newspaper mentioned gunplay."

"Ask that asshole Cunningham," Tyler said, pulling the cap's bill low on his forehead. He seemed more restless now, fidgeting with his mustache, his eyes darting back toward the men's toilet. "Fucker was out there trying to cut our grader into sardine cans."

"Well well well," someone said in a loud booming voice, one of the men in cammo standing near the entrance. A crash helmet tucked under his arm, the husky dirt-biker made his way back toward them, road dust puffing from his fatigues, his large bearded face flushed from this unexpected discovery. "Look who's here, boys! Our favorite mine rat! Must be our lucky day."

He set the helmet on the bar near Tyler and laughed again, a deep happy growl like the roar from a dancing bear. "Didn't ever expect to see us again, did you, mine rat?"

Kurt now understood why Tyler kept glancing toward the toilet. There was a window in there just large enough for a mine rat to slip out.

"What's the matter, fella? Cat got your tongue? You didn't seem so timid that day behind a twelve-gauge shotgun." He was a big son of a bitch, at least 250 pounds, a thatch of coarse hair on the back of each hand. His dark beard flowed down his neck into the cammo jacket. "Hey, boys, this is the gopher turd that trashed Harry's bike! Him and that crazy old man."

His five comrades swaggered back to join the fun. Sewn to each man's jacket sleeve was a patch depicting

a dirt bike surrounded by the words THE AUTOBAHN SOCI-
ETY. Kurt had heard of them and their lame redneck
pun. A gang of mindless yahoos out of Grand Junction,
insurance men and plumbers who spent their weekends
in the mountains, buzzing up and down nonmotorized
hiking trails, scaring off backpackers, their noxious gas
fumes lingering for hours in the woods. Nobody liked
dirt-bikers. Not even the macho bow hunters.

"You owe me for that bike," said a short fat man, his
dust goggles pulled up high on his blistered forehead.
"It was brand spanking new, junior."

Harry looked a little softer than the others, a dentist
maybe. He needed sunscreen. In a couple of days his
entire face and ears and the dome of that melon-shaped
bald head were going to peel off in long papery strips.

"You can have it back," Tyler mumbled, hunching
his shoulders slightly as though expecting a blow. "I
can't use it anymore."

"So you admit you did steal it, you fucking little
mine rat!" Harry the dentist was incredulous.

"Confiscated," Tyler corrected. "Impounded."

Kurt realized that Harry and his riding club had
made the mistake of trespassing on Ned's mining property with their obnoxious noisemakers. They weren't
the first intruders to feel Ned's wrath.

"So where is it, butthole?" Harry demanded.

Tyler studied his beer. "Me and my partner dug a pit
and set it on fire and roasted some marshmellers over
it." He looked up at the men who had gathered close
by. "You boys ought to try it sometime. Flavor's a mite
gassy, but you get used to it."

They had surrounded Tyler now and were not

amused. "Get a rope!" roared the bearded biker. "Let's show the mine rat our favorite kind of drag race!"

His buddies laughed darkly, punched one another on the arm.

"Hey, you. Beard," Kurt said. "I'm trying to have a private conversation with this guy. Do you mind?"

The gathering grew silent. The Beard shoved off from the bar and set himself in a wide stance behind Kurt's shoulder. "Who is this big pile of shit?" he asked Tyler. "Your bodyguard, mine rat?"

Tyler sipped his beer. "He's a cop, Einstein," he said without looking up. He peeked at Kurt under the lowered bill of his gimme cap. "Or used to be."

"Well well well," the man said. He folded his padded arms and glared at Kurt. "A use-to-be cop. I guess that gives us something in common, mister. I'm in the cop business myself. Makes us damn near blood kin, don't it?"

Kurt glanced over his shoulder at him. Rent-a-cop. Security guard. A hard-on every night wearing his holster and badge. "I said I'm having a conversation here," he said. "I would appreciate some privacy."

The man turned to his buddies and laughed defiantly, his meaty cheeks beaming. This was the most fun he'd had in months. "The big guy's getting greedy!" he sneered. "He wants the mine rat all to himself!"

The others laughed, too, shifted about nervously. Kurt could see they weren't bar fighters, just weekend cowboys out for an adventure on their dip-shit scooters. Anything to make them forget they installed aluminum siding for a living in Grand Junction. The Beard standing over Kurt's shoulder was the only real threat.

"We got us a conflict here, Mr. Use-to-be," he said.

"This little peckerwood destroyed valuable club property, and we have very clear guidelines dealing with that kind of antisocial behavior. Specific policy in our by-laws. A sacred code."

His buddies grumbled in agreement, exchanged conspiratorial whispers. Their code had been tampered with.

Kurt swiveled slowly on the stool until he was eye level with the dirt-biker's sternum. "I have to be honest with you, brother," he said. "I'm starting to get bored with this. You're logging in on my time."

The Beard's brow was as prominent as a rock overhang. He narrowed his gaze at Kurt, his small eyes sinking farther into the dark recess of bone. "And what the fuck do I care about your time, Mr. Use-to-be?" he said.

Kurt looked at the bartender standing several feet away, both hands braced against the oakwood scrolling of the bar, his shoulders stooped, observing this interchange with a cigarette dangling from the corner of his mouth. Kurt wasn't sure whose side Skank was on. "Why don't you do everybody a favor and ask these gentlemen to walk away?" he said to him.

"Not my movie," Skank muttered, wagging his hands to absolve himself of any involvement. He turned his back and ambled farther down the bar.

"I guess it's just you and us and the mine rat," said the Beard. A vein bulged on his forehead as he stooped closer to breathe on Kurt. "You want to flip for him?"

"Your math is a little off, my friend," Kurt said. "It's you and me and this tube of pepper spray in my pocket."

The man straightened his wide shoulders and

squinted at Kurt, glanced uncertainly at his buddies. "Girl stuff," said a lanky rider wearing a Rockies baseball cap pulled tightly over long stringy hair. The others laughed.

"Hell, let's just forget about it and have a drink," said Harry the dentist. He had had enough excitement for one day. "I think I'm starting to dehydrate."

"Stop being such a wuss, Harry," said the lanky guy. His snarly hair and cap looked all of one piece, a clown's wig. "This prick shot at us with a shotgun and fucked up your bike. You leave your balls at home today, man? It's payback time."

Something in the shift of tension must have struck Tyler as critical. He chose this moment to break for the toilet but the Beard was surprisingly quick and cut him off, throwing a shoulder, tackling him to the floor. Kurt slid off the stool in a hurry, tugging the small container out of his pocket. He sprayed the three closest dirt-bikers and they clutched their faces, screaming, knocking over chairs as they stumbled backward, dropping to their knees. Pepper spray was nasty stuff, worse than Mace. Their day was ruined.

"Hey, whoa, hey, don't do it!" Harry cried out, wiggling his hands in front of him. He and the last biker backed quickly away from Kurt. "We are not a problem," Harry assured him, extending his arms in surrender.

The pungent mist lingered in the air, drifted around them in a bitter vapor. The Latino shuffleboard players jerked their shirts over their faces and rushed for the door. Kurt had caught a whiff of the spray himself and his eyes were beginning to burn. "Better fill up your sink," he shouted at Skank, who was fumbling around for something underneath the bar. "These boys need to stick their heads in some water. It's the only thing that'll help."

When he turned around, he saw that the Beard had trapped Tyler in a headlock on the floor. Kurt seized the man by the bushy hair. "Let him go," he said, pointing the sprayer at his eyes.

The biker released his grip and raised his hands. "Easy," he said.

Tyler was up on his feet immediately, adjusting his cap, wiping grit from his cheek. He kicked the biker in the ribs and the guy moaned, curling into a ball.

"That's enough," Kurt said, shoving Tyler toward the door, where Skank was waiting with a sawed-off ax handle. The bartender tapped it against his bony thigh, a steady, menacing cadence. He looked unsure of himself, unresolved about his role here.

Kurt bent down to advise the three men writhing on the floor. "Water," he told them. "Find a garden hose, or stick your head in a sink. You'll feel better in a couple of hours."

When they neared the bartender, Skank spread his legs and gripped the ax handle with both hands, like a cop with a billy. Tyler grabbed a chair, lofting it back over his shoulder. "Get out of the way, Skank, or I'll take you out," he said.

Kurt yanked the chair away from Tyler, took his arm, and escorted him past the bartender, brushing Skank aside with a persuasive forearm. "Get serious," he said, staring the skinny man in the eyes. Skank exhaled a shaky breath and backed off, searching desperately for the cigarette pack in his shirt pocket.

* * *

OUTSIDE, KURT SQUINTED painfully into the bright afternoon sunlight, relieved to breathe real air again. Six mud-caked dirt bikes rested against their kickstands like a formation of battle-weary recruits. He found a faucet protruding from the side of the building and soaked his handkerchief under the tap, pressing the cool wet cloth against his face. A bruise on his chest, a knot on the back of his head, now his eyes. He was going to be a lot happier when he was miles away from the Black Diamond Saloon and this day was over.

"Where's your truck, Tyler?"

"Back in Basalt," he said, rubbing at the red finger marks on his throat. "Came with a chick but she got pissed about something and split on me."

"Having a bad decade, man?" Kurt squeezed the handkerchief over his head, dribbling water into his hair. "Come on, I'll give you a ride."

They were almost to his Jeep when the tavern door flew open and the entire force of enraged dirt-bikers spilled out onto the sidewalk. The Beard had appropriated Skank's ax handle. He marched directly to the Jeep, his eyes fierce and unforgiving. "Eat this, asshole!" he howled, smashing Kurt's headlight with a furious swing.

Kurt pulled back the tarp in his backseat, jerked the lid off the dynamite case, and grabbed a DuPont Straight with a long attached fuse.

"Give me your lighter, Tyler."

"Unh-unh, man."

"Give it to me now or I'll leave you here."

Tyler reluctantly handed over the plastic Bic bulging

in his jeans, and Kurt lit the fuse. "Get your redneck butts back inside the bar," he told the congregation, "before this gets real ugly."

The fuse hissed loudly, a slow sulfurous burn. Kurt had no idea how much time he had before the flame reached the cap and everyone realized it was a dud.

"Jesus," Tyler said, his eyes wide, fixed on the burning fuse. He was the only one here who knew how much damage they were talking about. "Put that damn thing out, Muller. You're scaring me."

When Kurt looked up again, he saw that everyone had disappeared except the big guy with the ax handle. "It's your move, pardner," Kurt said, walking over to the collection of dusty Yamahas and lodging the fizzing dynamite stick between the spokes of a bike. "Now why don't you say you're sorry about that headlight and let's get on with our lives."

The biker stared in disbelief at the sputtering fuse rammed between the spokes. "Fuck you, man," he said. "You don't have the stones for this."

Kurt walked back and slid his long legs into the Jeep. "Next time try to sound more convincing," he said, cranking the engine.

Tyler was staring at the fuse, primitive man mesmerized by the magic of fire. Nearly half of the detonating cord was already gone.

"Better get in the Jeep, Tyler. I'm leaving."

As they drove away, Kurt adjusted the rearview mirror and watched the Beard extract the dynamite stick from the bike spokes and stomp on the blazing fuse. When it wouldn't snuff out he raced with the smoking stick toward the huge industrial Dumpster next to the building.

"Are you out of your fucking mind?" Tyler whined. He turned around in his seat to witness what was happening behind them. "That shit's not Play-Doh, man. You could have killed us all!"

"Relax, Tyler," Kurt laughed. "It's a dud."

Tyler toyed with his waxed mustache, blinking nervously.

"The whole box," Kurt grinned. He watched the dirt-biker hurl the stick into the metal Dumpster and sprint back to dive under a parked van. "I'm not kidding. It's bogus stuff. Worthless."

The sudden explosion ripped out the sides of the Dumpster, launching jagged metal panels thirty feet away. The ground shook, garbage rained down, a thick cloud of dust billowed high above the building.

"Uh-oh," Kurt said, slowing the Jeep. Time to have a serious talk with Miles Cunningham.

He stopped the vehicle and got out. The Beard was crawling out from under the Dodge van. He stood up and studied the wreckage with his hands on his hips. The others were outside now, Harry and the boys shouting irately and pointing at the smoldering warps of metal.

"Where are you going, Tyler?"

"I'm not riding in that Jeep," Tyler said, jerking his thumb at the tarp. He had hopped out and was heading off up the road toward the farmland outskirts of Carbondale. "I ain't goin' nowhere with you, Muller."

Kurt watched the big dirt-biker turn and glower up the road at him. Shielding his eyes from the sun, he raised his cammo sleeve high in the air and gave Kurt the finger.

"Suit yourself," Kurt said. "Those scooter boys will

be coming along any minute now. Maybe you can hitch a ride with them."

Tyler kept walking. "I'll take my chances," he shouted back over his shoulder.

Kurt slipped the Jeep in gear and edged up the road to roll alongside the young miner. "We didn't finish our conversation," he said. "You owe me some consideration, pal. By now they'd be dragging your ass behind one of those shitty bikes by a tote rope."

Tyler didn't respond, didn't look at Kurt, kept walking.

"Don't make me get out of this Jeep, son."

Kurt heard how his words sounded, the fatherly admonition reverberating back through his head. He saw a fleeting apparition of Lennon hitchhiking along a country road ten years from now, bitter and petulant, running away from home. His old man had finally driven him over the edge.

"Who was the woman?" Kurt asked him. "You owe me that much."

Tyler spoke without moving his eyes from the road ahead. "Get out of my life, Muller," he growled.

Lennon in ten years. Same attitude, same punishing rebuke. Kurt wondered if he should consider a good military academy while there was still time.

"Come on and get in," he said, his voice softer now, more conciliating. It was always this way with his own son. Bark and back off. "It's a long walk to Basalt."

8

TYLER'S FORD PICKUP sat in front of a rundown trailer house with geraniums withering in a flower box under the tin-foiled windows. The truck's windshield was spiderwebbed where someone had struck it with the baseball bat that lay in the tall weeds nearby.

"Fuck a duck," Tyler said, rubbing his day-old whiskers with a weary disbelief. He was making no effort to get out of the Jeep. "Girl's got a hair trigger, don't she? What's the difference between a chick with PMS and a pit bull?"

Kurt pinched the flesh between his eyes.

"A little lipstick," Tyler said.

Kurt left the engine idling in case the girlfriend decided to come outside and take another swing at the windshield. Or at them. "There's something that's been bothering me, Tyler," he said. "You know there's an accident up at the Ajax, maybe Ned's hurt, maybe he's dead. And your response is to pick up this gal here and head for a bar to drink beer and play a merry round of shuffleboard."

"Call it the Irish in me."

Kurt grabbed his ear and twisted. "Listen to me, you

chucklehead. I'm in no laughing mood. You think those dirt-bikers were a nightmare, wait till you spend eight hours in a talk tank with me and Muffin Brown."

"Oww," Tyler grimaced, slapping Kurt's hand away, stumbling out of the Jeep. "I'm turning you in for police brutality, Muller."

"Do that. Sit down at a tape recorder with my investigators and tell them all you want. Starting with why a man goes off partying when he knows his partner might be dead."

Tyler stood for several moments in silence, hands in his pockets, observing the damage to his pickup with a haggard resignation. MINERS DO IT DEEPER, said one bumper sticker. NUKE JANE FONDA AND THE BABY SEALS. EARTH FIRST! WE'LL MINE THE OTHER PLANETS WHEN WE GET THERE. The boy was such a sweetheart.

"If it was a mine accident," he said finally, his jawbone setting hard, "then Ned died doing what made him happy. You can't ask for anything more than that out of this life. There's no use crying about it when your number's called."

The macho fatalism of the Old West. Tink Tarver must have felt the same way.

"And if he was murdered?"

Tyler dug his hands deeper in his pockets, rattling change and his pocketknife and the other greasy trinkets that had found their way into his jeans. "If it was murder," he said, his voice as rough edged as the metal pieces in his pockets, "then somebody's gonna have to pay."

Kurt had wondered if the boy truly loved the old man, would grieve over him, and he thought he saw the signs of loss in that one brief moment. But there was something else inside those dull, impassive eyes—wariness and a stubborn secrecy, his own fierce code of silence. Kurt suspected that Tyler knew more than he was willing to divulge, and the knowledge was chewing slowly on his conscience.

"Let me take care of this, Tyler. Ned was my friend too." He studied the young man's chiseled features. "The best way you can help now is to come back to Aspen with me and talk to the officer in charge of the investigation. Tell her when you last saw Ned, what he talked about, what was bothering him, anything that seemed out of the ordinary. You listening? She'll also need your help up at the mine. We've got to inventory Ned's office and disarm that Airstream trailer. I don't want anybody else getting hurt up there."

Tyler reached in his shirt pocket for a pouch of Red Man tobacco. "I ain't talking to that little dyke Brown," he said. "She tried to break my neck with that cop choke hold."

The trailer's front door opened and a woman in jeans and a white peasant blouse stood watching them behind the dark screen. Kurt could make out the Bud can rising languorously to her mouth.

"Women are not your strong suit, are they, son?"

"What I hear, you're no expert on the subject yourself, Romeo."

Kurt smiled. No expert indeed. "Why don't you go tell that young lady you're sorry, for Chrissake, before she comes after us with a meat cleaver," he said. "Buy her some flowers, take her out to dinner."

Tyler stared at the screen door, hesitant, uncertain. "Jake Pfeil's sister," he said with a sour smirk, as though something wet and loose had shifted in his bowels.

"*What?*" Kurt glanced quickly at the figure in the doorway.

"You been asking who was with Cunningham that night at the road grader. It was that bitch that blew herself up with her own pipe bomb in Oregon." He stuffed a pinch of tobacco in his cheek. "Too bad she didn't do better work."

My god, Kurt thought. Kat Pfeil. Little Katrina. What was she doing back in Aspen?

"Her and that drunken shutterbug are mighty queer on trees," Tyler frowned. "If they had their way, the country'd go back to the hoot owls."

60 Minutes had featured her as an attractive, charismatic leader of the Northwest green movement, which was well known for its militant confrontations. Kurt knew she'd survived the blast, but soon afterward she had disappeared from the media attention that had once surrounded her.

"I'll talk to her," he said.

"Yeah, right. I bet you will," Tyler said, lifting the bill of his gimme cap to wipe his sweaty hairline. "The Mullers and the Pfeils. The Fords and the Rockefellers. You people always look after each other, don't you?"

"I'll handle this, Tyler. Stay away from her and Miles Cunningham. Are you listening to me?"

Tyler spit a long stream of tobacco, his line of sight directed at the woman behind the screen. "When you talk to that bitch," he said, sucking in a deep breath and pulling himself up to his full height of five foot eight, "tell her she ain't the only one in this valley that knows how things go boom in the night."

"Don't go making more trouble for yourself. I won't think twice about locking your gnarly ass in the county jail until this thing is over."

The woman opened the screen door and sat down on the front steps without uttering a word. She was dumpy and overweight and looked older than Tyler. Either she had been crying or her swollen eyes were the forewarning of a life spent inside a bottle. She smoked a cigarette and watched them both with sullen suspicion.

"Now go tell her you're sorry and then get in your truck," Kurt said. "I'm following you to Aspen."

9

He sat at a desk in the observation room, concealed from the interrogation by a two-way mirror, and tried to listen as a rookie deputy named Linda Ríos asked Tyler the usual questions: *Did Ned Carr seem despondent? Was he taking any medication? Can you recall the details of your last conversation with him?* But Kurt was distracted, his thoughts straying back nearly thirty years to that spring when he first noticed Jake's little sister had grown into a stunning beauty. He remembered how guilty he had felt about his secret crush on her, a freshman when he was a senior in high school, how he had hidden his attraction, even from his brother. Katrina Pfeil had stolen his boyish heart.

The last time they'd run into each other she was strolling along Hyman Avenue before it was bricked into a tourist mall, the summer after her college graduation. She had landed a job with the U.S. Fish and Wildlife Service and was leaving soon for a salmon hatchery in Oregon. A new boyfriend from Boulder, tall and long haired and reeking of weed, was hanging on her arm, smiling proudly. Kurt didn't give a damn. He was so happy to see Kat he had lifted her in his arms and swung her round and round like a squealing child. She told him she would write, and for years he waited patiently for the letters that never came.

Kurt had kept up with her mostly through rumors and gossip and the occasional press clipping. He knew that she had married, and that she and her husband had become central figures in the Green Briars, a group of guerrilla environmentalists who had been waging a protracted war against the corporate timber industry in the Pacific Northwest. One night two summers ago, after a week of tree sit-ins and violent confrontations with loggers in the Siskiyou forest, a pipe bomb exploded in the motel where they were sleeping. Her husband was killed, and while Kat was still unconscious and undergoing extensive surgery to save her life, the FBI informed the press that the couple had intended to plant the device in a local sawmill and were themselves the victims of their own negligence. The Bureau charged her with possession of illegal explosives and conspiracy, and as far as Kurt knew, the case was still dragging through the courts.

So why was Kat Pfeil back in Aspen after all these years? And why was she hanging out with Miles Cunningham? Ned had shot at them for trying to monkey-wrench his road grader, and a month later the old miner was blown to bits. Kurt didn't like how things were falling in place.

He picked up the phone and punched an outside line, wondering if Meg and the boys were back home from their outing. She answered on the second ring. "How are the guys?" he asked.

"They're fine," she said. "It's amazing how resilient kids are. I'm sure Ned's death will sink in sooner or later and we'll have some serious comforting ahead of us. Like maybe for the next ten years."

The next ten years. He realized suddenly that it wasn't Lennon he had envisioned walking down that country road, running away from home. It was Hunter.

"But right now they're out in the yard kicking a soccer ball," she said, "yelping and rolling around like two pups."

He told her that something unexpected had come up and he might be out later than he'd planned. "Do you remember Jake Pfeil's sister?"

"Yeees," she said, drawing out the word as if to focus her recollection. "Beautiful girl. Didn't she become some kind of loony ecoterrorist? My lord, what a family."

"She's back in the valley. I have to track her down and talk to her about Ned."

A long silence on Meg's end. She didn't want to hear about police work. "Don't worry, Kojak," she said, "dinner will be a-waitin' on the stove."

"Mmmm, tofu burgers. The boys are in for a real treat."

"Ha ha," she said. "Those kids could use a day without meat. You, too, Muscle Beachboy."

"God, I miss that. Kojak. Muscle Beachboy. No woman has ever called me those things quite like you do."

She laughed, a luscious, throaty sound he hadn't heard in a long time. They were making their way back to a genial friendship. Their son deserved the effort.

"How are the bruises, Kurt? You feeling okay?"

"Don't ask. I need drugs."

"I suppose you've forgotten there are other ways to deal with pain."

They had been through years of meditation together. Yoga. Massage therapy. Pursuits that seemed as far away now as the Korean War.

"Tell you what, little Sufi girl," he said, testing her sense of humor, "when I come home why don't we light some candles and incense, put on a Cat Stevens album, and rub each other down with patchouli oil? That ought to get rid of my headache."

He could feel her quick smile, the way her playful eyes crinkled with mischief. "In your dreams, Beachboy," she said.

The door creaked behind him and Muffin Brown slipped into the room.

"Gotta go," he said to Meg. "See you later this evening."

Muffin dragged back a chair. "Hot date tonight, Kurt?"

He blushed.

"The word patchouli was before my time," she said. "Tell me, does it leave an aftertaste?"

He shot her a sidelong glance and then resumed watching the two people in the interrogation room. "Why did you assign a rookie to this case?"

"Rookies need to break in somewhere. I like Linda. She's intense and she's got a good head for small details. This case is the right fit for her."

A former schoolteacher from Alamosa, Linda Ríos had been recruited in Muffin's effort to hire more Spanish-speaking officers for the valley.

"You're not treating this like a homicide, Muffin."

"Unless your boy breaks down and confesses," she

said, "it's not a homicide until Lorenzo Banks tells us it is."

He rose from the desk, as impatient with the way things were going as Tyler appeared to be, slouched over the interrogation table, grunting monosyllabic responses. "One minute Ned was worried about somebody coming after him," he said, "the next minute he was dead. That sounds like homicide to me."

He walked to the door and was almost out of the room when she called his name. "Thanks for bringing him in, partner." She nodded at the glass. "I don't know anyone else who could've done that without a fight on their hands."

"Piece of cake," he said.

10

By the time he veered off the paved road a half mile
north of Ashcroft and stopped to lock the hubs on his
old Willys, the sun had long disappeared behind the Elk
Range and the narrow valley was imbued with a soft
violet light. Within fifty yards the Jeep was rocking
along a rutted four-wheel-only track that followed Ex-
press Creek up to Taylor Lake at 12,000 feet. Snowmelt
gorged the creek, a splashing rush of white water
through this wilderness of blue spruce and lodgepole
pines, the hiss as palpable as the alpine chill descending
over the forest.

He hadn't been to the Pfeil family cabin in thirty
years and missed the secluded turnoff, a small breach in
the trees. Smelling woodsmoke, he retraced his route,
searching for dark wisps from the chimney, and finally
located the old passage into deeper woods. The cabin
was still the same modest pine-log hideaway that Rudi
Pfeil had built in the '50s as a weekend retreat from the
pressures of running a virgin ski resort, a place where
he could take his family to hike and fish and escape the
telephone. It appeared as if no improvements had been
made to the structure in all these years. The exterior

needed a fresh stain-coating, the front porch sagged toward one end, shingles were missing here and there on the roof. Kurt parked next to a glossy white GMC pickup and wondered if the Pfeils still owned this property. It was the only place in the valley Kat would still feel at home.

For several minutes he sat behind the wheel with the engine dead, waiting for guard dogs or a demented caretaker with a sawed-off shotgun, trying to recall his last visit here. Jake Pfeil had thrown a wild victory party the night their football team won the district championship, Kurt's sophomore year. The first time he'd ever gotten drunk. He smiled now, picturing that younger self stumbling out into the snow to barf all over his lumberjack shirt and then pass out. Bert and Jake had dragged him by his ankles through forty yards of ice and brush and dropped him fully clothed into the steaming Swedish bath. A week later John Kennedy was assassinated and the parties ended out here forever, the whole world darkened by mourning. It seemed like such a long time ago.

When Kurt was satisfied he wouldn't be shot for trespassing, he crawled out of the Jeep and walked to the door. No lights on inside, no response to his knocks. He knew better than to peek through a window. If Kat Pfeil was here, she deserved her privacy. He would leave a note and return in the morning.

As he started back to the Jeep for paper and pen he noticed white smoke roiling through the dense underbrush south of the cabin and stopped to watch the ghostly vapor whirl up into the grainy blue dusk. Steam was rising from that old Swedish bath. Was someone down there? He followed the footpath leading to where

Rudi Pfeil had devised his most clever addition to the hideaway, his pride and joy. Kurt recollected that creek water was pumped through a primitive boiler shed and then piped into a bowl-shaped sitting pool lined bottom and sides with granite boulders. When he was growing up there were scandalous rumors that their parents liked to slip off down this path late at night to drink brandy and soak together in the nude.

The trail gave out unexpectedly and he had to battle his way through chokecherry and kinnikinnick, dodging the spruce branches scratching at his face and a mess of snowbrush underfoot. He stopped in a small clearing to orient himself and pick needles out of his hair, then spied vapor coiling up through the foliage ahead. He continued on until he caught sight of the old boiler shed—and a woman sitting motionless in the steaming pool. Her eyes were closed, sleek black hair curling onto her bare shoulders. From this distance her face was still an artist's study in delicate bones, the vision of beauty Kurt had dreamed about every night on his army bunk in Germany. Jake's little sister.

She swayed her floating arms, disturbing the fervid water, brewing up another cloud of steam. Kurt stepped back into the thicket, suddenly unsure of what to say under these circumstances, how to introduce himself, knowing that he should return to the cabin and wait there. But she stood up then, steam billowing around her tall willowy figure, and he was unable to pull himself away. She reached for a towel lying on a boulder and began to pat herself dry, her body angled in profile. The girl of his adolescent dreams at forty-two, if his math was correct, her buttocks as smooth and taut as a ballerina's, a small breast buried in the towel.

Could this woman have murdered Ned Carr?

Bent over slightly, drying her hair now, she shifted in the pool until she was facing Kurt. An evening breeze parted the heavy steam and he could see the surgery scars that crosshatched the left side of her body from rib cage to knee. Her breast was partially gone, the stitched flesh of a mastectomy, but he knew it wasn't cancer that had nearly taken her life two years ago in a Siskiyou motel. Remembering her flawless beauty as a young girl, the band of freckles across her bare shoulders in a sundress, Kurt felt ashamed of himself for staring at her like this, yet he couldn't take his eyes off her damaged body.

His mind registered the hammer cock a full second before he heard the command. "Down on your knees, asshole," said a female voice behind him, furious and convincing, "or they'll find your body on the county road with a hole between your shoulder blades."

Kurt knelt down in the dewy spruce needles and placed his hands on his head.

"Keep your eyes on the ground and don't make any sudden moves," the woman said, her footsteps moving closer through the brush. She sounded like a female version of his old master sergeant. "Who are you with, creep? The Feebees? Or you some kind of hired timber thug?"

"Pitkin County Sheriff's Department," Kurt said. "Now I advise you to put down that gun."

He saw Kat look up from the bath, suddenly aware of voices. She fumbled for her robe and withdrew a pistol from the terry pocket, the last image in his mind before a boot sole found the middle of his back and thrust him facedown in the mulch. The sergeant had a leg like a rugby pro.

"Whoever the fuck you are," she said, searching his hip pocket for an ID, "somebody forgot to remind you it's against the law to wander around on private property without the court's permission."

"Is that you, Randy?" Kat called out from the pool. "What's going on?"

"Caught some jerk peeping around over here!" the woman shouted back, wrenching the wallet free of Kurt's pants. "Everything's cool, darlin'! I've got him neutralized. Need any help getting out?"

"No. I'm coming."

The woman kept her boot pressed to the small of Kurt's back. He raised his head and spit out a mouthful of damp soil. "When I get up from here, Randy," he said, "you and I may have to go three rounds, Marquess of Queensberry."

Her boot mashed harder. "Don't push your luck, creep," she said. "I'm fixing to hang your big ass up on one of these spruce limbs."

He could hear Kat making her way through the brush. "Who is it?" she asked, breathless from the effort.

"He's got a shield. Pitkin County cop. Take a look."

Kat's bare feet settled in the mulch a few inches from his eyes. There was a moment of silence while she studied the ID.

"Ever heard of him?"

Kat's muddy foot caught the side of Kurt's face and turned his head, forcing him to look up her long tanned leg into the folds of bathrobe. "Hello, Kurt," she said. "My, it's been a long time, hasn't it?"

"Hello, Kat," he said, mud and spruce needles blurring his vision.

"What are you doing snooping around out here?"

"Came to see how you're getting along." With her foot on his face he sounded like a man trying to speak his first words after a dentist's Novocain.

"And now that you've had a good look, what do you think? How am I getting along?"

He reached up and took hold of her ankle and removed her foot from his face. "I'm here on official police business, Kat," he managed to say. "I think we ought to handle this some other way."

Randy dug the gun barrel into his neck. "You know this guy?"

"Yeah, I'm afraid so," Kat said. "Since day one of the family saga. When I was growing up he was a nicer big brother than my own big brother. Weren't you, Kurt?"

The memory seemed to warm her. She didn't sound as hostile now.

"Kat," he said, "Ned Carr was killed in a mine explosion this morning. I came out here to ask you some questions. Now kindly tell your friend to take that gun out of my neck and let me up. Otherwise this could be a very long evening."

Kat knelt down beside him and raked the mud off his cheekbone with the nose of her pistol. "Why the hell should I know anything about Ned Carr?" she asked, plucking needles from his forehead.

"Isn't there someplace a little more comfortable where we can talk?"

She worked the stainless steel nose under his eye, deftly removing a wet clod. "I like you where I've got you," she said.

He laid his head on the ground and stared at her hand. "Your finger's on the trigger, Kat," he said.

"That's right," she said, delicately tracing the barrel across his mouth and down his chin.

"I hope you've got the safety on."

"If you're worried about safety," she said, "you should be carrying your own protection, darling."

Randy released her foot and straightened up. "Okay, Katrina, I can see you're getting off on this," she said. "I'm going back to the house before it gets any weirder. Anybody coming?"

EVERYTHING IN THE cabin was exactly as Kurt remembered it—the faux rawhide furniture arranged for conversation, the hand-carved wood tables and kerosene lanterns, the tchotchke shelves filled with Christa Pfeil's nutty collections of Swiss cowbells, beer steins, Hummel figurines, and salt-and-pepper shakers from the capitals of Europe.

Kat excused herself to get dressed and Randy invited Kurt to the kitchen for a glass of wine while she prepared dinner.

"You still want to go three rounds with me, Big Boy?" she grinned at him, setting her 9mm Glock on the counter and filling a glass with burgundy. "Or would you rather have a salad?"

He liked this woman. "Where did you get your training, Randy?"

"Ten years with Uncle Sam, ten years in the Sheriff's Department out in Curry County, Oregon. Hell, I was once an MP at Leavenworth. You mess with me, I'll take you to the mat."

She was smiling now, a stout, busty woman around fifty years old, her steel-gray hair cropped short on the sides and boxed in a half-inch flattop she had probably sported since boot camp. Her large upper body bulged under a hooded jogging sweatshirt with an Oregon State logo over the heart. When she removed her mirror shades Kurt was surprised to find striking blue eyes. His reaction did not escape her notice. Her smile slipped into something unexpectedly sly and knowing, and he realized that in spite of the tough-gal persona, this woman could turn on the charm.

"Why does Kat need a bodyguard?" he asked her.

Randy poured wine into two more glasses. "I don't really think of myself as a bodyguard," she said. "Just a friend with a Glock."

"Have there been death threats since the bombing?"

"My, my, twenty questions." She opened a cabinet and found a perfectly preserved McCoy salad bowl. "There were threats long before the pipe bomb, my friend. But you got one thing right. Ever since Siskiyou the termites have come out of the woodwork. Heavy breathers. Hate mail. Posters circulating around the hunting clubs with rifle crosshairs superimposed over her face. There are some real sick bastards in this world."

He turned on the sink tap, cupped icy water in his hands, and splashed his face, washing off the streak of mud. "So she got the hell out of Oregon," he said, examining his reflection in the kitchen window. "I don't blame her. How long have y'all been here?"

"Long enough to catch some skiing."

He wiped his face with a dish towel that smelled like raw onion. "So if you don't mind me asking, Randy, cop to cop," he said, watching her rummage through the ancient Frigidaire for garden vegetables, "how did an old bush ranger like you hook up with an outfit like the Green Briars?"

She raised up from the vegetable drawer and gave him a belligerent look. "I'm not a tree spiker," she snapped. "I don't give a shit about the Green Briars."

She came toward him with an armful of vegetables and stopped close enough to head-butt him on the chin. "See this, Big Boy?" she said, tapping her crooked nose. "Got it broke on Bald Mountain trying to break up a fight between the stompers and the hippies. Tell you the god's honest truth, I'm not fond of either side right now. Everybody in the woods is acting like a bunch of macho assholes."

Kurt sipped his wine, watching her place cucumbers and tomatoes on a cutting board. "So why did you go to work for Kat?"

"This is starting to sound a teensy bit like a police interrogation, is it not?"

"I'm trying to keep it friendly, Randy."

"Why don't you just tell me what you're after, Sherlock, and we can cut to the final credits."

He didn't know what he was after right now. Maybe just a few minutes alone with Kat, to see how she was putting her life back together.

Randy looked impatient with his slow response. "How long you known Katrina?" she asked.

"All her life."

She rubbed moisture from her forehead with a sweatshirt sleeve. "My partner and I were the first ones on the scene," she said, lowering her voice. "Only time I've ever seen that much blood was when an eighteen-wheeler hit a big buck on the coast highway." She glanced over her shoulder to make sure Kat was out of hearing range. "It didn't take a genius to figure out they'd been set up. Nobody goes to sleep with a pipe bomb full of finishing nails under their bed, not even a death-trip Muslim fanatic. But the Feebees blew in from Eugene and locked us local yokels out of the investigation right away. I tried to talk some sense at them but they refused to consider any other suspects. So I called the DA and told him the whole thing stunk and the next thing you know my boss was standing over my desk recommending that I give serious thought to early retirement. So I said 'fuck you people' and handed in my shield and drove up to the Portland hospital with a dozen roses to get a look at the big bad girl that had turned two law-enforcement agencies and a billion-dollar timber industry into a swarm of lying shit beetles."

Kurt wanted to believe that Kat was innocent. But he had read the reports implicating her in sabotage activities all over the Northwest.

"The Green Briars aren't exactly Eagle Scouts," he said.

"No, we're not." Kat was standing in the doorway. She had dressed in jeans and a fuzzy sweater with reindeer prancing across her chest. Her hair was dry now, a thick dark mass brushed away from her face. "But then the logging companies aren't exactly Sesame Street, are they?"

He brought her the extra glass of wine. "Peace," he said, a conciliating toast.

They clinked glasses. "Hear hear," she said.

In this light he could see that she was indeed older, though remarkably unchanged in all these years. Her dark eyes and long black lashes were still as enchanting, but now strands of silver laced her hair, one for every thousand. There was a small V-shaped scar just below her left ear where a bomb fragment had grooved her jawbone.

"Have you and Randy been swapping old cop tales?"

"The Big Boy wants to know what I'm doing here," Randy said, sliding chopped vegetables into the salad bowl with the edge of her knife.

"Randy is every woman's aspiration," Kat smiled. "A great cook with firearms training."

The limp he had noticed on their walk back from the bath seemed more pronounced as she escorted Kurt through the dim cabin and out to the rear deck. Summer was another month away in these mountains and the evening air had settled misty and cool over the croquet lawn, the wall of spruce trees along the creek now darkening into shadows. Kat sank down in the cushy pillows stuffed into a wicker rocking chair and propped her leg on an old Austrian milk stool. Though the bombing had taken place two years ago, it was clear that she still hadn't recovered completely. Perhaps she never would.

"Are you comfortable?" Kurt asked. "Can I get you anything?"

"How about a hip replacement? You any good at surgery?"

He sat in a lawn chair beside her and listened to the jays screeching in the distant pines. "I was very sorry to hear about it," he said, "especially what happened to your husband."

She dropped her eyes. "I got your card and the flowers. What a sweet thing to do. Imagine my surprise when I saw the name *Muller* on the envelope," she said. "Your mother was wonderful too. She sent a Care package of sweets and paperback romances. I got so bored in rehab I actually read a couple of them."

"We were thinking about the beautiful letter you wrote when Bert was killed," he said. "We never forget our old friends."

She rested her chin on a fist. "The Pfeils and the Mullers," she said wistfully. "We had it all. So what happened to the dream?"

He wondered where her brother, Jake, was now. Mexico, Colombia, Tahiti—still running from federal prosecutors for drug smuggling and murder. Some people even blamed Jake for Bert's death. He hadn't pushed Kurt's brother off Maroon Bells, but Kurt knew Jake's hand was somewhere close behind Bert's tragic dissipation and that final despairing plunge.

"It was a pretty fragile dream from the start," Kurt said. "And then the accountants and lawyers took over."

They sat in silence, mulling over their losses. Her parents were both dead, her husband. Kurt's father and brother. He could remember sunnier days out here on the deck, Rudi Pfeil's barbecue chicken and their elaborate summer picnics. An unspoken bond between privileged people who believed that the laughter would never vanish.

"This morning I was about twenty yards short of the morgue myself, Kat," he said, "when that explosion killed Ned Carr."

Her face grew somber. "My god," she said. "Tell me what happened."

"I'm not sure. But I don't like the way things are

adding up," he said. "Nobody in Aspen was happy about Ned bulldozing through a wilderness area to cut his road. I imagine you weren't too keen on it yourself, which is why you and Miles went out there to blowtorch Ned's grader." He sipped wine and studied her face in the evaporating light. "I want you to tell me you didn't take it one step farther, Kat."

She tapped the wineglass impatiently with her nails. "You want to know if that crazy bomb-throwing bitch has gone after another old earth raper," she said. "Is that what you're asking, Kurt?"

"I'm a cop now, Kat. It's my job to ask what you know about it—if maybe you've heard that somebody in the local green movement was pissed enough to take Ned out."

She stared coldly into his eyes. "You've turned out to be quite a prick, Sheriff Kurt," she said. "I think this visit is over. It's time for you to leave." She used both hands to lift her stiff leg from the milk stool and set her foot down on the redwood deck. "Or did you plan to wait around by my window until I'm undressed again?"

Heat bristled his face and he could feel himself glowing with embarrassment. He knew he deserved that. "The last thing I wanted was for us to get in a fight," he said.

"You should have thought about that before you accused me of murder. Or asked me to rat out my friends."

"I'm not accusing you of anything, Kat. But I have to find out what happened in that mine so that someday, when Ned's grandson is old enough to look me in the eye and ask how his grandpa died, I can tell him something we can both live with."

She stood up awkwardly, testing the weight on her leg. "I wish you the best of luck in your noble endeavor," she said. "Now if you don't mind, I'm going inside to help Randy. You know the way out."

He put his wine aside and rose to his feet. He wasn't going to let her off this easy. "Would you like me to unload the caltrops and rebar spikes before I go?" he said. "I've got your stash in the back of my Jeep."

"What are you talking about?"

"I liberated that box of night tools from Miles," he said sarcastically. "The stuff he's been storing for you in his bunker. If you want it back, give me a call sometime. I'm in the phone book."

He turned to leave but she grabbed his arm and spun him around, an impressive move for a lean woman with a bad leg.

"I have never made a bomb in my life, Kurt Muller," she said, her fingers digging into his bicep. "My husband and I gave up monkey-wrenching a good two years before the bombing. We even held a news conference to renounce tree spiking and make a public declaration of nonviolence," she said, suddenly overcome with emotion, "but the media never bothered to run it because the story wasn't fucking sexy enough for the six o'clock news."

He understood her frustration. For eleven years and counting he had had his own problems with the media.

"If you've given it up, Kat, why did you try to sabotage Ned's road grader?"

She released his arm with a shove. "I went along for the ride," she said, raking hair out of her eyes. "I thought I could talk Miles out of it." She shook her head, puzzled. "I didn't know he still had that box. I gave it to him for safekeeping about ten years ago, long before I met Michael." Her late husband. "I was worried about an FBI raid on this cabin."

He wanted to put aside all of this animosity and hug her the way he'd hugged her on Hyman Avenue the last time they'd seen each other. Two old friends spinning round and round in the street. "Why did you come back?" he asked her, something hurried and impatient in the inflection, a hint of his disappointment that she hadn't written or contacted him in twenty years.

The darkness was falling quickly and he could scarcely read the expression on her face. "A little R and R in the woods is good for the soul," she said. "You ought to try it sometime."

He smiled. An entire year of R & R hadn't made his sleepless nights any shorter. "Does anybody know you're out here?" he asked. He didn't want Tyler Rutledge to find out where she was staying.

"Nobody around here. I would appreciate it if you'd keep it confidential."

"You can trust me, Kat. You know that."

They stared at each other in silence while the first evening stars appeared above the valley curtain. This had not gone well.

"If you need police assistance for any reason," he said, "give me a call."

"I appreciate the thought," she said woodenly. "But Randy and I are used to taking care of ourselves."

BOUNCING BACK DOWN the rugged four-wheel Jeep track, he was angry with himself for being so clumsy and mindless and unprofessional, for failing to uncover any useful information during their discussion. Bright headlights torched into view about thirty yards ahead, a vehicle approaching at reckless speed. Kurt honked his horn and pulled over against the trees, giving the fool room enough to pass. "Idiot!" he yelled as the muddy Land-Rover gunned past him, swirling up clouds of dust into the open Jeep. Spitting a mouthful of grit, he caught a glimpse of the driver lighting a cigarette, tossing the match out the window at him. Miles Cunningham on his way to visit an old friend.

11

MEG HAD SEPARATED the two boys after their scuffle and sent them to different parts of the house. "Would you please talk to your son," she said when Kurt came in. "He's gotten very territorial."

Kurt rapped lightly on the closed bedroom door. "Hey, buddy," he said, "how are you doing in there? Can I come visit?" Hanging from the doorknob was a KEEP OUT, VARMINTS sign with Yosemite Sam brandishing cartoon six-guns.

Lennon was playing quietly on the floor with a motley brigade of plastic, detachable-limbed superheroes, leading them in battle against one another. He paid little notice to his father now sitting cross-legged on the carpet beside him.

"Did you have supper?" Kurt asked.

"Mom tried to poison us," Lennon said without looking up from the two warriors clashing in mortal combat on a shoe-box lid.

"Give her a chance," Kurt said. "Her food's a lot healthier for you than mine. I'm going to borrow some of her recipes."

"Guuuhhh," the boy said.

Kurt rested his back against the bunk bed and watched his son play. His headache had finally gone but he still felt beat up and tired. "Mom says you and Hunter were fussing at each other," he said, running his hand affectionately through his son's silky hair.

"I don't think Hunter is going to make a very good brother," Lennon said, humming now, rearranging warrior positions. "He doesn't know how to take care of toys."

"Well, sweetie, he doesn't have very many of his own," Kurt said. "I suppose he needs to learn proper toy maintenance. Maybe you'll just have to show him."

He couldn't imagine Ned buying any of the crap that parents were forced to buy for their kids. The old man hadn't had the money or the inclination. The Carrs didn't even own a television.

"He was smashing my rain stick against the wall," Lennon explained. The rain stick was a long slender gourd from Chile that made a gentle rain sound whenever you twirled it, a thousand tiny pebbles hissing down a stairway of needles. "He started jumping on my bed in his dirty shoes."

"Hmm."

Lennon required a tidy world. He was an only child used to order and tranquility.

"We'll have to teach him the house rules," Kurt said. "But let's not forget that he's our guest right now, and that guests get extra special attention in the Muller home."

"Yeah, right," the boy said cynically. "If we don't watch him, he's going to mess up the whole place."

"I don't understand this, Lennon. This afternoon you were very excited about him coming to live with us."

"That was before he tried to smash my rain stick."

Kurt wrapped his arms around his son and gave him a rough squeeze, rocking him back and forth, and Lennon's small hand reached up to pat Kurt on the ear. He turned his head and kissed his father's chin.

"I think Hunter's going to be with us for a while," Kurt said. At least until Kurt could meet with Corky Marcus, Ned's lawyer, and find out what legal provisions he had established for the child. "Let's not forget he lost his grandpa today, okay? That's got to be the worst feeling in the whole world. He needs us to be his family now. We can't let him down."

Lennon's forehead wrinkled in deep thought. "Okay, Dad," he said at last. "I'll give him another chance."

Kurt left the boy to his game and went to the kitchen, where Meg was preparing him a plate of salad, chick peas, and ratatouille. "I'm sorry there's no candlelight and Cat Stevens," she said, offering a tired smile. Copper-colored tails of hair curled with perspiration on her long neck. "I've got to run them a bath. Hunter smells like a goat."

"This is delicious," he said, forking food into his mouth. "Thanks for going to all the trouble."

"No trouble at all. Would you like me to spend the night?"

Instantly she realized how ambiguous it had sounded and blushed deeply, averting her eyes. "The boys—"

"There's nothing more appealing," he teased, "than

a woman who can cook like this and is willing to stay all night."

She glanced up at him through a wave of hair that had fallen in her eyes. "I know how the couch works," she said dryly. "I've had lots of experience, if you'll recall."

He wiped his mouth with a napkin. "I thought I was the one who always took the couch."

Perspiration beaded her top lip. She fluffed her shirt, fanning herself. "I'm very happy we didn't have twins, Kurt," she said with the hint of a smile.

"You're out of training, Peaches."

"Huh! Excuse me while I go run the bathwater, Colonel." She mock-saluted. "Hunter's out on the deck looking at the stars. I'm sure he could use some company."

Kurt made a quick phone call to locate Muffin Brown and, receiver at his ear, opened the French doors onto the dark deck. The temperature had dropped to forty-five degrees and the crickets had surrendered their night music to seek deeper shelter. Hunter was sitting on a bench by the hot tub, gazing upward at the crystalline constellations, his legs drawn tightly against his chest. The sight of this small motherless boy alone in the dark formed a hard lump in Kurt's throat.

"How did it go with Tyler?" he asked Muffin when she finally picked up her line. She was still at the office, clearing out paperwork.

"Pretty much a wash. He agreed to go up to the Ajax with two of the deputies and then managed to disappear on them."

Kurt sighed. "That little jerk."

"Got a strange phone call from Dan the Man Davenport a little while ago."

Dan Davenport was the sheriff of Garfield County, a serious, mustachioed lawman who had deputied under Kurt for four years before moving downvalley and running for office in a place more suited to his saddle-horn style. They were on good terms, mentor and student. A couple of years ago Kurt had helped him track down two drifters who had robbed and pistol-whipped a convenience store clerk in Carbondale.

"Something about an exploding Dumpster. He wanted to talk to you."

"Hmm. I'll give him a call," Kurt said. But not anytime soon. "Is our man in from Denver?"

"I'm leaving in a half hour to pick him up at the airport."

"I'll check back with you in the morning after I pay a visit to Lee Lamar," he said. Leighton F. Lamar III was the president of the Roaring Fork Ski Corporation and its majority stockholder. "I don't expect to learn much, but I figure somebody's got to talk to him about Ned. I'd like to know what kind of lease agreement the Skicorp had with the old man."

"Give my fond regards to Leighton F.," Muffin said. "Good luck getting past the hair spray."

Kurt picked up Hunter's padded jacket and walked out on the deck he and his brother had added to the house in the late '70s, when their mother still lived here. "Evening, Hunter," he said. "Mind if I join you?"

"Hi, Coach," Hunter said, his voice theatrically glum. He had been their leading scorer on the indoor soccer team Kurt had coached this past winter. An agile kid, smart on his feet, tireless. Lennon had played, too, but was less interested in kicking a ball than in wearing a cool uniform and drinking Squeezits after the games.

"It's pretty cold out here," Kurt said, bundling the jacket around Hunter's shoulders.

"It's okay, I'm used to it," the boy said.

Kurt straddled the bench and pulled Hunter into his lap. "How are you doing, champ? Everything okay?" he asked, enclosing the child in his arms. He was noticeably heavier than Lennon, a wild musky smell to his thick brown hair.

"Lennon's mad at me," he said. "He doesn't want me to live here."

Kurt gave him an affectionate squeeze. "He was upset about his toys getting broken," he said. "Sometimes friends have a misunderstanding over something. They fuss at each other and then make up. I'll bet he's already forgotten about it and if you walked back to his room right now he'd be happy to see you."

"He's got too many rules."

An unfettered boy, his backyard Queens Gulch and the Snowmass Wilderness, where only the laws of nature applied. No fences, no signs, nothing but you and the Big Outside. Live free or die.

"Even soccer's got rules," Kurt reminded him. "We don't have very many in our house, only a few for damage control. But let's not worry about rules tonight, okay?"

"Okay, Coach."

They watched the stars together in silence, that vast dark mystery of winking lights so sharply real at 8,000 feet, the Milky Way as stark and awesome from this cold perch as it was from few other places on earth. Kurt remembered lying on his barracks roof as a young soldier in Germany, homesick for the breathtaking clarity of this mountain sky.

"It's time for us to go back inside," he said. "Lennon's mom is running a bath for you guys."

The boy's breathing had become deep and somnolent, and Kurt wondered if he was falling asleep.

"I don't think I can stay here tonight," he said in a small sad voice.

"Why not, champ? Lennon's not angry anymore."

"I can't sleep without Sneak."

"Sneak? Is he your special friend?" Lennon had one, too, a stuffed white monkey named Jerry.

"Sneak the Snake. My pet garter."

"You sleep with a garter snake?" Kurt was relieved it wasn't a copperhead.

"No, silly," Hunter giggled. "He's in a terrarium."

"I'll go pick him up tomorrow."

"Sneak needs me tonight. I haven't fed him all day. He never goes to sleep without me," the boy declared. "And I can't leave my rock collection at home unprotected now that my grandpa is dead."

"We can pick up everything in the morning," Kurt assured him. "Your clothes, your pets. Anything you want."

"If you drive me up there right now I can jump out and run in and get them. I promise I'll be fast."

Kurt sighed. "It's pretty late, my man. You can make it without them for one night, can't you? I give you my word we'll pick them up first thing in the morning."

He felt the little boy's courage cave in, his body shudder with quick tears. "I gotta go home, Coach," he pleaded, his voice high and whimpery. "I can't leave Sneak alone tonight."

Kurt held him close. "Shhh, it's okay," he said, rocking him, "it's okay. I'll go get them for you. You just tell me where they are."

12

NED CARR OWNED a second mine, the Lone Ute, and had raised his family in a nearby cabin on the backside of Aspen Mountain, a designated wilderness area off limits to deep-powder skiers and hunters and ORVs, the terrain as obscure and uncharted as the dark side of the moon. To reach the remote site a traveler had to drive west out of town and circle around behind the mountain, climbing the steep Midnight Mine Road above Castle Creek.

It could be worse, Kurt thought, his tires churning sand as the Jeep swerved onto Ned's access road. *Somewhere at this very moment in America a father is rushing his child's forgotten Barney blanket through ribbons of honking freeway traffic in the dark, pouring rain. It could be worse.*

He gazed out over the black basin below, 30,000 acres of invisible woodlands without a flicker of light, finding it difficult to imagine that just over the peak to the north lay a glittering resort. The Willys's single intact headbeam swept across a graveyard of charred spruce stumps in a shallow pit where the miners had torched their bulldozer debris. Crusts of dirty snow still survived under the trees. Steering was less arduous on this bedrock stretch Ned had plowed through the forest to his property line, a half mile of old Jeep trail the miner had used without challenge for nearly fifty years, until last summer, when he'd decided to widen and blacktop the route and dig drainage culverts. With the exception of one doddering U.S. magistrate in Denver, no one in the entire state believed that Ned Carr's shoe-string enterprise required an asphalt road through sensitive national forest to accommodate more truck-hauling for his Lone Ute Mine.

Kurt soon came upon a dump truck and a heavily padlocked road grader parked side by side, blocking the right-of-way where their construction had advanced. A crudely lettered sign on the grader's door said WARNING! DO NOT TOUCH! MACHINES RIGED TO KILL. He was forced to squeeze the Jeep through a narrow passage between the back tires of the long spindly grader and a massive outcropping of dolomite. Driving another quarter mile over smooth blacktop, he eventually reached the chain-secured gate marked PROPERTY OF CARR MINING COMPANY, NO TRESPASING and stopped to let his headlight reveal the gloomy scene beyond the fence. The Carr cabin was dark and cheerless. The rusting, corrugated-tin head-frame of the Lone Ute Mine loomed in the murky shadows another fifty yards beyond.

Hadn't Muffin sent deputies out here to have a look around after the Ajax explosion? Why wasn't someone assigned to watch this place overnight?

Kurt grabbed a flashlight from his glove compartment and left the engine running, the high beam blazing. He spat on the gate, tossed a handful of sand against it, raked a finger across the iron-pipe bars, testing for an electric current. Satisfied that he wouldn't be knocked to his knees, he crawled over the top and jogged toward the cabin.

When Kurt was a boy the local conservationists, two or three odd bird-watchers with sherry in their flasks, had incited a tame philosophical debate over Ned's right to homestead here in a national forest and raise his children on public land. But in the early '60s a new congressional bill called the Mining Claim Occupancy Act had settled the issue decisively. Because he'd lived next to his mine for more than seven years, Ned was allowed complete title to his house and five surrounding acres. One final law-book anachronism from the Old West before the longhairs arrived in their earth sandals.

Kurt didn't know what to expect once he'd reached the creaking front porch. He was relieved when the door latch gave way without effort and he didn't have to break in. It was pitch black inside and cold, a peculiar farmhouse brew of kerosene and yeasty bread and a workingman's sweat. His flashlight beam danced over the cedar floorboards as he searched the wall for a switch. He knew that Ned had installed an electric generator some time ago but he was having no luck finding a wall plate. *To hell with it,* he thought, giving up. *Five minutes and I'm gone.*

He followed his own light into a small central room cramped with a woodstove and cane-bottom chairs and an old café booth Ned had acquired from Tink Tarver, the family dining table. The floor was matted down with animal-pelt rugs, beaver and raccoon and red fox. Mrs. Carr had died twenty years ago and the decor, if it could be called that, remained as she had kept things, a collection of family photographs and blue bottles and macramé wall hangings, the usual embroidered home-spun wisdom. *God Bless This Mess. Don't Laugh, It's Paid For*. It was nearly impossible to imagine their two children, Marie and Nathan, doing schoolwork for twelve years in such a claustrophobic environment.

He made his way into Hunter's bedroom, the roof-slanted space where the boy's mother and uncle had shared a childhood before him, and as the flashlight fluttered over objects in the dark enclosure, Kurt was surprised to discover a cozy arrangement that dupli-cated Lennon's own room at home. Ned had once asked Kurt for a list of the things that Lennon liked most, his favorite toys and books and wall decorations, and it now appeared as if Hunter and his grandpa had set about replicating the list. The beam illuminated wall posters of Disney movies and rock stars, a shelf full of kids' books, plastic mutants spread across the floor. Kurt was deeply touched. Despite his age and tempera-ment, the old man had tried his best to be a good parent.

The terrarium was an easy find. Kurt shined the light on Sneak the Snake to make sure he was asleep beneath his grass and rocks. There was a hand-scrawled note taped to the lid, Ned's unique brand of spelling: *Hi, Buster Brown. I love you and yor snake. Granpa*. It might have been written early this morning, shortly before Ned had left for the Ajax Mine.

The cigar box that housed Hunter's rock collection was hidden under the bed exactly where the boy had said to look. Kurt shook the box and opened it, admir-ing the selection of quartz and feldspar and mica, and a few stones he couldn't identify.

He was slowly retracing his steps to the front door, the terrarium and cigar box stacked against his chest, when he thought he heard a board creak somewhere in the cabin. He froze instantly and clicked off the flashlight. Blood pulsed in his ears. He thought he detected movement, another footstep, and knelt down quietly, setting the pile on the floor. *Dumbshit,* he cursed himself, irritated for not bringing his .45 from the Jeep. Irritated that the pepper-spray tube in his pocket was empty.

The sound had come from the old man's bedroom twenty feet away. Kurt lowered his shoulders and slipped quickly through the darkness, the unlit flashlight his only weapon. Squatting back on his heels, he waited by the bedroom door but heard only an old cabin groaning under its own weight in the cold wind. He laughed at himself and stood up, switching on the flashlight, directing the beam into Ned's messy room.

He had taken only three short steps when a blow knocked the light from his hand and he was shoved hard against the wall, his head slamming Sheetrock. A dark figure skirted past him and Kurt lunged wildly for his legs, catching an ankle. The intruder hit the cedar floor with a resounding *whump.* Kurt pounced on him quickly, but the man proved strong and deft, whoever he was, breaking Kurt's hold with a wrestler's grace. They rolled on the floor in the darkness and Kurt grabbed at the man's throat, ripping loose some shirt. He thought he had him until two rapid jabs struck his bruised sternum, curling Kurt like a fetus, the pain so intense he almost passed out. Doubled over and moaning, he watched the man bang out the cabin door and dash across the yard toward the woods, a swift, solid body fleeing through the white haze of Jeep light, his ponytail bouncing as he ran.

Kurt was clutching something in his hand. He struggled to his feet and retrieved the flashlight from the bedroom floor. It wasn't a piece of shirt but an ornament of some kind. A beaded choker, Native American, six bird bones the size of Kurt's little finger.

He found a wall phone in the kitchen beside an ancient cupboard and dialed the Sheriff's Department. The night dispatcher told him that Muffin hadn't returned from the airport.

"Kevin, I've just had an altercation up here at Ned Carr's cabin," Kurt said, holding his chest. "Somebody broke in. Why the hell wasn't there a deputy watching the place?"

"I don't know, Kurt. Triage, I guess. Was it a priority?"

"Triage my ass," Kurt said. The department was still treating Ned's death as an innocent mishap. "Assault on a police officer and possible burglary. *Make* it a priority." He could hear his voice gain heat, ratchet into a higher state of annoyance. "Send two deputies code three. I don't have all night. I've got to bring a child his pet snake before bedtime."

The dispatcher hesitated. "Snake, sir?"

"Did I stutter, Kevin?"

"Sorry, sir." Another pause. "I didn't realize you were back on duty."

13

DAYLIGHT STREAMED THROUGH the chalet windows. He shook Meg's shoulder gently. "Good morning," he whispered.

"What time is it?" she asked in a deep, sleepy voice, her eyes still shut. "Are the boys awake?"

"Not yet, so let's not make any noise," he said, kneeling beside her. "I think I remember how you like it."

She unfurled the blanket, sat up, and took the cup of coffee. She was wearing one of his old T-shirts, John Prine on tour.

"How was it?" he asked, pressing the couch springs.

She shrugged. "How well I remember," she said, scraping film off her lips with a fingernail, taking a sip from the mug.

"You can have the bed tonight."

"Mmm, this is good." Her eyes blinked over the coffee steam. "The boys talked about going for a hike on the Rio Grande Trail this morning. Want to come along?"

"I'd love to but I've got some work to do." He truly

didn't want to spoil the moment with cop talk. "How long can you stay with us?"

She thought it over. "Maybe another night. But we need to discuss what we're going to do, Kurt. Do we have a plan?"

Their weekly arrangement called for her to pick up Lennon after school on Friday and bring him back home Sunday morning. Having Hunter would complicate matters.

"Do you have to get permission from what's his name, your Buddhist guru, to stay a few days?"

"Don't be a jerk."

"I'd hate to see you get grounded by the man."

She blew on the coffee and smiled coyly. She knew he was digging for something, prying into the details of her private life. He was curious about that Zen master she lived with.

"Am I still dreaming," she asked, closing her eyes, "or do I smell blueberry pancakes?" When they were married she had always made a fuss over his Saturday morning pancakes.

"Ready for a stack?" he asked, rising from the couch to check the griddle.

"If I didn't know better I'd think you were trying to impress me."

The kitchen was separated from the living room by a tiled counter with tall barstools. Kurt flipped the pancakes and speed-dialed Corky Marcus. He thought he heard the boys stirring in Lennon's bedroom.

"Hey, Corky, are you up, man?"

"It's Saturday morning, Kurt," said the weary attorney, "which means the inmates have been awake since dawn, banging their spoons against the bars." He had three boys by this marriage—six, eight, and ten years old. "Correct me if I'm wrong, but when I called last night the woman who answered your phone sounded suspiciously like Meg."

"Mm-hmm," Kurt said, watching Meg slide on her jeans. The Zen life had been good to her body. She was in better shape than a thirty-year-old. "She's helping out with the boys."

"I see," Corky said. He and his wife, Carole, had gone through the birthing course with Kurt and Meg, and now Lennon and Josh Marcus were in the same kindergarten class. Corky had been Kurt's attorney during the divorce. "Any chance you two might, you know—"

"Not much."

Lennon called out from the bedroom in a giggling singsong. "Mommm, oh, Mommmm! Are you still heeere?"

The two boys screeched, and then Hunter sang out, "Come and fiiind us, Missus Coooach!"

There was a proud smile that Meg and Kurt had always exchanged when Lennon did something adorable as a baby, and she gave him that smile now, mixed with a glimmer of regret. The question lingered between them still. *Should we have tried harder? Listen to what's at stake.* He returned the smile, conflicted, ambivalent, knowing how difficult it had been for her to live without Lennon.

"We're already off to the races here at *chez famille*," Corky said. "If my daily printout is correct, we've got one hockey, one baseball, and one birthday party at the Nature Center." He sighed. "Can we get together about

four in my office to look at Ned's will? If I'm still registering a pulse."

"Sure," Kurt said. "I'll furnish the caffeine."

Corky muffled the phone and shouted something at
one of his kids, then returned. "How is Hunter handling it?"

"So far, not bad. I've got Dr. Hales on the case."

Corky paused. "I don't know, Kurt. Something
weird was going on with Ned," he said. "After school
on Thursday he brings Hunter over to my car and asks
if the boy can spend the night with Josh. No explanation offered. He looked stressed, but then who could
ever tell with Ned? I thought maybe he wasn't feeling
well. The next morning he's dead."

Kurt watched Meg tiptoe in her bare feet to Lennon's
door and peek in. The boys were giggling, hiding somewhere in the room.

"Last week he calls me at the office and says he wants
to look over his will, make some changes. It doesn't
take a Mensa certificate to figure out Ned was expecting
something bad to happen. Maybe, God forbid, at his
own hand."

Kurt spooned pancake batter into three pools on the
hot griddle. "You can rule out suicide," he said, wondering again what the intruder was after in Ned's dark
cabin. "Somebody murdered him."

14

LEIGHTON F. LAMAR's "trophy home," as the real estate ads referred to the mansion, was 11,000 square feet of native stone and redwood beams perched conspicuously on the boundary of Little Nell, Aspen's most populated ski slope. When the grand residence was under construction, the local newspaper had made inquiries to the county commissioners, the zoning board, and the U.S. Forest Service, but no one could adequately explain how the communications tycoon had obtained permission to build in a major recreation area. Kurt knew that the mountain was a complex checkerboard of valid mine patents dating back to 1879 and public land preserved from development through various forest reserve acts; but it came as no surprise that Lamar had found his way around the petty laws that governed ordinary mortals. The man had friends in all the right places.

When Kurt arrived in his Willys an hour before noon, there were three vehicles parked in the Lamars' pea-gravel lot—a Jeep Cherokee, a Land-Rover, and a Suburban, their satin finishes gleaming in the morning sunlight. He got out and approached the wrought-iron gate on foot, noticing a tall man standing inside the courtyard, smoking a cigarette, one shoe resting on the rim of a mosaic fountain. Instead of buzzing the intercom Kurt waved him over, and as the man strode across the flagstones, moving toward him with a perceptible arrogance in his bearing, Kurt realized he knew this man and his walk and that defiant smirk that passed for a smile.

"Hello, Muller," the man said, flipping his cigarette butt between the gate bars. "It's been a while."

"Seems like only yesterday," Kurt said. "Enjoying your retirement, Staggs? I heard you were opening limo doors for Hollywood drugheads."

Staggs smiled darkly. "High-profile security," he said with an uncharacteristic measure of self-mockery. "What brings you up to the big house? You have business with the Lamars?"

"I'm here about a murder," Kurt said. "You remember how that works, don't you, Staggs? You were pretty good at it."

When Neal Staggs was a high-ranking FBI agent out of Denver he had hounded Kurt and the Pitkin County Sheriff's Department for four long years, monitoring the department's activities, wiretapping their phones, trying to link the Aspen office to drug dealing and murder. But last summer Staggs had stepped over the line when he'd led a SWAT team against a farmhouse of migrant workers downvalley, killing three innocent people, using the raid as a cover-up for a suspicious Bureau protection program. Kurt had been the one who'd exposed Staggs's misconduct, and as a result the agent was forced into early retirement after twenty-five years of service. Kurt had heard rumors that Staggs had become a special investigator for VIProtex International, security guardians of America's pampered VIPs, but he'd never expected to see him again in Aspen.

"I have an appointment with Lee Lamar," Kurt said, pushing the button on the intercom box attached to the gate. He studied the man's groomed gray hair and Marlboro looks, the Patagonia carryall vest and new Timberland puddle stompers, thinking that Staggs should be standing behind the bars of a federal cell instead of pulling down a six-figure salary as a designer security cop.

"There's been a change of plans this morning," Staggs said. "A minor emergency. You may have to take a rain check."

"I'd rather hear that from Lamar," Kurt said, punching the button again.

"Suit yourself," Staggs said, hunching his broad shoulders to light another cigarette.

The mansion's oakwood doors opened majestically and two people dressed in bird costumes stepped out into the courtyard. Lee Lamar had told Kurt by phone that he could give him half an hour of his time before he and his wife were scheduled to attend a fund-raiser for Friends of the Forest. He hadn't mentioned that it was a costume party.

"Good to see you, Kurt," Lamar said, waving a brown wing. "Give me a minute." His trim silver mustache and sculpted jaw were all that was visible beneath a fierce black beak. He managed the costume awkwardly, his feet clomping around inside menacing rubber talons.

Goshawk? Kurt wondered. *I'm here to interrogate a man dressed as a goshawk?*

Staggs walked back to meet his boss and take him aside for a private conference. Lamar's wife, the legendary folksinger Meredith Stone, continued on toward the parking lot in feathered legs, a plump, snow-white grouse with a paper ruff around her neck. Kurt opened the gate for her.

"White-tailed ptarmigan," she said, stopping to read his bewildered expression.

"Kurt Muller," he said, extending his hand.

She laughed. "Have you forgotten, Kurt, that we once shared a table at a museum gala?"

"I haven't forgotten," he said.

"We had a conversation about tattoos. You offered to show me the one you got in the army if I showed you mine."

The memory embarrassed him. "Please forgive me. I was drinking too much back then." It was just after the divorce.

"I still want to see it," she said. In her heyday that husky voice had melted the hearts of a million turtlenecked fans. "Reliable sources tell me there's nothing like it anywhere."

Meredith Stone had been a popular Greenwich Village folksinger in the early '60s, her songs recorded by Joan Baez and Judy Collins. But the British Invasion had sent her career into a tailspin and she'd dropped out of the celebrity scene to live on a secluded New Mexico goat farm and raise her three children from the brief, stormy affairs with a movie star and a well-known pop artist, devoting her life to environmental causes. The tabloids had feasted on her unlikely courtship with Lee Lamar. The couple had met by accident ten years ago in the bar of the Plaza Hotel. He was buying a cable network; she was lecturing at an Audubon conference on the importance of old growth forests in preserving endangered species. They argued over drinks, over dinner, and over the telephone for two weeks. A year later they were man and wife.

"Are you joining us for the party?" she asked. When Meredith Stone wasn't festooned as a white-tailed ptarmigan she was quite a beautiful woman. She no longer wore the waist-length honey-blond hair that had popularized her album covers, and she had put on a few pounds since the goat farm, but even now her classic bone structure could quiet a restaurant when she walked in the door.

"I need a few minutes with Lee this morning. Official business," he said, watching the two men in the courtyard, their lips moving silently, discussing urgent matters.

"Come with us up the mountain. You can talk on the way. That's more time than Lee gives anyone. Besides"—she smiled cleverly—"you never know who might show up at one of these shindigs."

"Lots of people in bird costumes, I imagine."

She hopped down the stone steps, her feathered feet locked together. "I doubt Katrina will wear a costume," she said. "I'm sure she thinks these fund-raisers are silly nonsense."

He looked at her. How did she know Kat? How did she know he knew Kat? How did she know he might be interested in seeing her again?

"Kurt!" Lee Lamar shouted from the courtyard. "Something's come up. Can you meet us at the gondola barn?" he asked, waddling toward the gate. "We can talk there. I don't want you to think I'm brushing you off."

OVERNIGHT, VANDALS HAD broken into the building that housed the Skicorp gondolas at the foot of Little Nell. The damage was minimal, in part due to the shrieking alarm system, but the perpetrators had managed to spray graffiti on two carriages and shove an ax handle into the cable's pulley winch before escaping unseen. By the time Kurt and the others had arrived, gondola service was in full operation. Two young women in shorts and Skicorp T-shirts were guiding incoming carriages to the yellow line, loading backpackers and picnic tourists, swinging them along the turnaround and up 3,000 feet of cable to the top of the mountain. In the service area a VIProtex photographer was taking pictures of the two sidelined carriages. *Die Ski corpse,* read one of the messages on the tinted Plexiglas door. The circled *A* symbol for anarchy was sprayed on the other.

"Did you check the tape in the surveillance cameras?" Lamar asked as he wobbled toward the carriages.

"Yes, sir," Staggs nodded. "Unfortunately they were blank. Either there was a malfunction or the damn things weren't on. I don't know how long they've been inoperative." He pointed to a man in blue coveralls standing in the bucket of a long-armed crane, inspecting one of the cameras high above. "We've got the Vidtec people looking at them now."

Kurt surveyed the graffiti. "High school seniors," he said. "They start doing stuff like this every year around graduation. Did you find any beer cans?"

Staggs shot him a disapproving look. "Monkey-wrenching ski property is on the rise nationwide," he said. "We've had recent reports from Idaho and New Mexico. Also a couple of felony incidents this season in Jackson Hole and Estes Park. It was only a matter of time before it hit the Aspen area."

Kurt was amused. Once a Fed, always a Fed. "This looks like a teenage prank to me," he said, "not the work of ecoterrorists wearing ski masks and combat boots. Have you contacted the city police?"

Staggs exchanged a quick glance with the man in the bird costume.

"I'm usually inclined to let VIProtex handle matters of this sort," said Lamar. "Mr. Staggs likes to do things his own way."

"I'm aware of how Mr. Staggs likes to do things," Kurt said.

He saw the hatred in Staggs's eyes. They had almost come to blows last summer and it wouldn't take much to get them going at each other now. Kurt had tainted the man's long and distinguished career, cut his pension in half.

"Maybe you don't read the papers, Muller. The West is a war zone right now," Staggs said, squaring around to engage Kurt face to face. "The maggots are crawling out from under every rock. If I thought there was a law-enforcement agency in this entire valley capable of comprehending the scope and magnitude of the problem, I would pull them in."

Kurt stared into those venomous eyes. "Are you talking about the Green Briars, Staggs?"

"Gentlemen," Lamar interrupted, "if you don't mind, I'd like to get on with my day. Meredith, darling," he said, "would you and Kurt please wait for me in one of the gondolas? I need to wrap this up with Neal."

"Come on, Kurt," Meredith said with an impatient sigh, extending her snowy wings. "Let's leave these two warriors to worry about the barbarians at the gate."

15

As THEIR GONDOLA rose higher into the brilliant sunshine and the rooftops of Aspen receded in the distance, Kurt peered through the Plexiglas at the magnificent cliffs and wedge-shaped fir stands passing underneath them. When Lee Lamar opened the Silver Queen Gondola in the mid-'80s, it was the longest and fastest ski lift in the world. From town to the crest of Ajax in fifteen minutes, the state-of-the-art passenger capsules sealed warmly and were equipped with audio speakers for messages and reports. Old-timers like Kurt didn't know what to make of such luxury. His earliest memory of skiing was riding up the mountain with his parents in an exposed chair lift, the cold wooden seat rocking back and forth in the icy wind.

"My gut tells me you were right about the vandalism," Lamar said, raising the beak from his forehead for a clearer view of Kurt sitting in the seat opposite. Two people in bulky bird costumes left little room for comfort in the vehicle. "But I pay VIProtex a healthy sum to stay on top of the game, and their man Staggs takes his job very seriously."

"I don't like him," Meredith said bluntly. "All this

high-tech monitoring he's doing is a waste of good money that could be going elsewhere."

"More to the Friends of the Forest, I suppose? Look at us, for god's sake." He flapped his wings, laughing at himself. "Aren't we doing enough for the cause, my dear? When it comes to cash flow, I'm their sitting duck!"

Before their marriage, Leighton F. Lamar III was considered one of the most ruthless, most humorless corporate executives in the world. But under Meredith's influence he had become an active environmentalist and a major contributor to green causes around the globe. Lamar had gone so far as to convert his horse ranches in Texas and Wyoming into wildlife preserves. None of his old friends would speak to him anymore.

"Staggs is trying to convince my husband that it's necessary to spy on the environmentalists in the valley," Meredith said with disapproval. "He wants to video meetings, compile computer data, god knows what. The jerk thinks these raging radicals, whoever they are, are going to bring the Skicorp to its knees with a can of spray paint."

"Now, darling," Lamar said. "No company secrets, please."

Kurt imagined that Miles was at the top of their list. "Staggs does good monitoring," he said. "He also opens mail and taps phones with the best of them. I can vouch for his work."

"Worry not." Lamar smiled at his two skeptical companions. "I've got him on a short leash."

They passed over the Ajax Mine and Kurt could see a shiny Pitco sheriff's car parked near the Airstream trailer. Lorenzo Banks was deep inside the shaft this morning, sifting through the rubble. He had thirty-six hours to find something before he was due back in Denver. Kurt had ten minutes until they reached the summit and the Lamars fluttered off to their avian fund-raiser.

"Who do you suppose Staggs would go after for Ned Carr's murder?" Kurt asked. He didn't have time to finesse this one. "The Sierra Club?"

The couple looked stunned. "The newspaper made no mention of murder," Lamar said in a quiet, reflective voice. "It sounded like a mine accident. Are you saying it was murder?"

"That's my bet," Kurt said, watching the charred mine adit disappear beneath them as the gondola crawled higher up the cable. "We'll know something soon. Maybe by the end of the day."

"My god," Meredith said, the crepe paper ruff crinkling as she gazed down at the mine. "Who would want to kill an old nut like Ned Carr?"

"He'd made so many enemies over the years," Kurt said, "it's hard to keep count without a score card."

Lamar appeared shaken by the disclosure. "He was a gigantic pain in the ass and fairly abusive to me personally," he said, "but I had a grudging respect for the old fart. He came up the hard way and he never compromised or backed down. Never. I admire someone who can outwit you at your own game."

"Was he outwitting you, Mr. Lamar?"

Lamar smiled wanly. "You tell me, Kurt. For a couple hundred bucks the man bought land nobody should've sold him. He built a home in a beautiful wilderness area of the Rockies. He sold thirty-five acres back to the Forest Service for a hundred times what he paid. And he took three generations of Skicorp owners to the cleaners—including your father's clique—soaking us for forty grand a year because his property happens to be right in the middle of one of the most glamorous ski runs in the world. Outwit me?" He laughed, a weary capitulation. "Hell, the man was twisting my tit every day of the year. He had something I wanted, and he knew it."

"I guess that's why I asked to speak with you, Mr. Lamar," Kurt said.

He didn't disapprove of this fellow as much as everyone else did. Unlike most graying barons in his tax bracket, Lee Lamar seemed ruled by boyish passions and momentary enthusiasms. He had captained his own orbit in the early, unnavigated ether of satellite telecommunications and cable networks, and the bottom line didn't matter to him anymore.

"I'm a cop and I have to ask this question. How bad did you want what Ned Carr had?"

Lamar eyed Kurt with what felt like a father's disapproval. He looked hurt.

"You're wasting your time, Kurt," Meredith said defensively, "if you think my husband had anything to do with Ned's death."

"It's okay, darling," Lamar said, patting her with a wing. "He's just doing his job."

In spite of the UV tint, sunshine blazed through the Plexiglas, heating the gondola to a summer broil. Kurt shifted uneasily in the seat. It was getting uncomfortable in this small tight enclosure.

"Of course I have a strong interest in Ned's property," Lamar said, his face growing stern. "Every year, when my lawyers negotiate the new lease, they're authorized to make him a generous offer for the Ajax Mine."

"Let me guess," Kurt smiled. "No deal."

"Ned was a stubborn son of a bitch. He loved the romance of the hardrock. Without his two mines he was just another sour old codger collecting SSI and spilling tapioca on his shirt. His work kept him going."

And his grandson, Kurt thought. He remembered the note taped to the terrarium.

"I even went so far as to propose a partnership, offering to eat his overhead and expenses, but he refused, of course."

There it was. A *partnership.*

"My most ingenious idea, if I do say so, was to suggest that we close down the silver operation altogether and conduct mine tours during the summer. Tourists love that kind of thing—it's straight out of the Old West. I told him the Skicorp would be happy to manage the business and send him a check every month, and all he had to do was lead a tour group now and then, whenever the spirit moved him."

Kurt knew that at $5.50 an ounce, silver was a losing proposition. But the old man didn't trust partners or accountants or bright offices full of computers. That's what was so puzzling about his last phone call.

"My husband did everything he could to accommodate that crusty old dinosaur," Meredith said. "Ned Carr was a bitter man. Angry at the world. Nothing was ever going to make him happy."

Their gondola had reached the final stretch of trampled field that served as a launching area for the Dipsy Doodle ski run in the winter season. Off to the right a group of Japanese tourists huddled around outdoor tables at the Sundeck restaurant, laughing at the robber jays swooping down to prey on leftover food. Birds of another feather were disembarking from gondolas in the station ahead, strutting off to their fund-raiser in flamboyant costumes.

"Look at Henley!" Meredith laughed, pointing.

"The Eagle?" Kurt said, turning to see.

"No, the Southwest willow flycatcher, if I'm not mistaken," she said.

At the landing Kurt helped her out of the gondola, then her husband, thanking them both for their time. He wondered if this patrician executive was capable of ordering a murder.

"Why don't you join us for lunch, Kurt?" Meredith suggested with an alluring smile. "You might find the company intriguing."

Partygoers were traipsing along the trail leading to a spruce-shaded ridge about fifty yards away, where servers wearing white dress jackets stood like royal sentries next to picnic tables engorged with colorful foods. Their fund-raiser was about the last place on earth Kurt wanted to be.

"Thanks for the invitation," he said, "but I didn't bring my tails."

He excused himself, explaining that he had to resume his work on the Carr investigation, and turned to catch the next gondola.

"Lee, you old bird!" chortled a short elderly matron emerging partially costumed from the rocking carriage. "Meredith! *Mein Gott,* this is fun! Do you recognize me? I'm a black-eared bushtit," the woman laughed heartily, showing off her ears polished with black greasepaint. "Sexually satisfied only above five thousand feet."

It was Else Prause, Kat Pfeil's aunt, a lively member of the old Austrian crowd and owner of an art gallery on Hopkins Street for over thirty years. At her side appeared her balding, bespectacled husband dragging behind a long iridescent cape that resembled a magpie tail.

"Do you know my niece Katrina?" Else asked. She hadn't lost an umlaut of her German accent since Kurt was a boy. "And her friend from—where is it, dear?—Ora-gawn?"

Kat Pfeil stepped out of the gondola, Randy close on her heels. The bodyguard was wearing a bulky green parka, mirror shades, a Seattle Seahawks cap concealing her flattop. She stopped and surveyed the scene, the outdoor restaurant tables and coin-operated telescopes angled toward the southern horizon, mountain bikers walking their wheels down the hike-and-bike trail.

"Well, look who's here," Meredith sang, giving Kurt a sidelong glance. "So nice to see you, Else. Darwin. Hello, Katrina."

"Let's get a move on, you turkeys," Lamar intoned. "Don't want to be late for the feed."

A ragtag group of revelers, including Aunt Else and her magpie husband, paraded off down the trail toward the picnic tables, a promenade of nightmarish bird people from a Hieronymus Bosch painting. Kat and Randy remained behind to say hello to Kurt.

"Is it my imagination," he said, "or did someone dump a gallon of LSD in the water supply?"

"The old town gets more bizarre every day," Kat

agreed. She was wearing comically oversized oval glasses and had glittered her cheeks with white flecks the size of a child's fingernail.

"Let me guess," Kurt said. "Spotted owl."

"I'm doing my best to blend in," she said dryly.

Behind menacing shades, her arms folded rigidly across the parka, Randy looked like one badass gum-chewing trooper. "Wearing that Glock today?" he asked her.

"You'll have to frisk me to find out, Big Boy," she said, offering the smallest hint of a smile.

"Randy, why don't you go ahead with the others," Kat said. "I'll catch up in a minute."

Randy touched the bill of her cap in a finger salute. "Will do, boss," she said.

Kat waited until the woman was several yards away before speaking. "I didn't expect to see you up here today," she said, sliding her hands into her jeans.

"I didn't expect to be here. I've got to get on back to work."

"Don't leave yet," she said, a surprising softness in her request. "Come take a walk with me."

Her limp appeared a burden on this rocky, uneven trail, the path descending and rising like the dorsal of a great lizard. She breathed heavily, her mouth open, her lungs struggling with the exertion in thinner air. He wondered if they should slow down and give her a rest.

"I was going to call you today," she said, pressing on. "I didn't like the way we left things last night. I'm sorry I got so angry and defensive."

"It was my fault. My approach wasn't very diplomatic."

"I want you to know I didn't have anything to do with Ned Carr's death and I don't know who did."

He stopped and smiled at her. He felt enormously relieved that she was being so direct. "Actually, Kat," he said, "I couldn't imagine that you were involved. But it was a good excuse to see you again. Twenty years is a long time."

Three mountain bikers rolled slowly around them, stirring dust. He wanted to ask her why she'd never written. Why she had let him go.

"I understand you have a son now."

He could feel his face glowing. "Lennon," he said. "He's a great kid."

"Is he old enough to fly-fish?"

When she was Lennon's age, her brother Jake and the two Muller boys had taken her down to the creek behind the Pfeil cabin and shown her how to cast a fly. Kurt remembered that morning with remarkable clarity.

"We've made a few trips to the Fryingpan," he said. "He's more interested in afternoon TV."

"I'd like to meet him," she said. "Why don't you bring him out tomorrow and we'll see if the rainbows are biting in the creek?"

She was making an effort to be friendly. "That's an invitation I won't turn down," he said. "Do you mind if we bring along Ned's grandson? He's staying with us now."

She removed the ludicrous owl-eye glasses. The alpine breeze fingered the dark hair away from her face. A lone bead of sweat trickled down her cheek. "Marie's son?" she asked with a frown.

He nodded. They had all attended the same Aspen schools for twelve years. Marie was a grade behind Kurt, two ahead of Kat. Everyone knew each other.

"Who is the boy's father?"

"I'm not sure anybody knows," Kurt said. "You remember what a free spirit Marie was when we were young. Well, she never slowed down. She had a weakness for the old freaks who make candles and hang around Renaissance fairs."

Kat smiled at some long-forgotten memory. "I always liked Marie. She organized the first Donovan fan club in the valley. We actually tried to get a mellow-yellow high off a stick of Juicy Fruit mushed in a rotten banana."

"I think I still have one of those in my deep freeze, if you want to split it with me."

She laughed and took his arm as they began walking again. He understood that her embrace was less an act of endearment than a need for physical support.

"My wife and I were with her in the same birthing class. She always came alone. I don't recall her ever mentioning a steady man in her life." He smiled sadly, remembering Marie's frantic energy, her effort to become the perfect single mother. "She picked Meg to be her breathing coach during Hunter's birth. We got the babies together in our playtime circle. At the time of the accident she was raising him by herself in an old house the other side of Mountain Valley."

Though he had tried to avoid such morbid reflection, Kurt sometimes found himself picturing the last moments of Marie's life. The wall of snow hurling her three hundred feet down the pass, snapping her bones, churning her body in ice as thick as wet cement. He was certain her final thoughts had been of her son, his name a mantra until the darkness rushed over her.

"The boy was living with Ned?" Kat asked.

"He was probably a better father to Hunter than he'd been to his own kids."

"The poor child must be traumatized beyond belief."

"So far, so good," Kurt said.

They had drawn near the party. Friends of the Forest, a hundred green socialites adorned as their favorite birds, strutting between tables, pecking at food. Randy was standing alone on a rock ledge thirty yards beyond the gathering, peering southward down into Annie Basin with her field binoculars.

"How do you know Meredith?" he asked Kat.

"Everybody in the movement knows Meredith," she said. "She was raising hell long before the rest of us." She watched the gathering with a bemused smile. "Though frankly I don't understand her marriage."

"The environmentalists now have one of the wealthiest men in the world on their side."

"Mmm," she said, a pondering nod. "Patronage for sex. I believe there's a name for that, Kurt."

He smiled, held up a hand. "Whoa. I thought you were friends. She seems very fond of you."

"We're friends," Kat said firmly. "I hate to sound so judgmental. I guess I'm just not willing to go that far for a cause."

The media had always portrayed Katrina Pfeil as someone who would do anything to further her issues. She had once chained herself to the top of an old-growth redwood. The Forest Service and the local Sheriff's Department spent two long days trying to haul her down.

"I wouldn't be too hard on her," he said. "Maybe she's really in love with the guy."

"Ah, yes, love. It makes fools of us all, doesn't it?"

They began walking again, quieted by her melancholy mood. Two mountain bikers, a young couple fit as Norsemen, called out a warning and swerved around them. Kurt wondered if people his age ever fell head over heels in love. He felt so intractable now, his passions buried, atrophied by neglect. He wasn't sure he could recognize the signs anymore.

"Miles ran me off the road heading for your place last night," he said. "Are you two old buddies?"

She smiled at something distant and dreamy. "I've known Miles since I was a college kid," she said. "I took a photography course from him one summer. It consisted of our class hiking up to remote lakes, eating peyote, and listening to Jimi Hendrix tapes. Miles was trying to free us from the frame."

"Did he tell you about my visit to his bunker?"

"Sure," she shrugged. "He thinks you've become a fascist cop."

"Is that what you think too?"

She stopped and studied his eyes. "I think your job must be very hard on you," she said, touching his cheek affectionately. "I hope it hasn't made you cynical. You were always a sweetheart."

Her face was flushed and damp. She raked her hands through her dark hair and it stayed pulled back, moistened by the hike. He pictured her slender body rising from the steam, the lovely sway of her waist and hips. In his memory there were no scars.

"I FOUND CARR'S other mine," Randy said, adjusting the binoculars.

Ned's stubborn enterprise had carved a barren spot in the fir forest two hundred yards below, the mine's adit surrounded by a slide area of gray silt that looked like the churned-up leavings of an enormous dirt-boring insect.

"The Lone Ute," Kurt said. "That cabin is where he lived."

The three of them were standing together on the rock ledge, staring down at the woodlands enveloping the backside of Aspen Mountain. A brisk spring wind rippled their clothes.

"Have a look at his sludge pond," Randy said, passing the binoculars to Kat. "What a lovely sight."

Kurt didn't need the glasses to find the pond, its surface as black and motionless as a tar pit. "For thirty years Ned let the weather wash his lead tailings down the mountain," he said, "until the EPA came along and made him put in that pond to collect the waste. Now the thing is leaking arsenic and sulfuric acid into the aquifer."

He had never understood the old man's strange romantic obsession with holes in the ground. What on earth had possessed him to undertake so much trouble, cause so much destruction and ill will, over so little return?

"Randy, if you walk into any hotel lobby in town you'll see photographs of how Aspen Mountain looked a hundred years ago," he said. "Those old hardrock stiffs didn't give a damn how ugly the land got as long as they were pulling up high-grade silver. When our parents came here after the war, the mountain was still crisscrossed with muddy mining roads, and the old chutes and headframes were falling to pieces everywhere you looked."

Kat searched Annie Basin with the binoculars. "The last good thing the Rumpf people did for the mountain was clean up the junk, seal off the mines, and give nature a chance to heal herself."

Kurt knew she had never been fond of her father and considered the entire early ski venture its own violation of the mountain.

"So how did this guy Ned get away with what he was doing?" Randy asked.

"The friggin' Mining Law of 1872," Kat said.

Kurt smiled at her. In their childhood they had heard their parents explain and condemn the law in a thousand angry conversations. He and Kat could issue a brief on the subject.

"To keep up a valid claim," he said, "all you have to show is a hundred dollars' worth of mine work a year. At least Ned was actually working his two shafts, waiting for silver to hit ten bucks an ounce someday so he could get serious about it. There was a guy named Cameron around the turn of the century who staked claims in the Grand Canyon, but instead of mining he built a hotel and livery business on the south rim and charged sightseers admission to use the trails. It took Teddy Roosevelt and the courts fifteen years to shut the bastard down."

"The Mining Law was supposed to stimulate western

expansion," Kat added, lowering the binoculars. "The agenda being to draw white people out to the godforsaken badlands to civilize the place. The original framers of the law would probably be surprised that a hundred and twenty-odd years later you can still get public land at 1872 prices, five dollars an acre. The title is yours free and clear—no government lease payments, no royalties to the national kitty—as long as you keep up the pretense you're mining."

Kurt could see sunlight shimmering off the tin roof of Ned's cabin down in the basin. When the deputies searched the place last night, they'd found no obvious signs of theft or vandalism. It seemed unlikely that the ponytailed man was a common looter—the cabin's remote location didn't lend itself to the average hit-and-run burglar. So what was he doing there?

"Six hundred million acres have been lost to the Mining Law," Kat said, shaking her head. "In the late nineteen thirties the Forest Service concluded that eighty-five percent of the claims hadn't produced a single nugget. A GAO study a couple of years ago showed that nobody had hit a shovel lick in eighty percent of the million claims they looked at. We're talking about con artists buying up sizable parcels of public land that have a fair-market value worth literally forty thousand times the five bucks an acre—land that belongs to you and me—and using it for their own personal gain. Condos, hunting lodges, pot farms. It's the biggest scam going, but the corporate mining lobby has stomped on every effort at reform. They don't want to pay what the land's worth, or kick in royalties to the federal government."

"When silver was money and the whole world

wanted it," Kurt said, "the law made sense. Men like Ned were doing what the microchip people are doing now. Filling a need, changing the future."

Randy squatted down and poked at the hard shale with a stick she'd found. "And as usual," she said, "leaving a mess for the mothers to clean up."

16

TYLER RUTLEDGE KNEW it was only a matter of time until someone made contact with him. The message had come from an unlikely source, a sheriff's deputy who had stopped Tyler's truck on the highway and told him that an unnamed party was interested in arranging a meeting. Tyler wadded up the warning ticket and tossed it back at the cop. "Somebody wants to talk to me," he said, "they can find me working the Lone Ute most any morning."

He was mucking loose rock near the top of a deep stope, forty yards inside the shaft, when he heard footsteps approaching, quiet voices echoing against the stone walls. He grabbed the twelve-gauge, pumped a shell into the chamber, and climbed quickly up the ladder to the main drift to wait for them behind an ore car. The floodlights were strong here and air from a five-inch ventilation hose cooled his wet shirt and sweating face.

Someone called his name. He didn't respond. Two men soon appeared in the tunnel, shielded their eyes against the blinding light, and stepped back out of the glare. "Sorry to drop in unannounced," said a tall, suave gray-haired man, his hands tucked in the pockets of a khaki fisherman's vest. "We didn't know how else to reach you, Tyler."

Tyler shrugged and pulled the Red Man pouch from his hip pocket. "You reached me," he said, fitting a wad into the corner of his mouth. "What's on your mind, boys? I got work to do."

"I think you've already met my associate."

The bearded man emerged from the shadows and smiled. "Hello, Tyler," he said, his small eyes disappearing into high, fatty cheekbones. Today he was wearing flannel instead of the cammo flak jacket. "How's your shuffleboard game?"

Tyler reached for the pump shotgun and braced it on the lip of the ore car. "What do you want?" he said, releasing the safety with an audible click. "You got about sixty seconds before I consider you a couple of dead trespassers."

"Relax, son," said the gray-haired man. "We're here to extend a friendly invitation. Our client would like to meet you. He's very interested in your future and is looking forward to working things out between you. He would be delighted if you'd be his guest for a few days. Call it a working vacation. Do you play golf?"

Tyler spit a stream of juice into the dirt. "Fuck golf," he said.

"Our client has considerable resources at his disposal, Tyler. I'm sure he can offer something in the way of recreation that will suit your pleasure. Why don't you let us arrange a get-together? Think of it as a nice break from"—he gazed around the narrow mine shaft—"your labor," he said. "This partnership is a once-in-a-lifetime opportunity, my friend, and believe me, everybody's going to walk away happy once the details are smoothed out."

Tyler didn't like the way this man talked. He sounded like a lawyer. Slick, condescending, the kind of silver-tongued bureaucrat who was making life miserable for everybody.

"Ned told me about your boss. He had a swell time drinking margaritas and playing all-night poker with the boss and his buddies."

"I'm sure he did," the gray-haired man smiled.

"And then he wound up dead."

The smile evaporated when Tyler raised the shotgun to his shoulder and aimed. "So which one of you motherfuckers rewired the charge?"

He watched the bearded fellow turn slowly and look back down the shaft toward the entrance.

"Take it easy, son," said the gray-haired man. "There's something in this for everyone. Why don't you at least come and hear what my client has to say?"

"Go tell your *client* to kiss my ass," Tyler said, sighting down the barrel at the man's chest. "Tell him if I ever find out for sure he killed my partner, I'm coming after him."

"You're making a foolish mistake here, Tyler. I wish I could talk some sense into you."

Tyler nudged the shotgun up and down. "Get off this property," he said, "and take the knuckle-dragger with you."

The bearded man grinned at Tyler's remark and turned again, waving his arm in a signal to someone back at the entrance. "Didn't your old man ever teach you not to point a gun at people?" he said with a threatening growl.

Then the mine went dark.

17

THE FIRST TWO reports sounded like doors slamming in the distance. They were followed by three echoing cracks and a quick blurt of gunfire.

"Jesus Christ!" Kat said. "Somebody's shooting down there."

"Where?" Kurt said, grabbing the binoculars from her. He scanned the woodland slope and discovered a puff of gray smoke drifting up from the Lone Ute adit. A Toyota 4 × 4 was spinning off past Ned's cabin, retreating rapidly into the trees. Where the hell was the deputy assigned to the place?

"Three men were running from the mine!" Kat said.

Kurt tossed her the binoculars. "Keep watching!" he said.

Racing over to the picnic tables, he shouted, "Who's got a cell phone? This is a police emergency! Does anybody have a cell phone?"

A half-dozen bird men produced phones.

"Phil, call nine-one-one and tell the Sheriff's Department to send deputies to the Lone Ute Mine," he instructed an architect whose kid played on their soccer team. "Tell the dispatcher the situation looks dangerous and there may be weapons involved. One of our men might be down."

A hush fell over the party. Kurt pulled the shield from his hip pocket and held it up to a trio of mountain bikers wheeling along the path nearby. "Pitkin County Sheriff's Department!" he said, slowing them to a stop. "I need your bike."

"No way, dude," said an incredulous young man wearing a Day-Glo Lycra riding suit.

"You'll get it back," Kurt said, taking hold of the handlebar. "If anything happens to it, the department will reimburse you."

The rider began to protest. He didn't expect Kurt to rip his bicycle out from under him. "Hey, man, you can't do that!" the young man shouted.

Kurt peddled quickly over to the rock ledge, where Kat stood peering down at the forest below. "I don't see anybody, Kurt," she said, the binoculars pressed to her eyes. "There was a truck but it's gone."

"How about Tyler Rutledge?"

"No."

"Give me your Glock, Randy," he said.

Randy stared at him. "No can do," she said, chewing gum with a stoic detachment.

"If you're worried about Kat, go tell those people over there to call Miles on their phone. He'll meet you with a *trunkload* of guns at the gondola station," he said. "Now give me your Glock."

"What the hell do you think you're going to do, hotshot?" Randy asked.

"Take the shortcut," he said. He would lose nearly an hour if he rode the gondola back down, got in his Jeep, and drove the roads to Annie Basin.

"You're going straight down the mountain on a *bicycle*?" Randy smirked.

"Un-hunh," he said.

"Give him your gun, Randy," Kat said, lowering the glasses. "We'll be okay."

Randy took her time considering the order. "I'm doing this against my better judgment," she said, unzipping the parka and reaching in to her shoulder holster.

Kurt released the Glock's magazine, zipped the clip into his jacket pocket, and shoved the unloaded pistol in his waistband. "Later, dudes," he said, launching himself past the bike's irate owner, speeding for the old Jeep trail over Richmond Hill and down into the basin.

"Kurt, be careful!" he heard Kat shout after him.

He rode the brakes down the rugged switchbacks through the trees, fishtailing around rockslide talus and patches of black ice, his legs growing rubbery and weak. He was thankful there were no hikers today, so early in the season. Sweat poured down his face, ribs, calves. The stiff wind whipped his long hair into greasy snarls. There was a scary moment, right before the final plummet past Ned's property fence, when the back wheel began to wobble and he thought he'd blown a tire.

He could see the tall corrugated headframe of the Lone Ute poking up in the forest and skidded to a stop. Abandoning the bike, he rolled under the barbed wire fence and snapped the magazine into the 9mm as he stumbled down the hillside toward the mine. To slow his lumbering descent he latched on to the trunk of an Engelmann spruce and knelt quickly to catch his breath, spitting a dry cotton wad, his heart pounding so hard he thought it might burst through his shirt.

From this knoll he had a clear view of Ned's cabin and the entrance to the mine. Tyler's pickup with the spiderwebbed windshield was parked next to an old yellow school bus used as a storage shed, but there was no sign of him or the deputy. Kurt waited, breathing through his open mouth, trying to get a bead on the situation before rushing ahead. He smelled heavy cordite, a sure sign there had been gunplay. Was anyone still here? An eerie silence had settled over the work site.

He gave himself two minutes to steady his breathing, then raised the Glock shoulder high and dashed for the black hole in the mountainside. When he reached the adit he found spatters of blood on the ground by the entrance, a thin trail leading out to the clearing where the Toyota 4×4 must have been parked. Somebody had taken a bullet.

He shielded himself behind a splintery support beam and shouted into the dark shaft. "Sheriff's Department! Is anybody in the mine?"

His voice echoed back at him. There was no visibility beyond the first twenty feet. He waited, counting silently, giving them a chance to respond.

"This is Kurt Muller with the police! If anybody is in the mine, I want you to come forward and identify yourself!"

The thought of exposing himself to the long dark tunnel churned his stomach. Ned's explosion was fresh on his mind.

"Tyler Rutledge!" he called. "Are you in there? Come out and identify yourself!"

At first he thought it was wind howling through the shaft. The sound was faint, plaintive, a human voice moaning deep inside the mine.

No no no, he thought. *I can't do this. What happened to the deputy on duty? And where are the goddamned lights to this place?*

Like a diver before a plunge, he sucked in a quick breath and held it, then scurried into the mine, sliding his hand along the cold rock wall at eye level, searching for the fuse box. It had to be there somewhere. Fuse box and throw switch. Miners were practical people. This was where they would locate the juice.

The box was close by, all right, with just enough light from outside to show Kurt what he didn't want to see. Wires dangled like entrails from the box's open door. Someone had jerked everything loose.

The moaning was louder now, a man in serious pain. *No,* he told himself, staring down the shaft into utter darkness. He sat down in the packed dirt and placed the Glock next to him on the ground. He couldn't do this. He had seen the rescue men carry Billy Nichols's small broken body out of a mine. He had watched them unzip the black bag that held together what was left of his brother after a fall from Maroon Bells. He just couldn't do this. He had been a fool to dash down here without proper backup.

He thought he could hear the word *please* in the feeble keening moan. How much longer would it take the 911 call to arrive? Twenty minutes? Thirty? Maybe he should run to Ned's cabin and call for EMS assistance as well. Somebody with more experience at tunnel rescue.

Please. A small desperate prayer echoing in the gloom.

Kurt rose to his feet. Was it Tyler? he wondered. The

deputy? Somebody wounded in an exchange with three men in the Toyota 4 × 4?

He stuck the pistol in his belt and gazed far into the shaft, the darkness dropping like a black curtain beyond the slanting rays of sunlight.

What if it was your boy? What if Lennon was down there in the dark with a hole through his chest?

Kurt turned and sprinted out of the mine for Tyler's pickup. He threw open the passenger door and popped the glove compartment. Among the yellowing traffic tickets and screwdrivers and coils of electrician's tape he found what he was looking for. A long silver flashlight. The batteries were weak, but they would have to do.

For forty yards or so the shaft was as straight as a chalk line, and Kurt followed the narrow-gauge tracks into deeper opacity, the air thick with bitter cordite. The moaning was sporadic now, and every long silence urged him on. The flashlight beam fluttered and grew dim, and he stopped to tap the light against his thigh, the walls closing in around him like a cold black membrane.

When he reached the ore car his beam danced over a shotgun lying where it had dropped on a pile of mine rubble. Blood spotted the dirt floor, trailed away. His light traced the red splatters to a junction of several shafts—at least three narrow crawl spaces tunneling upward at forty-five degrees from each other, and a gaping hole in the floor that appeared to be a deep vertical stope. As he drew closer he could hear the moans again, and he was fairly certain they were coming from the bottom of that hole.

"Tyler!" he called, kneeling down to peer over the

edge. The hair on his arms stood on end as the stope sucked the chilled air around him, a swift downward draft, the dank odor of an ancient cavern. "Tyler, are you down there, man?"

The flashlight beam flickered weakly over the terrible blackness. He saw a body curled up on a steplike ledge about twenty feet below. The beam dimmed again and he tapped the thing against his hip, shaking the batteries. The light blinked, shrank to a match flare, and died. He tapped it again but nothing happened. The darkness was total, unlike anything he had ever experienced. He couldn't see the dials on his watch.

Easy, he told himself. *Don't panic. Keep it together.*

He heard footsteps behind him, someone so close he could smell his sweat. "Who's there?" Kurt said, his heart in his throat.

He wheeled around and stood up, pointing his pistol, but the darkness confused his sense of direction. Another footstep crunched over loose rock and Kurt swung the pistol toward the sound, upsetting his balance. He tried to plant a foot behind him for support but the dirt gave way and his leg buckled and instantly he was sliding down the stope, losing the gun, the flashlight, clawing desperately at the soft clay walls, screaming, grabbing at anything that would slow his fall into the bottomless void that had swallowed Billy Nichols. His head ricocheted off something sharp and there was a white flash behind his eyes and then everything stopped abruptly.

He was lying on his back, alive, his bones intact. He had come to rest on a bed of soft wet poppies. *Now I lay me down to sleep,* he thought, soil raining over him from the grave digger's spade.

18

"THE BOY DIDN'T need that," said a deep voice, someone standing over him.

Kurt raised his head but thought he was dreaming. There was a penlight shining in his eyes. "Ned?" he said.

"He was damn near dead without you falling on him."

The bed of poppies was the moaning man. Kurt had landed on top of Tyler Rutledge.

"Get a grip, hoss," said the voice behind the light. "We've gotta haul him up out of here before he bleeds to death."

Kurt tried to sit up. His head swirled, the back of his shirt was wet with Tyler's blood. "You're not dead," he managed to say.

"You musta hit your head."

"Is it really you?"

"We've run into each other before," the man said. "You have something that belongs to me."

Strong hands searched through Kurt's tangled jacket, turning out empty pockets.

"Who the hell *are* you?" Kurt asked. He couldn't

decipher the man's face but he realized now it wasn't
Ned Carr.

"I'm the Lone Ute, Tonto," the man said with a
raspy laugh. "What the hell did you do with my
neckpiece?"

"It's in an evidence Baggie in the Pitkin County
Sheriff's Department."

"Shit." The man stood up. "Next time I see you, you
better give it back. Now roll out of the way so I can get
to that boy."

Kurt began to crawl away and then froze, feeling the
cold suction of air whistling up the stope. "Where's the
drop-off?" he asked, panic-stricken.

"Don't move any more thataway," the man said,
aiming the tiny light toward the black chasm. "It's
about twenty levels straight down to the flooded shafts,
and then another twenty full of water."

He stuck the light in his mouth and squatted down,
grappling Tyler by the limp arms and hoisting him over
his shoulder like a sack of grain. "You coming or staying?"

"You've got the only light," Kurt said, rising un-
steadily to his feet.

"There's a ladder over here," the man said. "Give me
a hand with this little turd."

The penlight was useless beyond five or six feet. The
man pointed the way, directing Kurt up the ladder as
far as the light would penetrate; then Kurt was on his
own, securing one hand over the other as he climbed
cautiously into the overhead darkness. At the top he
steadied himself on a wooden platform that croaked
and swayed beneath his boots. He waited nervously, his

arms aloft for balance, watching the meager light bob upward along the ladder, the man bearing Tyler's unconscious body over one shoulder, an impressive feat of strength. Kurt could bench-press 250 pounds but he wasn't sure he could do what this fellow was doing.

The penlight clamped between his teeth, the man grunted something incomprehensible when he reached the platform. Kurt bent down to grab Tyler and drag him up.

"Your turn," the man huffed, panting like a dray horse as he dropped down to rest next to the body.

Kurt laid his ear on Tyler's bloody chest and listened for a heartbeat. Pressing three fingers to his neck, he could detect a weak pulse.

"Were you in the firefight?" he asked the man.

"No," he said, his lungs heaving.

"What are you doing here? Why were you in Ned's cabin last night?"

The man remained silent, breathing hard.

"Did you see what happened?"

"Some of it."

"I'm a cop," Kurt said.

"I know who you are. Let's get the fuck out of here."

Their respiration was more labored now, and Kurt wondered if someone had cut off the oxygen in the ventilation hose. He knew they had to move quickly before their endurance played out.

"Which way?" he said, managing to load Tyler over his shoulder with the man's help.

"Follow me."

Kurt held on to the man's shirttail and they inched ahead in the darkness, the penlight's small ray butterflying over the shaft floor at their feet. After several minutes he stopped to rest.

"Hey!" he called out as the ponytailed man continued on, the light shrinking in the distance. "Hey, hold up! I'm taking a break."

"Just keep heading where you're heading," the man's voice echoed back at him. "Keep your feet between the rail tracks. You'll be all right."

"Get your ass back here with that light!"

The man's laughter floated like a black ribbon in the enclosing gloom and then quickly vanished. Kurt took a deep breath, hefted the body in his arms, and pressed on, sweat streaming down his face, his mind wandering into fathomless waters. Soon he was adrift in a cold damp place, weightless, gasping for air, the fear so cruel he felt the blood chilling in his veins. He thought he might have been floating for three days and three nights in the belly of a giant sea beast, like Jonah, tossed into this murky abyss by an angry God. Were those human voices he was hearing, the mariners who had hurled him overboard?

"Pitkin County Sheriff's Department! Please identify yourself!"

Bright lights exploded down the tunnel, blinding him. The sudden flash threw off his equilibrium and he sank to his knees, surrendering Tyler to the ground in front of him.

"Kurt, is that you?" A woman's voice. Muffin Brown. "Bring the stretchers!" she commanded. "Let's get some help in here!"

He shielded his face with his hands, the intense spotlight like an ice sliver plunged between his eyes. "Take this man to the hospital," he mumbled. "He's almost dead."

He could hear footsteps running toward him, Muffin calling his name again. And then he collapsed headlong into the ancient seabed, the bottom of the earth.

19

HE WOKE UP in a hospital bed with an IV tube in his arm. Muffin was sitting in a chair across the room. "Hey, hero," she smiled, coming over to squeeze his hand. "Back from the land of Nod?"

"How's Tyler?"

"Still in surgery," she said, her face darkening. "Two gunshot wounds. One shattered his forearm, the other punctured a lung. He's barely hanging on. If you hadn't got to him when you did, he'd be dead by now."

Kurt groped around to find the bed's adjustment button. "Raise me up," he said. "What am I doing in here?"

"Well, for one thing you were hallucinating like a madman and the doctor thought you might've suffered some oxygen loss to the brain," she said. "Not that anyone would notice. How long were you in the mine?"

"I don't know."

"You were pretty disoriented, Kurt. You kept babbling about an Indian."

"Did you talk to him?"

"Who?"

"The Lone Ute. Did he come out of the mine?"

She patted his hand and pressed a button, raising him to a sitting position. "Your electrolytes are real low and you're dehydrated," she said, nodding at the IV, "and they want to get your blood pressure down."

"There was another guy in there with us. Without him we'd both still be halfway to hell."

"And this guy was an Indian."

"I think so. The same guy I wrestled with in Ned's place."

He could see the confusion in her face. "How do you know that?"

He shrugged. "He was looking for his choker."

Her eyes narrowed with faint amusement. "He wears a choker?"

"It's an Indian thing."

She nodded, patted his hand again, rearranged the sheet.

"Stop doing that," he said. "I'm not nuts. Where the devil is the nurse?" He found the call button and buzzed for assistance. "I'm getting out of here. I've got to meet Corky Marcus at four o'clock."

"Don't be a jerk, Kurt. They want to keep you under observation for twenty-four hours. You've been through a lot and your body's run down. You could use the rest."

"I feel ducky. I just need somebody to take this goddamn tube out of my arm."

"You're one stubborn son of a bitch," Muffin said, her hands on her hips.

"Would you please get the nurse."

"The department can handle this one, Kurt. We won't fall apart if you take a day off. We've managed just fine for the past year without you."

It caught him off guard, a sudden, unexpected moment of doubt. She had jabbed him in the one place he was vulnerable. The department could do without him. Ten years in the ring, his back against the ropes every day, body slams from the commissioners, the media, the FBI. A ruined marriage, a dead brother. None of that counted. The department would survive no matter who was in charge. Kurt Muller was replaceable.

"I'm glad to hear that," he said, trying to contain his resentment. "Then maybe you can explain where your deputy was—the one who was supposed to be on duty watching the Carr property when all this shooting went down."

Muffin was prepared for criticism. "Tyler chased him off," she said. "He showed up around ten o'clock and told our man to take a hike, he didn't need a watchdog."

"It wasn't Tyler's call."

"Gillespie didn't want a confrontation. He figured it was broad daylight, give Tyler some space. Who's going to come messing around in the middle of the day?"

"Try three assholes in a Toyota four-by-four," he said. "Tyler must've popped one of them. Have you checked all the valley clinics for gunshot victims?"

"We're on it, Kurt," she said, her annoyance growing. "We've sampled the blood on the ground outside the mine. We've got our men in the shaft, collecting evidence, trying to reconstruct what happened. Forensics is looking at a bullet fragment from Tyler's arm. We've even taken a statement from your old chum."

He looked puzzled. What old chum?

"Jake's sister, the tree humper with binoculars," she said, reading his confusion.

Kurt was still feeling drowsy but his head was slowly beginning to clear. They must have shot him up with something. "What about Lorenzo Banks?" he said. "Has he found anything in the Ajax?"

"Not a neon arrow, if that's what you mean. When I left him he was still poking around in the rubble. He had ruled out all the textbook devices with wires and timers. But he's got a long way to go."

There had to be a connection between what had happened to Ned and the shootout with Tyler. Maybe the men in the Toyota were those dirt-bikers from the Black Diamond. Maybe they had already dealt with the old man who had violated their code.

"Tyler and I had a nasty run-in yesterday with some bubbas in the Autobahn Society," he told her. "Let's pull them in for questioning. They were mad enough to lynch the poor bastard."

He could almost hear the gears clicking in Muffin's head. "Did this run-in take place at a notorious gin joint in Bonedale?" she asked with a sly intonation. "And did it result in a demolished Dumpster?"

"I refuse to answer that without my attorney present."

"I had another conversation with Sheriff Dan the Man this morning, Kurt," she said. "He's very interested in talking to you."

"Where is that damn nurse?" he said, pressing the call button again. "I've gotta get out of here. Hospitals make me paranoid."

At that moment the nurse entered the room. "Knock knock," she said, a tall pretty woman named Sally who had helped Dr. Perry administer four stitches to Kurt's forehead last summer. "How are you feeling, Kurt? Did you need something?"

"Yeah, Sally, I need to be released."

She exchanged glances with Muffin. "I'm afraid that's not a good idea," the nurse said. "The doctor thinks you ought to take it easy for a day or so. We've got to get some fluids back in you."

"Can I please speak with him? Is he in the building?" He had considered removing the IV himself, putting on his pants, and walking out of here.

Dr. Perry arrived with surprising haste and spent twenty minutes trying to talk Kurt out of leaving. Finally the young physician gave in. "All right, Kurt, if you're this damned sure of yourself," he said, clearly exasperated by Kurt's stubbornness, "you must be feeling okay. But take it easy for a couple of days, will you? You may think you're twenty-five, my friend," he said, wagging the clipboard at him, "but the charts show me otherwise."

20

KURT WAS AN hour late for his appointment with Corky Marcus, but as he strode across the Hyman Avenue cobblestones and glanced up through the branches of the planted cottonwoods, he could see a light in the window of Corky's attic office and knew he was still at work. For most of his life Corky Marcus had been a practicing attorney, Harvard Law, third in his class, an ardent civil rights activist who had spilled his blood in Alabama with the Freedom Riders. During those dark early days of the movement he had wandered the back roads of the Deep South, registering black voters, and later had worked for Head Start and VISTA and a host of noble causes. But in the lean Reagan years, to pay his bills and send two children from a previous marriage to college, Corky had represented a cadre of bib-overall pot growers hiding out in the rural West and soon became known as a drug lawyer, much to his chagrin. After one of his outlaw clients turned a shotgun on himself and his two young daughters in an Idaho cabin, Corky gave up his practice altogether and had now become everybody's favorite fourth-grade teacher at Aspen Elementary. "I go to work in the morning with a smile on my face," he'd told Kurt recently, "and I come home with a smile on my face. I should've done this a long time ago."

Corky still maintained a shrinking backlist of clients, a half-dozen locals for whom he felt loyalty and obligation, the ones who had been with him from the beginning in Aspen, sixteen years now. But he did not love the law anymore and his people knew that if their case required sincere emotional commitment, they were better off with someone else.

In an alcove between a souvenir shop and a busy Thai café there was an inconspicuous stairwell leading up to Corky's office. Kurt mounted the stairs, feeling somewhat fuzzy and out of sorts, a side effect of the drugs, he suspected, and not stress or exhaustion, as the doctor had surmised. The shower and change of clothing had not revived him entirely.

The office door was open. Behind an ornate mahogany desk strewn with assignments and folders and children's drawings, Corky sat scribbling on a stack of fourth-grade homework, making smiley-face notations with a red pen, licking on stars. "Yo, Kurt," he said, peering up through thick horn-rim glasses. "I'd given up on you. Haven't you heard of a marvelous new invention called the telephone?"

"Sorry, Corky," Kurt said, flopping down on a dusty couch by the bay windows. "I was in the hospital."

Corky smiled his homely smile. "And I thought my kids came up with the best excuses."

Meg had once described Corky as Woody Allen on skis. Short, sinewy and fit, mid-fifties, beaglelike, his unkempt mop of hair only now beginning to gray. He was the smartest man Kurt had ever met. Politics, literature, art, the long-term fiduciary implications of your charitable remainder unitrust. Corky Marcus had an inexhaustible command of the large, the small, the merely comic.

"Somebody tried to kill Tyler Rutledge in the Lone Ute Mine. He was in surgery for about four hours this afternoon. His chances of survival aren't real good."

Corky frowned, locked his hands behind his head, and leaned back in the old high-backed leather chair, exposing salt rings in the armpits of his zip-up gray jogging jacket. His T-shirt declared FILM IS ART, THEATER IS LIFE, TELEVISION IS FURNITURE.

"The two of them back to back. I'm no metaphysician," Corky said, "but this is way off the chance graph."

"You said it yourself. Ned was acting strange, and now this." Kurt had sunk so deeply in the spongy couch cushions his bottom was dragging against a spring. He pulled himself to his feet and stood by the window. "When he told you he wanted to change his will, did he say what he had in mind?"

"No," Corky said, rising from the imposing chair to search through a tray of papers located on a file cabinet. "He was coming in next week. We would talk."

"He didn't mention any new business associates?"

"None," Corky said, raising a curious eyebrow. "What makes you ask?"

"Something he said the night before he died. He'd cut a deal with the devil."

"Mmm. That was always my line when I was a lawyer."

He found the folder he was looking for and sat down again. Behind him towered his bookshelves of legal tomes, hiking guides, favorite novels, cookbooks, volumes on teaching techniques and child psychology. The small office was stuffed so full of books and file cabinets and creeping plants, there was little room for his Soloflex muscle machine.

"I pulled his file last night," Corky said. "He emended his will three years ago, our last official interaction. Estate planning is all I've been handling for him. I know bupkis about his other litigation."

"Didn't you represent him against the Sierra Club and the county during the sound-ordinance beef?" A legal battle over the times of day Ned could set off his blasting charges.

"Please," Corky raised a hand. "Don't remind me. The worst mistake of my legal career. Well, close. I took his case because Marie had just been killed and I felt sorry for Hunter." Corky knew Marie from the same birthing class, the monthly reunions. "Never again. I can't afford to make more enemies in this life. I told Ned he would have to find someone else to fight his mine skirmishes for him. Christ, I'm a card-carrying member of the Wilderness Society!"

Kurt looked out the window. The row of century-old brick buildings cast a long shadow over the pedestrian mall below. Foot traffic was light this time of year, the shoulder season between skiing and the summer crowds. A couple of shopgirls were chatting quietly on a bench beneath the cottonwoods, taking a cigarette break from their slacker jobs.

"You've read the will," Kurt said. "Who gets those two worthless mines if Tyler dies?"

Corky hesitated. "Is this an official police inquiry?"

Kurt shrugged. "Sure," he said.

"If I don't give you the information you'll go to the DA and get the court to open the will, am I correct?"

"That's about the size of it, Corkus."

"Well, then," he smiled, "as the executor of my client's estate, I judge it in everyone's best interest to reveal the contents of the will during the present inquiry."

Kurt shook his head wearily. "Shakespeare was right, wasn't he?"

"Why do you think I'm teaching fourth grade?"

"Less paperwork, better food."

Corky opened the file in front of him. "This may come as a surprise, Sheriff Muller, but Tyler Rutledge is not the beneficiary of the mines. He is a salaried employee of the Carr Mining Company and not a business partner."

"He understands that?"

"Of course," Corky nodded. "Though I doubt he and Ned ever seriously discussed the business end of the enterprise. Ned was a very private cuss—the word *sneaky* comes to mind—and Tyler didn't give a damn about financial arrangements as long as he could spend his life digging for silver and pulling down a paycheck every month."

"So who were Ned's partners? And who is the beneficiary?"

Corky threw up his hands. "He didn't believe in partners, which is why I am frankly surprised you think there was something rational behind Ned's midnight rantings," he said, leafing through the pages. "And the beneficiary is obvious." His knobby chin lifted and he gazed across the big desk at Kurt. "His grandson, Hunter."

Kurt had overlooked the obvious. He hadn't even considered Hunter. There was a sudden, unsettling flutter in his stomach. "Well, now, I guess that brings us around to the original purpose of this meeting," he said, resting his weight on the round arm of the couch. "Who did Ned name to be the boy's guardian?"

The old man trusted no one, Kurt thought. *Who the hell would he appoint? Tink Tarver?*

"Here it is," Corky said, finding the typewritten page. "This is what we worked on three years ago. My language, of course." He began to read: "In the event of my death I insist that every effort be made to locate my son, Nathan Daniel Carr, through whatever investigative means are necessary, to place in his guardianship my grandson and legal ward, Hunter James Carr, son of Marie Carr and sole beneficiary of the Carr Mining Company."

"Nathan?" Kurt said, surprised. "Does anybody know where he is?"

If he was still alive, Nathan Carr would be Kat Pfeil's age, early forties. Kurt recalled that once, while pushing the kids in their strollers along the Rio Grande Trail, Marie had mentioned that she hadn't seen or heard from her brother in fifteen years. Father and son had had a falling out when Nathan was in college and the boy had angrily disappeared from their lives. From time to time rumors had surfaced about him. He was a male prostitute in San Francisco. He was confined to an institution for violent schizophrenics. He had died of a drug overdose in Morocco. Marie discounted them all. She had known her brother as a gentle, introspective boy who had spent too much of his childhood fighting leukemia in a Denver hospital, protracted treatments that had forced Ned to sell off thirty-five acres of mine land on the ski side of Aspen Mountain. Wherever he was, Marie had insisted, whatever he was doing, he was better off a thousand miles from the foul air of the mines.

"I've never met the man," Corky said. "But your department should have no problem tracking him down."

"I'll get Muffin on it right away. If we have to, we'll contact my dear old friends in the FBI."

They stared at each other for several seconds without speaking.

"Nathan?" Kurt said, shaking his head skeptically, concerned about Hunter's well-being. "He didn't even show up for Marie's funeral. Do you suppose he's alive?"

"If he's not one hundred and ten percent mentally competent, socially adjusted, and financially stable, we won't release Hunter into his custody."

"Can you do that? Do you have the power?"

"I got the power," Corky nodded, straight-faced. "And I got all the time in the world."

Hunter had lived with them for only twenty-four hours but Kurt could already see how difficult this was going to be. The boy packed off to live with a total stranger. He would be terrified, Lennon brokenhearted. Kurt simply wouldn't accept a decision that turned Hunter over to someone who had never raised a child. *What if you and Meg were killed and it was Lennon?* he asked himself. It always came down to that. What if it was your kid?

"I'm not letting that child go live with a flake," Kurt said.

"Relax, Kurt. We don't know if Nathan Carr can be found, dead or alive. Let's take this one step at a time. No need to panic yet. Have a little faith in my abilities."

Kurt smiled at him. If there was anyone you wanted on your side in a judicial street fight, it was Corky Marcus. "Who else knows about this will?" he asked.

"Nobody."

"Not even Tyler?"

Corky shook his head. "Not that I'm aware," he said. "Unless Ned confided in him, which I doubt. The old boy was anything but loose of tongue."

Kurt stood up and walked over to examine the gallery of framed black-and-white photographs arranged on the wall. A young preppie Corky Marcus talking with Stokely Carmichael and John Lewis on the porch of a southern Negro farmhouse. A hirsute Corky Marcus laughing with Abbie Hoffman outside a courtroom. Corky with Bobby Kennedy, with William Kunstler, with a young and beautiful Petra Kelly.

"What about his other lawyers?" Kurt asked. "Who's been handling his mine litigation since you gave it up?"

"A good question."

"The sound-ordinance hearings were four or five years ago, Corky. Since then Ned's been in court at least twice that I know of. The EPA jerked him in for violation of the clean-water regs, and the county and the Sierra Club teamed up against him again over that damned access road. So who took his case, if you didn't?"

Corky rocked back in the chair, pondering the question, his bushy eyebrows joined in a serious intensity. "If I'm not mistaken," he said, searching his memory, "the Free West people sent one of their pro bono attorneys to help him out."

"Who are they?"

"The Free West Rebellion? You know who they are, Kurt. Paranoid neo-Nazis who think the federal government is run by the Trilateral Commission, the environmentalists are all druid priests, and everybody but John Wayne is trying to take away their individual freedom."

Kurt knew who they were. The monikers changed from year to year, but the agenda remained the same. "They have their own lawyers?"

"About six years ago an attorney named Arnold Metcalf set up a legal foundation for them. The Free West Legal Coalition, run out of an office in Colorado Springs," Corky said. "He was some kind of general counsel in the Interior Department during the Reagan administration, but George Bush was too much of an environmental president for him, so he packed up his briefcase and came on back to Colorado to start his foundation. The green groups were pinning the strip miners and the logging industry to the wall, and Metcalf showed up just in time to lead the counterattack."

"But why Ned? He didn't strike me as a movement type."

"He's the perfect poster boy. A real working miner, the little man hurt by the EPA, the Clean Air and Water Acts, the Wilderness Act. They've got a whole raft of lawyers they farm out to support their reactionary causes. A couple of years ago Congress made noises about repealing the Mining Law of 1872 and it set them off."

He bent down behind the desk, opened a

minirefrigerator, and pulled out two beers. "Happy hour yet?" he said, waving the cans.

"I better not. I'm pumped full of chemicals."

Corky shrugged. "I can see them adopting Ned as a pet project. Miner in trouble, his property rights in jeopardy, the entire free-enterprise system at stake. They like to take on the big Constitutional issues," he said. "And they never turn down an opportunity to battle the Hydra-headed beast—the federal agencies and the environmental groups."

Kurt shook his head. "Poor Ned," he said. "When you're that unpopular, you take your friends where you can find them."

Corky poured beer into a frosty mug from the fridge. "Especially when the fees are waived."

Kurt picked up the telephone and dialed home. He was worried now, this business about Hunter as sole beneficiary. No one answered; the machine played his voice message. Meg and the boys must have gone on their hike.

"Hi, Peaches, it's me checking in. I'll be home in fifteen minutes. When you and the guys come in, could you please stay put till I get there."

Unless something was terribly wrong, Kurt and Corky were the only two people who knew the content of the will. Still, Kurt felt uneasy.

"By the way," Corky said, paging through the folder in front of him, "Ned mentioned you in the settlement. I believe he left you something."

Kurt was astonished. He watched his friend's smile cross the threshold into wicked amusement.

"Ah, yes, here it is," Corky said, lifting the page. "You get the Airstream trailer."

21

A PITCO CRUISER was parked between Ned's rickety office and the Airstream trailer, and Kurt could see Muffin sitting behind the wheel, drinking coffee from a foam cup. When she heard his Jeep she stepped out and nodded at him with a tired grin. She looked sleep-pinched and rumpled, as if she'd spent the night in the car. She hadn't bothered to brush her short tousled hair.

"You're looking rested," she said as he walked up the hill toward her.

"Is Lorenzo in the mine?"

"Been there since daybreak. The man isn't human."

"Anybody helping him?"

"He prefers to work alone." She offered Kurt the cup. "Like some breakfast?"

"No, thanks, I'm stuffed. Meg made waffles."

"Well, now, isn't that special," Muffin said, resting back against the cruiser door. "Sunday morning waffles. The very definition of domestic bliss."

They had discussed Meg's return only in the most superficial manner, but Kurt suspected that Muffin resented the abrupt reappearance of Lennon's mother and now felt left out of the picture. During the two years of Meg's absence Muffin had stepped in as the perfect doting aunt, baby-sitting the child, buying him clothes and toys, caring for him when he was sick. She was a constant in his life, female and nurturing. Now Meg's presence had loosened the bonds of affection between the child and the young overworked officer who had no other passions but her job and a needy six-year-old. Kurt could plainly see that she missed the boy.

"What do you have on the shooting?" he asked.

She emptied the last inch of coffee onto the ground and tossed the cup in the cruiser's open window. "We ran a quick check on the health facilities from here to Glenwood and there weren't any gunshot wounds reported yesterday," she said, "but we'll stay on it. I sent two deputies to Carbondale to question the bartender at the Black Diamond. He had a sudden case of amnesia and couldn't remember names. He claims he didn't know the dirt-bikers who hassled you and Tyler."

"He's lying. They're regulars."

"If we want to shake him down we'll have to get Garfield County involved, but Dan the Man will probably bottom-shelf anything for us until you go down there and talk to him about that Dumpster."

"I'll give him a call." He looked up at the mine adit, listening for signs of Lorenzo at work. "Let's go see how our guy is doing."

Muffin ventured into the lighted shaft while Kurt remained outside. He had no desire to enter another mine anytime soon.

In a short while the two cops issued from the tunnel, Lorenzo removing his respirator and rubber gloves, laughing a huge friendly laugh, happy to see Kurt.

"Looking good, Lorenzo," he grinned, giving the man a power shake and a back-clapping bear hug.

"Nothing to it, big fella."

Lorenzo Banks was a tall, slender African American, his hair and mustache graying now after twenty years with the Denver police. He had served in the same demolitions unit in Vietnam with Kurt's brother and had helped spread Bert's ashes on the mountain not a hundred yards from this mine. Kurt hadn't seen him since the funeral five years ago.

"How you been getting along?" Lorenzo asked with a wide smile. "I read about that mess last summer. Man, you kicked some ass."

"I hope I never have to go through that again. How are things in Denver?"

"Like everywhere else. Going down the shitter one spoonful at a time."

He unzipped his police coveralls and reached inside to remove a pack of Camels from his shirt pocket, offering them around, with no takers. He seemed relieved to have this break and led Kurt and Muffin over to the spreading shade of a Douglas fir, where he'd stashed a gym bag full of diet Cokes and breakfast sweets.

"I know you want to make a case for homicide here, Kurt," Lorenzo said, sitting down against the tree trunk, his knees spread, the cigarette smoldering from a dangling hand. "But my guess at this time is I'll have to call it inconclusive. I can't find any clear evidence of a bomb device. If somebody did the old man, they kept it simple. A rigged stick set in one of the shot holes."

The cheapest method of blasting ore, he explained, and the one preferred by old hardrock miners like Ned, was to drill shot holes in a circular pattern around the target area, like the numbers on a clock, and fill the holes with sticks of dynamite wired to a blaster back at the mine's entrance.

"I don't know. Maybe they used a tiny heat or motion sensor, so when the man checked his charge, the stick went off. One goes off, they all do. If that's what went down, it's damn near impossible to trace."

Muffin pitched a wood chip at a marmot peeking out from behind a pile of split logs. "Sounds too easy," she said.

"Maybe," Lorenzo shrugged, taking a drag from his cigarette. "In my experience the real pro always finds the path of least resistance." His brow wrinkled as he gazed at Kurt. "Your brother and me, we learned that in Nam."

22

THAT AFTERNOON KURT and the two boys picked budding yellow roses from the bush beneath the kitchen window and took them to the hospital for Tyler. Kurt left the children with Nickelodeon magazines in the waiting room and wandered down a corridor to the soft-lit Intensive Care Unit where Deputy Bill Gillespie was posted outside a door.

"How's he doing?" Kurt asked.

"Still unconscious."

Tyler's parents were keeping a quiet bedside vigil. Kurt didn't know them well, though he had patronized their trading post many times over the years, searching for the odd items he couldn't find anywhere else, snowshoes the shape of tennis rackets and earflap wool hats and army-surplus foldup tinware for camping. Mrs. Rutledge accepted the roses and her husband embraced Kurt in burly mountain-man arms, thanking him for pulling their son out of the mine. There was an intense sadness in the room, a premonition of death, and the three of them didn't know what to say to each other so they stood in silence over the bandaged body. Tyler was as pale and gaunt as a wax figure. The tube down his throat forced oxygen into his lungs, sustaining his life. It was difficult to look at him in such a helpless state.

Kurt could feel the couple's collective grief like an invisible fist squeezing at his own heart. He stayed as long as he could, managing to hide the unexpected emotion that had surfaced in him, then said good-bye, giving his word that he would bring their son's assailants to justice.

He walked back to the waiting room and sat for several moments between the two boys, holding them close to his side while they flipped casually through their magazines, glancing up at his face from time to time, asking if he was okay, confused by Kurt's brooding silence, his inability to speak. By slow measure he recovered, leading the children out of the hospital hand in hand, guiding their steps to the waiting Jeep, promising himself he would never let something like that happen to them.

WHEN THEY ARRIVED at the Pfeil cabin Randy came out and waved from the front porch, welcoming them like a grandmother eagerly awaiting her kin. "I know all about boys. I've got a big one in college," she beamed, hugging Hunter and Lennon to her ample bosom as though she expected to greet them like this every Sunday for the rest of their lives. "Come on, gentlemen, let's get busy. I'll show you where the tackle's stored."

She told Kurt that Kat was off in the woods taking rifle practice. "Head up the path and look for a bunker," she said, pointing.

"A bunker?"

"Our latest addition to the homey atmosphere."

The new bunker had been dug in the forest floor beneath the pines, its roof and narrow enclosure reinforced with hundred-pound cement bags. Kurt could hear muffled .30-06 reports as he neared the structure, a paramilitary shooting gallery that bore Miles Cunningham's distinctive influence. He shouted Kat's name several times before the gunfire ceased. A moment passed and then the heavy iron door croaked open and her face peeked out through a dark wedge.

"Whatever happened to that declaration of nonviolence?" Kurt asked.

She stepped into the morning sunlight and removed the ear protectors, shaking out her hair. He could see the hunting rifle propped against the bags inside, a red-dot laser scope attached to the long barrel. "Howdy, Kurt," she smiled, squinting, studying his face. She was wearing cutoffs and a T-shirt, her bare legs long and tanned except for two belly-white scars on her left thigh and the crescent where a metal plate had been inserted into her knee. "I tried to see you at the hospital but they wouldn't allow visitors."

"I got your note," he said. "Thanks for coming."

Walking back toward the cabin he told her about Tyler's condition and thanked her for cooperating with the Sheriff's Department in their long interview.

"That cop Muffin Brown doesn't like me very much," she said. "I think she was worried I would frag her patrol car."

He smiled. "Don't be offended. Muffin treats me the same way."

They emerged from the woods to find Randy and the boys rummaging through an old tackle shed on the edge of the yard.

"Did you get a good look at those three men in the Toyota?" he asked.

"They were a long way off, Kurt. But as I told Miz Brown, I think one of them was wearing a uniform shirt."

"What kind of uniform?"

"I'm not sure. Maybe forest-green, like the one she was wearing when we spoke."

Pitkin County Sheriff's Department? One of their own?

"Did any of the men look wounded?"

"Not that I noticed. But it happened so fast, and then you grabbed the binoculars."

Randy had dragged a snarl of fly rods into the yard and was untangling them with the boys' help. "When was the last time this gear saw any action?" she asked.

Kat struggled to remember. "Probably ten years ago," she said, lost in a momentary reverie. "When Michael and I were here."

The memory of her dead husband shadowed her face. Kurt took her hand. "Come on," he said. "Let's go lose some flies."

The fishing party followed a winding path through the spruce grove down to the creek. White water splashed around barricades of smooth river boulders, but in the shadows near the bank the stream ran with less force and there were clear pools where Kat tested her fly. Kurt spent the better part of the next hour coaching the boys, demonstrating wrist technique, freeing line hung up in the branches. Lennon eventually grew heat-flushed and frustrated that the trout weren't biting and abandoned his rig with grumpy impatience.

He dug the Walkman out of his backpack and joined Randy on a flat benchlike rock ledge.

"This may not be your sport, Sport," she said, offering him the Gatorade bottle. "My kids didn't much like to fish either."

"I like karate," Lennon declared. "I just got my orange belt."

"All right, champ!" she said, chucking him under the chin.

Kurt squatted down on his haunches. "How many kids do you have, Randy?"

"Two was plenty," she said. "My daughter is twenty-five, making a good living as a graphic designer in Portland. Doesn't look like she'll get married anytime soon. My son is a junior at Oregon State, majoring in grunge bands, far as I can tell. Lord knows what he's going to do with his life."

Kurt smiled, knowing he would be uttering those same words soon enough. "Are you still married?"

She shook her head slowly. He couldn't interpret the expression behind her mirror shades and pulled-down cap bill. "My husband was a logger for Georgia-Pacific. A redwood jumped free of a weak choker and crushed him to death when the kids were little. I guess that's maybe why I was drawn to Kat. I knew what she was going through."

Kurt moved over beside his son and used a shirt-sleeve to wipe beads of sweat from the boy's soft cheeks and nose. Lennon was absorbed in the headphones now, his heels tapping against the rock, oblivious to moody fish and creek-spray and the bristling afternoon sun. They watched Kat roam downstream to check on Hunter, a solid chunk of childbone casting from the shallow inlet with the determination of a fanatic middle-aged sportsman. Kat laid aside her own fly rod and stooped over him, locking her arm around his chest, guiding his chubby wrist and the action of the long arcing line. They practiced this routine together, thirty strokes, fifty. The trout weren't biting today.

"Well, campers," Randy yawned, stretching her arms, "I hope y'all don't mind hamburgers."

The light was beginning to soften now, a breeze stirring high in the trees, and Randy and Lennon walked back to the cabin to start the grill. Kat gathered her gear and came over to sit beside Kurt on the ledge.

"Stubborn kid," she said, watching Hunter whip the air with his line. "He'll be out here till midnight with a Coleman lantern if we let him."

"I remember being like that," Kurt said fondly. "Lennon's different. He's inherited his mother's artistic temperament. I suspect I've got a painter or a poet on my hands."

"Lennon is adorable. What a beautiful boy!"

"He got his mother's looks as well."

She closed her eyes, entranced by the mist in her face, the wind blowing her hair. "I'm sorry it didn't work out for you and Meg," she said.

"We're trying to become friends again. Lennon needs some stability. The cop's life has been tough on him."

He stole the moment to study her face, the long beautiful lashes and lovely mouth, wishing she would remain in that pose for the rest of the afternoon while he obsessed over her features one small detail at a time.

"Have you thought about giving it up?"

"I'm on official leave. I've got six weeks to make up

my mind. I don't know what I'll decide. I haven't had a real job in eleven years. That scares me."

She reached over and gave his hand an affectionate squeeze. "You can always come to work for me in Oregon," she said. "Have you ever blown up a logging yarder?" She opened her eyes, smiled sardonically at him. "Just kidding, Kurt. You can relax."

He laughed, realizing that she considered Oregon her home now and would no doubt return after her recuperation.

"You're a smart, decent man, Kurt Muller," she said. "The right thing will come along and you'll know it."

Did she mean the right *woman?* he wondered. He looked at her and returned the smile. She leaned over and kissed him gently on the lips, her face lingering close to his, her eyes bright and inviting. He was both surprised and exhilarated. He caught his breath and kissed her again.

"If I'd known you were this tasty," she whispered, her voice husky, tantalizing, "I would've done this twenty years ago."

He glanced over to make sure Hunter was still facing the stream, preoccupied with his casting, and kissed her once more. They enjoyed each other's lips for as long as they dared, and then he draped his arm around her shoulders and they sank back against the stone. There was a long, comforting silence between them. They watched the child loop his line high in the air, a figure eight suspended for the briefest moment, dying over the water. Kurt wanted everything to stay like this forever. Katrina Pfeil in his arms, the creek running strong, the sky as pure and milky blue as he'd ever seen it, a little boy learning to fish. It all felt too perfect.

Somewhere near the border of his awareness a nebulous sorrow was intruding, taking solid shape, finding its dark legs.

"Ned's will names Nathan as the guardian," he said, surprising himself with this sudden revelation, breaking their snug silence. He didn't know why he was thinking about this now, in this exquisite, untroubled moment.

"Hmh?" she said. She had gone drowsy in the shaft of sunlight falling on his warm chest.

"Nathan Carr is Hunter's designated guardian."

"Nathan Carr?" she said dreamily. "Now there's a flash from the past. Is he still alive? I thought he was killed in a car wreck."

"We're running him down by computer. Should know something tomorrow or Tuesday. No one is sure if he's dead or alive."

She sat up, pushing the hair out of her eyes. "Nathan was a sweet kid. Our class visited him one time on a field trip to Denver, when he was in the hospital. I haven't seen him since high school."

"I don't know what was going on in Ned's head when he made that decision," Kurt said, watching Hunter fiddle with the homemade fly on the end of his line. "The child is much better off with us."

Kat slid her hand underneath the hair on his shirt collar, massaged his neck. "I'm sorry, Kurt," she said. "If there's any way I can help . . ."

He closed his eyes. "You're helping already."

They held each other and kissed again, a long arousing embrace. When he opened his eyes, peering over Kat's shoulder, he saw Lennon watching them from the trees.

"I got bored and came back to fish some more," his son said.

"Great!" Kurt said, unfurling himself from Kat's arms. "Let's go show those rainbows who's the boss."

Lennon was walking toward them, his rosy face as solemn as a marble statesman's. "Is she your girl-friend?" he asked.

Kurt didn't know what to respond. Kat looked away, embarrassed.

"She's my good friend," Kurt said. "We're getting to know each other better."

Lennon stopped and stared at them. "Does kissing and all that mushy stuff help people get to know each other better?"

Kurt stood up and raked at his son's sweaty hair. "It doesn't hurt," he grinned, exchanging glances with Kat, her entire body fighting the urge to laugh.

"Come on," Kurt said. "Let's find your rig."

"I can fish by myself," Lennon said indignantly, his eyes searching for the fly rod he had left on the rocks. "You can go back to your kissing, Dad."

He pulled away from his father and headed down the creek bank.

"I'll get you started," Kurt said, following after him.

"No!" Lennon said, wheeling around in anger. He was clearly upset by what he had witnessed. "I can do it by myself."

Kurt knew that the boy had been holding on to the vain hope that his parents would reconcile. He watched his son shuffle across the talus, kicking at loose rocks, choosing an aimless, meandering journey toward the water.

"Sorry about that, Kurt," Kat said. "I should have been more considerate."

"It's okay," he smiled at her. "It's time my son and I made some adjustments."

Lennon picked up his fly rod and waved to Hunter, who waved back and called out something Kurt couldn't hear. In a short while the two boys were standing side by side, giggling and nudging at each other, trying to tangle lines out over the creek.

23

IN THE VIOLET twilight they ate their paper-plate hamburgers at a picnic table on the back deck, the evening chill nestling around them, ground fog drifting slowly across the lawn, dew dripping from the spruce trees like a gentle rain. Thunder echoed down the valley, a low menacing rumble that made the boys *wooo* nervously. Late spring could bring a downpour, it could bring snow.

"My ears are getting cold," said Lennon.

"You boys ever play Monopoly or Parcheesi?" Randy asked, blowing on her coffee. "I found some old board games left over from when Miss Katrina was a kid."

They settled down for the evening around the dining-room table to play Monopoly on a board held together by masking tape as dry and yellow as a mummy's bandage. Kat brought in bowls of strawberries and cream for dessert while the game rolled on endlessly through negotiations and arguments, insider trading, under-the-table chicanery. The boys embraced the competition with a fierce personal devotion, and Kurt realized he was witnessing how small children grew up to become county commissioners and dirt-pimp developers.

Around eight o'clock he said, "Hey, guys, we better wrap this up. We've got to get on home. There's school tomorrow." And Ned's funeral, he reminded himself.

Though their eyes were drooping with fatigue, the boys protested, feisty to the last barter. "Just a little while longer, Coach," Hunter said in a deep, sleepy voice, his jaw clenching, hungry for one final free-and-clear land deed.

Kurt noticed a sudden, strange look on Randy's face. She glanced out the patio doors. He watched her rise from her chair and go quietly to the picture window. The fog was heavy against the glass and she used her fist to rub off condensation, a clear circle she could peer through into the impenetrable night. She scanned the dark deck from one end to the other. "I'm going to go take a walk around," she said. "Be back in a few minutes."

She slipped on her parka and checked the chamber of the .38 police special tucked inside the pocket, then slid back the glass door and disappeared into the fog.

"Why is Randy going outside with a gun?" Lennon asked.

"She gets a little paranoid sometimes," Kat said, rolling the dice. "It's nothing to worry about, honey. She probably heard a bear in the garbage."

"Oooh, let's go check it out!" Hunter beamed.

"Let's finish this last round, Bubba Wayne," said Kurt. "It's getting near your bedtime."

Kat and Hunter were dickering over a property swap, Park Place for Atlantic Avenue, when Kurt heard a noise outside. He looked up to see a fireball materialize in the darkness like a streaking meteorite, growing larger as it hurled toward the window.

"Get down!" he shouted, yanking his son off the chair.

The glass exploded and flames spread across the dining room, a burning splash of fuel oil. Kurt shouldered the heavy wooden table onto its side, creating a barrier against the river of fire flowing all around them.

Kat had thrown herself on Hunter, dragging him to the floor behind their cover. Flames climbed up the table, ignited the carpet underneath them. "My god, Kurt!" she screamed. "What's happening?"

"Grab Hunter!" he shouted, rushing Lennon down the steps into the smoky living room. The child clung to his father's chest like a terrified cat, silent and trembling. Kurt fell to his knees and quickly inspected the boy's hair, his arms and pants. He wasn't burned but Kurt could smell the melted rubber on his own Reeboks. When he turned, peering back through the smoke, Kat tumbled over him with Hunter in her arms, and they all scattered across the rug.

"Where's Randy?" she yelled, rising to her knees, gazing toward the elevated dining room engulfed in flames. The curtains, the upended chairs, the glass case filled with her mother's bric-a-brac, all of it blazing wildly. Black smoke roiled into their faces and the boys began to choke.

"Let's get these boys out of here!" Kurt yelled. The fire was roaring so loudly he could barely make himself heard. "Everybody listen, now. Don't stand up. Follow me on your hands and knees."

"Daddy, don't leave me!" Lennon pleaded, clutching at his father.

Kurt's heart nearly burst with the sound of those words. "I'll never leave you, baby. Hang on to my jacket!"

The fuming smoke obscured visibility to two or three feet. Kurt crawled quickly toward the front of the cabin, feeling Lennon's small hands groping at him, struggling to keep up with the father he couldn't see. When Kurt flung open the door, heat rushed over them, seeking outside air, a suction of dancing sparks.

"Stay on your bellies!" he said, pulling the two children onto the dark porch. He didn't know if there were snipers hiding in the woods. "Keep the boys down, Kat. I'll get the truck."

He lowered his head and raced for the GMC pickup parked twenty yards away in the heavy fog. With every stride he expected a bullet in the back. As he drew near the vehicle he could see Randy sitting behind the steering wheel, staring ahead, her eyes fixed on a thousand yards of empty night.

"Randy!" he shouted. "What the hell are you doing? The cabin's on fire!"

When he opened the door her large body keeled over against him. Warm blood soaked his shirt from the gaping hole in her neck.

"Jesus Christ!" he said, shuddering from the shock. Her eyes were open but he couldn't feel a pulse. "Come on, darlin', let's get the fuck out of here!" Gripping her by the pants and parka, he boosted her limp body over the wheel skirt and rolled her into the truck bed.

Motors were revving somewhere close by, the familiar buzz of 250cc engines. A headlight flared in the murky woods, then a second one. Dirt bikes hurtled through the fog toward the cabin. Kurt jumped into the pickup, switched on the ignition, and sped directly at them, flashing the high beams into their helmet visors. The bikers veered around him, hook-sliding across the gravel drive, borne away by their own reckless momentum.

"Let's go!" Kurt screamed, skidding up to the porch and shoving open the passenger door.

Kat lay on top of the boys, shielding them from the swarm of floating embers. The entire cabin was raging now, consumed by fire, the windows popping like flashbulbs. She hustled the boys into the cab and pressed their squirming bodies down on the floorboard while Kurt peeled off for the road, forcing the pickup to forty, forty-five miles per hour down the single-lane Jeep track through dense fog. The ground was slick from rain; tree limbs lurched out at both doors. One careless move on this wet trail and the GMC would pinwheel into the woods.

"We can't leave Randy!" Kat screamed, as though waking suddenly from a nightmare. When she looked through the back glass at the blazing cabin she saw her unconscious friend in the truck bed, rolling in her own blood. "My god, Kurt!"

"She's been shot."

"Oh, god, this is all my fault!"

The dirt bikes were fifteen yards behind them, closing quickly, a third one joining the chase.

"I've got to help her!" Kat cried, kicking open the passenger door.

She grabbed the door frame and started to swing around into the rear bed but Kurt seized her arm and pulled her back inside.

"Stay here, Kat! You'll get yourself killed!"

A pistol cracked behind them and his side mirror shattered. He flinched, jerking the wheel involuntarily, and the GMC fishtailed in soft mud, sideswiping a tree on the passenger side, ripping the swinging door off its hinges. The boys were screaming now, and Kurt fought the wheel as they careened back across the narrow trail, scraping bushes against his window.

"You wearing a firearm?" Kat said, yanking at his jacket.

"No. It's in my Jeep."

There were two more wild gunshots but he knew they couldn't handle their bikes at top speed and fire with accuracy.

"Damn!" Kat said, throwing junk out of the glove compartment. "I thought she kept a gun in here!"

When he glanced in the rearview mirror, he saw one of the bikes moving agilely past the pickup's tailgate, the rider raising his pistol to shoot out the tire. Kurt slammed the brakes and swerved, bumping the man into the dark pines.

"What was that?" Kat shouted, looking over her shoulder through the glass.

"One down."

Lennon had started to cry and Kurt reached over to rub his wet cheek. "Easy, champ. We'll hit Castle Creek Road in a few minutes and they'll never catch this big hog."

Wind swirled through the open door like a riptide, sucking loose debris out into the darkness. Kat held on to the boys, hugging their necks. In the headlight beams the fog hung suspended like stiff angel's hair, obscuring the trail ahead. Kurt knew they were approaching a sharp cutback, but if he tried to make it at this speed he would roll the truck. If he slowed down, the bikers would surely overtake them.

He caught sight of a vehicle's headlights angling up from the creek to their right, a strange apparition, someone trailblazing through the rugged woods at high speed. "Hold on, everybody," he said, "we've got more company."

The vehicle bounded onto the trail just ahead of them, a tan Jeep Wrangler, and Kurt swerved wide, trying to pass in the narrow aperture between trees. But the Wrangler kept pace hub to hub, honking his horn until Kurt turned and glared out the empty door frame. The driver raised a huge .44 Magnum to show Kurt what he was packing. There was nothing between the children and that weapon. *Ram him,* he thought. Then suddenly the driver motioned with the pistol, signaling Kurt to move ahead, a long black ponytail whipping back and forth across the man's thick shoulders as he waved his arm.

"I'll be damned," Kurt mumbled to himself. "It's you!"

"Who, Kurt?" Kat asked, lifting her head to peer out the gaping hole. "Are there more of them?"

Kurt stomped the accelerator and the GMC surged forward. The Wrangler dropped behind them and hooked in a half turn, sliding sideways, blowing mud, guttering to a dead stop across the trail. There was a commotion of squealing bike brakes, booming gunshots. In the rearview mirror Kurt watched the Wrangler lights shrink in the distance, and soon every trace of the man and his Jeep was swallowed by the fog. *Can he hold them off?* he wondered. *Will he make it out?* Within a few breathless seconds he had negotiated that final sharp cutback and they were on their way to the highway.

24

IN THE EMERGENCY room Muffin cradled Lennon in her lap, his eyes drooping and his hair wet with rain and body heat. The evening had been too much for him and he was slowly deflating into sleep.

"Do you have any idea who they were?" she asked Kat, who occupied the chair beside them, bundled snugly in a blanket, her shaky hands wrapped around a steaming cup of hospital coffee.

"She's had death threats for a couple of years now," Kurt said. He was holding Hunter, the child's clothes reeking of smoke.

"I'm asking *her*, Kurt," Muffin said, her eyes darting at him, then back to the shivering woman. "Do you know why they did this, Miss Pfeil?"

She stared at the tile floor. "I'm not a very popular person in some circles," she said in a distant voice.

"Is that why you hired a bodyguard?"

Kat nodded.

"We'll need your complete cooperation, ma'am. If you've kept a file of hate mail, or tape-recorded any threatening phone calls, I want access to the materials. We'll probably have to pull in the FBI."

Kat lifted her chin and fixed her teary eyes on the deputy sheriff. "When you talk to them," she said with a cold hostility, "why don't you ask the FBI who killed my husband."

Muffin lowered her eyes impatiently, then looked at Kurt. "I see you two have a lot in common."

The doctor on call appeared, his soft-soled shoes squeaking over polished tile. Kurt knew by his long gray countenance that the news was not good. They were informed that Randy could not be resuscitated. Kat covered her face with her hands and began to weep. Kurt placed a consoling arm around her blanket-draped shoulder.

"We've dispatched two fire trucks and several armed deputies to your residence," Muffin assured her. "I should hear back from them real soon."

Kurt hadn't told Muffin about the Lone Ute, how he had materialized out of nowhere and blocked off the Jeep track, giving them time to escape. He was in no mood for her skepticism. And he was beginning to question his own sanity. Who was that man?

"Make sure Forensics goes over every inch of the truck," he said.

There was a sudden disturbance at the ambulance entrance, where a deputy had been stationed to monitor visitors. Meg had arrived and was arguing with the young cop, jerking her arm from his grip.

"It's okay, Hal," Kurt waved to the deputy. He had phoned Meg and asked her to come. "Let her through."

Haphazardly dressed in unlaced hiking boots and a thrown-on ski jacket, Meg stormed toward him, her face pale with rage. Behind her walked a lean middle-aged man with thinning gray hair stretched tightly over his scalp and tied back in a small knot behind his head. Her housemate, the Zen master. Her probable lover.

"Lennon, are you okay, baby?" She lifted the groggy boy from the comfort of Muffin's lap, his long arms clutching for his mother. At six years old he was already half her size.

"Hi, Mom," he said in a sleepy voice, burying his face in her neck. "We had to escape a fire."

She hugged him close, her hand pressed to the back of his head. "These boys are coming with me," she said, glaring over her son's shoulder at Kurt. "I don't want them anywhere near you, Kurt Muller."

"All right, Meg," he said calmly, standing, his hands on Hunter's shoulders. He had already decided that Meg should take them for the next few days.

"Goddammit, Kurt, I thought you learned your lesson last summer," she fumed. "What are you doing to this boy? It took him nine months to start sleeping by himself again. He's still having nightmares. You can't keep doing this! I won't let you."

"Meg, this isn't the time to talk," he said, gently rubbing Lennon's back.

She swung the boy away from him. "We're leaving!" she announced to her companion. The man was wearing a quilted Tibetan jacket of some sort and black slippers, a tiny hoop earring. In spite of these affectations he struck Kurt as having a kind and thoughtful face. His eyes glowed with sympathy, pained by the anguish in the room. Kurt was glad he was here to help Meg get through this.

"We'll assign two deputies to escort you home," he said, turning to Muffin for confirmation.

"We don't need your deputies," Meg objected. "We don't want you people in our lives."

She handed Lennon to her companion, took Hunter by the hand, and angrily marched the small troop to the door. Kurt didn't like the way his son had surrendered himself willingly, familiarly, to the man in the silken jacket. His heart sank at the sight of his child's head resting on somebody else's shoulder.

"Stop them a minute, Hal," he said, signaling the deputy. He leaned close to Muffin, a confidential aside. "I want those boys driven in a county squad car," he said quietly, "and I want at least two deputies watching Meg's place for the next forty-eight hours. Let's start with Dotson and Florio." Two men in whom he had absolute trust.

Muffin viewed this with reservation. "Do you think that's necessary, Kurt? We're spreading our guys pretty thin."

"I'm not so sure they were trying to kill Kat," he said, glancing at the distraught woman grieving silently in her chair. "They might have been after Hunter."

Muffin's face transformed quickly, a look of horror. She was speechless.

"I'll brief you about it as soon as we get some time together," he said. "Those kids aren't leaving the building without police protection."

Meg's protestations to the deputy were growing louder.

"Okay, I'll handle this one," Muffin said, nodding toward the brewing argument with a wicked glimmer in her eyes. Kurt suspected she had wanted to give Meg a piece of her mind for a long time now. "You make the arrangements for the Pfeil woman." She hitched her gun belt, shot him one last accusatory regard before joining the fracas. "That shouldn't be too hard for you, Kurt."

25

THEY WERE ALONE now in the waiting room except for the stern-jawed deputy at the door and a Latino couple huddled anxiously in the far corner. A restive silence always hovered over emergency rooms, a suspicious promise of hope. But for Kurt and the woman under his arm there were no lingering illusions.

"You can stay at our house tonight," he said. "I'll assign some deputies to stand guard."

She patted his leg. "I can't do that to you, Kurt," she said. "You've gone through enough already because of me."

"It's not your fault, Kat. You didn't throw the firebomb. Don't be so hard on yourself."

She wiped tears from her cheeks and stood up, dropping the blanket from her shoulders. "I can't stay at your home," she said. "Everybody near me ends up dead."

She walked away from him and stood at the plate-glass window with her arms folded, staring defiantly into the darkness.

"Why don't you step away from the glass," he said.

The bombing flashed through his mind. The flaming

tail streaking out of the black mist, scattering their lives in fire. The boys weren't the only ones who would wake in a cold terror, tonight and for many nights to come.

"I thought I could escape it, Kurt. Hide out in the mountains for a few months, get myself back together. I need more surgery and I figured this was a pretty good place to lay low and recuperate. I should've known better. I let myself get too goddamned soft."

She hadn't budged an inch from the window. He studied her troubled reflection in the glass. "Who was it, Kat?" he asked. "The timber companies?"

She shrugged, silent and brooding, and he wondered if she would tell him if she knew. "Whoever killed Randy and burned down my house has bought themselves a world of hurt," she said.

He put his hand on her shoulder but she flinched away from him.

"Let the Sheriff's Department handle it, Kat," he said. "You've already gone through enough."

Her expression was hard and cold. "Last time I heard a cop tell me that," she said, "my husband was in the morgue and I couldn't move anything but my little finger. After the cops got through being my friend, I was knee deep in hospital bills and lawyers' fees, and the Feds were threatening me with serious jail time for something I didn't do. Pardon me if I sound a little skeptical, Kurt. I know you mean well, but you're playing in a different league now."

"I'm going to find out who did this, Kat. The boys could've been killed."

She nodded, gazing blankly into the nighttime. "I'm sorry, Kurt. I wish I could change everything. I shouldn't have dragged you and the children into my life." She sighed, gave his hand an affectionate squeeze, then turned and limped off toward the hospital corridor. "I'm tired and my leg is bothering me," she said over her shoulder. "I need to rest."

"Come on. I'll take you to my place."

"I won't do that to you, Kurt. Wait there while I make a phone call."

He watched her use the phone at the nurses' station. She talked to someone, waited, then replaced the receiver with visible frustration.

"Private listing, naturally," she said, leaning against the desk for support. He could see that she was fading fast. "And I can't remember the goddamned number." She peered up at him, blew a strand of hair out of her eyes. "Give a girl a lift, sailor?"

THE LAMAR MANSION glowed like an ocean liner on the slope of Aspen Mountain. When the deputy pulled the Pitco unit into the spotlighted parking lot out front, a half-dozen people were walking to their cars and Kurt had the sense that a small informal party was breaking up. He left Kat to doze in the backseat and climbed the stone steps to the intercom box at the wrought-iron gates. A housekeeper with an Hispanic accent responded to the buzz, and he asked for Meredith.

"I'm sorry, sir, the reading group is finish already. Was she expecting you?"

"This is an emergency," he said, staring up at the small surveillance camera recording his presence. "Could you please tell her Kat Pfeil needs her immediate assistance."

After a long humming silence Meredith's voice rang

out with the clarity of tapped crystal: "Hello, Kurt." She was viewing him on the monitor. "Is Katrina in some kind of trouble?"

"Somebody tried to kill her tonight, Meredith. They burned down her cabin."

"Oh, my god!"

"She asked me to bring her here. May we come in?"

"Yes, of course. I'll send Gloria out to let you in."

Meredith met them in the foyer and rushed forward to embrace Kat. "You poor dear," she said, throwing her arms around the exhausted woman. Meredith was barefoot, dressed in jogging sweats, her famous hair tied back with a band. She looked ready for a workout at the Nordic Club.

"I'm sorry to barge in like this," Kat said, barely able to hold up her chin. "I think I need to lie down. My leg feels like an anchor."

"Of course, of course," Meredith said, sliding an affectionate hand up and down Kat's back. "Don't you worry about a thing, darling. Gloria, help me take Miss Pfeil to the sequoia room."

The three women disappeared instantly and Kurt was left wondering what to do with himself until Meredith returned and he could explain the situation to her, the need for heightened security. He hoped that Neal Staggs's VIProtex men were stationed about the premises, checking the locks, watching the grounds. The surveillance cameras, the stone walls surrounding the mansion, were precisely what Kat needed to ensure a good night's rest.

Kurt heard a murmur of soft voices and ventured down the steps to a railed gallery overlooking the cavernous living room. Massive redwood beams braced the bowed ceiling like ribs on an ancient ship. The space below was designed for large gatherings, a showcase of opulent divans and love seats and settees, silent and dusky as a vault, a weak fire flickering in the giant hearth. There were dozens of these places in Aspen and Starwood, monster homes for monster appetites, the architecture as uninspired as an industrial drum. He was considering a return to the foyer when he noticed a golf ball gliding smoothly across fifty feet of virginal carpet and plinking against the base of a lamp. A balding, potbellied man wearing an epaulet safari shirt strode into view in his snakeskin cowboy boots, a putter resting over one shoulder, whiskey tumbler in hand. He stopped to tilt back his head for a long drink and noticed Kurt staring down at him.

"Jesus, Muller," he said. "Is there nowhere on this planet that's safe from your interminable surveillance?"

"The dynamite wasn't dead, Miles. I blew the fuck out of a Dumpster."

Miles Cunningham tucked the putter under his arm like a British swagger stick. "Well done," he said.

Kurt couldn't imagine what Miles was doing here. He was surprised the Lamars allowed him on the premises. "Somebody firebombed Kat's cabin tonight," he told the aging photographer. "Randy's dead."

Miles lowered his drinking hand, stunned. He looked as if someone had clubbed him across the skull with his own putter. This was the first moment in several years that Kurt had witnessed an expression of concern on the man's bloated face.

"Fucking curs," he mumbled, slurring, his eyes narrowed fiercely. "So they finally tracked her down."

Kurt descended the staircase into the dim living

room. "Who did this, Miles?" He expected an accusation against the FBI. Or the timber industry in Oregon.

Miles let the putter drop to the carpet. He finished his drink, trying to collect himself. Sweat beaded his forehead. They hadn't trusted each other in a long time and it appeared as if nothing would change that now.

"My son and Hunter Carr could've burned to death in that fire." His calm words reverberated in the silence. "Randy was shot to death. If you have any idea who was involved," he said, "I want you to start talking."

A moment passed, a dark and fathomless silence filling the capacious chamber. Kurt felt like a lost swimmer drifting deeper into an underground pool inhabited by eyeless fish.

"It's time you caught up with the rest of us, Kurt," said a voice above. Meredith was looking down from the railed balcony. "Come to my study," she said. "You can judge for yourself who's behind this madness."

Meredith's study was tucked away in a corner of the bottom floor, a cozy room crammed with built-in cedar bookshelves and a long conference table spread with magazines, sheets of Miles's slides, stacks of photocopied articles. Used glasses and empty snack bowls were scattered about, and Kurt realized that the guests had been here for some sort of study group.

Meredith stooped over the table, selecting stapled documents. "We've been tracking the antigreens for four or five years now, Kurt," she said. "They're becoming as organized as the environmental movement. The difference is, they like their guns. We have strong evidence that they've been hiring thugs all over the country to eliminate their opposition. Here, read as many of these as you can," she said, handing him an armload of articles. "We're keeping tabs on some of these organizations and their financial backers. There are scads of them now, primarily out here in the mountain states—a loose coalition calling themselves the Free West Rebellion. They pretend to be a grass-roots movement, but most of them are front groups for the corporate honchos in oil, ranching, timber, and mining."

"And for the Japs who make all those little noisemakers buzzing up and down my backyard," Miles added.

Meredith found more publications, piled them on Kurt's collection. "Photographs of Free West leaders partying with industry CEOs show up with suspicious regularity in their newsletters," she said.

"I know about these people," Kurt said, recalling his conversation with Corky Marcus.

"They think the greens and the EPA have gone too far and they're fighting back," Meredith said. "The shit they're doing has for the most part escaped the news media. There's a rumor they have a special forces unit called the Night Clubbers—a bunch of Neanderthals in charge of their countersurveillance and thuggery."

"And you think these Night Clubbers have gone after Kat?" Kurt said, thumbing through the pages.

"Unfortunately no one has ever proved that the Night Clubbers really exist," Meredith said.

The moment the flames crashed through the window, Kurt had assumed it was the same killers who had pipe-bombed Kat and her husband in Oregon. But now he wasn't so sure.

"One miner dead, one miner hurt real bad, and the next day a well-known green is firebombed," he said, eyeing Meredith and Miles. "That sounds like retaliation to me." Maybe Neal Staggs was right for once. "Is there some kind of guerrilla war going on between you people?"

He watched them trade looks. "The war has been going on for decades, Kurt," Meredith said. "It's just starting to get real nasty."

Kurt held a sheet of slides to the light. Head shots mostly, men in gray suits. "Considering what happened to Kat and Randy, do either of you feel you need police protection?"

Meredith shook her head, smiled. "As you can see," she said, "I'm well watched after."

Miles knelt down and withdrew a Beretta .22 automatic from inside his cowboy boot. "A man had best carry his own life insurance," he said, palming the small assassin's pistol. "Save your boy scouts for the DUIs out on the highway."

Kurt felt his jaw clench. "Kat Pfeil told me she didn't need any protection, either," he said. "And now her bodyguard is dead and her place has been torched to the ground. Time for a reality check, Miles."

HE ASKED TO look in on Kat before leaving, and Meredith led him to the guest wing and down a long quiet corridor lined with family photographs of smiling backcountry campers and ski parties out on the slopes. "If there's any way I can help Kat," she said, "please call on me. I'll do whatever it takes to nail those bastards."

"This may help," he said, indicating the stack of articles under his arm. "You've given me enough bedtime reading for a month."

They stopped in front of Kat's door. "You know,

Meredith, in the old days, when one of our buddies did something wild ass and stupid, we called it revolutionary," he said, "and we stood behind it, right or wrong. I'm wondering if you and your little tea group are still operating under that same misguided principle."

"What are you driving at?" she asked, raising a defiant eyebrow.

"If you knew that somebody in the green movement killed Ned Carr, would you report it?"

She folded her arms across the jogging sweatshirt. "I don't condone murder under any circumstances, Kurt," she said.

"You didn't answer my question. Would you report it?"

"Yes, I would," she said coldly. "Now listen to me. I don't know who killed Ned Carr, and neither does my husband. I hope we never have this conversation again."

Kurt leaned against the doorjamb. "Is Lee in your study group? He doesn't seem to be around tonight. Does he know about your research?"

"Lee is a very busy man. When you run a worldwide communications network and one of the most popular ski companies on the planet, you don't have time for study groups. Now if you'll excuse me, I have other guests to attend to."

After Meredith walked away, Kurt knuckled lightly on Kat's door. He heard faint footsteps, a low voice: "Who is it?"

"Kurt. I hope I didn't wake you up."

The door cracked open and Kat reached out for his hand, pulling him quickly into the dark room. She locked the door behind them and sagged into his arms.

He could feel her lean, sinewy body beneath the silk pajamas. "I'm glad you're still here," she said, kissing him on the chin, her breath minty from toothpaste. The stack of articles fell, pages fluttering like the wings of a nocturnal bird.

"What was that?" she said, startled, nervous.

He hugged her closer. "My homework assignment. I'll get them later. How are you doing?"

"I'm having trouble calming down," she said, leading him by the hand through the darkness to a window seat. "Stay with me awhile."

"Can I get you anything? Some brandy?"

"No, just sit with me. I'll be all right."

She stretched her legs across the cushion and lay back in Kurt's arms. Out the window, beyond the compound walls, shadowy moonlight softened the dark fir groves higher up the slope. They held each other in a long consoling silence and Kurt expelled a weary breath, releasing all the tensions of the past few hours. He buried his face in her wet hair, its sweet fragrance of herbal shampoo.

"Randy was right," she said. Her heart was beating rapidly beneath his hand. "We shouldn't have started. That's my fault too. I should've kicked you off my property the minute I laid eyes on you."

"Kat."

"Then those boys would be home sleeping in their own beds, where they belong."

"You don't have to do this to yourself."

She began to shiver violently, as if she'd succumbed to a sudden, racking fever, and he held her the way he held Lennon when the child was ill, rocking her slowly, coaxing her into the soothing rhythms of his own heart.

"Kurt," she said, squeezing his arms tighter around her, "when the bomb went off I was five months pregnant. I lost a husband and a daughter too."

He kissed her hair. "Jesus, Kat, I'm sorry."

"Michael pampered the hell out of me. We both knew the baby was a blessing at forty. We talked about leaving Oregon for a while, raising her in a quiet country town somewhere—maybe Aspen—till she was old enough to understand our work." Warm teardrops wet his arms. "Now that part of my life is over and done with too."

She unbuttoned her pajama shirt and slid his hand against the rough puckered skin where her breast had been. "This is who I am now," she said. "Dry as a stick, inside and out. When a pipe bomb goes off under your belly, everything dies."

He slowly withdrew his hand and held her close. She began to weep, and he understood that this was what she needed most of all. There were worse things than reliving the terrible moments that have shattered your life. Forgetting was the greater sin.

The woman in his arms eventually cried herself to sleep and he found himself drifting down the cold dark corridors that haunted his own dreams. Somber images floated through his mind, two boys wandering among broken tombstones, his brother's fractured face staring up at him from the body bag, a knife blade at his son's throat. He was hopelessly lost in the black labyrinth when a loud thumping noise startled him and he sat up. It might have been the bedroom door. He listened hard, rubbing his face and eyes to wake himself, waiting, his mind straining against the silence.

Convinced it had been a dream, he lifted Kat into his arms and took her to the bed, placing her head on a lacy pillow, buttoning her pajama shirt, drawing the covers around her. He kissed her forehead and groped his way toward the door, his boots soon shuffling over loose paper, the sound like footsteps through dry leaves. Remembering the pages now, he bent down and gathered them up, then backed out of the room, closing the door with a light click. Turning, he stumbled headlong over a body lying in the hallway and the pages again scattered in the air.

"God damn!" he said, rolling to his feet, crouching, ready to swing.

"Mmumfrdlphart," muttered the figure sprawled across a golf club. "Frdlmmummerphut."

"Miles, you asshole. That's a good way to get your jaw broken."

"Hmm, hmmm. Wha? Christus! Whah's that? Charlie incoming? Suck on this, yellow man!" he mumbled, attempting a lazy swing of the golf club at Kurt, the putter rising scarcely an inch off the floor.

"You're drunk, man. What the fuck are you doing there?"

A rotten breath escaped Miles's mouth, a long hissing sound like a punctured tire. He lifted his face from the carpet and peered up at Kurt through bleary eyes. "Must've blacked out in the shelling," he said. "How long have I been in this trench?"

"You need to sober up and go home."

Kurt knew the phone number for Tipsy Taxi.

"Mercy Jesus," Miles moaned, sitting up, holding his

head, collapsing back against the wall. "What were they firing at us? Howitzers?"

Kurt knelt down and began collecting the pages again. "Get ahold of yourself, buddy. It's the nineties."

Miles stared ahead, motionless, his eyes open but watery and unfocused, his mouth slack, a trickle of drool running down his chin. Sweat drenched his wide forehead, his neck, soaked a large circle through his safari shirt. He had lost one of his cowboy boots and it was nowhere in view.

"Are you going to be okay, Miles?" Kurt asked, touching the man's clammy wrist to check his pulse.

Miles gripped Kurt's hand with surprising strength, a clamp like a machinist's vise. "She was a fine woman, Muller," he said, his words finding greater clarity now. "I think I was halfway in love with her."

And then it all became clear. The late-night visits to the cabin, the stoic loyalty.

"Rare is the woman who appreciates a pearl-grip Colt."

Miles and Randy. The perfect match.

"I'm sorry, Miles. I liked her too."

The man's nails were embedded in Kurt's wrist, digging deeper, an unconscious fury. "Tell me we're going to find the swine that did that to her," he said. "Say it, Muller. Tell me we're going to hang their shriveled balls from a lamppost."

Kurt needed all of his strength to extract Miles's fingers from his wrist. There were four deep gouge marks, the skin broken, drawing blood.

"You want to help me, you've got to clean up your act, Miles. I can't use a drunk."

Kurt heard Meredith coming down the corridor, approaching them swiftly in a monogrammed bathrobe, the housekeeper struggling to keep up with her. "Miles, I thought you went home an hour ago," Meredith said. "We've been looking all over the place for you. Security noticed your Land-Rover in the lot and thought something might have happened."

Miles blinked, sweat pouring down his face. "Got to keep an eye on Katrina," he muttered. His eyes rolled back in his head and his upper body toppled sideways into a heap of rumpled clothing. He was down for the count.

Kurt reached into Miles's one intact boot and freed the Beretta from an ankle holster. He didn't want the man to blow his foot off.

Meredith spoke to Gloria in Spanish. *Prepare another room.*

26

IT WAS MIDNIGHT when Gloria let him out through the wrought-iron gates and he slid into the squad car waiting for him. The closed vehicle smelled like Chinese food. Resting on the backseat were a couple of dog-eared paperback mysteries, a plastic clothes hamper full of dirty laundry, and a gooey container, the source of the odor. Kurt rolled down his window.

"How is the green goddess?" Muffin asked, guiding the car back down the private road toward town. "Did you tuck her in?"

"She's hurting. She needs about twelve hours of sleep."

"I'm surprised you didn't stay to make sure she got it."

He ignored her cynical smile and asked about the boys.

"They're fine. Dotson and Florio are watching the house in Basalt. But I came very close to punching out your hysterical ex. You have remarkable taste in women, Muller."

"Meg's a mother." He felt the need to defend her. "I

don't blame her one bit for being pissed about what happened."

Muffin raked a hand through her hair, a familiar sign of her frustration. "The cabin was totaled," she said. "The firemen had a fight on their hands keeping the blaze out of the woods. They're still out there."

"Any sign of the bikers? I bumped one of them into the trees."

She shook her head. "Our guys saw lots of tire tracks in the mush, but by the time the fire trucks passed through there, the road was a mess."

She drove him to the impound area behind the county jail. The deputies had towed Kurt's Jeep back to town. He got out and inspected the smoky upholstery, looking for burns. The old Willys had escaped unscathed.

He reached under the driver's seat, reassured to find the .45 still in its holster where he kept it. Muffin raised the hood and they both leaned in for a closer examination, checking hoses and belts, their heads bobbing within inches of each other. "What are you going to do now?" she asked him, tugging on a wire.

"Go home and go to bed," he said. "Want to come?"

"What an intriguing offer." She straightened up and wiped her oily hands on her pants. "Thanks, but I've got laundry to do."

Things had been awkward between them for several months now, ever since he had taken R & R leave, so he was glad they could still tease each other with a smile on their faces. Their friendship was changing, undergoing mysterious strains he could never have imagined a year ago.

"So what have we got here, Kurt? I'm drawing

blanks," she said. "You've talked to Tyler and you've talked to Katrina Pfeil. Are they trying to kill each other? The miners against the tree humpers?"

He slid behind the wheel of the Jeep and turned the key. "It's possible," he said, as perplexed as she was. "Except that a man in a coma has a very hard time tossing a firebomb."

"Maybe he's got friends we don't know about."

They both knew Tyler didn't have a friend in the world. "Yeah, go drag Tink Tarver out of bed and book him," he said. "I've always suspected that little pud was a bomb-throwing anarchist."

She slapped the side of the Jeep, a ranch girl swatting the haunches of a slow work animal, moving it along. "Gotta log some time. Reports to file," she said, backing away. "See you at the funeral. Get some sleep."

In spite of the hour, he had no intention of going home. He drove downvalley along the dark two-lane highway toward Basalt, dodging bloody roadkills, the nighttime as dense and unyielding as the bottom of a lagoon, the pastures and river trees and shale walls of the valley lost in a murky black liquid without depth or dimension. A cold wind whipped through the roofless Jeep, pinching him awake. His body sagged against the backrest, tired and leaden, but his thoughts raced in frantic circles, fueled by adrenaline and a father's apprehensions.

The old two-story farmhouse was hidden in a willow glade beside a strip of crumbling road that had been the main highway thirty years ago, before the new bypass. The turnoff was easy to miss at night, especially with only one headlight, but Kurt slowed down and crept over a bumpy cattle guard, making his way past the mailboxes toward the Pitco unit blocking further entrance. The cruiser's spotlight flashed on and lasered into his eyes, blinding him. He stopped abruptly and raised his head above the windshield, blocking his face with a hand. "It's Muller!" he called out, waving. "Turn that damn thing off!"

"Come ahead, Kurt," the deputy said, killing the light.

Kurt got out and joined Gill Dotson in the cruiser. Gill was a large friendly farmboy from Minnesota, well liked in the department, a superb backcountry skier and the leader of their special rescue squad. They sat in the dark vehicle waiting for the other deputy, Joey Florio, to return from his rounds of the quiet house and the garden out back. A soft light glowed within the bottom floor, but upstairs was black and silent. Kurt wondered where the boys were sleeping. He wondered why Lennon had not told him about Meg's friend, the man on whose shoulder he had so readily dozed. He wondered, too, if Lennon understood that his mother had found someone else to love and that life would be different now.

"Why are we watching the kids, Kurt?" Gill asked, sipping from a milk carton.

"Just a precaution."

"Who would want to hurt a child?"

"Whoever threw that Molotov didn't give a shit who they hurt."

A flashlight beam danced across the yard, Joey Florio circling back from the rear of the house. He stopped and shone the light on a wood-slat swing creaking from a rusty chain between two willows. His long white ray scanned the fence line and a small orchard of pear trees.

"What's your impression of the guy with Meg?" Kurt asked the deputy. He had hired Gill eight or nine years ago, provided what little training he required, trusted him like a favorite nephew. If somebody wearing a Pitkin County uniform was dirty in all of this, it wasn't Gill Dotson. Or Joey Florio, whom Kurt had known since junior high.

"Is he the new love interest?"

"Looks that way," Kurt said.

"He seems all right. One of those New Age feely-touchy types, but harmless. You want me to do a background check on him?"

"You're reading my mind again."

"When we change shifts," Gill shrugged, "I'll let the air out of his tires."

"Let's cut him some slack, Gill. He's a man who travels a loftier path."

"You're a wonderful human being. I mean that."

"These are two souls struggling to achieve a higher level of Tantric fulfillment."

"Is that like holding off until she gets hers first?"

"This is my ex-wife we're talking about, Gill."

"Okay, what are we giving them, six months?"

"Two months, max. If they're still together we'll slice off his valve stems."

"I'm glad you're being grown up about this."

Joey Florio opened the back door, tossed his flashlight onto the seat, and slid in. "Hey there, Kurt," he said. "Everything's tight as a tick. The boys are asleep."

Kurt watched the dark windows on the upper floor. As he told the deputies about the firebomb exploding into the Pfeil cabin, his voice began to quaver slightly and he struggled to control his anger, remembering that first frenzied moment of fear and helplessness. Lennon's words still echoed through his head. *Daddy, don't leave me.*

"A fucking firebomb," Joey said. "Things are a lot stranger around here than when we were kids, Kurt."

"Who's got the Oreos?" Gill asked.

Kurt handed him the bag. "An eyewitness says that one of the perps in the Tyler Rutledge shooting was wearing our colors," he told them. "You guys have any idea if that could be so?"

"Not possible," Joey said.

"Who's the witness?" Gill asked.

"Somebody watching through binoculars. Keep this to yourselves. We may have a roach in our popcorn."

"Come on," Joey scoffed. "That's bullshit, Kurt. Our posse squeaks when they walk."

Joey was probably right. Kat could have been mistaken about the uniform. There had been no serious incidents of department misconduct in Kurt's ten years as sheriff.

"I hope you're right, Joey. But I want you guys to keep your eyes open. You see anything unusual, get in touch with me."

There was a short, unsettling silence. "What kind of things are we talking about, Kurt?"

Kurt had been working this over in his mind ever since Kat's remark. "Did anybody show up on duty today wearing a bandage? Maybe an arm or leg taped up?"

The two men mumbled, shook their heads. They

hadn't noticed anything like that. Kurt explained that one of Tyler's assailants had been wounded.

"Does Muffin know about this eyewitness?" Gill asked.

"Yeah, but she doesn't believe the make either."

Joey rustled the Oreos bag. "So why do you believe it, Kurt?"

"I'm covering all the bases. I don't want it to be true any more than you do."

Eliminating these two men and Muffin, that left a dozen deputies in the department. Kurt had hired them, sent them through the training program in Glenwood Springs, nurtured their careers. They were a family. If there was a bad mutt in the litter, Kurt felt responsible. He hadn't spent enough time with his deputies in the past couple of years and didn't know them anymore.

"I'm not starting a witch hunt here," he said. "I don't care if somebody's wasting Xerox paper. But if you notice one of our compadres going through some funny changes, give me a call."

Joey snickered in the backseat. "Jeez. Cops going through funny changes. What are you, Kurt?" he said with a mouthful of cookie. "Hard up for phone calls?"

27

By the time he arrived at the Black Diamond Saloon it was nearly two in the morning. Sunday night, closing time, the slowest hour of the week. There were no dirt bikes out front, only two Harleys and a couple of pick-ups. He parked in the dark lot across the street and watched the stragglers weave out to their vehicles, a skinny-necked cowboy with a drunk woman hanging on him, slurring her laughter, and a few minutes later, half a dozen Mexican migrants piling into the other truck bed and howling off into the night. Soon a Garfield County patrol unit cruised by, the deputy slowing down to look for DUIs, and Kurt sank behind the wheel, in no mood to get hauled down to the sheriff's office to discuss those twisted sheets of metal stacked up across the road, the remnants of what used to be a Dumpster.

After the deputy had rolled out of sight, two Bandidos swaggered through the doors to rev up their Harleys and roar away, and soon the lights began to dim inside. A battered old Studebaker was parked near the rear of the saloon, the last car in the lot. Kurt suspected that junker was Skank's ride home and sped across the road with his headbeams off.

He tried the back door but it was locked, so he stepped around the corner of the building into deeper darkness and waited. In a few moments the door opened and a tall stooped figure emerged, mumbling to himself, rattling a ring of keys.

"Hello, Skank," Kurt said. The bartender was startled and whirled around to face him. "How about one for the road?"

Kurt never saw the knife. There was a swish across his forearm, a quick stinging slice of skin. Kicking out hard, he caught Skank in the crotch and slammed him against the brick wall, and the knife clattered to the ground. He dragged the bartender to his feet, twisted his arm behind his back, and smashed his face against the wall. "Is that any way to treat an old friend?" he said, booting away the six-inch switchblade lying near his feet.

"Who the fuck *are* you, man? What do you want?"

"I'm looking for a name and I think you can supply it, Skank. Let's go back inside, shall we? We don't want to wake the neighbors."

There was a single light on inside, a buzzing fluorescent tube hanging twelve feet above the row of liquor bottles. His arm pinned behind his back, Skank marched obediently ahead, offering little resistance to the big man behind him. Kurt drew him to a halt at the bar sink, a deep basin filled with murky gray water, a scum of suds.

"I know who you are, dude," Skank said. "You're the motherfucker who blew up that Dumpster out back."

"Wrong," Kurt said. "Your buddy the dirt-biker blew up the Dumpster."

"It was your stick, man. You fucking lit it."

"Well, Skank, you may have me on a technicality. Let's call it a draw. You tell me the name of the guy who threw the stick and I won't dunk your ugly face in this sink."

Kurt's jacket sleeve was slit open, the denim stained with his blood. The wound wasn't deep but it stung like a razor cut.

"The cops are after your ass," Skank said, nervously twisting at a long string of hair. "They've been in here taking notes."

"His name, Skank. What's the Beard's name?"

"Some uniforms from Pitkin County were here yesterday asking the same thing. I'll tell you what I told them. I don't know none of those guys. They blow in on the weekends and drink their beer and shoot some pool and then they ride off into the sunset. Hiyo, Silver, kemosabe. I don't keep their time sheets."

Kurt grabbed him by the neck, shoved his head under the dirty water, yanked him up quickly. Skank gasped for air, a mass of long wet hair concealing his face like kelp.

"You're going to have to do something about the way you wash glasses in this establishment, Skank. One call to the Health Department and they'll shut you down."

"Fucking shithead!"

Kurt shoved his head under again. "I'm sorry, I didn't hear you very clear. Did you mention a name?"

Skank fought back but was no match for Kurt's

strength. He came up coughing, spitting water, cursing the man who had a grip on his arm and neck.

"I guess I'm just in a bad mood tonight, Skank. Somebody tried to kill my little boy and his friend. You have any kids?"

The bartender nodded, his head dangling over the basin, dripping like a wet dog. "Little girl in Rifle," he sputtered. "Lives with her mother."

"Then maybe you can understand why I'm so upset. Now if you just tell me the guy's name, I'll walk away and we can stop all this foolishness."

"I don't—"

Kurt squeezed Skank's neck, the signal he was going swimming again. "Okay, okay," the bartender said. "His name is J.J. That's all I know."

"And where does this J.J. live?"

"I don't know."

Kurt dunked him again, holding his head down for at least ten seconds. When he dragged him up, Skank said, "Junction! That bike club in Junction!"

"Good, Skank. Now I'm going to give you a chance to catch your breath and clear your head. I want you to think very carefully. Does J.J. have a last name? This is crucial. If you can't remember his last name, I may have to consider other forms of memory therapy."

Skank was breathing hard, his elbows resting on the basin. Cheese-colored foam clung to his hair. "I can't do this anymore, man. You've got to stop."

"Ask yourself this, Skank. What has this guy J.J. done for me that's worth another twenty seconds in the nastiest water in Bonedale?"

The bartender straightened up, pushed the hair out

of his face with his free hand, wiped at his wet wind-breaker. "J.J. tried to hurt your kid?" he asked.

"I don't know," Kurt said. "I want to talk to him."

Skank sniffed, harked up a wad of phlegm, and spit, his eyes blinking rapidly. "J.J. Chilcutt," he said. "Works for some security outfit in Grand Junction. That's all I know about him, man. You want to dunk me again, fuck you. I ain't saying another word."

Kurt released him with a shove. "You pulled a knife on an officer of the law," he said, removing his jacket and rolling back the bloody shirtsleeve to examine the cut. "You could do time for that, asshole. Keep that in mind when I walk out of here. If I find out you've contacted this J.J. Chilcutt about our conversation here tonight, I'll be back to press charges."

Kurt found the switchblade on the ground outside the back door and tossed the knife into his glove compartment. He got behind the wheel and drove the deserted orchard road back to Highway 82, praying he would get out of Garfield County without being pulled over for a missing headlight.

28

THE JIGGLING SOUND woke her, a turning doorknob. She reached for Kurt but he wasn't there. The bed beside her was empty. Maybe he had accidentally locked himself out. "Kurt, is that you?" she asked in a drowsy moan.

"Miss Pfeil," said a male voice in the hallway.

She rolled out of bed quickly and searched the darkness for her clothes. "Who is it?" she asked.

"Security, ma'am. Is everything all right?" A deep growling voice. Why was he still working the doorknob?

"Everything's fine," she said, slipping into her jeans. "I was asleep."

"Just a precaution, ma'am. We've had some reports. May I come in and check your room?"

She gazed out the window. It was the middle of the night, maybe four A.M. The moon was down and a light rain speckled the pane. She couldn't get the damned boot on her bad foot.

"That won't be necessary," she said. "I'll be all right. I've got a gun."

The doorknob continued to twist, a faint, menacing

tick, and she had the feeling he was jimmying the lock with a tool. If only she did have that Lady Smith that Randy had trained her to use.

"There's a message here I'm supposed to deliver."

"What kind of message?" She was stalling for time, pulling on her sweater, her heart speeding wildly. "Who's it from?"

"It's a note, ma'am. Is there any reason why you won't open the door?"

"Yes, there is. I'm undressed and in bed."

She unlatched the window, opened it to the night. A strong cold wind hurled the curtains in her face. It was too dark to see what was below. A hedge, a patio table, a spinning central air unit. The drop might be five feet, it might be twenty. She couldn't remember which floor she was on.

"Could you please come back in a couple of hours? I'm sure the message can wait."

"Not this message," the man said. "I'm told it's very urgent. Here, I'll slip it under the door for you."

She heard a soft scraping sound, and something disturbed the wide strip of light under the door. A piece of paper.

"I'll check on you a little later, Miss Pfeil. Sorry to bother you."

Her eyes had adjusted to the unlit room and she could make out the paper on the floor. Who the hell had sent her a note? She didn't believe for a second that the man was gone.

Crossing the room in quiet steps, she knelt down and picked up the paper, then retrieved the cigarette lighter from her pants pocket. The flame revealed the scrawled words. *Boom you're dead bitch.*

"Sooner or later," said the deep voice on the other side of the door.

Kat gasped, struggled to catch her breath, leaned all her weight against the door.

"You're running out of places to hide, kitty cat." His voice was an obscene whisper only three inches from her ear.

She wadded up the note and threw it on the floor. "I've got a message for you, too, asshole," she said, "and for those limp dicks you work for. That little red dot you feel on the back of your neck is my way of playing tag."

He shouldered the door hard, cracking wood, knocking Kat to the carpet. She dragged herself to her feet and hobbled as fast as she could to the window. On the third blow the door was forced open and the man stepped into the room, a large silhouette backlit by creamy light from the corridor. Shadow obscured his face.

"Here, kitty, kitty," he growled, moving slowly toward her, a bandaged hand hanging like a club at his side. "How many lives you got left, pretty Kat?"

She hopped up onto the window seat. The curtains were floating around her like gossamer streamers. "Enough to fuck you up real bad," she said, and then turned and leapt into the darkness.

29

KURT STUCK HIS head under the cold shower stream to shock himself awake. He had had only three hours of sleep but Ned's funeral was at eight and Meg was bringing the boys here beforehand to try on the two pint-sized suits packed away in a trunk, hand-me-downs from Kurt's childhood. It was going to be a hard day on everyone. He let the water run awhile longer over his thick hair, then stood back and washed out the cut where the knife had sliced his forearm. When he turned off the faucet and slid aside the shower curtain, some-one was waiting for him.

"I should've taken you up on your offer, Kurt," she said, staring at him across the large bathroom.

"Jesus Christ, Kat, you scared the shit out of me," he said, grabbing a towel to cover himself. "What happened?"

"Some guy broke into my room," she said, un-screwing the cap on his after-shave, smelling the green liquid. "He knew all about me. Had to be one of the bastards behind the firebomb."

"Are you all right?"

"I jumped out a window."

He saw now that her jeans and sweater were spattered with mud and that she was leaving a puddle on the tile. Her hair was messy and damp and pulled back behind her ears.

"Where were the Lamars and their high-priced security people?"

"A very good question," she said, toeing off one muddy boot, then the other. "I don't know how the guy could get in a place like that. Unless . . ."

He stepped out of the tub, the towel cinched at his waist. "Unless the fucker was *with* security," he said.

"Exactly," she said, unzipping her jeans and dropping them to the floor with a heavy wet thud.

"VIProtex," he said. Neal Staggs. The son of a bitch was always lurking around the edges.

She came up close to him and pulled the sweater over her head, discarding it in the trail of clothing. "I'm too tired to worry about my vanity," she said, pressing her scarred chest against him in a long embrace. "So please don't stare at me. I need a shower bad."

He could feel the tension and fear deep down in her bones. "Did he hurt you?" he asked.

She rested her head against his dripping chest. "I got the worst of it from the rosebushes."

He kissed her matted hair. "Do you think you could describe the guy to one of my deputies?" he asked. "Did you get a good look at him?"

She untied the knot at his waist and the towel slipped to the floor. "Not as good as this," she said, her hands sliding down his back to rest on his buttocks. "Come in with me." She took his hand and stepped awkwardly into the tub. "I'm cold and I can't bend my legs this morning. You'll have to kneel down and wash them for me."

HE STAYED IN the bathroom a few minutes longer to dress the knife wound, and when he opened the door he found her lying on his bed, the sheet wrapped mummylike around her long slender figure. "Meg left a few things behind. They're in that bottom drawer," he said, pointing to an old dresser that had belonged to his parents. "I don't know if anything is your size, but you're welcome to them."

She smiled at him, her wet hair fanned out on the pillow. "Do men always keep the underthings of their ex-wives?"

Only the ones who are foolish enough to think their wives might be coming back, he thought. But he offered no explanation.

"How is your arm?" she asked, patting the bed beside her. "Your doctor should have a look at it."

"I'm okay," he said, crawling in next to her.

She propped herself up on an elbow, ran her finger across the fading tattoo above his bicep. "This is incredible, you know," she said, placing a gentle kiss there. "Where did you get it?"

It always embarrassed him to talk about the tattoo when he was sober. "I was a wet-nosed soldier boy stationed in Germany," he said, cringing at the memory. "*Fasching,* the winter of sixty-nine. My buddies and I were so wasted we could barely stand up. They got skulls and daggers and 'Born to raise hell.' I told the little tattoo man what I wanted and he started to bawl like a baby. Pretty soon everybody in the shop was crying. Can you believe he did this from memory? He'd seen it on television like everybody else in the world. It took him hours. I think I was stone cold sober by the time he was through. My buddies were long gone."

"It's the sweetest thing I've ever seen on a man," she said, caressing his face. "If I'd been there, I would've cried too."

She kissed him, and as the kiss lingered on, he began to unfurl the sheet around her. "It's so bright in here," she said. "Can we pull the drapes?"

"Kat," he said, "you don't have to hide from me."

His hand roamed softly over the cesarean scar on her belly, stroked her damaged knee. "Let's take it slow and easy, okay?" she whispered. "I haven't been with anyone in a long time."

It had been a long time for him as well. He kissed her breast, imagining that they were young again, discovering love's delicate friction, their blushing bodies strong and flawless and pure.

"I'm sorry, Kurt," she said, flinching suddenly, her body tensing beneath him. "It hurts too bad."

He pulled away, rolled over on his back.

"My doctor warned me there might be a problem." She was panting now, her skin glazed with sweat. Not from arousal but from the shock of intense pain. "He said I might need surgery."

Kurt leaned over to kiss her. "We'll find a way," he said. "There's no hurry."

They lay side by side, their respiration calming into a single shared cadence, her head floating on his chest. He had closed his eyes and was drifting into a mindless euphoria when he felt her fingers spidering up his thigh. "Do you have another one of these?" she asked, peeling off the condom that still clung to him like the wrinkled digit of a medical glove.

"Un-hunh," he said, pointing drowsily to the open drawer of the night table.

"Lucky for you," she said, nibbling at his belly button, "they didn't get my tongue."

THE PLEASURE WAS so intoxicating he nodded off afterward, faintly aware that she had crawled under his arm to nuzzle and rest. When he heard footsteps bounding up the stairwell to his bedroom he knew who they belonged to, the boys arriving to try on suits for the funeral, but he couldn't rouse himself from the deep, comforting slumber.

"Hi, Dad, I'm home!" Lennon called out, bursting into the room.

Hunter was right behind him. "Hey, wake up, Coach!" he shouted. "Time to get a move on!"

"Oh, lord," Kurt said, reaching over to shake Kat. His hand groped at empty sheet.

"Let's wrestle," Lennon said, diving on his father, pinning him to the mattress. Hunter piled on top.

"Some other time, guys," Meg's voice rang across the room. She was standing in the doorway, wearing a formal dress he hadn't seen her wear in ages. "Kurt, do you have any idea what time it is? The funeral is in half an hour."

"Okay, boys, run on downstairs till I get dressed," he said, shooing them off his back. He looked around the room, expecting Kat to emerge from a closet or step out of the bathroom. There was a note lying next to her pillow.

"Come on now," Meg said, "let's give Kurt some privacy."

He waited for the boys to race away, then picked up the note. *Took your suggestion and borrowed some clothes. I am off. Have to phone Randy's daughter in Portland. Not looking forward to that. Don't know when you and I will see each other again, Kurt. Maybe when all the darkness is gone. Love, K.*

"Kurt," Meg said. He glanced up. She was still at the door, watching him read the note. "I'm sorry I was so bent out of shape last night. I apologize for making a scene."

He tucked the sheet around his waist and stood up. "It's okay, Peaches," he said. "You had good reason to be upset."

He waded toward the bathroom, dragging the sheet behind him like a regal train. In the dresser mirror he saw her eyes following his awkward movement. "Did the boys sleep okay?" he asked, pausing at the door before going in. "Is something wrong?"

"The room is still the same, isn't it?" she said, gazing about with a wistful dreaminess. "You haven't made many changes."

The bedroom was a large undivided space, the entire upper floor of the house, glass doors opening onto a narrow sundeck. Most of the furniture had been in place for forty years, lugged here from Chicago and Austria by his parents. Three of Meg's photographs were hanging on the walls where she'd left them, mountain landscapes from her earlier life as an amateur photographer.

"I'm one of those guys who likes everything just the

way it was," he said, realizing she hadn't been in this room since their divorce three years ago.

She stepped over to a chest of drawers and studied a framed photo of Lennon when he was eleven months old. They had made a special trip to the mall in Glenwood Springs for this, and Kurt remembered the ordeal as if it were last week. The fussy families ahead of them in line, the photographer trying to prop up Lennon with a backrest so he wouldn't keel over.

"How involved are you in this thing with Kat Pfeil?" she asked, lifting the photograph, examining it closely.

"What do you mean?"

"Trouble seems to follow her around, Kurt."

He exhaled deeply. "I'm going to find out who tried to kill her," he said, "and who almost killed our son. It's my job. If that kind of talk scares you, Meg, maybe you and the Zen master ought to check in to an ashram till this is over."

Whenever she grew angry or frightened, a red rash blotched the skin on her neck. There it was, blooming bright.

"Lennon loves you very much," she said. "Please don't do anything that puts your life at risk. I don't want him growing up without you."

She was telling him he had done a good job raising their son, and her words meant a great deal to him at that moment. "I'll be careful, Meg," he said. "I don't want him to have another father."

They stared at each other, understanding what was left unsaid. That no matter how complicated their lives would become, tugged about by other loves, an indelible bond remained between them forever. Their beautiful son.

"Tell me it's going to be all right, Kurt," she said. "Whatever happens, I want to stay good enough friends to hold your hand at his high school graduation."

He smiled at the thought. "I'll be so old you'll have to push me into the auditorium in a wheelchair."

It made her smile too. "You know I will," she said, and he believed her.

30

THE REMAINS OF Ned Carr were laid to rest, according to his wishes, in the overgrown cemetery at the foot of Ute Trail. A light rain drizzled on the handful of mourners tromping through the cottonwood thicket scattered with fallen tombstones, forgotten miners who had perished in outbreaks of cholera and diphtheria, their markers quarried out of Colorado marble and returning slowly to the elements. On the way to the grave site Lennon and Hunter stopped to scrape mud from a crumbling headstone, deciphering the inscription like excited archaeologists in a Greek necropolis.

"Look at this one, Dad!" Lennon waved. "It says, 'Sleep now, angel.'"

Hunter sounded out the rest of the sentence: "'You . . . are in . . . God's . . . hands.'"

"Let's go, boys," Kurt said. "You're getting your suits dirty."

He and his brother had roamed through this cemetery when they were kids, searching the brush for ornate stones and the rusty spike fences that enclosed families of means. Too many children were buried here, their tiny graves outlined with creek rocks. It had been a hard life, the winters long and unforgiving. Foolish dreamers pursuing deep veins of silver.

"This place is great!" Lennon announced. "This is where I want to be buried!"

"Not me," said Hunter, his jacket sleeves soaked to the elbows. "I want to be buried next to my mom."

Kurt worried about him. The child hadn't shown any emotion since the initial shock of hearing that his grandfather was dead. He had asked only one question: *Is my grandpa in heaven with my mother?* Kurt had told him, *Yes, you bet he is,* and that seemed to satisfy him, erase all his doubts. He was a contented boy again, cared for, safe, lost in childhood adventures with a best friend. His grandpa was in God's hands. The monsters hadn't yet stirred under the bed.

Father McCabe led the gathering in prayer and sprinkled the casket. Lennon and Hunter looked like handsome little gentlemen in their white summer suits and clip-on ties, vintage relics from the Muller brothers, circa 1953. The Lamars were present, well dressed and stoic, and Tyler's parents, ashen from grief and fatigue. Corky Marcus wore his last remaining three-piece lawyer suit and stood holding an umbrella over his son Joshua. Halfway through the ceremony there was a loud rustling in the tall green bushes and Tink Tarver materialized out of the foliage like a wild-eyed Caliban, his Radio Flyer wagon in tow. He doffed his beret and bowed his head, and after the final prayer was uttered, and the mountain columbines were placed on the casket by the two boys, the old man lifted the tongue of his red wagon and disappeared into the thicket.

The rain had finally stopped. Kurt made his way over to Meredith Stone, who was standing off by herself near a cottonwood tree, waiting for her husband to finish his conversation with Corky Marcus.

"Hello, Meredith," he said. "How is Kat this morning?"

"Sleeping well, I expect," she said. "I'll check on her when we get home. Would you like to join us for breakfast?"

She was wearing makeup and matching Navajo jewelry that ornamented her neck, wrists, and earlobes. This was the way she had always appeared in magazines, effortlessly beautiful, exuding intelligence and a casual elegance.

"Maybe Lee ought to spend his money on a more reliable security setup," he said. "Somebody broke into her room and she had to jump out a window to get away."

She looked stunned. "If that's a joke, Kurt," she said, her face growing stern, "it's not a very funny one."

"She's all right—she came over to my place."

"You're serious, aren't you?" She turned to locate her husband. "Someone broke into our house? That doesn't seem possible. I've got to speak to Lee about this."

Lamar was now talking with the priest, a hand on the pastor's shoulder.

"Before this goes any further than you and me," Kurt said, "let me talk to Neal Staggs first." He suspected that Staggs was the key to what was going on. "Do you know where I can find him?"

Her brow wrinkled. "He has an office here,"

she said. "I'd like to have a word with that prick my-self."

"Where is his office?"

"VIProtex rents space from us in the Silver Queen," she said. The posh new hotel Lee Lamar had built at the foot of Aspen Mountain. "But let us take care of this ourselves, Kurt. Kat was our guest.. If I know Lee, he'll rattle cages until he finds out what went wrong."

"Do you think you could persuade him not to rattle any cages until after I speak with Staggs?"

With a quick smile she studied his face. "There's something you're not telling me, Sheriff."

"Staggs and I go back a long way. I don't want to bore you with the details. When I get through with him, you can have what's left."

She thought it over, her smile darkening. Clearly she had no sympathy for Neal Staggs. "I'll wait till lunch before I tell Lee about the break-in," she said. "But only on one condition."

"Okay."

"I want to see Katrina. I feel horrible about what happened. Tell me where she is."

"I don't know where she is. She left me a note and then disappeared."

Her look was cool and probing. "You'll hear from her again."

He hoped she was right, but Kat Pfeil was proving to be as elusive as her brother the drug lord. "She and I have a truckload of unfinished police business to tie up," he said. "You hear from her first, tell her I'm looking for her. I hear from her, I'll make sure she gives you a call. Deal?"

She gave him that heartbreaking smile from her old

publicity photos. Every now and then she did something like that to remind him who she was. Who she had been. "Deal," she said. "You've got till noon. That noise you hear will be Lee going through the roof."

31

HE ARRIVED AT the courthouse before the shift change and walked into the department's squad room, a remodeled basement space of cluttered cubicles and soft-humming computers. The room always smelled like scorched coffee crusted at the bottom of a glass pot. Sitting at Gill Dotson's desk, Kurt pecked at the keyboard, searching through state files for the police record on one J.J. Chilcutt. Within seconds he'd found him. James Joseph Chilcutt had two priors, a DUI five years ago and a recent assault-and-battery against his wife, who had subsequently dropped the charges. His address and phone number were listed in Grand Junction, and the name of his employer. VIProtex International.

Bingo, he thought, clasping his hands. The connection he was looking for.

And then he noticed something else in the man's records. U.S. Army, 1967–73, distinguished service in Vietnam. Explosive Ordnance Disposal, MACV-SOG. The same demolitions task force as Kurt's brother.

He picked up the phone and dialed the Banks home in Denver. A teenage boy answered, and Kurt asked to speak with his father. "Did I catch you at a bad time, Lorenzo?" he said when the man came on the line.

"I was just about to head downtown, Kurt," he said. "Hey, sorry I couldn't be more definitive about the mine explosion. I didn't feel I could call it one way or the other. I know that doesn't help your case, man, but I would be lying if I said otherwise. Maybe you should bring in the ATF. They've got more sensitive equipment and they're better trained at that kind of thing."

"You did a great job, Lorenzo, and we all appreciate it. That's not why I'm calling."

Kurt asked if he had ever heard the name James Joseph Chilcutt.

"J.J.? Hell yes, I know him. Your brother knew him too. He was in our unit. J.J. was one seriously disturbed individual. Only man I know who got his rocks off crawling down VC tunnels with plastique hanging off his back. He was too big for the work but the brass didn't want to discourage a man who so dearly loved his job. J.J. still living out in Junction?"

"Yes, he is."

"Next time you see that boy, tell him Lorenzo Banks says to kiss his ass."

"I'll do that."

THE VIPROTEX OFFICE was located off the hotel lobby at the end of a long corridor with polished wood floors and potted ferns. A discreet brass nameplate identified the door. The small reception area gave the impression of a therapist's waiting room, soft carpet and soothing earth tones, comfortable fabric couches, the lamps dimmed to an amber repose. There was no crude suggestion of surveillance cameras or monitors, no tape reels spinning. This was where the clients met for introductions, warm handshakes, reassurances.

"May I help you?" the receptionist asked with a brittle smile. Rigid as a ruler, frosted hair, bright lipstick, her face narrow and pinched. Staggs must have brought her in from out of town. No one in Aspen except a handful of real estate weasels dressed up like that to sit behind a desk all day and take phone messages.

"Is Neal Staggs in today? I would like to see him, please."

"I'm sorry, sir. He's leaving town this morning and won't be back until next week."

Kurt glanced at the closed doors in the rear where a crew-cut young man sat reading a magazine in a straight-backed chair. He looked up, a rookie guard outfitted in a starch-pressed VIProtex uniform, his hollow eyes meeting Kurt's. He was the kind of unambitious grunt, confused and amorphously angry, who had always made the perfect foot soldier.

"That's too bad," Kurt said, offering his best smile, trying to thaw the woman's chilly exterior. He was wearing a dark blue suit he'd chosen for the funeral and knew how dignified and imposing he appeared, how remarkably *adult*. "I was hoping to catch him before he got away. We go back a few years."

"Oh, I see." Not one corpuscle of human emotion.

"In fact," he said, gazing around the reception room, "I didn't know Neal had a branch office here until just this morning."

"Yes, sir, we've been here four months."

He studied the hard lines around her mouth. "You're from Denver, aren't you?"

A faint glimmer in her eyes, an arctic wind shifting the snowscape. "How did you know that?"

He rested his hands on the desk and leaned closer, lowering his voice. "When Neal was in the Denver office, he and I worked some of the same cases."

A weak winter sun shone over the ice plates. The frozen crust was beginning to soften. "Are you with the Bureau, Mr.—"

The young guard was watching them now, eavesdropping. Kurt lowered his voice to a whisper. "No, I'm not, Miz Barnstone," he said, reading the nameplate on her desk. Hazel Barnstone. "But Neal and I have similar professional interests. Would you tell him I'm here to see him."

He watched the word *snitch* cross her thoughts. The words *lowlife paid government informant*. "I'm sorry, sir," she said, "Mr. Staggs is making last-minute preparations for his trip and is unavailable right now. If you give me your name and phone number I will let him know you came by. Perhaps you would like to schedule an appointment for next week."

He had abandoned all hope of charming this woman. He was prepared to drop his shield on her desk and say, *Okay, sister, buzz that asshole and tell him this is police business*, but he didn't want to lose Staggs out a back door, or be forced to wait until his lawyer arrived. "Miz Barnstone," he said in a final effort, "do this little favor for me, I'll do one for you."

There was the suggestion of a smile at the corners of her hard mouth, a cold, perverse twitch. "What makes you think you could possibly do something for me?" she asked, her eyes narrowing darkly.

"You've never seen my tattoo."

"No," she said with a flash of small sharp teeth. "And it isn't likely you'll ever see mine. Good day, sir."

At that moment the hall door swished open and a young limousine driver rushed in. "Sorry I'm running late," he huffed, his face flushed with heat and embarrassment. "I had some trouble finding your suite."

Hazel Barnstone stood up from the chair, attempting to direct the young driver's attention, her bright lips moving quickly, speaking clipped phrases.

"Are you Mr. Staggs?" he said to Kurt, extending a hand, his chest heaving from the sprint through the lobby. "Don't worry, sir. I'll get you to the airport with time to spare."

"Young man!" the receptionist said in a shrill voice. "Please have a seat. I will let you know when your client is ready to leave."

The driver smiled sheepishly at Kurt, apologized again, shuffled toward a couch. Hazel Barnstone circled around the desk and marched briskly across the carpet in her white leather heels to open the door for Kurt, showing him the way out.

"I will tell Mr. Staggs you were here," she said, her voice as barren as a tundra. "What did you say your name is?"

The security guard was on his feet now, moving bovinely toward the commotion, his shoulders rolled up around his neck like a stiff little bull.

"Tell Staggs his old Aspen buddy came calling," Kurt said, lingering at the open door to stare down the young guard approaching him.

"Shall I say it was the old buddy with a tattoo?" she asked snidely.

"The old buddy who fucked up his retirement pension. He'll know who I am."

FOLLOWING A LIMOUSINE was the easiest tail Kurt had ever handled. At the airport the driver shuttled Staggs to the hangar that housed the private planes of movie stars and Wall Street traders, and carried two bags for him to a waiting Lear. As soon as Staggs was aboard, Kurt wheeled his Jeep into an EMPLOYEES ONLY space next to the service shed where Wing Taylor could be found day or night, chewing out his crew, filing paperwork, monitoring the weather.

Kurt tapped on the glass wall that separated Wing from the noise and grease. The man looked up from a newspaper, grinned, and waved Kurt in. "Morning, son," he said. "Long time no see. What brings you to the pit?"

"I need to know where a plane is going," Kurt said.

"Not a problem. Give me a few details."

"How about that one right there," Kurt said, pointing out the window at the Learjet taxiing across the wet tarmac.

"No brainer, Kurt. That's the VIProtex jet. Two guys going to Colorado Springs this morning."

"*Two* guys?"

"The first one's been here an hour, poking around the shop, shooting the shit with my mechanics. I had to go out and tell him to wait in the designated area. Something falls on his bad hand, I'm screwed. Insurance don't cover that."

"The guy had a bad hand?"

"Bandaged, anyway. Don't make any difference, I cain't let people wander around my shop."

"What did he look like?"

"Like a goddamned Viking. Big fella with a beard."

Wing Taylor was pushing seventy, gap toothed, a stout, balding man with curly white muttonchop sideburns that had been out of style for at least twenty years. A sheriff prior to Kurt had officially deputized Wing and the old pilot was proud of his association with law enforcement. He showed up for every department picnic and fund-raiser, plastered his truck with supportive cop stickers, sent baskets of fruit to everyone at Christmas. The department hired him out several times a year, especially in avalanche season. There wasn't a better pilot in the valley.

"You feel like a trip to Colorado Springs today?" Kurt asked him.

Wing's Irish face glowed with excitement. "Back by suppertime?"

"I can't promise."

"Let me call the wife," he said. "I'll have you in the air in fifteen minutes."

Kurt watched the Learjet roll down the strip for take-off. "Make it ten," he said.

32

THEY HEADED DUE east out of the rain clouds, the Turbo Commander climbing above the rugged, snowcapped peaks of the Sawatch Range, a dramatic spectacle of alpine cirques and blue mountain lakes, the pinnacle of the Continental Divide. But Kurt was exhausted, light-headed in flight, and the awesome beauty didn't prevent him from nodding off. By the time they were sailing over the Pike National Forest he was fast asleep and didn't wake until the plane's wheels touched earth in Colorado Springs and Wing gave him a shake.

"Here we are, bub."

"Wait for my call," Kurt mumbled at the pilot. "I might be gone two or three hours."

He didn't know how he was going to find Staggs, who was at least half an hour ahead of them by now. Groggy and floating, he made his way to the airport's limousine service counter and smiled at the young woman behind the desk. "Two of my colleagues in law enforcement grabbed a limo a little while ago," he said, showing her his badge. It was a long shot, but what did he have to lose. "We were supposed to hook up and ride together but my flight was delayed. Is there anything available right now?"

"Certainly, sir," she said, a perky blonde with a sunny disposition. "Your friends were the two gentlemen from Aspen, right?"

"Very good," he smiled. "I can see you're more on top of things this morning than I am."

She pecked away at her computer. "We aren't as busy as we were yesterday," she said, "when the golfers came in for the tournament."

"How long is the ride?" He checked his watch ostentatiously. "Can we make it by noon?" He didn't have a clue where he was going.

Click, click. "The Palmer Country Club is only twenty minutes away, sir." She waited for the screen, glanced up at him, smiled. "One of our drivers should be returning shortly. How many bags?"

"None. I'm just here for the day."

"No clubs, sir?"

Clubs? He hesitated. "No."

"I read about the tournament in the paper," she said, tapping her printout button. "Sounds like a worthy cause. My grandfather did some ranching down near Pagosa Springs."

What was this all about? "So they covered us in the paper," he said.

"Yes, sir. I think I still have yesterday's *Gazette* in the office, if you'd like to see it."

As the LIMOUSINE transported him into the city, Kurt read the back-page newspaper article about the golf tournament, a benefit for something called the Ranch

Relief Fund. What caught his eye was the sponsor, the Free West Legal Coalition. Their executive director, Arnold Metcalf, explained that the fund "aids those folks whose livelihood has been threatened by unnecessary federal regulations. It's a shame," Metcalf was quoted as saying, "that the good people who put food on our tables are struggling to stay in business because Washington bureaucrats and the environmental lobby have tied their hands and won't let them do what they've been doing successfully for generations."

Arnold Metcalf, he thought. The lawyer Corky had told him about. Was Staggs playing in this tournament for pleasure, he wondered, or was he here on security business for the Free West Legal Coalition?

The limo ride was Kurt's first trip through the boulevards of Colorado Springs. He was well aware that this place was a strategic military encampment, the nerve center for the North American Air Defense Command, the U.S. ballistic missile force, and the Space Command satellite surveillance systems, all secured in hollowed-out Cheyenne Mountain nearby. The few times in his life he had passed through this area on I-25 he hadn't slowed down long enough to acknowledge the sprawling Air Force Academy with its smooth green landscaping, or the city itself, which impressed him as one big water-sucking, artificial lawn planted on the last prairie mesa before the Front Range of the Rockies. Ever since his unhappy two-year stint in the U.S. Army, 1968–70, he had avoided all things military—base areas, vet hangouts, commissaries—so on those long vacation trips to New Mexico he was relieved when Colorado Springs was behind him, receding farther into the rearview mirror, an orderly grid with timed sprinkler systems and cheap Sunday buffets and a hundred thousand aging, buzz-cut hardasses living out their circumscribed years among the fading ribbons and bronze stars on their mantelpieces.

"How long ago did you drop off my two friends?" Kurt asked the driver.

"About an hour ago, sir."

They drove into the scrub-oak foothills below Cheyenne Mountain, an exclusive planned community of $300,000 homes, impressive views of Pikes Peak, their own man-made lakes. On the sylvan grounds near the country-club entrance there was a tastefully constructed sign welcoming the public to the tournament. The limousine rolled down a long pine-shaded lane to the club headquarters, a Tudor castle rising out of the greenery. Kurt tipped the young man generously and crossed the wooden footbridge over a stagnant, moat-like pond covered with lily pads. In the castle's palatial lobby a handful of women wearing paper name-tags sat at a long table, greeting visitors, handing out brochures, taking money. A pair of uniformed VIProtex security guards strolled about, keeping a watchful eye on the proceedings.

"You're not too late, dear," said a friendly older lady named Mabel Dishburger. Her eyes darted about behind librarian bifocals as she collected materials for him from five different stacks. "They haven't made it to the second tee. There's still plenty of afternoon left."

Kurt returned her smile. "I'm expecting some friends," he told her. "I'll go wait for them out front."

He had no intention of shelling out money for a benefit golf tournament. Instead he walked outside and wove his way through a trellised rose garden leading to the rear of the grand old edifice, where a group of teenage caddies lounged around by the golf carts. Kurt picked out a wisecracking carrottop who could have passed for Lennon's older brother and slipped a ten-dollar bill into his shirt pocket. "Take me out to the action," he said.

The caddie studied Kurt's suit lapels. "You're supposed to get one of those little pins when you register, mister."

Kurt found another ten in his wallet. "Here's my registration form," he said, adding the bill to the boy's pocket. "Let's take a ride."

The caddie drove Kurt down two hundred yards of fairway past the first flag. They could see the crowd off to the right, maybe a hundred people shading themselves under a stand of ponderosa pines. The golfers themselves were scattered out over several acres of stunning scenery, little safaris of Ban-Lon bwanas trailed by their baggage bearers. Striped canvas-roofed carts meandered about the course like lost ice cream trucks.

"Are there any celebrities playing in this tournament?" Kurt asked the driver.

"Yes, sir," the boy assured him. He named three circuit pros Kurt had never heard of, the ne'er-do-well son of a famous television comedian, and a macho deep-voiced movie actor known for minor cowboy roles.

"I'm looking for two people," Kurt told the driver. "I don't know if they're playing or watching. Let's try that group over there," he said, pointing to a sizable party off near a water trap.

"I'm not authorized to drive around the course during the tournament, sir."

"Okay, my friend, I don't want to get you in trouble." Kurt showed him his badge. "Help me find these guys and you can split."

Within a quarter of an hour they had located Neal Staggs walking with his party less than fifty yards from the second flag. Five middle-aged men chatting among themselves, including two casually dressed Asians wearing blue sun visors, their golf balls dotting the green ahead. The caddies marched in the rear, heavy bags slung over their shoulders, and behind them all, idling along like a protective patrol car, crept a lone white cart driven by a man holding the wheel with a heavily bandaged hand.

"Pull up behind that cart," Kurt instructed the driver.

He gave the boy the last five-dollar bill in his wallet, hopped out, and jogged over to the cart, sliding into the passenger seat alongside J.J. Chilcutt. "Afternoon, J.J.," he said. "What happened to your hand? Hurt it blowing up that Dumpster?"

Chilcutt recoiled, startled, his deep-set eyes showing an unexpected panic in a man so large and fierce-looking. Surprise was a wonderful thing. The cart rolled to a stop.

"Or did Tyler nick you with some bird shot?"

Chilcutt turned his large body to study Kurt. "Where the fuck did you come from, man?"

"Dropped out of the sky," he said. "I thought it was time you and I had a conversation about demolitions."

Neal Staggs had glanced back over his shoulder, walked on a few steps, and then turned around in a full standstill, wondering why the cart was not moving. Wondering who the hell was sitting next to his man.

"You knew my brother, didn't you, J.J.?" he said.

"Bert Muller, same unit in Nam. I've heard you guys could blow up a VC tunnel with nothing but a bottle of nail polish and a Zippo lighter. I guess that means you know how to set dynamite too," Kurt said, his words scraping at the back of his throat, dry and angry. "And how to mix a Molotov."

None of this made the slightest impression on Chilcutt. He glared at Kurt with cold, unflinching scorn. "I don't see your pin," he said. "We got strict rules here. No pay, no play. My orders are to throw gate-crashers out in the street."

They stared at each other. A vicious loathing settled in the bones of Chilcutt's face. Moments passed.

"I'm still sitting here, J.J. Why don't you make your move? Nothing would give me greater pleasure than to shove that bad hand up your ass."

Chilcutt laughed, a wicked sound deep in his bear-like chest. "The word on the street," he said, "is you won't be able to hide behind that badge much longer, Mr. Use-to-be. And when your time's up, I'll be waiting for you."

"Funny," Kurt said, watching Staggs stride back toward them, his face vexed and impatient. "Your boss used to say the same thing until somebody stomped all over his nice button-down career. You might want to give that some thought, shithead."

Kurt saw the harsh light of recognition flare in Neal Staggs's eyes as he approached the cart. "What the hell are you doing here, Muller? Get out of there. You're holding up the round." He retrieved a putter from a bag in the rear of the vehicle. "J.J., stop fucking around and drive this thing up near the green."

"It's not his fault," Kurt said. "I detained him over a missing headlight."

The ex-agent tested the putter's grip. Kurt wondered if he was going to bash him in the head with it. "I don't know why you're here, Muller, but whatever the reason, it can wait," Staggs said. "In case you haven't noticed, there's a golf tournament going on. If I have to, I'll call security backup and have you removed."

Kurt watched the crowd bulge out to the taped-off viewing area at the base of a sand bunker. An exuberant gathering dressed in shorts and T-shirts, amusing themselves in the warm afternoon sun. A local TV station was there with their minicam, the reporter speaking into a mike. Kurt thought he recognized someone standing behind the crew, a solid build, arms folded across his chest, observing the action, his long ponytail hanging out the back of a baseball cap.

"I've got some questions for your man J.J. concerning one homicide and one attempted homicide in my jurisdiction," Kurt told Staggs. "Convince me he'll come back to Aspen tomorrow morning for questioning and I'll get out of your hair so you can go on with your game."

He didn't have anything solid to charge Chilcutt with. He just wanted to sweat him out.

Staggs glowered at the driver. "What's this all about, J.J.?"

"He's just yanking us off, boss. The guy's a joke. Give me the nod and I'll drag his butt out of here."

One of the men in Staggs's golf party had doubled back to investigate the delay. "Is there a problem here, Neal?" he asked. "Why the holdup?"

"Everything's under control, Mr. Metcalf," Staggs apologized. "We're on our way."

So this was Arnold Metcalf. He appeared to be in his late fifties, as tall as Kurt at six feet four, a rawboned man with a high glistening forehead and dark sunglasses. His tan was genuine and he walked with the lanky stride of a ranch foreman, which made it difficult to imagine him wearing a three-piece suit at the head of a long teakwood table in the boardroom of his law foundation.

Kurt slid out of the cart and nudged past Staggs, extending his hand to the attorney who had organized this event. "Hello, Mr. Metcalf," he said, smiling affably. "It's a pleasure to meet you, sir. I'm Kurt Muller from the Pitkin County Sheriff's Department. If I'm not mistaken, you and I had a mutual friend in Aspen."

"I see," Metcalf said, shaking Kurt's hand tentatively, his eyes ranging toward Staggs for some plausible explanation for this interruption.

"His name was Ned Carr," Kurt said. "I believe your people represented him in a lawsuit last year."

"Yes, we did," Metcalf nodded formally. "I was very sorry to hear about Ned's death. Our coalition plans to make a contribution in his name to an organization that was very close to his heart—the American Institute for the Preservation of Free Enterprise. Individuals like Ned are in damn short supply these days."

This guy was bullshit. Ned didn't believe in any organization beyond the math columns in his own checkbook.

"We're treating Ned's death as a possible homicide, Mr. Metcalf," Kurt said. "I would like to ask you some questions about your relationship with the deceased."

Arnold Metcalf looked at Staggs and laughed. He spread his arms in the direction of the waiting audience. "You've caught me at an inconvenient moment, Sheriff. I'm trying to raise money to help people like Ned Carr survive against the odds." The genial smile remained in place. "Why don't you make an appointment with my secretary," he said with a note of good-humored exasperation. "We're in the phone book."

Kurt didn't have another day to waste. "This is police business, sir. I'll be waiting for you when the tournament's over." He turned and regarded J.J. Chilcutt. "And I'll be waiting for you, too, my friend. Pitkin County Courthouse, tomorrow morning at nine."

33

By THE TIME he'd made his way down the grassy slope to the stringed-off gallery, the man was no longer standing where Kurt had seen him. He couldn't be certain it was the Lone Ute, only a vague suspicion, something in his bearing, and the ponytail. As he ambled through the flock of sedate, leisure-class retirees, searching for the Denver Nuggets cap, Kurt's eye wandered toward the woods seventy yards beyond, where a solitary figure was heading into the trees. He recognized the loping movement of that body, the swinging tail of dark hair, from the night the intruder had bolted from Ned's cabin. It had to be him.

A wall of ponderosas rose up abruptly at the outer boundary of the manicured course. Kurt buttoned his jacket, tucked in his tie, and sprinted for the spot where the man had gone in. Huffing hard, he slipped between the first tall trunks into a hidden undergrowth of juniper bushes. He knew how foolish he must have looked thrashing through the forest in a suit and tie, slapping branches out of his face, collecting loose mulch in his dress shoes. He stopped to listen for footsteps in the woodland ahead but heard no sounds except birdsong and his own labored breathing. Out of public view now, he pulled the Smith & Wesson .45 from his shoulder holster and snapped open the chamber, checking the rounds. He didn't know what to expect. Maybe the man he'd seen wasn't the Lone Ute after all, just some innocent golf groupie in need of a long private piss.

He thumb-latched the pistol back in the holster and pressed on through the thicket, looking for a trail of any kind, five good yards of clearing. Sunshine fought its way down through the towering limbs overhead, a haze of pollen suspended in the slanting shafts of light. In this jungle it was impossible to quiet his clumsy passage. He searched the brushwood around him for something out of place, a snatch of clothing, a pair of watchful eyes. It had been years since he'd gone hunting for game and he realized that his stalking skills had all but vanished. He recalled how he'd made himself invisible as a young boy with a pellet rifle, becoming a leaf, a twig. Slowing respiration, relaxing his body, flowing into the chlorophyll.

He held his breath and squatted down on his haunches, closing his eyes, listening. Birds twittered; a wasp buzzed nearby in the trapped, musty heat. After a few moments he heard a branch snap and opened his eyes, gazing into the foliage at knee level, waiting for other signs. There was no motion anywhere, the branches so still he wondered if the air ever stirred beneath this impenetrable canopy of bark and hanging vines. The man, whoever he was, had been swallowed whole, consumed by wood spiders. Or more than likely he had finished his business and returned to the course.

Kurt smiled at his folly and bent over to untie his dusty shoe, shake out the soil and cool leaves. He heard a footstep and glanced up, oblivious to the whooshing limb until it clubbed the back of his head.

34

A SHARP-TOED COWBOY boot nudged at his ribs. When he opened his eyes there was a man standing over him, pointing a pistol at Kurt's face. He knew instantly it was his own Smith & Wesson. "Sorry I had to hit you, hoss," the man said. "I saw you had a gun."

Kurt sat up, touched the broken skin on the back of his neck, rubbed blood between his fingers. Six more weeks of stress leave, then all this relaxation was over.

"That's the second time you've nailed me," Kurt said, his head still ringing from the blow. "I'm starting to wonder about our friendship."

In the mottled forest light he could see the man clearly for the first time. He was older than Kurt had imagined, maybe fifty, thick shoulders, an expanding beltline, his handsome Indian features beginning to line and sag with age. His nose had been broken long ago and had never been reset. Those dark puffy eyes retained the haunting hardness of a man who had done serious time.

"We need to get something straight," the Indian said. "I don't want to keep looking over my shoulder to see where you are."

Reaching into his hip pocket he withdrew a wallet and tossed it at Kurt. A private investigator's license, state of Colorado. The name under the photograph read *Jesse Nighthawk,* with an address in Durango.

"We're working the same case," Jesse Nighthawk said. "Ned Carr was an old friend of mine."

Kurt was momentarily speechless. He handed him back the wallet and stood up, removing his jacket, brushing leaves from his pants. "What happened with the dirt-bikers?" he asked.

"I started shooting that big forty-four and they scattered."

He snapped open the revolver, emptied the chambers into his hand, and slid the bullets into his pocket.

"I owe you," Kurt said.

Nighthawk returned the unloaded pistol grip-forward. "You still have something that belongs to me," he said. The eagle-bone choker. "I want it back."

IN THE REAR of the Tudor castle a patio café looked out over the first tee and the immaculate course stretching far into the distance. The waitresses were dressed as English milkmaids. The menu explained that General William Jackson Palmer, the founder of Colorado Springs and original owner of these grounds, was obsessed with British history and had attempted to fashion his early settlement as a small-scale London.

Kurt and Jesse Nighthawk sat at a table whose umbrella resembled a sixteenth-century silk parasol. From the outset their waitress had cast a suspicious eye on the ponytailed man wearing a Nuggets baseball cap, but Kurt's well-heeled presence seemed to neutralize the tension. She hadn't noticed the blood on his shirt collar.

"Whose party are you with?" she asked, her pencil poised.

"Neal Staggs and J.J. Chilcutt," Kurt responded without hesitation, and the young woman wrote something on their ticket.

Over sandwiches Kurt asked Jesse Nighthawk why he was involved in the investigation. "You said you were an old friend of Ned's. Is your interest personal," he asked, "or are you working for somebody?"

Nighthawk regarded him with patient eyes. "A little of both. These are lean times and I usually take PI work where I can get it," he said. "Right now I'm on a retainer with an outfit called SPIRITT." He pulled out his wallet and removed a business card, dropping it on the table in front of Kurt. "Here, I can't ever remember what the damn letters stand for." *The Society for the Preservation of Indian Resources in the Tribal Territories*, headquartered in Santa Fe. "It's a coalition of Native tribes, maybe twenty, twenty-five of them. Cherokee, Hopi, Sioux, all the major players. These bloods have their shit together. About ten years ago they set up a corporation to manage business on Indian lands. Oil and gas, uranium, commercial fishing, the whole nine yards. The idea was to run the store real slick, like Exxon and Anaconda. So they hired an OPEC engineer to oversee field operations, a Jewish lawyer to handle contracts, and a Japanese marketing analyst to keep the books and supervise investments. Nobody on the team but all-stars."

"Good move," Kurt said, smiling appreciatively.

Nighthawk remained expressionless, imperturbable.

"Ned phoned me about three weeks ago to say he wanted SPIRITT to manage his mine operations after he passed on. A custodianship until his grandson reaches twenty-one," he said. "Then the young man can do whatever he wants with them."

This was the last thing Kurt expected to hear today. Ned turning his two mines over to Indians.

"The SPIRITT lawyers were supposed to meet with Ned this week to see what he had in mind," Nighthawk explained, "and then they were all going to sit down with that lawyer who manages his estate and put everything in writing." He sat back in his chair and wiped mustard from his fingers, his head fixed proudly on a huge neck. "But somebody dropped the hammer on the old boy before the deal could go down, and now it's like the phone conversation never happened. SPIRITT's pissed at me because their pricey lawyers got jazzed up over the idea and logged some expensive case time for nothing." He moved his head slightly, cracking his neck. "My credibility is shit at the home office."

"So you want to know what went wrong?"

Nighthawk nodded.

Kurt understood now why he had been poking around in the Carr cabin. "The other night at Ned's place," he said. "You were looking for something."

"A document, a note to himself, a phone bill. Hell, I didn't care. Anything I could use to trace names, enemies. I'm going to find out who trashed this deal, and why. My reputation is on the line—and my meal ticket."

"I've got to be honest with you, Jesse. I'm having trouble with this." There were loose ends dangling all over the man's story. "Why would Ned want you people to run his mines instead of Tyler Rutledge?"

Jesse Nighthawk shrugged, as lost for explanation as the next man. "I've known Tyler since he was a wiseass teenager," he said. "I don't think Ned intended to cut him out altogether. But Tyler's a fuckup and Ned probably didn't trust him to pay the bills and negotiate the leases and do all the things you have to do to keep that two-bit business in the black. SPIRITT is a proven expert in resource management."

Kurt couldn't argue with the fact that Tyler was less than reliable. "You'll have to forgive me if my questions sound a little skeptical. I've been a cop too long," he said. "Let's start at the beginning and go real slow."

He had seen a lot of Ned and Hunter during the past four years but had never heard the old man mention Jesse Nighthawk. "How do you know Ned Carr?"

Kurt could see by the defiant look on the man's face that he was not accustomed to explaining himself. He seemed to be considering whether to tolerate this inquiry or stand up and go his own way. Finally he relaxed, folded his hands, rested them next to his plate. "Ned saved my life," he said.

Kurt stared at him.

"I'm an alcoholic. Ned was my AA sponsor. If he hadn't come along when he did, I'd be dead of cirrhosis by now, another Indian statistic."

Kurt had heard that Ned was a heavy drinker in his youth. "You met him in AA?"

"No, I met Ned about fifteen years ago in Gunnison," he said, cocking his head to one side, "back when I was a wrangler for the Ute tribal ranch out at Pinecrest. In those days I spent most of my Saturday nights in the county drunk tank. Ned had the hots for some ol' gal in town and came to see her every once in a while. On his birthday him and the girlfriend got carried away and started shooting off fireworks and the Sheriff's Department busted him, and Ned gave them some shit so they threw his butt in the slammer with me and five or six unhappy Ute brothers. At first I thought, hey, this fat old goat-roper is going to get his ass kicked. But Ned was such a good bullshitter he had everybody laughing. He sat down in a corner of the cell and started telling weird ghost stories, and the next thing you know, the drunks were so scared they went crawling under their blankets. They thought Ned was *ini'putc'*, the Ghost himself."

Kurt smiled, remembering how Lennon and Hunter had always been frightened and enthralled by the old man's tales.

"After everybody nodded off, me and Ned got to talking and he invited me to come visit his mines in Aspen. The only mining I knew about was the uranium strip mining where I grew up, the reservation south of Cortez. I didn't want anything to do with mining. It was the miners that had chased our people out of the mountains into the desert. Hell, because of gold and silver we ended up living in a shithole wasteland even the buzzards wouldn't fly over."

Kurt had immersed himself in Native American books as a twelve-year-old boy and knew Ute history. The Blue Sky People, the People of the Shining Mountains, seven distinct bands spread across what was now Colorado. They had summered in the Roaring Fork Valley, preserved their game in the ice caves of the Grottos. Toward the end of the Civil War the government had bribed them to move west of the Continental Divide, promised money and livestock and generous provisions if they would leave the mountains to white men with gold fever. Half of Colorado would always be Ute, the government pledged in writing, a treaty guaranteed forever. The bands complied, but the bounty was never delivered. Less than twenty years later the government seized the rest of Colorado and divided the Utes into three reservations. By that time the bands had dwindled in number and spirit and offered only isolated resistance. The great graying Ouray, appointed chief of the Utes by long-coats in Washington, was content with his farmhouse and sheep and annual government stipend, and he remained silent and accommodating during the relocation.

"About a year later I lost my job and was feeling pretty sorry for myself and started hanging out with an old army buddy in Basalt, another unemployed alcoholic, and one night we got fucked up and started a fight with some rednecks in a bar and your county boys stormed in and hauled us to the lockup in Aspen. Somehow I remembered Ned's name and asked a deputy to call him for me, and I'll be damn if the old man didn't show up that night and chew my ass out for being a bonehead drunk. Ned was AA and recognized a loser when he saw one. He offered to post my bail if I would stick around and go to the meetings with him. Cookies and milk or a week in the calaboose."

Kurt struggled to remember what he was doing fifteen years ago, when this was taking place. When the idea of running for Pitkin County sheriff would have seemed a twisted joke. "How long did you stay in Aspen?"

"About six months. I got with the program and dried out, and I've been sober ever since. Well, for the most part." He raised the glass of diet Coke, his lined face softening into a small, tight grin. "Ned was a good man and treated me like a son, but Jesus, there was hell to pay. Every morning at daybreak he'd drag my carcass into the Lone Ute Mine and we'd blast and drill and muck all day till my hands were bloody and raw. I was indebted to him for turning my life around, but then there I was again, a drunken Injun breaking my back for the white man." He shook his head, smiling at himself now, the luxury of time and distance. "I don't regret what I learned about hardrock mining. But after working with Ned Carr for six months, I never wanted to step foot in another dark hole in the ground as long as I lived."

"So that's why you knew your way around the Lone Ute," Kurt said.

Nighthawk nodded.

"What's your read on the Ajax explosion?"

"It's easy to short out blasting wire, make a spark. I could have done it myself."

Maybe so, Kurt thought, but it wasn't easy fooling an expert like Lorenzo Banks. "Who's your leading suspect?"

Nighthawk's dark eyes grew narrow and severe. "Same as yours," he said. "Ain't that why we're both here?"

Kurt gazed past the aging club members eating salads at their patio tables to watch a groundskeeper blow leaves off the fairway with his power pack. The golfers and their audience were out there somewhere, the sixth or seventh hole by now, chasing little white balls into a cup. "What do you know about Chilcutt?" he asked.

Nighthawk squinted, surprised to hear the name. "Who the hell is Chilcutt?"

Kurt looked at him. "We must be on different pages," he said. "I'm after Neal Staggs and his VIProtex operative, J.J. Chilcutt. Who are you after?"

Nighthawk stuffed the last morsel of sandwich into his mouth. "VIProtex are just the hatchet men, like the Pinkertons used to be," he said. "Night Clubbers, that's what they call them. A small gang of VIPro hit men taking care of business for the big ranchers and the energy companies. I'm pretty sure VIPro talent was hired to pull the trigger on a Navajo brother trying to stop the logging of grandfather trees in New Mexico. They've got access to sophisticated computer networks and all the surveillance toys a high-tech security company can buy. Which is why they're so slick at locating targets, going in fast, and disappearing without a smell."

If this was true, Kurt thought, the possibilities were endless. A timber corporation wants to eliminate an old enemy in the green movement, they use VIProtex Central to track her down and then call on their local operatives to ride up in the night and throw a firebomb through her window. VIProtex was providing a private army for the power brokers.

"But why would they want to kill an old miner?" Kurt said, thinking aloud, his mind groping through the options. Ned was an industry poster boy, as Corky Marcus had pointed out.

Nighthawk smiled at him. "Shouldn't that be obvious, my friend?" he said. "Ned was going native."

Kurt stared blankly at the man, still unable to plug in all the loose connections. Still struggling to believe that Ned had made such a deliberate decision.

"He'd spread his blanket with the Red Man," Nighthawk said. "Some folks would consider him a traitor to his race."

That was possible, Kurt thought. A warped allegiance at stake, a broken promise, a breach of faith. Something larger than money. You surely wouldn't kill a man over the silver in those mines, not at $5.50 an ounce. But one thing was bothering Kurt: How did anyone know that Ned was negotiating such an arrangement with the Indians?

"If VIProtex does its killing for hire," Kurt said, "who hired them to blow up Ned?" The Skicorp? he wondered. Had Lee Lamar become incensed that the Indians might obstruct the old lease agreement and shut down the black-diamond ski trails around Ajax Mine?

"If you don't know the answer to that, how the hell did you end up here?" Nighthawk asked, somewhat confused by Kurt's ignorance.

"I followed Staggs from Aspen," Kurt said. "I'm going to nail him and Chilcutt on three or four counts, if I can make 'em stick. If there's money behind them, I want to know who it is."

Jesse Nighthawk wiped his mouth with a cloth napkin. A dark delight stirred behind those piercing eyes. "The VIPro boys are bootlicks. The dude you were shaking hands with out there"—he nodded toward the course—"is the one you want."

35

KURT ADJUSTED THE binoculars to get a clear look at the intense concentration on Arnold Metcalf's face as he settled over his putt on the ninth green. "What can you tell me about him?" he asked, watching the tall man limber his wrists and eye the flag fifty feet from his spiked shoes.

"His law foundation has built up a fat endowment— a paper trail of write-off contributions from all the usual suspects," Nighthawk said, snapping photographs with a telephoto lens. "Metcalf is so flush he can send hotshot lawyers to put out every green fire in the West, free of charge. When he needs muscle," he said, "he calls on his pals at VIProtex."

Nighthawk had led Kurt back to the woods, where the Jeep Wrangler was hidden, and then he'd driven them out here to the ninth hole, an unauthorized vehicle leaving tire tracks in the soft grass.

"Check out the Asians," Nighthawk said, his shutter whirring.

Kurt moved his sight slowly, locating the two men near the outer skirt of the green. They were engaged in an animated discussion about how the shorter one should play the roll down the long smooth slope.

"The little Jap is Colonel Yukio Komatsu," Nighthawk said, "a retired military man and a higher-up in the Church of World Unity. He's one of Father Ke's inner circle."

"Father Ke?" Kurt said, lowering the binoculars. "You're pulling my chain, right? Not *the* Father Ke."

"Father Ke is a high-dollar contributor to the Free West cause," Nighthawk said, peering through the camera. "He owns cattle ranches and fish hatcheries out here, and he's a major stockholder in the Japanese auto cartel."

Father Ke was the shady leader of a worldwide religious cult. His followers were the lost souls selling flowers on city street corners.

"If the greens succeed in shutting down wilderness and national forests to dirt bikes and four-wheelers," Nighthawk said, "the Japanese manufacturers are going to take a beating in the billion-dollar rec market. They were the ones behind the National Recreational Trails Act in ninety-one, courtesy of our environmental president. Thirty mill a year, taxpayers' tab, to cut new ORV trails for the yahoos."

Kurt slowly scanned the golfers and caddies spread out around the green. "So this is what you do for SPIR-ITT?" he said. "Take pictures, collect data, eyeball the players."

"You got it, hoss. I show up wherever Free West is throwing a party. Back at the home office they download my legwork into their big computer system and the magic begins. Business affiliations, board memberships, cross-references, name-and-photo makes, who's in bed with who. When the time is right, we'll turn it all over to the Justice Department."

"You have evidence they're breaking the law?"

"It'll happen," Nighthawk said, clicking away. "Sooner or later these nimrods are gonna slip up and our lawyers will be all over them like flies on a dead dog. We'll pop a Night Clubber for jamming somebody," he said, glancing sideways at Kurt, "burning down a cabin, whatever. And then their ball game's over."

Kurt found Staggs conversing with a white-haired gentleman wearing sunglasses and one of those natty Scottish golf hats from the 1920s. "How did you happen to be in the Ashcroft woods last night," he asked, "when the Pfeil cabin was firebombed?"

Nighthawk wandered away from the Jeep, stopping to frame the golfers from another angle. "Keeping an eye on my business partner," he said.

Kurt lowered the binoculars again. He was slow to make the connection. "Hunter?" he said.

"Something happens to the boy," Nighthawk said, "we'll never get that mine thing straightened out."

A feeling of dread suddenly overcame Kurt. "You think they're after Hunter now?" he asked.

Nighthawk shrugged. "They got Ned, then they got Tyler," he said. "Maybe somebody wants those mines real bad. The boy is the only one in their way."

Kurt's stomach dropped. He didn't want to hear out loud the voice he'd been hearing in the back of his head. "Can I use your car phone?" he said, glancing into the Wrangler.

"Go ahead. I'll send Pitkin County the bill."

Kurt checked his watch. Well after three o'clock. The

boys were out of school now, on their way back to Basalt. He phoned the Sheriff's Department in Aspen and asked for Muffin Brown.

"Not a very good connection," she complained. "Where are you, Kurt?"

"Colorado Springs. I'll tell you about it later," he said. "Just calling to make sure you have someone assigned to the boys."

"Gervin and Miller on this shift," she said. "They're escorting Meg and the boys back to Basalt about now. Is something wrong?"

"I hope not," he said, still pondering the possibility that one of their cops might be dirty. "We'll talk when I get back. Make sure Hunter stays under protection around the clock."

"Should I be worried, Kurt, or are you just being a paranoid father?"

He watched Jesse Nighthawk amble toward the green and drop to one knee, *click click click*. "Do you know if anybody in the department is moonlighting for VIProtex International?" he asked her.

"VIProtex?" she said. "The high-profile security people?"

"Right. They have an office in Aspen."

"Not that I know of," she said. "I would have heard."

"Do me a favor, Muff, and check that out. Go through the personnel records. See if anyone's ever worked for them."

The phone line crackled. "Jesus, Kurt. At least give me a good reason I'm going to spend my day digging through a hundred pounds of ancient paperwork."

"If there's a bad cop mixed up in the Tyler Rutledge

shooting," he said, "chances are he's got a VIProtex match. I'll explain it when I get back."

He latched the phone in place and walked over to where Nighthawk was squatting behind a scrub oak, changing the film in his camera.

"Did you notice the little dude wearing the funky hat?" he asked Kurt. "He's an engineer with Riebeeck Mining."

"The South Africans?"

"Yeah. They're in South America now, too, and Canada. I've heard they're looking over a piece in Montana."

"Some serious foreign interest in this Free West Rebellion."

Nighthawk looked up at him, closing one eye in a squint. "Birds of a feather. They do a lot of jawboning about property rights and the Fifth Amendment and the erosion of freedom," he said, "but when the rubber hits the road, it all comes down to money. Whose stock is up, who's losing their investment."

Kurt smiled. "My, but you're a cynical fellow. Aren't you forgetting who this benefit is for?" he said. "Ranch relief, the family farmer. The little people squeezed out of their livelihood by the spotted owl."

Nighthawk stood up, peered through his viewer. "I'd like to get in a plane and drop about eight million leaflets over every redneck trailer park in the West," he said, "and show all the Gomers a bar chart of where their jobs are going. Machines are replacing thousands of them, and the rest is being shopped out to Mexico and Indonesia for one tenth the labor cost. The owl's got nothing to do with it."

Security had spotted the Wrangler. Two carts were now approaching, swift, soundless vehicles with yellow lights flashing on their roofs. Kurt could see uniformed men coordinating their strategy on walkie-talkies, dashing toward them with military haste. "We've got company," he said.

Nighthawk raised his head from the viewer. "Fuck," he said, his expression souring. "I was just getting warmed up. Ah, well." He seemed resigned to such an outcome. This had no doubt happened before. "Enough pictures for one day. Time to go to the house."

He trotted back to the Wrangler and swung his camera into the rear hold. "You coming, hoss?" he said, quickly firing up the engine.

The first cart was bearing down on them, a battery-powered whine. The two guards looked like hard-nosed Marine recruits patrolling a barbed-wire perimeter.

"You go ahead," Kurt said, glancing over at the golfers. "I want to talk to Metcalf."

"Yeah, right. Best of luck." Nighthawk waved two fingers, his tires spinning. "Catch you on the flip-flop!"

Gunning for the woods, he plowed a pair of ugly ruts through the smooth carpet grass, damp sod spewing up behind the Wrangler. Kurt watched the security carts veer off after him, sparrows chasing the cunning falcon. Even if he stopped to change his oil they would never catch that man.

He walked down the hill to join the admiring audience. The tournament was over for the day and the participants loitered around the green, exchanging handshakes, reliving key moments along the course. He followed the TV camera crew as it moved in close, the reporter pulling Arnold Metcalf aside for his comments. Kurt hadn't noticed the three weathered ranchers until Metcalf collared them from the crowd.

"These folks are what this is all about," he smiled into the minicam lens. "Come on up here, gentlemen, and tell Channel Two what's been happening to your families since the federal government started meddling in your business."

The ranchers were shy men wearing cowboy hats and pearl-button dress shirts. It seemed unlikely that they had ever set foot on a golf course in their lives and they looked reluctant and uncomfortable in front of a camera. The reporter was having trouble getting them to take the bait.

"You're not going to do anything stupid, are you, Muller?"

Neal Staggs was standing on one side of him, J.J. Chilcutt on the other.

"I don't know, Staggs," Kurt said, turning to regard them. "I've got this overwhelming urge to drop my drawers."

Staggs removed his sun visor and wiped his face and neck with a towel hanging over his shoulder. The band had left a dark wet impression through his graying hair. He looked like he needed a cigarette. "What's it going to take for you to leave Mr. Metcalf alone?" he asked.

Kurt watched the attorney forcing a laugh at something one of the ranchers had said, his long arms wrapped around the fellow as if they were old bronco busters from the rodeo circuit. The cowboy movie star had joined them now, and in his presence the ranchers were as giddy as schoolboys. Metcalf saw Kurt staring at him, and his camera smile quickly faded.

"A half hour of his time," Kurt said. "Five o'clock. He can name the place."

36

THE FREE WEST Legal Coalition occupied a large corner suite on the twentieth floor of a downtown office building, one of the few high-rises of that scale in Colorado Springs. The open reception area exuded a casual folksiness, the walls filled with traditional Western paintings, Remington and Russell, wagon trains through dramatic gorges, lone Indian scouts gazing out over the endless prairie. But in spite of the ambient summer light, the lawyers themselves roamed furrow-browed down the corridors in their serious pursuits, self-important and loud, briefcases knocking at their knees. An amiable young secretary led Kurt back to Arnold Metcalf's office, and on the way they passed the ranchers from the golf tournament, hats in hand, hair slicked flat with pomade, touring an arcade of bronze cowboy sculpture with a chatty young law clerk wearing a turquoise bolo tie.

Metcalf answered the door himself with a drink in his hand. He was dressed in the same sporty clothes he'd worn on the course. "Come in, Sheriff Muller," he said. "I've had my girl pull together the Carr file. We usually require a little more lead time for these reviews, but I can see you're a man in a hurry. And I certainly want to help your investigation any way I can. Ned Carr was a good friend."

Neal Staggs was standing at the tinted glass wall that faced west toward snow-shrouded Pikes Peak and a blue cloudless sky blemished only by a thin white vapor trail. Staggs, too, had a drink in his hand.

"I think you two know each other," Metcalf said.

Kurt nodded.

"Thanks for your help today, Neal. I'll touch base with you later this evening," Metcalf said. "Better ice that shoulder if you expect to catch the pros on the back nine."

"I'll stay if you need me," Staggs said, eyeing Kurt with his usual distrust.

"The sheriff and I will be fine." Smiling handsomely, Metcalf turned to Kurt. "Unless he intends to pull that revolver on me."

Kurt glanced quickly at his suit jacket like a man checking his fly. The .45 was perfectly concealed.

Metcalf laughed at his confusion. "Don't be alarmed, Sheriff. We make a sonic-wave readout of everyone who comes through reception. It's just a precaution. You never know when some lunatic ecoterrorist might try to disrupt our work here."

Staggs set down his drink and shook hands with Metcalf, exchanging words Kurt couldn't hear.

"Staggs," Kurt said, demanding his attention. "I want to see Chilcutt in my office tomorrow morning."

"You'll have to discuss that with our lawyer," Staggs said, hitching his chin toward Metcalf, one final gesture of defiance before leaving the room.

Metcalf extended his hand toward a small conference

table located within a few steps of a fully stocked bar.
"A drink before we get started, Sheriff?"

"No, thanks," he said. "Does your foundation represent VIProtex, Mr. Metcalf?"

"Yes, that's correct." The attorney offered Kurt a
chair at the cherrywood table and sat before a hefty file,
the only object on an otherwise spotless surface that
smelled of fresh lemon oil. "VIProtex and all of its
employees," Metcalf said, peering at Kurt over the
frame of his reading glasses. "I'm not sure I can free up
someone to appear with Mr. Chilcutt on such short
notice. Could you give us an extra day or so?"

Above the visor line on his tanned forehead his scalp
appeared pale and rubbery under baby-fine sprigs of
hair, a suggestion that he sometimes wore a hairpiece.

"Does Chilcutt need a lawyer, Mr. Metcalf?"

Metcalf smiled, his crow's feet wrinkling. "*Sheriff,*"
he said in mock disbelief. "Even in the People's Repub-
lic of Aspen a man is entitled to counsel, is he not?"

"I'm an easy guy to get along with," Kurt said. "Let's
make it Wednesday. Not a day later. Don't force me to
issue a warrant."

Metcalf removed his glasses with a quick flourish, a
practiced mannerism from the courtroom. "That
shouldn't be necessary, sir. I hope we can all remain
friends. We have Ned Carr's interest in common."

"Good."

The attorney opened the file. "I was disturbed to
hear that Ned's death might've been a homicide," he
said, flipping through the pages. "But frankly, it
shouldn't surprise me. All his life Ned waged war
against the obstructionists and their government toad-
ies. With deranged felons like the Green Briars running

loose, spiking trees and blowing up machinery, it was only a matter of time before they killed a defenseless old miner. Ned was an easy target. He didn't have the resources for state-of-the-art security."

"Like you have here," Kurt said, surveying the spacious office. This was the choice corner of the building, glass walls in a ninety-degree wedge, an impressive panorama of the Front Range and the scrubby mesa to the north.

"He liked doing things his own way," Metcalf said. "The old-fashioned way. We offered to help him tech up, but he wasn't interested."

Across the room, above the rich leather couch in a cozy sitting area, hung a huge oil painting of a frostbitten mail rider struggling his way through a fierce blizzard, the horse and saddlebagged mule tromping bravely onward in belly-high snow. A vivid portrait of the old-fashioned way.

"You think it was the Green Briars, Mr. Metcalf?"

"That would be my first guess. Or someone like them. When we were handling Ned's case we became well aware of his formidable opposition in Aspen. It's not a friendly place for people who don't toe the liberal party line. Hell, our attorneys had their tires slashed on two occasions. And look what the animal nuts have been trying to do there—outlaw fur, for god's sake! We might as well have been trying our case in Haight-Ashbury."

"You won, Mr. Metcalf. Ned got his access road."

The attorney lowered his voice, as if they were fellow conspirators in some dark plot. "I'm beginning to believe it will be easier to establish democracy in Communist Russia than in some of our federal districts. You may not be aware of the figures, but the environmental lobby is spending three billion dollars a year to mangle the free enterprise system. We were very fortunate to get a sympathetic bench."

Kurt knew that Metcalf could go on in this vein for quite some time. "What was your relationship with Ned?" he asked, shifting focus. "Tell me how your foundation works."

Metcalf sipped his Scotch. "We represent the little guy against the Robert Redfords of the world," he smiled. "There's so much celebrity money behind the Sierra Club, the Audubon Society, and the Wildlife Federation that people like Ned Carr can't afford to go head to head with them, certainly not through the judicial process. We take their cases pro bono, so the mom-and-pop ranchers and loggers and weekend miners will have something left in the bank when it's all over."

"Do you represent the larger corporations as well? Say, the big timber companies in the Northwest?"

"Only the clients who can prove need. Right now we've got a case pending in the state of Washington over fishing rights. The Northwest Indians have taken it upon themselves to cut off access to a public river where salmon fishermen have been making a living for four generations. And in Wyoming we're helping out an old boy who shot a wolf he caught eating his livestock. The goddamn Fish and Wildlife Service threw him in jail!"

Kurt had read about the shooting. The old boy had killed one of the sixteen gray wolves reintroduced into the wild near Yellowstone and was busted when he tried to sell the pelt to a small-time furrier.

"There are at least three dozen cases on our plate,"

Metcalf said. "Honest, hardworking folks who've been snared up in the huge net the EPA and the greens have thrown over this country. The American people are being hog-tied by laws and regulations, Sheriff, and they're not happy about it. Constitutional rights are at stake. The business climate is being destroyed by all the litigation costs and restraints. We've got to get our national agenda back on track. That's what the Free West Rebellion is all about." He smiled at some private thought. "We'll dump tea in the harbor if we have to."

Kurt had been hearing speeches like this for years. "When you were working with Ned, did he ever talk about death threats?"

"Certainly," Metcalf said. "But most of the threats were related to his mining operations and his property. He mentioned names, yes. One of our clerks took notes," he said, turning pages in the file, looking through memoranda. "I'm sure it's all in here somewhere. I'll have my secretary make a copy for you. Perhaps the names are worth pursuing. There was an alcoholic photographer in Aspen, if I remember correctly, whom Ned held in highest contempt. A man who had harassed him for decades. Others as well, though I can't list them for you without reference to the notes."

"I would appreciate any information you have on record."

The attorney pushed the file away, sat back in the regal chair, and sipped his drink. "I liked Ned very much," he said with a fond smile, removing his reading glasses. "More than that—I respected him. He reminded me of an uncle of mine, my mother's brother, a strange old hermit who did some mining out at Cripple

Creek and came down to see us from time to time when I was growing up. Men like that are our national heritage."

Kurt realized he had two choices now: either sit here and listen to more pious homage to the Great Frontier Spirit or jerk this guy's rope to see how loud the bell would ring.

"Mr. Metcalf, were you aware that Ned had planned to will custodianship of his mines to a group of Indians?"

Kurt expected a visible reaction but the man showed no emotion whatsoever. More evidence of his courtroom training. He undoubtedly played a mean game of poker.

"What's your source of information, Sheriff?"

Kurt hesitated before answering. "A birdy told me. In fact," he said, "it was a large nighthawk."

Metcalf's eyes hardened. "You say Ned had *planned* to do this. Do you have confirmation that this transaction actually took place?"

Kurt waited, his mind racing to fabricate something believable. "No," he admitted finally.

Metcalf studied him with disappointment. "I don't know what his game is," the attorney said, lacing his fingers, "but your nighthawk is seriously misinformed. Ned Carr made no such determination. The idea is ludicrous."

"What makes you so sure of that, Mr. Metcalf?"

He placed his fingers under his chin. "As Ned's attorney, I am privy to his last will and testament, Sheriff Muller. Believe me, there is no provision to include Indians."

Kurt could feel the color surge across his face. Arnold Metcalf had access to the will? "Are you saying that you are the executor of the Carr estate?"

A courtly nod. "Our legal foundation is, yes."

"That's odd, Mr. Metcalf. Two days ago Ned's will was read to me by an attorney in Aspen. Corky Marcus has been Ned's executor for as long as I can remember. It will come as a surprise to him that he has been replaced."

Metcalf rose from the table to freshen his drink. He stood at the bar and dropped ice into his glass, a splash of Scotch.

"When Ned came to us he was a defeated man," he said, swirling the liquid in the tumbler. "He had more problems than Job, and even his longtime attorney, Mr. Marcus, wouldn't take his case. I don't blame Ned for feeling that Marcus had turned his back on him. He certainly had. Ned didn't have an ally in the world. But then he found us, and we were very pleased to join his battle in the trenches. I'm sure he thought of us as his savior, poor man. And maybe we were," he said with a wistful sigh, "for a little while. We did everything we could for him, Sheriff. We even loaned him money when he needed it. No one should be surprised that Ned Carr chose our foundation to handle his estate for him. We were the only people on God's green earth who cared whether that old miner breathed another breath."

No, there were others, Kurt thought, the rare souls who really loved the old man. Tyler. Hunter. Maybe Tink Tarver. Not enough to argue over.

"So you're telling me that Ned made out another will."

"That is correct. According to Ned's stated wishes,

the new will supersedes any document in Mr. Marcus's possession."

Something smelled in the room, and it wasn't the expensive Scotch. If Ned had created a second will, why had he phoned Corky last week to tell him he wanted to make changes in the will they had written together three years ago?

"May I see it?" Kurt said.

Metcalf offered him a rogue's grin. "Sheriff Muller," he said, his crow's feet dancing, "I'm sure you're aware that there is a proper time and place for the disposition of matters like these." He brought the glass to his lips. "Right now you and I are just a couple of old boys sitting around on a sunny afternoon shooting the shit."

Kurt reached over and tapped the file folder. "It's gotta be in here, Arnold," he said. "Read it to me."

Metcalf's smile was beginning to chill. "At the appropriate time."

"What's wrong with now?" Kurt asked, opening the stiff cover.

The top document was a hand-scrawled letter from Ned to their legal foundation. Metcalf reached down, closed the cover, and slid the file out of Kurt's reach. "I'm sorry, Sheriff," he said, his brow creasing, "these papers are confidential. But if you'd like, I'll have my girl go through them and photocopy anything that looks relevant to the investigation."

"That's very generous of you," Kurt said, rising from the chair to meet Metcalf eye to eye. "Now when can I see the will?"

The attorney did not flinch. "As I've said, Sheriff. At the appropriate time."

"Aspen is a small town, Arnold. The judge is a good

friend of mine. We play poker at the same table every Wednesday night." A bald-faced lie. The district judge and Kurt Muller had crossed swords on many occasions in court and did not run in the same social circles. "If I ask him to, he'll subpoena the will as evidence in a murder investigation. I hope I don't have to do that. I hope we can all remain friends here, with Ned's interest in common."

Metcalf strolled across his office to the glass wall. Sipping his drink, the other hand tucked casually in the pocket of his cotton trousers, he stood gazing out at the mountains, his back to Kurt. "You're a Colorado boy," he said absently. "Your parents moved here when you were only two years old."

Kurt was a little unnerved that he would know this about him. What else did the man know?

"Look at this view," he said. "I'm sure you appreciate this magnificent country as much as I do."

Kurt wandered over to admire the scenery. This time of year the Front Range appeared green and enchanting, with long cornices of snow above 11,000 feet. To the northwest he could see the Garden of the Gods, strange red-sandstone formations jutting out of the brushy foothills, a magic place revered by cliff-dwelling Anasazi.

"I suspect that Neal Staggs is wrong about you," Metcalf said, his eyes fixed on some distant peak. "He thinks you're like all the knee-jerk trustafarians in Aspen, trendy and corrupt. But I know something about your family stock, Sheriff Muller, and what your parents went through to build their dream in a forsaken mining dump nobody would've given a dime for. Like Ned Carr, they rolled up their sleeves and made their shaky enterprise work, in spite of the odds. You've been through it with them, my friend. It's in your blood." He spoke with the certainty of a minister. "That's why this investigation is important to you, isn't it? You don't want to lose Ned. He wasn't so different from your father, another incurable romantic. They were both stubborn dreamers."

"Some dreams turn into nightmares, Mr. Metcalf."

The attorney's chin moved slightly and his eyes embraced Kurt with an unexpected warmth. "Don't be offended, Sheriff. None of us has their strength of character," he said, his voice softening. "We're all spectators now, experiencing everything through a glowing idiot box. The best we can do is keep their spirit alive a few years longer, so our grandchildren will get a taste of it before the world we once enjoyed is taken from us."

Kurt looked over at the painting above the couch. A fearless messenger trooping westward through blizzards and Indian attack, bringing order to man's rightful dominion. It was the way Arnold Metcalf saw himself and his destiny.

"I don't share your brand of nostalgia, Mr. Metcalf. And just for the record," Kurt said, "I've never wanted to follow in my father's footsteps."

"That's a pity. Jacob Rumpf and his team were admirable visionaries. Where would this country be without their kind of ambition?"

The city lay at their feet, a modest downtown business district and bordering tree-shaded neighborhoods, the modern developments rolling away across a busy interstate into a quaint enclave of Old West storefronts and vintage redbrick hotels. Though he had never been there, Kurt recognized that locale for what it was, another early mining settlement turned tourist attraction, the saloons and dry goods emporiums now a home for art galleries and T-shirt shops. The Rumpf legacy in its final stages of ambition.

"Sheriff Muller, there's plenty of room in our coalition for sympathetic peace officers," Metcalf said, his eyes following the traffic twenty stories below. "We have friends wearing badges in every western state. I would like to think that you could become one of those friends. We welcome the opportunity to supply information and assistance to any law enforcement department open to our mission."

Our mission. Like Jesse Nighthawk these people were monitoring their enemies, collecting data, recording names. They were also unleashing the pit bulls whenever it suited their mission.

"I'm not much of a joiner, Mr. Metcalf."

The attorney gave a slight shrug. "One doesn't have to carry our business card to be an ally," he said. "There are a hundred ways to help." He looked at Kurt again, studied his face. Something sinister resided in the man's cold, unyielding stare. "I have never heard anyone complain about the amenities that come with being associated with our cause."

One of the subtlest inferences of a payoff Kurt had ever witnessed. Arnold Metcalf was truly a professional.

"We will talk again, Mr. Metcalf," he said, checking his watch. "I'm due back in Aspen tonight. I expect a phone message confirming a Wednesday appointment with J.J. Chilcutt. And a definitive date for the reading of Ned's will. Don't disappoint me."

He strode across the soft beige carpet and had almost reached the door when a nagging thought wouldn't let him leave. "You mentioned that you loaned Ned some money," he said, his hand on the doorknob.

Metcalf was still standing at the glass wall. Afternoon sunlight shone around his tall, lanky frame, a luminous corona. He shook the ice in his tumbler.

"Did he ever pay you back?"

"It was a business arrangement."

"Yes, of course it was. But did he pay back the loan?"

He could feel Metcalf's condescending smile across the room. "Sheriff, you ought to know by now that I don't reveal the details of Free West transactions."

Cut a deal with the devil but the dirty bastard double-crossed me, Ned had told him in that final phone call. *I tried to burn 'em at their own game. Now they're coming after me.*

"How much of his mining operation do you own, Mr. Metcalf?"

The attorney remained silent, staring blankly through empty space.

"He traded you a piece of his mines in exchange for your help, didn't he, sir?"

Metcalf walked over and placed the empty glass on his cherrywood desk, a large, uncluttered piece of furniture that took up considerable space in the corner where the walls met. "There was nothing out of the ordinary about our partnership with Ned Carr," he said impatiently. "We made a separate loan agreement, the kind arranged every day by banks and lending institutions throughout the world."

"A loan payback to a nonprofit foundation?"

"Any incidental revenue is put to nonprofit use, I assure you. If you're confused about 501-C regulations,

Sheriff Muller, perhaps you ought to consult your department's legal counsel in Aspen. He will inform you about the myriad routine transactions that take place at nonprofit institutions and universities."

Kurt looked at Ned's file on the conference table. "How much of him did you own?" he asked again, the bitterness showing this time.

Metcalf glanced down at his desk, tracing his finger across an appointment calendar. "I have to be somewhere for dinner, Sheriff," he said in a remote voice. "I'm afraid I don't have time to give you a crash course in estate planning. Why don't you consult an attorney," he said, his eyes flashing across the room, "and then we will talk."

Ned, you stubborn old fool, Kurt thought. *Was there no one in the whole world to turn to but this thief? Did you become so desperate to hold on to the thing you loved the most, you were willing to give up part to save the whole?*

"You're one clever son of a bitch, aren't you, Arnold old boy?"

Metcalf pressed an intercom buzzer on his desk. "Good day, Sheriff," he said, his expression as cold as the ice in his glass. "My secretary will see you to the elevators."

"Those ranchers down the hall," Kurt said. "How much of their land are you going to take?"

"I'm a busy man, Sheriff. We will continue this conversation some other time."

"We're a long way from finished with each other," Kurt said.

Metcalf's response worked its way from mild annoyance to outright scorn. "You're beginning to disappoint me, Mr. Muller."

"If I were you, Arnold, I would start to worry."

A VIProtex security guard appeared suddenly in the office doorway. "Is everything all right, Mr. Metcalf?" he asked, a hand resting on his weapon.

"Ken, would you and Miss Thorpe please escort my friend to the elevators. He seems to have lost his direction."

"My pleasure, sir."

The guard stepped back out of the door, waiting for Kurt to join him in the corridor.

"What's that noise, Arnold?" Kurt said. "Do you hear it?"

The secretary had arrived now, breathless from the quick jog.

"It's getting louder. Can't you hear it?"

Metcalf stared at the security guard, raised an impatient eyebrow.

"Sounds like there's a crack in your foundation," Kurt said.

37

WING TAYLOR BROUGHT the plane down in a misty gray nightfall, the tires hissing through shallow rain puddles on the runway. Kurt had radioed ahead and Muffin was waiting for him outside the hangar. Darkness hovered over the eastern mountains and a frosty wind blew in their faces. "I found something in the personnel files," she said, hunching her shoulders, her hands stuffed in a department windbreaker.

She drove them to the hospital and they marched down the corridor with an urgent stride. When the automatic doors swung open at ICU, Kurt could see Joey Florio at his post, arms locked behind his back, observing the activity in Tyler's room. "He's had a couple of seizures," he told them in a cautious whisper. "It's not looking good."

Dr. Perry and two nurses were rushing around the bed, a somber team applying electroshock to the young man's greased chest. A few feet away the Rutledges held each other, the mother's face buried in her husband's neck. The lines on the monitor blipped, flattened, blipped again, a graph of receding life force. Kurt closed his eyes and said a prayer for everyone in the room.

After a moment he looked over at Joey Florio still positioned in the doorway, his head bowed, a small man with a thick black mustache. Muffin was waiting in the corridor behind Joey, her cap resting against a knee, watching Kurt with bitter determination in her eyes. They had already discussed what had to be done.

AT TEN O'CLOCK the deputy arrived to relieve Muffin at her station outside the door. Kurt could hear their voices.

"Didn't expect to find *you* here. Where's Florio?"

"He's been having some personal problems. I had to fill in."

"His old lady again?" The deputy laughed.

"Murphy will relieve you at two."

"How's our boy? Still hanging in there?"

"There was a bad scare early on. They had to zap his chest. But he seems to have stabilized." Her voice grew clearer as she stepped into the dark room. "The monitors look good right now. The nurse just left. She'll be back every half hour to check on him."

Wavy orange graph lines from the two monitor screens provided the only light in the room.

"He's one tough little fucker."

"Yeah, he is. You need anything before I go?"

"How about a bottle of Jack and that pretty nurse named Sally."

"Your wife must be one lucky woman."

"Jesus, Brown, lighten up."

"Murphy will be on at two. See you later, stud."

* * *

THE MINUTES CREPT by in the dead quiet of the room. Clothes hangers rattled at his slightest move. Through the crack between the closet doors Kurt could make out the swaddled figure hooked up to monitors and dripping plastic bags. From time to time saliva gurgled through the tube in his mouth. Outside the dark window a light wet snow had begun to fall, softly ticking against the glass. The morning Lennon was born, a young deer had appeared out there, nibbling in the aspen glade, and Kurt had held the baby up to the window, showing the animal his newborn son. That memory comforted him now in this place where sons were all too quickly gone.

The nurse came in periodically, read the monitors, scribbled notes on a chart. She examined bags, adjusted valves, a flurry of efficient clicking sounds. He could hear the deputy making small talk with her in the corridor. More than once it occurred to Kurt that nothing was going to happen tonight. That he had misjudged intentions, miscalculated the timing and method. Throughout the long tedious wait he held on to the only thing he knew for certain: If Tyler Rutledge lived, he was a problem for the triggermen. And their employer. Sooner or later they had to make their move.

After nearly three hours, bone tired, his concentration wavering, he slumped down on the floor of the tight enclosure, his weary mind conjuring images of Kat Pfeil in his arms. He wondered where she was tonight. If she was safe. If she was thinking about him.

Footsteps entered the room, not the nurse's quick, soft-soled pace but a man's creaking boots. A shadow drifted past the crack, moving toward the bed. Kurt stood up quietly and nudged open the closet door an extra inch. The deputy was standing next to the safety railing, staring down at the motionless figure. Kurt slipped the .45 from his holster, a light scrape of leather, and bit his lip, waiting.

The deputy quickly scanned the room. Perhaps he had heard the sound. He glanced back toward the lighted corridor, then at the faintly glowing screens. He raised his eyes and searched the ceiling, turning full circle, making certain he hadn't overlooked a video camera. He studied the patient for some time, touched his bare arm above the gauze wrapping. Finally, in one swift movement, he slid a rubber glove over his right hand, reached down, and turned off the oxygen flow to the respirator.

What are you going to do now? Kurt wondered. The man remained at the bedside, watching the screen's respiration line wiggle and dip. He was practiced at his technique, confident, as if he'd done this sort of thing before. Perhaps he intended only to weaken Tyler, then turn the air back on at some critical moment, after it was too late, and let the boy sputter out on his own. When the nurse came in and found her patient dead, who would question what had happened, especially after the problems earlier this evening? The heroic med-tech systems were up and running but Tyler's body could no longer respond.

Kurt kneed open the closet door. "You didn't have to go to so much trouble, Gillespie," he said, stepping out with his pistol gripped in both hands, pointed at the man. "Tyler died four hours ago."

Startled, Gillespie banged against the monitor stand. The graphs went haywire, a buzzer sounded.

"You know the routine, Bill. Step out where I can see you. Hands on your head, kneel down real slow."

"What are you going to do if I say, 'Fuck you, Muller'? Shoot me?" the deputy said. "I don't think so. You're too smart a guy to fire a gun in an IC unit. Smart guys like you know a round might go through one of these cheap-shit walls and hit some crip in the next room."

He whipped the 9mm service revolver from his holster with impressive speed. "Me, I'm not so smart as you," he said, leveling the weapon at Kurt. "I'm not so nice either. Move out of the way and let me pass, motherfucker, and everybody rides off into the sunset."

"Where you going, Bill? Muffin and half the department are waiting for you outside."

The deputy's top lip glistened with sweat. His mind was working hard, turning over the possibilities.

"Put down the piece, Bill. We'll find you a good lawyer. We're not after you," he said. *Unless you pulled the trigger on Tyler, you son of a bitch.* "You know how it works. Tell us who you're working for, you may not do any time at all."

"I been a cop thirty years, Muller. I ain't going to the pen, not even for a weekend visit." He cocked the hammer. "Now get out of my way."

Gillespie took a step closer to the bed and the bandaged corpse rose up and seized the pistol hand and slammed it downward with incredible force, cracking the deputy's forearm against the bed rail. The gun dropped like a flower petal onto the sheets. Joey Florio rolled through a tangle of plastic tubing and grappled Gillespie around the neck, riding him to the tile floor. They ended up wrestling under a wreck of aluminum trays and fallen IV stands, and Kurt piled on top of them both, finding Gillespie's wrist and handcuffing him to the leg of the bed.

"God damn, Joey," Kurt huffed, standing up slowly, pulling the radio from his belt. "Why'd you wait so long?"

Joey Florio was on his feet now, unraveling the gauze around his head, snapping off tubing taped to his hairy body. "I couldn't move, man. You have any idea what it's like to lie in a bed like that for three hours? My brain went numb." He wadded up a fist-sized ball of adhesive tape and flung it at Gillespie, smacking him in the head. "Next time *I* wait in the closet."

Gill Dotson jarred open the door to the linen shelf above the closet and dangled his long legs over the side. "Hey, Florio, could we get a second take on that Hulk Hogan airplane spin?" He had videotaped everything from a drill hole in the door. "A little sloppy on the takedown."

"Bite my ass, Dotson."

Kurt radioed Muffin, who was waiting in the parking lot with three deputies as backup. "Come on in, partner," he said, still panting from the scuffle. "We got his whole nightclub act live and in color."

38

IF THE COPS had pooled bets on Bill Gillespie's one phone call, Kurt would have won big money. After his brief telephone conversation the deputy returned to the interrogation table a dispirited man. He asked for a cigarette and smoked nervously, his eyes cast on the floor.

"Staggs is in Colorado Springs at a golf tournament," Kurt said. Gillespie's face betrayed his surprise that Kurt was one step ahead.

"It's going to take a while for the local VIPro office to get in touch with him," Kurt said, "and then it's going to take a while longer for Staggs to line up a lawyer. We're looking at noon the earliest, Bill. That gives us about eleven hours to chat."

A graying, angular man, the deputy appeared gaunt around the mouth, exhausted. "Don't treat me like a punk, Muller. I been at this game a lot longer than you have," he said. "I don't talk without a lawyer."

"Suit yourself, Bill. But let me give you a few things to think about while you've got some time on your hands."

He told the deputy that somebody would go down for murder now that Tyler was dead. "I've got a witness

that says there were three of you at the Lone Ute Mine,"
he explained patiently. "But my guess is that all three of
you didn't pull a trigger. Who's it going to be, Bill? You
or the bad boy?"

Muffin was pacing back and forth in front of the
two-way mirror. She had discovered the VIProtex connection in Gillespie's file, a letter of recommendation
from the branch chief in Albuquerque, for whom the
cop had done a little moonlighting. "Don't be stupid,
man," she said. "You're not in that deep. Do yourself a
favor. Give us a reason to go easy on you."

Though there was an ashtray in plain sight, Gillespie
dropped his cigarette on the floor and ground the
burning tip into the carpet, leaving a large black
smudge. "Do me a favor and go easy on my dick, sweetheart," he said.

She lunged at him, grabbed his shirt collar. Kurt had
to restrain her from smashing the man's face against
the table.

Gillespie laughed at them. "This jam session is
over," he said, straightening his shirt, "until I hear
from my lawyer."

KURT WENT HOME to a dark house dusted with snow. A
white envelope had been slipped under the front door,
his name addressed in a familiar handwriting. He
stepped inside the mud porch and flipped on a switch.
Just got off the phone with Randy's daughter in Portland,
the letter said, *which is why this note may sound so
scattered and emotional. I'm sitting here at Miles' place,
drinking his bourbon and thinking about parents and
children. You are a wonderful father, Kurt. Seeing you*

*and Lennon together, feeling the love between you, made
me regret I didn't have a child with Michael.*

*Miles has agreed to drive me to California, where I can
stay with friends until my life settles down. I realize I am
a material witness to murder and arson, and I will cooperate with your department in whatever way I can. (You
know as much as I do about the incident.) Maybe a written deposition would be the best thing for now. You can
leave messages for me on Miles' phone recorder. After the
insanity of the past 24 hours, I am not willing to hang
around Aspen any longer. I'm sorry if this poses a problem for your investigation.*

*Please take care of yourself and the boys. You are a
dear sweet man and I wish things had turned out different for us. I can understand now why the adolescent Katrina P. had such a crush on you, and why it's lasted all
these years. With love, K.*

He sat on the bunk bed in Lennon's chill room,
moonlight shaping strange silhouettes out of the toys
scattered across the floor, and longed to hold the child
in his arms. Slumped forward, wrists dangling between
his knees, he imagined himself as an old man, alone
and grieving in a room that had once been his son's,
the playthings just as the boy had left them thirty years
before. In that same moment he saw Tyler's parents
sitting on a bed like this one, holding each other in the
empty, desolate chamber of one heart, inconsolable and
lost now that their only child was gone. He began to
tremble. He didn't want to believe that something like
that could ever happen to the boy who slept in this bed.
He didn't want to believe that parents sometimes outlived their children.

Laying his head on the Lion King pillow, he gathered

Lennon's stuffed friends around him, a dozen creatures that comforted the boy every night, Jerry the Monkey and Weebok and the Wild Thing and some whose names Kurt could not recall. He didn't intend to fall asleep, but he woke just before dawn with a burning pain where Skank had cut him with the switchblade. Over the bathroom sink he rolled back his sleeve and ripped off the stained bandage. His arm was red and swollen from wrist to elbow and pus oozed from the long shallow scratch. He applied a clean dressing, taped down the gauze, and looked at himself in the mirror, wondering why he had aged ten years in the last five days. Trying to rouse himself, force life back into those stone-hard features, he splashed water in his face and smoothed back his hair, then went into the cold living room to make a fire in the woodstove.

The answering machine indicated three blinking messages. The first was from a Free West attorney representing James Joseph Chilcutt. He sounded like a mature middle-aged man, relaxed, optimistic. No rookies for J.J. Chilcutt. If he was implicated in three murders and brought to trial, revelations about VIProtex's relationship with Free West would destroy Metcalf's credibility and jeopardize his foundation's legal status, as well as threaten him with criminal prosecution.

". . . sorry to say when Mr. Metcalf spoke with you he wasn't aware that James would be out of state on assignment today and for the rest of the week," the voice informed him. *James.* As if he knew the prick. "I hope it won't be too much of an inconvenience to schedule the meeting for next week."

The first thing Kurt was going to do when he returned to the office this morning was issue an arrest warrant, drag Chilcutt's ass back to Pitkin County.

"Hello, Kurt. I've been thinking about you all day. Did you find my note?" Kat Pfeil's lovely resonant voice. "Miles and I had a disagreement and we parted company somewhere near Moab. I wish I could see you right now. I need a friend. It's that time of night when I get so depressed and angry. I'm feeling like there's only one thing I can do to make things right, but I know if you were here you'd talk me out of it."

Kat, he thought, *why did I let you get away?* His mind raced over the ways he could contact her. The Utah state police? If only she would call again. And where the hell was Miles?

He telephoned the photographer's cabin and got the recorder. Kurt's message was brief but firm, insisting that Miles call him as soon as possible. Then he phoned the department and found Linda Ríos on duty. "Linda, I want you to pull up a plate for me," he said, giving her Miles's name and the make of his Land-Rover. "Call me back when you have it." He would ask the Utah troopers for assistance in tracking them down.

Dazed from lack of sleep, he went to the kitchen to brew coffee and then realized he hadn't listened to the third message on his machine. He punched the button that rewound the recorder, and skipped to the last call. It was Hunter's small, formal telephone voice asking for his pet snake again and his box of rocks. He missed Sneak terribly and pleaded for Kurt to bring his things to Meg's farmhouse. "I hid the box under Lennon's bed so nobody would find the rock my grandpa said to never let anyone have. . . ."

Kurt sighed and rubbed his bristly face. He wanted

to see the boys but he didn't know how soon he could—

He stopped abruptly and punched the button a second time, replaying the message. Hunter's words were unmistakable: "I hid the box under Lennon's bed so nobody would find the rock my grandpa said to never let anyone have."

Hurrying into the room he slid to his knees and dragged the rattling cigar box from under the bed. Samples of feldspar, mica, granite, quartz, marble. And one slate-gray chunk he couldn't identify, chisel marks grooving the sides, a rough-edged piece that fit snugly in the palm of his large hand. A rock the old man didn't want anyone to see.

He stood at the window, hefting the ore in his hand, feeling its weight and sharp facets. A hazy blue light was rising over the valley. There was a trace of snow on the juniper windbreak and the meadow below the house. From this promontory on Red Mountain he could see lights in the sleepy village of Aspen, and the tiny stark headlamp from an ATV bobbing along the slope of the ski mountain, ascending into the cottony clouds obscuring the peak. At this distance the Ajax Mine adit could not be marked by the naked eye, but he knew exactly where it was.

He turned the fragment over in his hand, examining its color in the soft light from the window, then stared again at the mountain. Deep inside that tunneled-out heap of dirt and hardrock, perhaps down in the hollow center Kurt had feared would someday collapse upon his entire world, Ned Carr had found something worth killing him for.

FOR AT LEAST twenty years Tink Tarver's neighbors had been trying to have his property condemned, his house torn down board by board. It was unclear how the old pack rat had survived the periodic health and safety inspections for so long. From time to time Kurt had sent county prisoners to help him clean up the scrap metal lying around his yard, but Tink had grown increasingly resistant and the last time had chased off some poor hungover DUI with a tar-paper knife.

Ever since Kurt could remember, a tanklike '52 De Soto had hunkered undriven in front of Tink's house, and the car had now been transformed into a flower planter, long tendrils of ivy spilling out the windows, tall sunflowers poking their heads up through rust holes in the roof. He unwired the gate and made his way across the dead yard, a dumping ground for lumber and ancient appliances and lawn mower parts and threadbare tires that lay about randomly, wherever they had rolled to a stop. It was just after six A.M. and the Radio Flyer was still parked by the front steps, a sign that Tink had not left for his morning rounds of the town Dumpsters and trash heaps. Kurt knocked and stood waiting in the cold, blowing on his hands to warm them, his breath becoming little white cuffs of vapor. When there was no answer he opened the creaky door and called the man's name. A half-dozen mangy cats rushed from the foul-smelling darkness to lick his boots and stare up at him through hollow eyes, mewing for food.

"Come on, guys," he said, stepping around them. "Take me to your leader."

Cat odor permeated the old house. He forced himself through the cluttered living room, where a quilt-draped army cot served as Tink's bed. More cats emerged from under sour laundry piles and cardboard boxes, a feline army following him into a kitchen whose buckling linoleum floor was as sticky as fresh paint. Coffee brewed on a warm woodstove in the center of the room. Two scrawny toms licked at the crusty dishes piled in the sink. Tink's false teeth soaked in a jelly glass on the windowsill. Kurt could hear an electric arcing noise coming from the rear of the house, where the old kook kept his workshop.

At the end of a dark hallway there was a door tacked with a sign that said ENTER AT YOUR OWN RISK. Bright sparks flashed within, the smell of burning coil. Kurt gave the door a cautious push. "Hey, Tink!" he called out above the welding din. He didn't want to spook the man. "It's Kurt Muller."

Tink valved off the torch, a makeshift device connected to a surplus airplane generator. He lifted his mask and squinted at Kurt, deep lines etching his forehead, scarlike furrows from nose to jawbone. He looked astonished that someone might actually find him in all this junk.

"Pretty damn early in the morning to come calling, son. I ain't had my second cup."

He was wearing a tattered bathrobe, laceless army boots. Grizzly, week-old whiskers stubbled his sharp chin. He reached over to a flattened beer can serving as an ashtray, withdrew the wet stub of a roll-your-own, and plugged it in the corner of his mouth.

"There's something I want you to look at," Kurt said.

He nudged aside the cats purling around his ankles and walked over to place the rock on the welding bench. Tink stared at it, glanced warily at Kurt, dragged on the cold cigarette. The old man was an expert assayer and at one time, twenty-five, thirty years ago, had been the only reliable authority in the entire valley. His gravimetric setup still inhabited the far corner of the shop, an alchemist's secret laboratory, weighing scales and stained beakers, a Bunsen burner as charred as a chimney brick. If anyone this side of Leadville could compute the composition of that ore, Tink Tarver was the man.

"Can you assay it for me? I want to know what it is."

The junk man raised one wiry eyebrow. Without his teeth he sounded like Gabby Hayes. "Where did you get that from?" he asked.

"From a cigar box, Tink. What does it matter? Can you figure out its makeup?"

Tink picked up the silver-gray chunk with a grimy hand and brought it close to his eyes. He turned the piece slowly round and round. "You got this from Ned, didn't you, son?"

Kurt wasn't surprised. He suspected that Tink knew

much more than he was willing to let on. "How do you know that?"

An orange tabby jumped up into the old man's lap and he dropped it back on the floor like a bundle of rags. "I seen it before," he said.

"He showed it to you?"

Tink nodded.

"What is it?"

Tink examined the rock one last turn and set it on the bench like a chess piece. "It's the closest damn thing to pure platinum I've ever seen," he said. "Worth many times what silver's going for. Rare as a hen's tooth."

"Platinum?" Kurt said. "Where did it come from?"

Tink lifted a shaving mug full of black coffee. "According to Ned, it come from the Lone Ute Mine," he said, winking one eye as he drank.

The shop walls were braced from floor to ceiling with board shelves containing jars of nails, screws, bolts, unidentified gelatinous suspensions. A collection of dead things floated in brackish liquids. Tarantula, scorpion, coral snake. The fetus of a baby pig.

"But you got to consider that Ned was a notorious liar, like ever' Pickax Pete in the history of the trade," Tink said. "Hell, he mighta swiped that rock in South America, for all I know. Miners love a good leg-pulling."

"What would lying get him?"

"Your wallet, son. Anytime some hardrock stiff tells you he's made a big strike and there's three backers lined up in Mexico City, hold on to your hip pocket."

Kurt looked at the ore. "How long ago did you assay this for him?"

"I reckon it was last fall. 'Bout the time he was drawing fire from the owl lovers."

"Did anyone else know about the platinum?"

Tink massaged the back of his neck. He seemed annoyed at Kurt. But then he always seemed annoyed about something. "You're not catching on here, son," he said. "I knew that rascal fifty years and in all that time I never heard him once tell the truth about a damn thing, not even what he had for breakfast. After a while he tells you something, you figure it's just another nursery rhyme."

"Okay, fine, Tink. What nursery rhyme did he tell you about the platinum?"

The old man spit the wet cigarette butt on the floor and fumbled in his bathrobe pockets for rolling papers and a small cloth bag of tobacco. "You got any store-bought smokes?" he asked.

"No."

"Figures."

He sprinkled tobacco on a creased paper, rolled and licked, taking his sweet time, pulling the bag string with his teeth. Kurt felt like twisting one of his jug ears to hurry him along. Finally the man peered up at him and spoke.

"He told me he'd sold off a piece of his works to a big outfit, and that they'd brought in their own engineers and shovel jocks to give his mine the once-over. Said they went in deep and messed around for a week, and then come back two or three times with more hot-shot foreign experts and such, and that that hunk of ore sitting right there was from a seam they found about ten levels down." He puffed his cigarette, squinting through the smoke. "That was his story, son. A platinum strike. I shelved it alongside the one about the president of Mexico asking him to come down and run their bureau of mines."

"Is it possible, Tink? I've never heard of any big platinum strikes in this country."

The old man made a face. "What the old-timers called white gold comes up with the native silver. High-grade platinum showed up in that big copper mine down in the San Juans, and they shipped a lot out of the old Boss Mine at Goodsprings, Nevada, and from the iron hat at the New Rambler in Wyoming. Trouble is, the South Africans got their gatekeepers in all the fancy labs in Denver and Reno. Any platinum or rhodium they see gets reported to Johanniesburg first."

The South Africans, Kurt thought. Gentlemen in natty golf hats.

"Did Ned tell you the name of the outfit?" he asked. If the old codger had heard a name—Metcalf, Free West, anything remotely close—the DA could pull him in for corroborating testimony. Maybe. If the grand jury believed a man who kept a pig fetus in a jar.

"Did he mention who they were?" He repeated the question.

Tink rubbed his nose with the back of his cigarette hand. "Nah," he said, draining his cup. "And I didn't ask."

40

KURT MADE A pot of coffee and sat in an old recliner in the book-lined study that had once been his father's office, trying to focus his thoughts and weave together the strands from this tangled weed lot of an investigation. Corky Marcus possessed a document naming Hunter as the heir to the mines. Jesse Nighthawk said that Ned had wanted SPIRITT to manage the day-to-day operations until the boy turned twenty-one. But Arnold Metcalf insisted that the Free West Legal Coalition was the sole executor of Ned's estate, and it was likely that they now owned part of the mining enterprise itself, probably in exchange for legal favors or a forgiven loan. Perhaps this entire scenario made sense only in a perverse logic that Ned Carr alone could have constructed, his final twisted joke. Cowboys and Indians in an alliance of mutual distrust, overseeing one of the few platinum strikes in the continental U.S. The perfect composition of checks and balances, with Hunter benefiting no matter what happened between the uneasy partners. If this was what Ned had in mind, he was one ingenious old coot.

So what went wrong?

Kurt drank his coffee and shuffled through the stack of photocopied articles Meredith had given him, choosing one at random, reading about the origins of the Free West Rebellion and the oil and mining corporations that were its most loyal financial supporters. It occurred to him that Meredith and her reading group and every environmentalist in Colorado were going to be outraged when they learned that a major platinum-mining operation would soon be under way in the national forest on the backside of Aspen Mountain. More truck traffic and noise, a bigger tailings pond for the acids and cyanides, maybe a stamp mill to pound the ore. No wonder Ned and his Free West legal counsel had fought so hard to widen and pave the access road. It was crucial to their future endeavor.

Something nasty and ratlike began gnawing at the back of his mind and he stopped and removed his bifocals. What if Meredith and her allies had somehow known about the platinum? More than anyone in the Free West Rebellion, the greens would've been happy to see the old miner dead and buried. But who would they have hired to make the hit? Not J.J. Chilcutt from the other side. Miles and Kat Pfeil? They weren't the killing kind.

He picked up the rock fragment, lying like a paperweight on the pages, and scratched at the hard surface with his thumbnail. *It's easy to short out blasting wire, make a spark,* Jesse Nighthawk had told him. *I could have done it myself.*

Kurt went to his father's work desk and dialed the rotor on an antique black telephone. Directory assistance in Santa Fe, New Mexico, had no listing for the acronym SPIRITT. The operator requested more information and Kurt remembered the *Society* and the *Indian*, thought the *P* might stand for *Protection*. It was close enough.

"I hope I'm not calling too early," he said to the young woman whose verbal rhythms sounded Hispanic. "I'm trying to reach Jesse Nighthawk. He gave me this number."

"One moment, sir."

She put him on hold and returned after a long wait. "I'm sorry, sir, but Mr. Nighthawk cannot be reached at this number. He is no longer employed by us."

Kurt squeezed until the rock bit into his palm. He identified himself as the sheriff of Pitkin County, Colorado. "Is there somebody I can talk to who might have worked with him?"

She hesitated, a low-level administrative assistant not paid enough to make these decisions. "I don't think so, sir. He hasn't been associated with our organization for three or four months."

"May I please speak with the head of your security division?"

"Our security division?"

"Yes. Whoever's in charge of your building security."

Another pause. "One moment, sir."

This time the wait was even longer, and Kurt wondered if his line was blinking away in some unattended office, possibly the janitor's storeroom. He was about to hang up and call again when a male voice came on the line.

"Alvin Birch. What can I do for you?"

Alvin Birch sounded like an older man, Native American, whose larynx had been graded with a gravel rake. He sounded like someone you didn't want to fuck with. Kurt inquired politely about Birch's title.

"Security," the man said gruffly. "Who am I talking to?"

Kurt introduced himself as the sheriff and asked if Birch knew Jesse Nighthawk.

"Is Jesse in trouble with the law?" Birch asked with a knowing weariness, a familiarity with such matters.

"I'm not sure yet," Kurt said. "He told me he worked for SPIRITT and now I find out he doesn't. I met him at a Free West golf benefit in Colorado Springs yesterday. He said your organization had hired him to take photographs."

The man breathed into the line, and Kurt imagined a large chest with heaving lungs. "It's been a while since we've needed his services," he said.

"I see. Is there a reason why he doesn't work for you anymore?"

A measured hesitation. Several slow, wheezing breaths. "Do you mind if I verify your status with the Pitkin County Sheriff's Department?"

"Verify away." Kurt gave him the phone number of the department and his social security number. "You want to call me back when you feel like talking, Mr. Birch?"

"Information about our employees is strictly private. There's not much I can tell you, buddy."

"Tell me this much. Is Jesse a good man? Or should I be worried?"

"You want to hire him to do a job?" he asked. "Is that what we're talking about?"

Kurt thought it over. "Something like that," he said. "I'm looking for a character reference."

"Me myself, I got along just fine with Jesse," Alvin Birch said. "No complaints about his work. He rubbed our legal eagles the wrong way. Maybe you better talk to them."

Kurt made a joke about lawyers. Could anyone get along with them? They both laughed.

"You have any idea how I can get in touch with him?" Kurt asked. "Is he still living in Durango?"

"Far as I know. I haven't talked to him in a couple of months."

"You have his phone number?"

"Sorry, brother," he said. "I cain't help you out on that one."

Kurt thanked Alvin Birch and hung up. He tried directory assistance in Durango, Colorado, and was given the number for Nighthawk Investigations. After three rings, a taped message with Jesse's deep, polished voice began to play. Kurt pressed his finger on the receiver button and canceled the call.

If Jesse Nighthawk wasn't on the SPIRITT payroll, who was he taking pictures for? The private dicks Kurt had worked with wouldn't walk a dog unless somebody else was covering their time.

Rhombic shaped and dull, the platinum ore lay on the desk in front of him, the source of so much grief. It didn't look like something a man should lose his life over. Kurt understood now why Jesse Nighthawk had broken into Ned's cabin that night. He was searching for solid proof. A rock in a child's cigar box.

IN LESS THAN fifteen minutes Kurt was sitting in his Jeep in front of the elementary school, watching parents in bumper-to-bumper vehicles stop and let out their kids. He was usually in that line, giving Lennon one last squeeze, reminding him about the homework pages and signed forms in his backpack, urging the dreamy boy to walk quickly out of the weather. There were only two weeks left until his graduation from kindergarten, another milestone that had come and gone too fast. Kurt wished he could slow everything down, drag out these innocent moments a little longer. But the months were already running away from them, turning into years.

He watched the county squad car slip into the stream of traffic. Kurt got out of his Jeep and crossed the street to meet Lennon and Hunter at the sidewalk. This was his only chance to see them today.

"Hi, Dad," Lennon said with that familiar pale, sleep-faced expression he always wore this time of morning. Kurt knelt down and hugged his son, helping him put on his backpack.

"How is everything, champ?"

"Fine," the boy said cheerfully. "We're helping Bhajan plant a garden."

"Bhajan?"

Meg opened the passenger door and said good morning. She seemed happy to see Kurt here.

"Bhajan is Mom's friend," Lennon explained.

"I see," he said, smiling at Meg. Bhajan indeed.

"Hi, Coach," Hunter said, hopping out of the back-seat. "We got to ride in this awesome police car!"

Deputy Mac Murphy waved from behind the wheel.

"Just for a few more days," Kurt said, as much for Meg's benefit as for theirs. "Everything's going to be normal again real soon."

Two of their classmates walked past the squad car and stopped to admire it. "What did you guys do?" asked a girl named Lauren.

"We were playing Monopoly and the cabin blew up," Lennon said.

"Way cool," she said, and they all turned and raced one another toward the classrooms, their backpacks rattling.

Kurt and Meg stood together and shouted their good-byes, watching the children disappear into the corridor. Horns were tooting now, the late arrivals urging Mac Murphy to move along out of the drop-off area. Caffeinated mothers who didn't care who he was.

"I'm glad to hear things will be normal soon," Meg said, turning to glare at someone honking impatiently from a Saab. "Is that a prediction or a promise?"

"It's a promise, Meg. I'm going to bust the people who did this to us."

To *us*. As if they were all one big happy family.

"The boys are still pretty nervous, Kurt," she said. "Yesterday Hunter wanted me to close all the blinds in the house in broad daylight. He thought that would keep the firebombs away."

"Jesus." Kurt shook his head, angry at himself, blaming his own lack of vigilance for what had happened.

"Are you okay?" she asked, touching his forehead, the side of his face. "Your face is red. You feel warm. Have you got a fever?"

It was true, he wasn't feeling well. His arm throbbed and he suspected he needed an antibiotic for the infection. "It's been a rough week," he said.

Horns were honking again. She gave him a quick

hug and crawled back into the squad car, rolling down the window. "Tell your friend she ought to take better care of you," she smiled.

"My friend?" he said, confused, half asleep on his feet.

She raised her chin toward the parking lot across the street. Muffin Brown was sitting in her unit next to Kurt's Jeep, eating breakfast from a paper bag.

"At least you both share the same lifestyle," Meg said.

The squad car pulled away into the chaos of departing traffic and Kurt returned to the lot. Muffin acknowledged him with a finger raised from the foam cup at her lips. "I thought I would find you here," she said, brushing Egg McMuffin crumbs from her lap.

He folded his arms and rested his butt against her back door. "What's the word on Gillespie?" he asked.

"He finally heard from his lawyer. The guy's flying in from Colorado Springs around noon. Corporate jet. Impressive representation for a man living on a deputy's salary."

Kurt watched the last of the mothers trail off toward the exit. "They're not getting away with this," he said. "I don't care who's involved."

Muffin stepped out of the Pitco unit and stood next to him, her back braced against the driver's door. Steam whiffed from the cup in her hand. "We located Nathan Carr," she said. "He's a high-school chemistry teacher in Seattle. Two kids, seven and ten. Boy and girl."

The news was an unpleasant shock. He would never give voice to such a dark thought, but Kurt had been hoping that Nathan was dead.

"I asked him if he knew his sister had a kid and he

said he'd heard. Said he'd been planning a trip to Aspen this summer to see his father and the boy."

"How thoughtful of him."

"I couldn't get a read on whether he was willing to take Hunter. He seemed pretty upset by Ned's death. I'm sure he needs some time to process it all."

Hunter in Seattle. City life. How could he possibly adjust to such a vastly different world? He would miss these mountains. And Lennon. *Maybe he doesn't want the child,* Kurt thought. *He has two of his own.*

"What kind of guy would have to think about taking his dead sister's son?"

Muffin finished her coffee and tossed the container on the rising knoll of cups littering the back floorboard. She extended her arms and squatted in a deep knee bend, joggling herself awake. "Kurt," she said, "I hope you're preparing yourself for what's coming."

He watched the windows of a classroom. He could see children gathered around their teacher, jumping up and down, arms outstretched like beggars, eager for whatever she was handing out.

"If Nathan Carr decides to accept custody of Hunter, there's nothing we can do about it."

He shoved off from the patrol unit and circled around to his Jeep. "Thanks for the consoling advice," he said. "You can always be counted on to cheer me up, Brown."

"Are you coming in to meet Gillespie's lawyer?"

"I'd love to see the weasel's face when he watches the video of his boy switching off the oxygen. But if I'm not there by noon, start without me. You and Dotson can handle him."

"What the hell's more important than the Gillespie interrogation, Kurt?"

Finding Jesse Nighthawk, he thought. "I'll be in touch."

He drove to the airport hangar and tracked down Wing Taylor wandering through the welders' shop with a crumpled invoice in his hand, bawling out everyone in his path. When he saw Kurt he stopped and grinned, tonguing the wet cigar stub to the other side of his mouth.

"Hey, Wing," Kurt said. "You ready to ramble?"

"Goddamn right," Wing said. "Anything but this."

41

THEIR FLIGHT TOOK them over the Gunnison Gorge, a steep-walled trench the river had scoured through ten million years of sediment down to the deep, ancient gneiss, and in a short while they were soaring above the broken necks of vanished volcanoes in the Uncompahgre Wilderness, a landscape of snow-packed summits and long green valleys as stunning as the glacial basins of Switzerland. An hour and 150 sky miles from their departure they landed on a sand-blown runway at the desert edge of the Southern Ute Reservation. It was late morning. Kurt instructed Wing Taylor to stay with the plane while he went into the La Plata County Airport terminal and rented the only available Jeep from the only rental agency in the building. Durango was fifteen miles away.

He remembered fragments of that sleepy cowboy town he'd passed through with his family as a boy, on their way to Mesa Verde, and a stoned road-trip in a VW microbus with Meg and Bert and Bert's girlfriend, Maya Dahl, a peyote pilgrimage to Anasazi holy places in the remote canyons of the Southwest. Today, making his way along this flat, parched country where the Utes had been interned for more than a century, he decided it was time to introduce Lennon and Hunter to the awesome sandstone balconies of the Cliff Palace just west of here, and to the kivas and pictographs scattered across these desolate mesas. The boys were at the perfect age to wonder.

He crossed the highway bridge over the shaded Animas River, noticing a band of kayakers fighting the spring-melt waters below, and cruised into the old part of town, a gentrified historical district with upscale boutiques and bistros and a refurbished Victorian hotel. Tourists waited at the antique depot to ride the famous narrow-gauge railway up to the ghost town of Silverton, forty-five miles north in the San Juans.

Kurt parked on the street and found the address listed for Nighthawk Investigations, but it turned out to be a storefront art gallery located between a health-food café and an India import shop. He checked the address again and then wandered up and down the block, searching for some sign of a detective agency, a security company, a collection agency. There were waterbeds, used books, Western boots, and tofu—but no shamus. As a last resort he returned to the art gallery and stepped inside, rattling the dried gourd shells lacing the door. It was a newly remodeled space featuring Native American pottery and basketwork under a double row of track lighting. The pleasant, high-country aroma of piñon emanated from a burning stick of incense. An attractive young dark-haired woman, possibly Ute, sat behind a desk in a sunlit corner, typing on a computer. She glanced over and smiled. "If I can help you with anything," she said in a soft voice, "just let me know."

He lifted a clay serving bowl and examined the simple markings. "I'm looking for a man named Jesse Nighthawk," he said.

She pointed indifferently toward a door in the rear, a subtle admonition that said *Oh, you're one of those people,* and continued with her work as if he had never appeared.

The door gave way into a dim workshop area filled with packing crates and sheets of bubble wrap. A long scarred table was scattered with black markers, rolls of tape, cutting blades. The place smelled like sawdust and damp cardboard. He was about to turn around and ask the young woman again when he noticed another door, its paint shedding in loose green curls. The john? he wondered, walking over to try the knob.

"Close the fucking door!" snapped the bulky figure bent over a developer tray in a red-lit darkroom.

"Hello, Jesse. How's the picture business?"

Nighthawk spun around at the sound of the voice and came toward him, but Kurt drew the .45. "Relax," he said, showing the weapon. "I'm not here to pop your balloon. Unless there's something you've forgotten to tell me about Ned Carr."

A slow recognition passed over the man's face. "Muller?" he said. "Jesus Christ, man. What are you doing here?"

"I like to drop in at odd times myself, Jesse. Keeps everybody honest."

There were a dozen eight-by-tens drying on a line. Kurt yanked one free, an excellent close-up of Arnold Metcalf standing on the golf green next to that South African mining engineer in the natty hat.

"Why don't we go somewhere and have a nice long talk," Kurt suggested.

"Whatever you say, hoss. You've got the gun."

Nighthawk pulled back a heavy black curtain and they entered a small storage room with a single transom window high above. Misshapen rectangles of sunlight had bleached out the old political posters tacked on the wall. BIA = CIA. FREE LEONARD PELTIER. ALCATRAZ FOR THE INDIANS. Judging by the columns of books wobbling among the uncrated pottery, Jesse Nighthawk was a voracious reader of anthropology and science fiction, with an impressive collection of *Playboys* yellowing in another corner.

"Have a seat there," Kurt said, motioning the gun at a metal chair. He didn't want Jesse sitting behind that industrial desk, where there was probably a pistol in one of its drawers.

"You can put that thing away, Muller. I'm not going to jump you."

Nighthawk sat in the chair and folded his large arms across his chest. An inch of hairless flab was visible between his beltline and the bottom of the tight Los Lobos T-shirt he was wearing. "Where I come from," he said, "we've got better ways to treat a man who's saved your life."

"You lied to me, Jesse," Kurt said, slipping the .45 back in his shoulder holster. "You haven't worked for SPIRITT in a good long while. So who are you taking these pictures for?" he asked, dropping the photo of Arnold Metcalf in the detective's lap.

"For the only boss who can tolerate my wicked ways," he said with a cunning grin, tapping his chest. "Numero uno."

"Bullshit." Kurt peered around the dusty room. "You can't afford to work for yourself. I don't believe you."

"I hope this doesn't come as a big surprise, Muller, but I don't give a rat's ass what you believe."

Kurt pulled the chunk of platinum ore from his jacket pocket and held it out in his open palm. "This is what you were looking for that night in Ned's cabin," he said. "Isn't it, Jesse?"

Nighthawk stared at the rock.

"Yeah, it's high-grade platinum, all right. And it's from the Lone Ute, unless Ned was pulling everybody's leg. You want it so bad?" he said, pitching the fragment at Nighthawk. "You can have it. But tell your clients if they're after the mine, they're too late. Metcalf and his South Africans have already dug around in the stopes and they know it's platinum rich. They've got paperwork that says they're in charge of Ned's holdings."

Nighthawk leaned forward, his forearms resting on his knees. He tossed the rock in the air, caught it, felt its weight, turned the piece over in his hand, studying the rough texture. "Ned cut them in at forty percent," he said after a long silence. "Do the math. That's still not enough to call the shots at a stockholders' meeting."

"Where did you come up with that?"

Nighthawk flashed his dark eyes. "He told me."

"When he called and told you he wanted SPIRITT to run his mines?"

"That's right. The kid takes the other sixty percent. If Metcalf shows you something that says different, check to see if the signature's dry."

"And you're still saying that Ned wanted your people to manage Hunter's sixty percent."

"Just like I told you, hoss. Until the boy is twenty-one."

"Can you prove that? The forty-sixty split?"

Nighthawk shook his head slowly. "Why do you think they offed him when they did?" he said. "They knew I didn't have anything in black and white, and they wanted to make sure it stayed that way."

"Arnold Metcalf's got paper, and you've got squat."

"Squat plus zilch, my friend. Don't I know it."

"He's a big-time lawyer, Jesse. He's got a whole kennel full of hotshot legal counsel with Ivy League pedigrees. What's going to stop them from cooking up a will that says the Free West Coalition is the sole guardian of the Ned Carr mines?"

He studied Kurt through small mischievous eyes, his huge head canted slightly on a thick neck. "You and me," he said with a grin.

Kurt stared back at him and began to laugh. "They've got lawyers, guns, and money. We've got squat plus zilch."

Nighthawk began to laugh now too. "They don't stand a fucking chance," he said.

Kurt wiped at his eye with a finger, trying to get control of himself. Trying to wrap his mind around this whole ludicrous situation, the sixty-forty algebra of murder. Something besides the math wasn't adding up.

"I'm hearing a little voice in the back of my head, Jesse. A little voice that's wondering what's in this for you," he said. "SPIRITT let you go, so there's no use pretending you're winning one for the brothers. Who are you doing this for?"

Nighthawk stood up and tossed the rock on a mess of shipping papers. The surface of the desk was so cluttered with photo contact sheets and scribbled notes it would take another geologist to find that chunk of ore again. He began to rummage through the chaos, searching for something, and worked his way slowly around the desk to the drawers.

"I'm in it for the same reason you are, Muller," he said, reaching down for the drawer handle.

"Don't do it, Jesse," Kurt said, unholstering the .45 under his jacket.

Nighthawk stared at the gun. "There's something I want to show you," he said, his hand slowly disappearing behind the desk.

Kurt cocked the hammer. "Raise your hands where I can see them and step away from the desk," he said. "I don't want this to get rude."

Nighthawk narrowed his eyes at him, stubbornly held his ground.

"Raise your hands, man. Do it now."

Slowly, reluctantly, the detective lifted his hands above his head. "You people have no honor," he said bitterly.

Brandishing the pistol, Kurt walked around the desk and glanced at the rust-pocked drawer.

"There's something I wanted to show you, asshole," Nighthawk said. "I think it's probably in the top left-hand side. Open it yourself."

Kurt stared at the drawer. A trip-wired latch was the oldest trick in the book. J.J. Chilcutt would have rigged it to blow off an intruder's hand. Maybe Jesse Nighthawk possessed those same perverse skills.

"Step out of the way," Kurt said, and Nighthawk did so with a disgusted shake of the head. Kurt knelt down and searched for loose wires, metal tubing, anything out of the ordinary. "Okay," he said, standing, backing away several steps, the gun still in his hand. "Go ahead and open it."

Nighthawk hesitated, his mouth forming a wicked smile.

"Open it, Jesse. Show me what you want to show me. Let's see what you've got in there."

Nighthawk lowered his hands. "I'm not sure you can handle this, Muller," he said, his smile turning darker.

Kurt shrugged. "Then don't waste my time, man."

Nighthawk stepped forward and opened the drawer. When nothing happened, he glared at Kurt with up-turned palms, like a magician after a coin trick. "You look a little nervous, hoss," he said. "Did you expect a rattlesnake?"

Kurt glanced in the drawer. More receipts, invoices, scraps of paper.

"With your permission," Nighthawk said with a sar-castic nod.

"Go real slow."

It didn't take him long to find the object. A six-by-nine photograph in a bronze frame. He handed the glass-encased picture to Kurt. "Don't drop it," he said. "It's my only one."

Kurt recognized her instantly. Marie Carr was smil-ing at the camera, holding her baby swaddled in a crib blanket. And looming behind her, his arms around both mother and child, an ageless Jesse Nighthawk.

Heat rushed up the back of Kurt's neck. "My god," he said, laying his gun on the desk.

"Like I told you, I'm in this for the same reason you are," he grinned sheepishly. "For the boy."

Jesse Nighthawk was Hunter's father. Kurt sank

down on the green vinyl cushion of an old slat-backed office chair and gazed at the photograph in his hands. "You and Marie," he said, hearing the astonishment in his voice.

Nighthawk nodded. "We got to know each other when I was working the mines with Ned," he said. "The old man eventually found out about us and chased my ass off with a shotgun. But Marie and me saddled up every once in a while, whenever we crossed paths and the spirit moved us. She claimed the pregnancy was an accident, but I knew better. She was thirty-eight and running out of biology."

Kurt was surprised at himself for the sudden protectiveness he felt toward Marie and her son. "Where were you during the shitwork, man? My ex-wife stood by her through the birth," he said. "You never came around after Hunter was born."

He was beginning to sound like an angry brother.

"I came around," Nighthawk said firmly. "I walked the floor with that child when he had colic. I changed his diapers and rocked him to sleep chanting the old songs of the Bear Dance. Come daybreak I was always gone. It worked out better that way."

Kurt placed the bronze frame upright on the desk. "Hunter needed a father who was there for him. Especially after Marie was killed."

Nighthawk peered down at him, his small dark eyes set fiercely above the crooked septum. "That pretty lady you saw out in the gallery is my daughter, Muller," he said. "I've got three of them, all grown up now, on their own. Me and their mother have been trying to stay married for thirty years and believe me, it's been a dogfight. I've done near everything a bad drunk could do to ruin that poor woman's life. But things have been fairly decent between us for the past three or four years and I don't want to hurt her anymore. If she knew I'd sired a son with a white woman, her and the girls would hang my nuts from a tepee pole. Which is why this information will not leave the room."

Kurt had no intention of telling anyone about this. "Did Ned know you were Hunter's father?"

Nighthawk nodded. "Marie must have told him," he said. "That's why he got in touch with me, I suppose. He knew how much I cared about his daughter. And our son."

He explained that Ned had asked him to look after the boy's interest in the shit storm that was coming, to find somebody worthy and reliable who was experienced in mine management and who wouldn't be intimidated by Ned's other partners.

"When I told him about SPIRITT he nearly busted a gut laughing. He thought it was the greatest idea he'd ever heard. Indians running a mine in Aspen."

"Did he say why he was pissed at his partners?"

"He thought they'd double-crossed him. The way it shook out, he'd gone to Metcalf for legal help and ended up giving them a piece of his action as a loan payback. He didn't count on them bringing in a big South African corporation to run their end of the business. You know Ned. He didn't trust foreigners and he didn't like committees and corporate boards and he sure as hell didn't want anybody telling him how to mine."

"And you think Metcalf had Ned killed because it looked like he was going to sabotage their deal?"

Nighthawk nodded again. "He went right ahead and

told Metcalf he was bringing in SPIRITT to manage Hunter's majority share. Fucking lawyer must've filled his shorts every time he pictured a bunch of wild-eyed Indians dancing around his precious platinum strike. Wasn't exactly what he had in mind."

A phone rang somewhere under the mounds of paperwork. Nighthawk glanced at his watch. Before he could find the knob to the answering machine, a female voice began speaking: "Hello, Jesse, I'm here at the airport and—"

Shuffling aside lading bills, he finally located the volume switch and killed the voice. "I've got someone in my office," he said into the phone receiver. "Can you call back in ten minutes?"

Though Kurt had heard only a few words, the voice sounded familiar. Did he know the speaker?

"Yeah, fine," Nighthawk said, listening to the line. "Good. Ten minutes."

He hung up and checked his watch again. "You gonna shoot me," he asked, pointing at the .45 on the desk, "or can I get back to work now? My youngest is still in college and I've got bills to pay."

Kurt stood up and holstered the pistol. "Sounds like you're a busy man," he said. "Do all your clients fly in to see you?"

"Only the rich ranch wives who think their husbands are down here sleeping with Mexican girls."

He led Kurt through the darkroom and workshop back into the white-walled gallery, where he introduced his daughter as a grad student in art history at the University of Arizona. The young woman showed less animosity when she learned that Kurt was the sheriff of

Pitkin County and not some scumbag wife beater buying motel photographs from her father.

The two men stepped out onto the sidewalk in front of the gallery. "How's all this going to play out, Jesse?" Kurt asked.

"You tell me," Nighthawk said. "You're the cop. I'm just a blood with some snapshots in a can."

Kurt thought about Bill Gillespie. If they could sweat him out, this prom was over.

He slipped on his sunglasses. "Be seeing you, Jesse. Come visit your son," he said in a quiet voice, "before Nate Carr shows up and takes him back to Seattle."

Nighthawk looked stunned. The way he must've looked thirty seconds after his nose was broken.

"Nothing I can do about it," Kurt said. "It's in the will. Ned wanted Hunter to live with Marie's brother."

The man's face had collapsed. He was devastated by the news. "Seattle?" he said weakly, his stricken expression showing the true measure of his feeling for the boy.

Kurt reached in his jacket for the department evidence Baggie he had brought with him. "Here," he said, emptying out the eagle-bone choker. "I believe this is yours."

Nighthawk held the choker in his hand, absently fingering the beads, his thoughts distant and troubled. He seemed neither surprised nor especially grateful for the return.

"You're his father, Jesse. Show the boy you love him," Kurt said, "before he's gone for good."

He rambled off down the sidewalk with his hands in his pockets and an inexplicable anger welling in his chest. He was three blocks away, standing in front of an old-time hobby shop, studying the model airplanes behind the plate-glass window, when he realized how much he missed his own father. How much he missed those things that had vanished from his life forever.

42

KURT SAT NURSING an iced tea in a crowded sidewalk café across the street from the gallery. His table was shielded from public view by a boisterous kayak club from Farmington, New Mexico. It was a good place to watch the entrance to the gallery, the only way in and out, if his observation was correct. The woman's phone call had made Jesse more nervous than he ought to have been. Kurt was still struggling to place that voice when a taxi rolled up to the curb, the same model of mellow-yellow Suburban from the early '80s that had been a popular cab in Aspen during the funkier years. *So this is where all those junkers went,* he thought, leaning forward to see who would step out of the passenger door. The taxi pulled away, leaving a woman standing alone on the sidewalk. She was wearing tight-fitting jeans, a faded denim jacket, designer cowgirl boots. One of the young kayakers at the next table noticed her and whistled, stirring some attention. She turned and smiled appreciatively, giving him a coy wave before slinging a canvas tote bag over one shoulder and striding for the gallery door. Though she had tried to disguise herself with oversized sunglasses and a Dallas Cowboys cap tucked low on her forehead, it was impossible to conceal that remarkable smile, still melting boyish hearts after all these years. This woman wasn't a ranch wife here to expose an infidelity. Jesse had lied again. It was Meredith Stone.

Kurt wondered how these two had come together. Had Meredith hired him to take photographs in Colorado Springs, her own private attempt at surveillance of the Free West antigreens? Or was she using him for some darker purpose?

Nearly an hour later the gallery door opened and two figures shuffled into the sunlight. Nighthawk was carrying a gym bag. He took Meredith's arm and escorted her across the street to a narrow parking lot wedged between two buildings. They stopped to talk to the Latino attendant and then disappeared from view. Kurt dropped bills on the table and hurried to his rental Jeep a half block away.

He had no problem picking up the tan Wrangler as it swerved out of the lot and cruised down Main Street, retracing the same route Kurt had taken from the airport. Soon they were speeding along out in the scrub-brush desert, veering off toward the small terminal shimmering in the midday heat. He suspected that Meredith had flown here in Lee Lamar's personal Lear, and that she was transporting Jesse back to Aspen with her.

The Wrangler entered a gate leading to the hangar where private aircraft were serviced, a prominent sign warning AUTHORIZED VEHICLES ONLY. Kurt lagged behind and returned the Jeep to its rental space in an adjacent lot. He found Wing Taylor polishing off his third beer at a hot dog counter, flirting with the Native American girl forking wieners on a grill. By the time the two men had boarded the Turbo Commander with traffic-control permission to fly, Meredith's jet was already airborne.

"I'll find out where they're headed," Wing said, flipping switches, the engines kicking on with a shuddering roar. His face was flushed from the expectation of a chase.

"My guess is back to Aspen."

"Let me confirm that."

He grabbed the mike and contacted the tower. Kurt was confused when he learned the Lear's destination. He thought perhaps there was a mixup in transmission and asked the pilot to double check, but Wing's old buddy in the tower repeated the information with absolute certainty. The Lamar Learjet was on its way to Las Vegas.

43

WING HAD THEM on the ground in less than two hours. As they taxied toward the hangar, heat wavered off the desert floor like gasoline fumes, a glaring white afternoon in the early days of a Nevada summer. To the south and west, flintlike ridges jagged the horizon, barren mountains hewed out of hard stone.

"They're here," Wing said, pointing toward a row of private planes where the Lamar Lear was being refueled. When Kurt didn't respond he said, "You all right, son? You look a little peaked."

For the duration of the flight Kurt had felt weak and somewhat disoriented. Now his wounded arm ached from wrist to shoulder and his head began to spin when he unfastened his seat belt and tried to stand up. Wing gripped him around the waist and walked him over to a passenger seat.

"You better rest a spell," the old pilot said, helping him sit down. "I don't like the way you're acting. Might have a touch of air sickness."

Kurt closed his eyes and immediately blanked out, then jerked awake, gazing around the plane, staring at the man beside him, trying to remember where he was.

He checked his watch and saw that it was almost three o'clock.

"We need to get some water in you," Wing said. "You're probably dehydrated."

Kurt's head was filled with cotton. "Let's go see why we're here," he said.

In the hangar they stopped at a maintenance crew's water cooler and Kurt drank until a cold shiver coursed through his body. He knew he had a low-grade fever but he couldn't let it slow him down.

"How the hell you going to find them?" Wing asked, watching him guzzle another paper cup of water. "They could be holed up in a hotel room making whoopee for three days."

"I'll find them," Kurt said.

In the passenger terminal hordes of shaggy young people wearing tie-dyed T-shirts and tattered jeans were milling about with backpacks humped over their shoulders, and in his feverish state Kurt wondered if he'd stepped through a time warp, or was having an acid flashback, until two impish girls with rings in their eyebrows asked if he had a car and he learned they were all in town for a Pearl Jam concert. Finding his way to a telephone was like a walkabout in a Bedouin camp, clusters of ragtag worshipers huddled on the ground around their meager possessions, chanting the music of some arcane tribal rite, waiting for the miraculous. Up the stairs in a mezzanine area, polyester retirees were emptying their last change into the slots and video poker machines, one final spasm of hope before boarding their planes back to the ranch-styles. Kurt stuck a finger in his ear and dialed long distance to Miles Cunningham's cabin. Watching an elderly lady in a bad blond wig dump coin after coin into the same slot, he realized he was no different from her, another fool in Vegas playing the long odds, stacking all his chips on one big pass. If he didn't make contact with Miles, Kurt knew he might have to cut his losses and join the lines of disappointed seniors on the next ride out.

The answering machine played its usual recording, a piece of the Nixon resignation speech. After the beep Kurt began to babble, making no sense even to himself, eventually demanding that Miles inform the Pitkin County Sheriff's Department of his whereabouts. He was halfway through his parting string of expletives when a voice interrupted him.

"Jesus, Muller, get a grip. Next time try the decaf."

"Miles, you asshole, I need some information. I'm in Las Vegas tailing Meredith Stone."

"Nice assignment. Say hello to Jimmy Hoffa for me. Last time I saw him he was swimming in the foundation of the Tropicana."

Kurt sighed. The dinging noise from the slot machines was driving him mad, the trapped air smelled like hair spray and cigarettes, and he was sweating through his cotton sport jacket. "Listen, man," he said, "I'm in no mood for bullshit. I know you and Kat split up in Utah. Did she come to Vegas? Is that why Meredith is here?"

A long pause, the hum of telephone wire. "Meredith is worried about her," Miles said. "Guilt trip over the break-in. She knows somebody's trying to kill Kat, so she hired a private dick to help find her. Wants to set the girl up in a safe little condo in Malibu. Ahh, the rich are different from you and me."

"What happened in Utah?"

"She's wired tight, Kurt. I've never seen her like that," Miles said with unexpected concern. "The crazy woman stole my Land-Rover while I was asleep and left me to die among Mormons."

"Why did she leave?"

"We had a fight. She wanted to go through Vegas and stir some shit at the Free West convention, but I said no way. I didn't want her anywhere near those swine. They're the ones trying to blow her away."

A Free West convention in Las Vegas. Of course.

"There's dynamite in the Rover, Kurt. Plus two handguns and her hunting rifle."

"Jesus Christ," he said, blowing out a weary lungful of air.

"She was seriously pissed about what happened to Randy. And speed-rapping about her dead husband. I didn't like the look in her eye. Tombstones and *calaveras,* man. The chick was beginning to scare me."

"Where is the convention?"

"The Sahara," Miles said. "Same place they have the *Soldier of Fortune* bash every year."

"Meredith is there looking for her?"

"With the gumshoe. Some big Indian dude. Things could get gnarly."

Kurt knew what was different about this conversation. It was late afternoon and Miles Cunningham sounded stone-cold sober. "Okay, man. Thanks," he said. "I'll go get Kat out of there."

"Kurt," Miles said, holding him on the line for one last word. "Katrina is tribe. *La gente.* Don't let anything else happen to her. The shitbirds have already pecked a large hole in her life. That's got to stop."

44

As HIS TAXI approached the Sahara Hotel at the north end of the Strip, Kurt counted a half-dozen people suspended from ropes on the outer wall of the aging edifice, making their way down from the rooftop to the pool area ten stories below. He thought perhaps they were window washers engaged in a marathon cleaning effort until the driver laughed and said, "Look at those maniacs! Bunch of badasses called the Green Briars. It's their protest against the convention. The cops and firemen are waiting for them with a big butterfly net."

The driver stopped his cab in the parking lot behind a phalanx of police cars. "Sorry, buddy," he said. "This is as close as I'm getting. These people are gonna kill each other."

Outside the main entrance to the hotel, a scuffle had broken out between a band of protesters and some good old boys wearing gimme caps. The police were dragging people apart, leading away one disorderly bush hippie in handcuffs, a stout, bearded man Kurt recognized as the volatile founder of the Green Briars. The two sides were shouting at each other, exchanging insults. Uniformed VIProtex security guards had formed a column at the lobby doors and were trying to contain the angry Free West mob inside the building. Kurt walked over to search for Meredith and Jesse Nighthawk among the placard-wielding greens. There were at least two dozen of them, and except for the graying hair and more sensible footwear, these protesters had the anger and narrow-eyed intensity of another era, an earlier movement.

"Is Meredith Stone here?" he asked a gaunt middle-aged woman with a salt-and-pepper braid down her back.

"Meredith Stone the singer?" the woman smirked, bending over to retrieve a mangled sign that said EVERY-BODY LIVES DOWNSTREAM. "You must be lost, man. The concert's out at the stadium."

"I'm an old friend of hers from Aspen," he said, raising his voice to be heard above the din. "I was supposed to meet her here today."

"Try the piano bar at the Sands," she said, stumbling backward as the police and security guards began forcing their group farther away from the lobby doors.

"How about Katrina Pfeil? Have you seen her around?"

The woman gave him a quick, suspicious look. "You some kind of undercover cop, mister?"

"Sheriff in Aspen."

Her eyes wandered over him, then toward the policemen barking orders. "I've heard the Aspen sheriff is one of the good guys," she said. "Why don't you tell your cop brothers to lighten up?"

Kurt was shoved in the back. "Keep moving, pal," the VIProtex guard told him. "Out to the sidewalk. This is private hotel property here."

Kurt spun around and faced the tall guard, nose to nose. The fever had put him in a foul mood. "Go ahead and push me again, asshole," he said, ready to believe that this pencil-necked rent-a-cop was one of the Night Clubbers who had firebombed the Pfeil cabin.

The woman with the braid grabbed his arm and pulled him along. "Chill out, Aspen Sheriff," she said. "Not used to taking orders, are you?"

Reluctantly he retreated across the parking lot with the protesters. A beer bottle splattered near them, hurled from a passing van. In spite of police containment, more conventioneers had spilled out of the lobby and were screaming threats. A green with a bloody lip strode out to challenge somebody to a fistfight, but three comrades rushed over to restrain him.

The woman was still clutching Kurt's arm. "You asked about Meredith Stone," she said, watching her friends guide the angry man back to the sidewalk. "She's probably in the hotel. I talked to her about an hour ago and she was going in to check out the convention."

"Thanks," Kurt said. "If you see her or Kat Pfeil, tell them I'm here looking for them."

HE ANGLED BACK through rows of parked automobiles to the rear entrance of the Sahara, where passengers were disembarking from a chartered bus. Not eager to draw attention to himself, he slipped into the line filing into the hotel. "Here for the convention?" he asked the young man walking next to him.

"They give us the day off, full pay, to come on this trip," the boy grinned, his bottom lip fat with Skoal.

"The whole plant shut down just so's they'd have some warm bodies here. Tell you the truth, I don't even know what it's all about. But who's gonna bitch? Las Vegas beats the hell out of hauling ore on a hot day in Elko."

"You drive a truck for the mine up there?"

"Not today I don't. No siree. Today I play blackjack till I bust the house."

Standing at the registration tables in the lobby, watching the participants mill about, Kurt thought at first that it was a Monster Wheels trade show. He had never seen so many spit cups and teased-up bottle blondes in one location. The information packet was crammed with schedules, exhibit maps, association newsletters, advertisements for recreational vehicles and hunting gear. Kurt flipped through the pages, boning up on what to expect from this gathering. He learned from the official program that Arnold Metcalf would be the guest of honor at the Free West banquet this evening, the recipient of a lifetime achievement award presented by a Republican congressman from Arizona. Kurt was about to dump the entire folder into a casino trash can when he noticed something out of place among the glossy materials, a sheet of plain white paper bearing the photocopied photograph of a smiling Arnold Metcalf shaking hands with the controversial cult leader Father Ke. He stopped and studied the flyer. The hand-lettered inscription read, *Why are these men smiling? Because they're getting away with investing your money and your cause in a cult religion. Ask Arnold Metcalf why he and Father Ke are such good friends.*

"Your Green Briar pals must be wetting themselves with delight."

Neal Staggs had appeared suddenly out of the stream

of passersby. Wearing a dark Brooks Brothers suit and striped tie, the formal persona he'd always projected as the FBI special agent assigned to Aspen, he looked conspicuously overdressed in this assembly. "When you find out how they were able to tamper with the packets," he said, eyeing the flyer in Kurt's hand, "please pass on my professional admiration. I respect anyone who is deft at dirty tricks."

Sooner or later Kurt was going to put this man away. His people had blown up Ned Carr, shot Tyler Rutledge, and left a gaping hole in Randy's neck. J.J. Chilcutt may not have done the work alone, but Staggs knew every name involved. He had no doubt awarded the contracts.

"It isn't looking good for you and your goons, Staggs. Last night we busted Bill Gillespie at the hospital. We've got him on tape."

Staggs smiled arrogantly. "Am I supposed to know who that is?"

"My guess is Gillespie will spill his guts to save his own worthless ass. Better find yourself a good lawyer. A smarter one than Arnold Metcalf."

He could see the hatred manifest itself in Staggs's eyes, a dark fury as cold and deadly as the glow from a black star. He was a social architect with uncompromising convictions and an immutable blueprint for the way things ought to proceed, and Kurt Muller had spilled large stains on his designs. First a year ago, and now this inconvenience.

"I know about the Night Clubbers, Staggs, and how your company is using them to bash the greens." Kurt reached into his pocket. "Here's a quarter," he said, the silver coin pinched between his fingers. "Call the home office and tell them it's over. Tell them somebody on their payroll is going to jail. Maybe the new branch chief at the Aspen desk."

Staggs's false smile flattened into a sneer. "You have an inflated view of your talents, Muller," he said. "You need to come back down to earth. These allegations are getting wildly out of hand."

Kurt tugged at the discreet badge on Staggs's lapel. *Convention Security.* "This VIProtex gig was a natural for an old spook like you, wasn't it, pal? The world of karma according to Neal Staggs. You couldn't get at them last time around, with all those Bureau regs and oversight committees, so you're getting at them now. The maggots under every rock."

"Let's just say I enjoy my work," Staggs said. "Like your girlfriend enjoys hers." He plucked the flyer from Kurt's hand. "Is Miss Pfeil here today?" He glanced at the picture of Metcalf and Father Ke, then smiled ominously at Kurt. "I certainly hope so. I've heard so much about her. I look forward to making her acquaintance."

"If anything happens to her," Kurt said, "I'm coming after you, Staggs. Personally."

With a slow one-handed clutch Staggs wadded the flyer into a tight ball. "This is no time to lose control of your emotions, my friend," he said. "If I remember my own fieldwork correctly, this is the part of the climb where the footing gets treacherous and a man has to be very careful. One false step and you're sliding face first down nine hundred feet of rock. And you know what a mess that can be."

The reference to Bert's death provoked the inner rage Staggs had intended, but Kurt composed a calm smile. "Have a good time at the tables, Staggs. Spend your money while you still have it." He watched mom-and-pop gamblers waltz out of the casino and crowd onto an escalator. "The take-home pay won't be as good at Leavenworth."

Staggs's eyes shifted right, then left, determining if anyone was close enough to hear him. He leaned forward, leading with his chin, and spoke softly. "What makes you think you've got anything on me, cowboy?"

Kurt took a step closer, erasing the comfort zone between them. "Bill Gillespie," he mock-whispered.

Staggs laughed, a tight clucking sound. He reached in his trousers, rattling change. "Here's a quarter," he said, flipping a coin that bounced off Kurt's chest and fell to the carpet. "Call your office. You haven't checked in lately."

What the hell was he talking about?

"Enjoy the convention, Muller. If you see Miss Pfeil before I do, tell her I hope we'll get together someday soon. Her limp intrigues me."

As swiftly as he had appeared, Neal Staggs was gone, riding up the escalator with two VIProtex guards and the crush of conventioneers. Kurt walked over to the pay phones and called the Pitkin County Sheriff's Department.

"Where are you, Kurt?" Muffin said in a shrill voice. "We've been looking all over the county for you. Gillespie's dead."

He didn't believe her. It wasn't possible.

Stretching out the metal phone cord, he looked quickly up the escalator. Staggs was near the top now, smiling down at him with a smug, victorious contempt.

"Looks like he ingested something and took his own life. The medical examiner is with the body. He'll have a prelim soon and we should know if the substance is an easy trace. Jesus, Kurt. This is fucked."

"How did it happen, Muffin?" he asked, struggling to control his temper.

"I don't know. We searched him head to toe before we booked him. We searched the lawyer when he came in at noon. Maybe there was something sewn in his pants."

Kurt knew that the police searches would make it impossible for the DA to prove culpability of any sort.

"This is going to damage the department big time, Kurt," she said. "I would appreciate it if you'd come in and lend a hand. The press is already lining up in the hall with gym paddles."

"Don't beat yourself up. Gillespie was somebody's hired soldier. He did what he had to do. I doubt if anybody could've stopped him."

"This case is slipping away from us, Kurt. Without Gillespie we've got nothing."

"Hang in there," he said. "I'll be back as soon as I find Kat Pfeil. Don't release a statement to the media until I look it over."

"Where are you?" she asked. "I hear a lot of background noise."

"Vegas," he said. "Free West is having a convention here."

A long silence. He thought she might have hung up. "Book the Peter Lawford suite at the Flamingo," she said finally. "The green goddess will appreciate the walk-down tub."

He groaned impatiently, feeling his warm forehead with the back of his hand. "Make sure you double the security around Hunter," he said. "These people mean serious business."

The line crackled from her erratic breathing. "Done," she said. "And Kurt . . ."

He waited.

"Ignore that remark. You know I didn't mean anything by it. It's just cop talk."

"Muffin."

"Yeah?"

"Don't lose any more suspects while I'm gone."

He followed the crowds up the escalator to the second floor. He knew it wouldn't be easy finding Kat in this madhouse, but he had to get to her before Staggs did.

The banner above the entrance to the Sahara's exhibit hall said WELCOME TO THE REBELLION. Inside the grand space, scores of Free West supporters ambled past product displays and partitioned booths where industry associations had set up shop, a clamorous medina of professional lobbyists whose logos brazenly declared them defenders, advocates, alliances, policy projects, research centers, bureaus, institutes, federations, foundations, committees, councils, conferences, societies, coalitions, alerts, and citizens for. Though Free West affected the appearance of a spreading, uncontainable grass-roots movement, Kurt could think of no other cause that had sprung to life virtually overnight with well-paid staffs, comfortable tower suites, and fat expense accounts bankrolled by corporate sugar daddies. As he ventured down the exhibition lanes, the noise and pageantry and sheer volume of information had a dizzying, hallucinatory effect on him. He felt like a man who had lost his way through some strange, chimerical theme park whose purpose was as vague and elusive as a fever dream.

To demonstrate their latest models, chainsaw manufacturers had hired flannel-shirted woodsmen to gnaw apart heavy redwood logs, and a sweet cloud of sawdust filled the air. Across the aisle, members of a group called the Timber Defense were handing out complimentary rolls of paper towels and bumper stickers that said HUNGRY AND OUT OF WORK? ROADKILL AN ENVIRONMENTALIST and EAT MORE SPOTTED OWL. Farther along, a farm-equipment salesman dressed in *Hee Haw* overalls invited Kurt to inspect his new line of tractors. "Hey there, cousin, come on in and crank these babies up!" Sequined showgirls with clipboards pressed to their ample bosoms surrounded Kurt quickly, soliciting his signature. When he stopped to thumb through the petitions—for lower grazing fees, a moratorium on endangered species, a ban on wolf reintroduction—he noticed the two VIProtex guards he had seen on the escalator with Staggs. They were following him.

In the next lane, eager trail-machine reps waved him over to climb aboard their ATVs, dirt bikes, and off-road minitrucks. "How you fixed for the outback, partner? Set your tail down in this four-wheeler and see how she suits you!" Three desert rats wearing Autobahn Society patches on their cammo jackets were fondling shiny handlebars with lust in their eyes, but Kurt didn't recognize any of them from the Black Diamond.

His head was burning, his arm had begun to throb, and he moved on in a feeble delirium, hoping to spot Kat Pfeil before he keeled over. The guards were still tailing him, making no effort to conceal their surveillance. As soon as he grabbed her he was leaving this place. Even if he had to throw her over his shoulder and run for it.

Suddenly there was a loud disturbance in another lane, a volley of shouted insults, and Kurt thought he recognized Kat's voice rising in anger. He trotted over to discover four beefy security guards wrestling a woman to the floor. "Leave her alone!" he said, rushing to her defense, pulling a guard off the squirming pile of limbs.

He was seized from behind, a forceful grip on his aching arm. "Don't be a problem, man," said one of the men who had been trailing him.

Kurt saw now that the woman wasn't Kat Pfeil but a protester who had infiltrated the convention with an armload of Green Briar leaflets, which were scattered about the floor like parade litter. Within seconds she was handcuffed and whisked toward an emergency exit.

"Be nice," said the second guard, the crew-cut little bull from the Aspen office. "You don't want to get dragged ass-end through the hotel like that chick, do you, ace?"

Kurt watched the guards hustle the woman through the exit door. "You boys are real heroes when the odds are four to one," he said, shaking himself loose.

"You wanna be a hero today?"

Kurt gazed around at the exhibits. "I'm just another curious citizen here for the hayride," he said. "You got a problem with that?"

"I got a problem with troublemakers," said the little bull. "They step out of line, I come down hard. Think about it, mister."

"Tell you what, junior. You decide to come down on

me, you better go find your daddy and all his friends. It's going to take more than four."

He nudged the guard aside and walked away. He'd had enough of this place and needed to sit down in a quiet corner, check his bandage, absorb some liquids, lower his body temperature. In his own twisted way Staggs had been right: Kurt had to get control of himself. Otherwise he was powerless to help Kat.

He roamed past an astonishing display of hunting rifles and skinning knives, and picked up a brochure about the Second Amendment from an NRA volunteer. Near an array of state-of-the-art, stainless-steel animal traps a knot of people had gathered around the Arizona congressman scheduled to present Arnold Metcalf with the achievement award. Short, stocky, jowl faced at forty, a thatch of thin blond hair combed across his pink scalp, the congressman was addressing the network news cameras, explaining his bill to abolish all federal environmental regulations. "We've got to place environmental responsibility in the hands of each state," he was saying as Kurt approached the back of the crowd. "Does some bean counter in Washington know what's best for the ranchers in my state or the rice growers in the Louisiana wetlands? I don't think so. The bureaucrats ought to stay out of our business and let the people of Arizona and Oregon and Colorado judge what works best for them!"

The only person not applauding was a tall, good-looking woman wearing a Dallas Cowboys cap and dark glasses. If Kurt hadn't seen her a few hours ago in Durango, he wouldn't have recognized Meredith Stone. She was standing behind the camera crew's light man, listening to the speech with hardened detachment. He surveyed the surrounding faces but didn't find Jesse Nighthawk among them.

Skirting the crowd, he slipped up behind Meredith and spoke over her shoulder. "You're pretty far out of your pond here, aren't you, my friend?"

"Kurt!" she said with surprise. "What the hell are you doing here?"

"Don't look at me when you speak. I'm being followed."

"Join the club," she said, nodding over at a VIPro guard feigning interest in starlight scopes and ultraviolet tracer powders.

Kurt saw his own pair circling the audience like sniffing hounds. "I talked to Miles. I know why you're here. Have you seen Kat?"

"No," she said, "and we've been up and down every row for an hour. I don't think she's in the hall."

"We can't let Staggs get his hands on her. She's pretty high up on their hit parade. If his boys pick her up we'll never see her again."

Meredith exhaled nervously. "Miles says she's loaded for bear. That scares me about her, Kurt. She seems like such a sensible girl. I can't imagine her with a bomb. What's she planning to *do*?"

"Let's not wait to find out. Where's Jesse?"

She looked back down the aisle past the gun displays. "We split up. He thought we could cover more ground that way," she said. "Are you all right, Kurt? You look . . . ill."

"I need some fresh air. This room is closing in on me," he said. "Where can we touch base if one of us finds Kat?"

"Lee has a suite at Caesars. Leave a message on our voice mail. Every hour on the hour."

They remained in the crowd without speaking for several moments longer, listening to the Arizona congressman field a soft question from a news reporter. *Is this the kind of turnout you expected, Congressman?*

"What are you going to do if you find her and she won't cooperate?" Kurt asked finally. "If she won't leave the building."

Meredith raised and lowered the bill of the Cowboys cap, airing out her hair. "That's what I've hired Jesse for," she said.

45

SMOKERS IDLED ABOUT the mezzanine, lanky men with crests of oiled hair, women in pastel pantsuits, and the air engulfing them was as thick and gray as a sweat lodge. He looked back to see if the VIProtex guards had followed him out of the hall, but there was no sign of them.

Kurt bought a soft drink at the cash bar and wandered down a corridor to find a quiet, out-of-the-way place to sit and ponder his next move. The first two doors he tried were locked. Toward the far end of the hallway a service entrance opened onto a stately banquet room, the lighting low and nocturnal over an elaborate arrangement of white tablecloths, drinking goblets, and fine silver. Twilight dimmed the arched glass panel behind the podium and stage, deep shadows gathering for the desert night. He could hear muted preparatory kitchenwork beyond the walls, but the room itself was as quiet as a chapel. He ventured down an aisle toward the podium and took a seat at a table set for ten. Stiff name cards positioned guests, listed their affiliations. *Ron Askew, Citizens for Abundant Game, Pocatello ID. Candy Tetlow, Alliance for Property Rights,*

Bellevue WA. A banner draped over the podium ex-
claimed FREE WEST, FREE FUTURE. This was where the
awards ceremony would take place. Kurt closed his eyes
and sipped the iced drink, a quick shiver racing
through him. This was where Arnold Metcalf would
receive a little gold plaque for founding a movement
that strove to turn back the clock twenty-five years and
eliminate any opposition in its way. That the bastard
had also eliminated salt-of-the-earth friends like Ned
Carr, when they refused to march in step, was appar-
ently of no consequence to Metcalf's political promot-
ers.

Kurt reached into his jacket pocket for the flyer he
had retrieved from the convention floor. It showed the
same picture he'd first seen in Nighthawk's darkroom,
Metcalf and the gentleman in the natty hat. The caption
read, *Ask Arnold Metcalf why he plays golf with the South
African mining industry. Foreigners like this man (right)
control 15 of the 25 largest gold mines in the U.S., most of
them on our public lands, royalty free.* Add a platinum
mine to that stat, he thought, wondering how the conventioneers, solid America-first patriots to a person,
would view all this foreign involvement. Had any of
them seen the photo of Metcalf shaking hands with the
fanatical Father Ke?

Near the podium there was a large oil painting
propped on an easel, the kind of popular western scene
Kurt had observed in Metcalf's law suites, a wagon
train circled for battle, pioneers firing rifles at ma-
rauding Indians on horseback. Something to auction
off during the banquet, or perhaps a door prize. *Most
environmentalists bagged this season.* When the red dot
appeared, he thought his eyes were playing tricks on

him. Then the dot moved, dancing across the canvas, fluttering like a firefly, settling lightly before flittering away. Kurt stood up and approached the stage. The red dot was not an hallucination. He watched it resurface on the podium and quiver around the dull metal mouthpiece of the microphone, finding its resting place at last. A small steady point of red light fixed where a man would stand and speak. Where the back of his head was exposed to the arched window.

Kurt edged along the carpeted stage and hid himself beside the curtain pulled back from the vaulting panel of glass. Below in the parking lot, another busload of people was emptying into the Sahara's rear lobby. VIProtex guards patrolled the area, directing foot traffic. There was a new construction under way less than a hundred yards from the hotel, an imposing gray concrete structure that looked like a multilevel parking garage. A cement mixer and other heavy machines were parked in a fenced-off site next to a trailer, but dusk had fallen and the work crews were gone. He looked again at the podium and watched the red dot jitter for one final moment and then disappear. Gazing out through the glass he tried to calculate her angle of sight. She was stationed on the second or third floor of that dark building. Hunkered down, scanning the stage, waiting for Arnold Metcalf with her laser scope.

46

THE PARKING GARAGE smelled of fresh paint and wet cement. He found the stairwell and slowly made his way up the steps of a vertical shaft as dark and claustrophobic as the Lone Ute Mine. The doors hadn't been hinged in place and a faint gray light seeped through the opening to the second floor. He stepped into the vast parking area and waited, his eyes struggling to focus beyond ten yards in the silent gloom. Paper cups and construction debris brushed underfoot as he walked to the retaining wall and peered over at the hotel, locating the arched window now blazing with light. Guests were arriving for the banquet. In a short while the master of ceremonies would mount the podium, welcome everyone, tell his lame jokes, introduce the guest of honor. *If I had a rifle where would I position myself?* From here it was a flat shot; a miss would bullet horizontally into a hundred innocent onlookers. *Get up higher,* he thought, *make sure the lead angles downward through his body to the carpet.*

At the doorway to the third level he stopped and drew a deep breath. The foundation wasn't entirely dry and the footing felt like packed wet beach sand. He could see where the pouring had ended, the open molds squared off, braced with steel rods, waiting for tomorrow's fill. Skirting along the retaining wall, he watched car lights swing in and out of the Sahara's loading zone below. When he came to the first support pillar he crouched down and steadied himself against the cool concrete column, considering whether to retrieve his .45 before proceeding ahead. Would she shoot him? Perhaps if he surprised her. Did he really know this woman? Not if she was capable of blowing somebody away with a sniper rifle. Cautiously, the breath burning in his lungs, he inclined his head out from the dusty pillar. A wire-thin stream of light was waiting for him, imprinting a red dot on his forehead like an Indian's Bindu point.

"I saw you at the window," she said, her voice a haunting echo in the vacant garage. "I wondered how long it would take you to find me."

As he rose slowly to full height, the laser beam tracked his eyes. "You don't need the weapon," he said.

They were immersed in darkness. He could decipher only the barest outline of the nest she'd made for herself at the wall, an overturned wheelbarrow, sacks of cement, cardboard packing stacked precariously like a child's fort.

"Shooting him won't end it, Kat," he said. "Their movement is too big for a couple of bullets. Somebody else will step up and wave the saber."

"These people killed Randy," she said. "Someone down there paid for the pipe bomb that murdered my husband and daughter."

She was standing near the shell of an elevator shaft, a ghostly framework of exposed iron beams. "How do you know it was Metcalf?" he asked her. The only sure bet was that VIProtex had done the dirty work.

"Metcalf is a good place to start," she said.

He moved toward her, searching for her eyes in the dark. "So this is how you're going to spend the rest of your life, Kat? Sitting on a rooftop with a rifle in your hands? Revenge is hard work, my dear. The list is a mighty long one."

Her body was backlit by the hotel's phosphorescent glow. She switched off the laser and lowered the rifle to her waist. "What about you, Kurt? What if Lennon had burned to death in the fire?" she asked, her voice so calm it was beginning to spook him. "Here, take a look for yourself," she said, shoving the rifle against his chest. "It's an easy shot. You just set the dot on the back of his skull and squeeze the trigger, and there's one less dirty son of a bitch on the planet. Maybe it won't solve every problem, but like I said, it's a start. Maybe you'll get caught and maybe you won't. It doesn't make a fucking bit of difference," she said, her words cracking now in the eerie stillness. "Because your life hasn't meant a thing since the day you lost him."

Kurt tossed the rifle into the cardboard packing and reached for her hand in the dark. She seemed reluctant to accept his embrace, her body stiffening, the bulky parka like a barricade between them. "Easy," she said, pulling away, her gloved hands pressed against his chest.

"No one can take away your pain, Kat," he said, holding those hands with a firm grip. "They may never bring in the bomber who killed your husband. But if you come back to Aspen with me, help me make a case against VIProtex for Randy's death, the bastards will at least know they've been danced with."

He heard a shoe scrape somewhere in the darkness. The fever had dulled his reflexes and he was slow to reach for the pistol in his shoulder holster.

"I wouldn't do that if I was you," said a low grumbling voice.

A light flashed in his eyes, the harsh beam trained on him from the corner of the elevator shaft.

"We'll shoot your girlfriend first."

Other flashlights torched on, a strategic spread of positions. White rays danced over Kurt and Kat as the holders closed ranks around them.

"Drop your hand to your side or the bitch takes one in the tit."

Kurt slid his hand away from his jacket. He recognized the voice. He knew who these men were. Night Clubbers.

"You're a pretty decent tracker, Mr. Use-to-be. We never would've found her without you."

Cement dust swirled like trapped smoke in the long flashlight beams. Kurt could see the bandaged hand behind the speaker's glowing light.

"Let him leave," Kat said, separating from Kurt's side. "You're not after him."

"That's very sweet of you, kitty cat," the voice said. "But I'm afraid it's too late to cut your boyfriend loose."

Slow, calculating footsteps scuffed across the hardening concrete. The lights drew nearer, brighter.

"The cops are down there busting protesters," Kurt said, glancing over his shoulder. "Another busful of people just pulled into the parking lot. How you going to take us out of here, Chilcutt?"

The man laughed, a deep wheezing sound. "That's the beauty of it, Muller. We don't have to. There's a special grave reserved for you two lovebirds right over there," he said, shining the beam on the rebars criss-crossing an open floor mold. "It's an old Vegas tradition. Where do you think all the knocked-up showgirls are buried?"

Low, menacing laughter from the men behind the flashlights. They were close enough now for Kurt to make out their gun belts and the stripe down their uniform pants.

"So y'all are the brave boys who're doing all the killing?" Kat said with an uneasy smile. "Why don't you come a little closer so I can get a look at your faces?"

The semicircle of lights had tightened around them but her challenge produced an unexpected halt in their movement.

"Seeing our faces won't do you any good, little pussy. Your nine lives are up."

A daring smile brushed across Kat's lips. "You're not afraid to show me your face, are you, hero? I want to see what kind of man goes around firebombing children."

Her audacity ignited Chilcutt's temper and he swung around the corner beam of the elevator shaft, bulling forward through the darkness until he was only a few short steps away from her. Raising the light to his bearded face, he gave her a savage sneer. "Here I am, bitch," he said, pointing a pistol at her head. "This is the last face you're ever gonna remember."

"Put down the gun," Kurt said.

Chilcutt whipped his arm sideways, aiming the pistol at Kurt's face. "You're a dead man, Muller," he said. Hammers cocked all around them, one behind every flashlight. "Wait your turn."

Before Kurt went down he was going to put a round through Chilcutt's heart.

"Shooting somebody up close is a messy business, isn't it, hero?" Kat said, her face composed in a strange, fearless smile. "It's a whole lot easier leaving a package under the bed and reading about it in tomorrow's newspaper."

She unzipped her parka and spread the folds. Chilcutt recoiled a step, cocking his own trigger. Two sticks of dynamite were taped to her chest in a spiral of coils. "So what's your professional opinion of *my* package?" she said, fingering a pair of small wires on the detonator. "How much of this floor do you think I can take out if I touch these wires together?"

Flashlights fluttered wildly as the men scurried off in every direction.

"Come back here!" Chilcutt shouted, enraged by the insubordination. Quick footsteps were echoing in the distance.

"Don't do it, Kat," Kurt said.

"You better leave too," she said. "This is between me and the hero."

"I'm not going anywhere."

Chilcutt was alone now, his solitary beam exposing the device on Kat's chest. "You know what they always say. If you want something done," he said, raising the pistol to her head with an exasperated sigh.

"Go on, Kurt. Get out of here. You've got two boys to look after."

"No!" he said. "Both of you back off! It doesn't have to happen this way!"

In the instant Chilcutt shifted his eyes to Kurt, she grabbed the man's wrist and rammed her head against his sternum, forcing him backward in an off-balance stumble. They grappled each other like clumsy dancers, the flashlight strobing around them. The gun went off in a flash of fire.

"Noooo!" Kurt screamed, racing toward them. He tried to reach them but tripped over a sawhorse and fell to his knees.

For one final moment their tangled bodies struggled at the edge of the dark shaft. Then they spun and crashed through a lattice of thin brace-rods, plunging out of sight.

The explosion lit the garage, a fireball of intense heat whooshing upward, following the air shaft like a burning bubble. He could smell his own singed hair. Something collapsed, splattering concrete like mud, and he gazed up from the floor to see the shaft frame listing badly, the structure slowly caving in. Black smoke billowed through the hole, wafting over him in a space as dark as hell itself. He crawled forward on his belly, calling her name, but he knew it was too late. *Two boys to look after,* he told himself, remembering her words, burying his face in his hands. *Go on. Move! Get out of here before the whole building comes down on you.*

47

PEOPLE SWARMED THE parking area, hotel doormen and security guards and chartered bus riders from Kingman, all of them jabbering about the explosion and pointing upward at the smoke belching from the dark structure. Kurt could hear a siren in the distance. Someone rushed up to him and said, "Are you all right, mister? You look hurt." His jacket was still smoldering and his eyebrows were gone. When he touched his forehead, a lock of hair crumbled into crisp ash.

In the Sahara's lobby the crowds parted for him, onlookers grimacing in disbelief. His face felt sunburned and his throat was parched. He didn't want to see himself in a mirror. A hotel valet said, "You'd better sit down, sir. You're in shock. EMS is on the way."

When he stepped off the escalator on the second floor someone grabbed his arm and he pivoted, raising a fist.

"Hold on, hoss," said Jesse Nighthawk, his stunned expression revealing just how bad Kurt must have looked. "What happened? You're messed up."

Meredith was with him. "My god, Kurt, take off that

jacket!" she said, pulling at a ragged sleeve. "We heard the boom. What's going on?"

"Kat's dead," he told her. "Here." He slung off his jacket and unstrapped the shoulder holster, handing it to Nighthawk. "Get rid of this for me. If I'm wearing it, I'll use it."

Conventioneers loitering in the mezzanine hurried out of his way.

"What do you mean she's dead?" Meredith said behind him, her voice trilling nervously. "Where are you going, Kurt? You need a doctor."

The banquet had been disrupted by the explosion and dozens of name-tagged guests were roaming the corridor like dazed inmates in an asylum. Inside the dining hall a hundred people had gathered onstage, huddling near the arched window for a view of the fire. A pair of VIProtex guards saw Kurt enter the room and marched toward him. Three others were waiting beside the stage. He studied their gun belts, the stripes down their pants, wanting some small detail to give away the ones behind the flashlights.

Only Arnold Metcalf and the Arizona congressman remained seated at their table. Sipping cocktails, conferring quietly, their demeanor seemed peevish and impatient, annoyed by the delay. Neal Staggs stood behind them, pressing an earplug with his index finger, auditing a message.

"Excuse me, sir," said one of the guards trying to intercept Kurt. "Your invitation, please."

Wending between tables, knocking chairs out of his way, Kurt outmaneuvered them, reaching the host's table first. His appearance shook the congressman. A look of terror overcame Metcalf's stolid bearing.

"Good lord, man!" said the congressman. "What's going on out there?"

Staggs rushed around the table, signaling to the other guards for more help.

"I'm here to update Mr. Metcalf's résumé for you," Kurt said, blinking, his thoughts growing fuzzier, more disjointed. "When you give him the lifetime achievement award tonight, Congressman, add the name Katrina Pfeil to his list of problems solved."

Two guards seized Kurt but he offered no resistance.

"Congratulations, Staggs," he said. "You can collect your bonus now. She's dead. But she took Chilcutt out with her. Go find yourself another bomber."

The congressman stood up. "Who is this guy?" he asked. "What on earth is he talking about?"

"These men are killers," Kurt said, pointing at Metcalf and Staggs. "You sure you want to break bread with killers, Congressman?"

Staggs snapped his fingers. "Take him out of here," he instructed the guards.

The disturbance had captured the attention of the few banquet guests still seated at their tables. They rose and drifted toward the confrontation. Workingpeople without style or pretense. Stubborn cusses like Ned Carr, tough, no nonsense, fiercely independent, holding on desperately to the only dream they knew. They deserved better than Arnold Metcalf.

"Folks, don't ever trust a slick lawyer like Metcalf with your money or your property," Kurt told them. "He'll trade everything you believe in to the highest bidder."

"Get him out of here!" Staggs commanded.

Kurt broke loose from the guards and threw a punch

at the ex-agent, missing badly, losing balance, falling to his knees. Hands were all over him at once, gripping his shirt, his legs, dragging him across the carpet. Bystanders were raising their voices but he couldn't understand a word. His body had gone limp, his head was spinning, his throat dry and burning.

"Let him go," he heard someone say. Jesse Nighthawk was standing in the doorway of the banquet hall, the .45 visible in his waistband. Two EMS medics were waiting behind him.

"Get away from him!" Meredith was on her knees beside Kurt, cradling his burning head in her lap. "We're taking this man to the hospital."

48

AFTER TWO DAYS in a Las Vegas hospital he was transported back to Aspen Valley for another week of intensive treatment. The burns were minor but the knife infection had spread rapidly and Dr. Perry placed him on round-the-clock IVs of antibiotics, glucose, and painkillers. He was unable to attend Tyler's funeral or to help in any way with the disposition of Kat's cremated remains, which were returned to her friends in Oregon to be spread over an old-growth forest in the Siskiyou Mountains. The outpouring of cards and flowers from Aspen well-wishers was overwhelming, both for Kat and for Kurt, but he had no appetite for visitors and didn't return phone calls. His only consolation came from seeing Lennon and Hunter every afternoon, listening to the comforting timbre of their voices while he floated off to neverland. Once, in the middle of a deep dream, he heard someone speak his name and thought it was his dead brother standing at the bedside.

"Bert, where have you been?" he asked.

"No, Kurt, it's Nathan Carr."

Nathan was a husky fellow with a trimmed beard

and round rimless glasses. He had a kind smile. Kurt reached out and squeezed his hand.

"This is my uncle," Hunter said, leaning against the man's leg. "He knew my mom."

"I wanted to come by and say hello," Nathan said. "I'll be here for a couple of weeks, straightening out Pop's affairs. We'll talk when you're feeling better."

"Nate," Kurt said, refusing to release his hand until he understood everything clearly. "He wears a size one shoe. He doesn't like milk on his cereal."

When Kurt opened his eyes again, the room was dark and silent. He wondered if he'd dreamed Nathan's appearance. A volunteer wheeled in the dinner cart, and there was a note from Miles under a coffee cup: *The shitbirds have come home to roost. But it ain't over till it's over.*

The same day, or maybe the next, Kurt woke from a nap to find Sheriff Dan the Man Davenport sitting in a chair across the room. "I figured this was the only way I could git you to tell me about that Dumpster," he said with a grin. "And I brung you a card signed by my boys in Garfield County."

Kurt was touched by everyone's sincerity. He didn't know what he'd done to receive so much attention. So much kindness.

Meredith arrived bearing magazines and chocolates, and the only good news he'd heard since this whole nightmare began. "Lee fired VIProtex as his security consultants," she told him. "It's got to be an incredible loss of revenue for them. We were using their services in three states. When the home office crunches those numbers, Neal Staggs may have to look for another job."

As he was dozing off one evening, the telephone rang on his bedside table. "Hello, little brother," the speaker said, the connection so poor he could've been calling from Borneo.

"Jake?" Kurt didn't believe he was hearing this man's voice again.

"Tell me what happened." Calm, businesslike.

"I'm a fool," he said in a sleepy mumble. "I didn't know they were following me and I led them straight to her."

Jake Pfeil sighed into the line, his helplessness audible from a million miles away. "You aren't a very good cop, little brother. Maybe you ought to go back to selling camping gear."

Kurt wasn't certain if this was real or another fever dream. He ran his hand over the condensation on a water pitcher and wet his face. "Your sister was a wonderful woman," he said. "I should have married her twenty years ago."

Listening to the connection was like dialing the bands on a shortwave radio, a warp of high-pitched frequencies and galactic wind and faint otherworldly voices.

"When she was just a little thing, three or four, I used to put her on my shoulders and hike up the mountain. She loved to pick serviceberries and bring them home to make pies with Mother. You and me and Bert, we showed her how to fly-fish in the creek."

"I haven't forgotten."

"You were there, little brother. You saw it all go down. How come you didn't help her?"

Every waking minute in this hospital bed Kurt had

been asking himself the same question. "I tried, Jake," he said. "She didn't want my help."

The line crackled, a catch in Jake's breath. "Who were they?" he asked. "Same people that hurt her in Oregon?"

"Same profile," Kurt said. "She must've been very good at what she did. They didn't want her back in the game."

"I'm acquainted with VIProtex. Some of my associates use their bodyguards," he said. "Is there a name in their organization I should direct my attention to?"

"An old friend of yours. Neal Staggs."

When Staggs was in the Denver bureau, he had conducted a decade-long investigation of Jake Pfeil's illegal drug activities. Because of Neal Staggs, Jake was living in a foreign country, a fugitive from justice, his American assets frozen, several million dollars in real estate and other investments.

"After the Feds put him out to pasture he went to work for VIProtex. Colorado region. He was at the Sahara for the convention."

"So that's what this is all about," Jake said. "Neal Staggs sticking another knife in my back. I should have killed that prick when I had the chance."

"Don't flatter yourself, Jake. Your sister's death is a lot bigger than your feud with Staggs."

Jake seemed to be evaluating the rebuke. "She was the last family I had in this world," he said finally. "They're all gone now. You know how it feels when you lose someone close. I've got a hole in my heart, little brother. When does that go away?"

"It never goes away, Jake. You learn to breathe different."

The phone static sounded like electron waves crashing over a dark metallic shore. "Who is this guy Arnold Metcalf?" Jake asked. "Did he have a problem with my sister?"

Kurt wasn't surprised to hear Jake say the man's name. "I don't know for certain."

"We both want the same thing here. Let me help."

"I'm not going to finger Metcalf for you, Jake. I don't know how involved he was. He's a rotten bastard, but I have no evidence that he was after Kat."

"I'm offering my services, little brother. I can accomplish in a few days what it will take your department two years to pull together."

"It may take two years, it may take three. We'll get it done. Don't become a player, Jake. I'll sleep better if you stay out."

"It's too late for that now. My sister's dead and I've got this hole in my heart. Something's got to make it go away."

"Don't, Jake." Kurt didn't know how many enemies Jake Pfeil had disposed of in his life.

"Are they taking good care of you, Kurt? Let them spoil you a little. You and me, we're the only ones left from the old days. We deserve attention."

Kurt had every reason to hate this man for the mess he'd made of Bert's life. And Meg's. But in that moment he felt only pity and sorrow and emptiness.

"Good night, little brother. Treat yourself right. You're not getting any younger."

Kurt lay awake for hours replaying the conversation in his mind. When he did finally drift off, numbed by Percodan, he dreamed the old dream of black corridors and creaking doors. He had found Kat alive in a dark room, standing in her pajamas near a window, the cold night wind blowing gauzy drapes around her slender body. *It will come to you,* she said, swaying her hands to catch the aspen leaves fluttering about the room. *The answer is always in the leaves.* He woke in a hot sweat and buzzed for the night nurse, begging for another painkiller.

The day before he was released from the hospital, the Las Vegas homicide investigator who had interviewed him in the emergency room flew to Aspen to question him again, and Kurt requested that Muffin Brown and Corky Marcus sit in on the discussion. Detective Nick DiMeo was clearly dubious about the larger implications of Kat's death and insisted on treating the case as a fatal confrontation between a security guard and a deranged Green Briar sniper.

"You're my only witness and you're telling me you can't ID a single perp because all you saw was their striped pants," the detective said. He was a career man with a Jersey accent, a cheap suit, and a chipped front tooth. Kurt didn't want to know where he'd received his training. "Am I correct about the pants, Sheriff Muller?"

"It was dark."

"And so is this investigation," DiMeo said, closing his notepad.

"I can ID James Joseph Chilcutt of Grand Junction, Colorado, and swear in court that he intended to kill us both."

DiMeo raised a skeptical eyebrow. "The VIProtex people say this Chilcutt was checking out a report about a possible sniper in the parking garage. They say you were in the convention hall earlier, causing trouble yourself. What were you doing in Vegas, Sheriff Muller? Why were you in the garage? Are you some kind of militant like the deceased Miss Pfeil?"

"I don't like the direction this conversation is taking," Corky said. "Is my client under investigation here?"

The homicide detective smiled caustically and slipped the notepad into his suit jacket. "Let me give your client some free advice," he said. "Next time he's in somebody else's jurisdiction it's common courtesy to inform law enforcement what he's doing on their stoop. Otherwise things can get real hinky. I see a man packing a piece in a shoulder holster, I'm going to pull my own. Do I make myself clear, people?"

"I'm sorry I didn't check in, Detective," Kurt said. "There was no time."

"Next time, make time. Good day, folks. Got a plane to catch." He dropped a business card on Kurt's sheeted legs. "You remember anything else about these assailants in the striped pants, give me a call."

After he left, Muffin stood up and kicked a chair. "That asshole is going to deep-six this whole case in his dead file."

Corky ran a hand through his mop of hair. "He came here to let you know he's doing you a big favor, one cop to another, by not coming after you, Kurt." He shook his head. "Next time you hear from him, a couple of years from now, he'll be calling in the debt."

Muffin walked to the window and stared out at the green glade encircling the picnic tables. A patient wearing a terry bathrobe was eating breakfast with her family. "Let's take this to Don," she said. Donald Harrigan was the local DA, a good man. "We've got enough to make a case in Pitkin County, don't we, Corky?"

Corky looked dispirited. "Did your demolitions expert determine that Ned's death was the result of intentional tampering?"

"No," Kurt said.

"Can anyone identify who shot Tyler in the Lone Ute?"

"No."

"Can you ID any of the dirt-bikers who chased you in the pickup?"

Kurt closed his eyes.

"We've got Gillespie on tape!" Muffin said. "Goddammit, that should count for something, Corky."

"Can you prove that the deceased police officer was employed by either VIProtex or Arnold Metcalf?"

There was a long silence. When Kurt opened his eyes, he saw that Muffin was sitting on the floor next to the central air panel, frustration souring her handsome face.

"I've got to get back to school," Corky said, rising from his chair with the legal briefcase he'd brought to impress the detective. Kurt knew it was stuffed with math tests and fourth-grade workbooks. "I'm sorry, guys. I wish I could be more optimistic. Don doesn't have jack to work with."

A quarter of an hour passed before Muffin said anything or budged from the floor. Kurt was depressed by his own inadequacy and extremely tired of lying in this bed. He stared out the large glass window, watching the aspen leaves quiver in the spring breeze, a magical green trembling that had never ceased to enchant him.

"Where did you get these?" Muffin asked, flipping

through the environmental magazines Meredith had left behind. "Jesus, Kurt. Maybe that guy DiMeo was right about you," she said, studying a photograph that had caught her eye. "Katrina and her friends must have rubbed off on you. Are you becoming some kind of ecomilitant tree hugger?"

She bumped the table inadvertently and the precarious stack of magazines tumbled to the floor. "Damn," she said, kneeling down to gather the scattered pages. "Sorry I messed up your little library here."

Kurt sat up in bed. He remembered something, the ghosts of a dream. *The answer is always in the leaves.* "Muffin," he said, "I want you to go to my house—to my father's study—and bring me that pile of articles on the desk next to the telephone."

Muffin stood up, her face red from exertion, and stashed the jumble of magazines on a dresser. "You don't have enough reading material here?" she asked, straightening the assortment of glossy covers.

"It's there somewhere," he said. "It's got to be."

"What, Kurt?"

"The thing that'll ruin his sleep."

He was going to read every bloody word of every bloody article ever published about the Free West Rebellion—spend the rest of his life in a library if he had to—until he found a way to stop Arnold Metcalf.

49

THE DISCLOSURE OF Ned Carr's final will and testament was scheduled for the first Wednesday in June, and Kurt flew to Colorado Springs with Nathan Carr, Hunter, and Corky Marcus to attend the reading. Security on the twentieth floor was even tighter than before. A VIProtex guard detained them at the entrance to the FWLC reception area and waved a metal-detector wand over the three adults, then released them into the custody of a squadron of lantern-jawed security officers who marched them like prisoners of war down the long sun-bathed corridor to Metcalf's suite. Kurt felt like Abu Nidal entering the UN.

When Metcalf introduced himself to Nathan and Hunter, the attorney appeared unusually tense, his high forehead glistening with perspiration. His eyes darted nervously at Kurt as if he expected something sudden and inappropriate to take place. "I'm very pleased to meet you, young man," he said, stooping to shake Hunter's hand. "I knew your grandfather quite well and respected his tenacious spirit."

Isn't that why you had him killed? Kurt wanted to ask. *That unpredictable spirit.*

Attended by efficient young clerks with unmistakable Ivy League breeding, the group settled around the conference table and Metcalf wasted no time getting the reading under way. The VIProtex guards stationed themselves close by, hands behind their backs, legs spread at parade rest, and the entire ceremony struck Kurt as ostentatious and excessively vigilant. He wondered why all the heightened security over a few harmless visitors from Aspen.

There were no surprises in the will. The FWLC draft nullified any previously existing wills, as they knew it would, naming Hunter as sole beneficiary of sixty percent of the "estate" and granting the other forty percent to the Free West Legal Coalition "for their outstanding generosity and support of my enterprise." Allegedly written by Ned himself, the narrative praised the law foundation as the savior of the independent hardrock miner in a hostile, overregulated world. *Couldn't have survived without their expertise. Came to my defense at a crucial moment in my life. Provided more than legal assistance. Courage, moral conviction, friendship.* Et cetera, et cetera. Not a word of it in Ned's singularly recognizable voice. And the spelling was no doubt perfect.

Afterward Arnold Metcalf sank back in his chair and whispered something to the clerk sitting beside him, and she rose to fix him a Scotch at the bar. "We're delighted to be your new partner, young Mr. Carr," he said to Hunter, who was occupied with the rules of a contest on the back of a Coke can and didn't appear to be listening. "We look forward to a long and prosperous friendship. I'm sure there will be many mutually beneficial projects in our future."

"I have a question," Hunter said, his chin resting on the table, tired and grumpy from the early-morning plane ride. Kurt was surprised that the child was attentive enough to speak.

"Yes, certainly," Metcalf said, peering over his reading glasses like a bemused librarian.

"Am I the boss?"

There was polite laughter around the table. "Yes, you are," Metcalf nodded. "The controlling interest."

"Then I don't want anybody going into the mines anymore. They're too dangerous. That's how my grandpa and Tyler got killed."

The law clerks exchanged glances. Metcalf eyed Kurt with suspicion, as if he'd coached the boy to say this. "We'll all have to be very careful, then, won't we?" the attorney said. "Human health and safety should be our primary concerns."

Nathan Carr was sitting back from the table with a leg crossed over his knee. "Hunter and I have discussed this a lot," he said. Nathan had turned out to be a patient, thoughtful man with a dry sense of humor, and Kurt had come to like him very much during the week he had stayed at the Muller home. "We've talked about shutting down any active operations, such as they are, and opening up the mines for guided tour groups. We'll need a sizable investment to make them people-ready, and insurance will be a bear, but Leighton Lamar has offered to help on our end."

"I see," said Metcalf, steepling his fingers.

"It's a clean, constructive way to keep my father's legacy alive," Nathan said. "Folks will get a chance to see what he's been doing for the past fifty years, and what the early miners started, without messing up the mountain and the backcountry any more than it already is."

Metcalf sipped his Scotch. This kind of talk made him uneasy.

"Sounds like a sensible solution to me," Kurt said, offering the attorney a dark ironic smile. "Especially since those old silver mines are flat-out worthless, Mr. Metcalf. Who could possibly be interested in working them again?"

Without recognizing Kurt's remarks, Metcalf jotted something on a yellow pad and handed the note to his assistant. "I see we have much to discuss at our first investors' meeting, gentlemen. Perhaps we should set a date."

After a brief interchange about calendars and commitments, the meeting was abruptly adjourned and the law clerks began to clear the conference table like frenzied waiters. Within minutes they had dashed out of the suite with armloads of documents, leaving the guards to watch over the Aspenites. Corky Marcus remained in his chair and took his time examining the will itself. "It's Ned's signature," he said to Kurt in a quiet aside. "Everything looks kosher on the face of it. I don't find any improprieties with they way they've managed this."

"Mr. Marcus, that's your copy to keep," Metcalf said from across the room. He had gone to the bar to splash more ice in his drink. "My staff will be happy to provide you with any other paperwork you require. If you like, we can copy Ned's correspondence with our foundation over the past two years."

"Thank you, Mr. Metcalf," Corky said. "I will take you up on that offer."

Kurt asked Corky to accompany Hunter and Nathan

back to the lobby. "Give me a few minutes alone with the new partner," he said.

Two of the guards remained with Kurt in the suite. He wandered over to the couch and stood looking at the large painting of the cowboy mail-carrier trudging through deep snow. "A party just isn't a party without our old friend Neal Staggs," he said. "Where was he today, Arnold? Have they reassigned him already? That fella can't keep a steady job, can he?"

"I'm a busy man, Muller. What's on your mind?"

"Platinum," Kurt said.

There was a long silence, and then Metcalf addressed the guards. "Wait outside the door, gentlemen. I'll call if I need you."

After they left, Kurt went to the bar and poured himself a Scotch on the rocks. Glenlivet 21. Nothing but the best for the Free West Legal Coalition. "I know about the South Africans," he said. "I know that Ned didn't want them messing around in his mines and threatened to poison the deal." He swirled the ice in his glass. "But there was too much money up for grabs to let him do that, wasn't there, Arnold?"

Metcalf sat behind his sprawling desk. He seemed worn down by the reading and loosened his tie. "Your speculations run to the melodramatic, my friend. But I will grant you this—there is money to be made," he said. "Enough to send the kid to the best schools and provide him with a lifestyle beyond his wildest dreams. And there's surely something in this for you too. The Carrs appreciate all you've done for them. Hell, if they don't cut you in, I will. Your persistence should be rewarded."

Perhaps it wasn't the reading that had produced this

weary look. But something was troubling Arnold Metcalf. Something had happened to ring this entire floor in paranoia.

"An extra fifty grand a year can buy a lot of toys for you and your son, Muller. Why don't you come to your senses and help me see this thing through? It doesn't have to be a war. Everybody can walk away a winner."

"I don't know, Arnold. I hear you saying those same words to Ned right before you had his brains blown out."

Metcalf's expression tightened. "Ned was getting long of tooth and had become overwrought and irrational," he said. "Still, we might have been able to work everything out had he not insisted on bringing in outside influences who do not share our philosophy. Our" —he paused, reflecting, tapping his fingertips together —"cultural values."

Kurt smiled at him. "You're talking about Indians, aren't you?"

The attorney showed no reaction. "I know the kind of stock you come from, Muller. You and I, we speak the same language. We wouldn't have had the misunderstandings that came between Ned Carr and me." He dawdled with the Scotch glass in front of him. "Why don't you take some time and reexamine your feelings about me and my organization? Consider the opportunities available. An arrangement like this could secure your son's future. Don't let anger be your guiding principle."

Kurt sipped the expensive Scotch and smiled again. "Arnold, you're a very good judge of character. I *am* from strong stock. I've got so much integrity and sound business sense I would be a fool to get involved with an organization that's in trouble with the IRS."

Metcalf stopped playing with his fingers. The statement had caused a sudden frown.

"You were right when you said I ought to learn more about the 501-C tax status," Kurt said. "So I did some research on that very topic and guess what I discovered? The IRS insists that a public-interest firm like yours cannot take on a case that directly benefits someone on your board, or a major contributor to your cause. You aren't allowed to provide insider profits to your sponsors, Arnold. But that's what this platinum deal looks like to me. The Riebeeck Mining Corporation is one of your most loyal supporters. Last year they contributed a hundred thousand dollars to the Free West Legal Coalition. And you've used your pro bono services for Ned Carr to send a big strike their way."

"You're grasping at straws," Metcalf said, taking a long drink of Scotch.

"Well, Arnold, that's what broke the camel's back, isn't it?" He reached in his suit jacket and withdrew a folded document. "Here's the letter from the IRS saying they intend to look into my allegations." He had enlisted Meredith and her reading group to help him with the research. "I've found four cases on your docket where a ruling in your favor will benefit Free West patrons and members of your board." He dropped the letter on Metcalf's desk. "Expect a phone call from the regional director in Denver, a man named Marvin Rainwater. He seems real interested in your story. If I were you, I'd warm up the shredders, Arnold. It would be a damned shame if you lost your nonprofit status."

He looked around the opulent suite. "You wouldn't be able to run this place anymore, would you?"

Kurt crossed the room and stopped to retrieve his old leather briefcase lying on the conference table. "Marvin Rainwater," he said, shaking his head. "You know, that almost sounds like an Indian name."

When he opened the door to leave, the two VIProtex guards were waiting for him in the corridor. Tall, stern young men, their arms rippling with pumped-up muscle, thumbs latched in their gun belts. Suddenly a tiny red light went on in the back of Kurt's head and he turned around, staring back at Metcalf across the long expanse of carpet. The man hadn't moved from his chair. He was gazing numbly at the letter on his desk.

"You've heard from Jake Pfeil," Kurt said.

Metcalf's eyes shifted uncertainly. Enough to tell him it was true.

"I've known Jake a long time," Kurt said. "He's a fair man. If you didn't have anything to do with his sister's death, you don't have anything to worry about." He studied the two guards, the arrogant set of their bodies. "But if you did, Arnold, all the security in the world won't stop him from killing you."

Metcalf stood up. The blinds had been drawn across those magnificent glass walls and there was scant natural sunlight in the suite. Without his glasses the attorney's eyes appeared dark and hollow. He looked like a marked man living out his days in a dingy hotel.

"So long, partner," Kurt said as the two guards came forward to escort him away. "See you on the tour bus."

50

TWO HUNDRED PEOPLE showed up for Hunter's going-away party on Aspen Mountain. At the boy's request, McDonald's catered the affair and provided a huge humming, air-filled Moon Walk for the kids to bounce around in. Despite the festive atmosphere and the many good friends gathered around the picnic tables, Kurt was in a melancholy mood and wandered away from the group to sit on a boulder and take in the expansive green silence of Annie Basin on the south side of the mountain. This was where he had stood with Kat and Randy only a month ago, surveying the forest with binoculars. Since that morning too much death and ill will had darkened Kurt's spirit, and he wondered if there was anything in this world that could patch the hole in his own heart.

"Mind if I join you?"

Meg looked remarkably euphoric today, exhilarated by all the children frolicking about the picnic site, somersaulting in the Moon Walk. This was her idea of heaven.

"The Carrs are nice people, Kurt," she said, sitting beside him on the boulder. "I just had a wonderful conversation with Susan." Nathan's wife. He had brought his family to Aspen to meet Hunter and see where Dad had grown up. "She said they intend to add on to the Carr cabin and come back for a month every summer. Maybe at Christmas to ski."

Kurt watched Nathan's children, Daniel and Claire, chase after Lennon in a game of tag. Kurt had spent the past few days with them and knew how fortunate Hunter was to be joining such a fine family.

"Is everything okay, Kurt? You're awfully quiet today."

He tried to smile but the effort seemed strained. "I know Hunter has to leave, but I feel bad for Lennon. For both of them. I guess I'm having trouble with all this loss."

She stood up and stepped to the rock ledge, gazing out over the basin. A solitary hawk circled the fir forest below.

"This has got to be a hard time for you. Maybe you should talk with someone professional."

He listened to the children shrieking, the burble of conversation. Talk was always inadequate.

"Were you in love with her?"

Ah, yes, love, Kat had once said to him. *It makes fools of us all.*

"Maybe," he said. "I was beginning to recognize the signs."

In the long ensuing silence he watched her wavy auburn hair ripple in the breeze and remembered the many years when it had fallen to the middle of her back, a frizzy luxurious mane. "You're pretty serious about that Bhajan guy, aren't you?" he said.

"We're thinking about having a baby."

It didn't come as a surprise. Meg was forty-three, facing her limitations. She had always wanted another child. "Then I won't be the only parent in a wheelchair at my kid's high school graduation," he said.

She smiled at his remark. "How do you think Lennon will feel about a new baby?"

"Excited. He's been wanting a brother or sister for a long time now."

She rolled her neck, a yoga exercise, and stared off into the hazy summer light. "And how about you?"

Struggling, he thought. *Still struggling.* "You're a grown-up, Meg. You don't need my permission to be happy."

She nodded slowly and turned around, toeing at a loose rock, nudging it away with the edge of her hiking boot. "I understand you're officially back on the job as the Pitkin County sheriff," she said.

He sighed deeply. "We need the income. I owe the town of Carbondale five thousand dollars. Don't ask why."

He expected one of her lectures on the dangers of the job. Instead she said, "I'm proud of you for the way you've handled this whole horrible mess. I may have to revise my opinion of you as a cop."

Muffin Brown blew a loud police whistle, capturing everyone's attention. Nathan and Susan Carr began to wave and call in the picnickers scattered about the area.

"They're opening gifts. Come on," Meg said, taking his arm. "Let's go see what kind of loot he's getting."

Hunter sat at a table piled with presents and tore into the wrappings, uncovering the mementos brought by townspeople. A silver aspen-leaf key chain, ski patches, local T-shirts, a Colorado refrigerator magnet, a Rockies baseball cap, a framed painting of the Roaring Fork River. Kurt and Lennon were giving him three polished stones for his rock collection. The children from his kindergarten class had made drawings of the school and pooled their money to buy a bat feeder. Watching Hunter grow more and more excited by the wonderful surprises, Kurt looked around for Lennon and saw that his son was standing next to Meg, caught up in the celebration as if it were his own. Several times they had discussed Hunter's leaving, and Lennon was philosophical about it. His friend would come back every summer. They could talk on the phone, write letters when they learned to write better. Kurt marveled at the innocent optimism of children. They refused to believe that the people they loved could disappear from their lives.

Preoccupied with his brooding thoughts, he hadn't noticed Jesse Nighthawk until the man emerged from the back of the crowd and pushed his way to the picnic table. Hunter was opening his last present but stopped abruptly when the imposing figure squatted down in front of him, a stranger wearing a black cowboy hat with a long feather stuck in the band. "Here ya go, young fella," he said, handing the boy a leather pouch. "I brought you something from our people."

Hunter stared at the man, then glanced sheepishly at Kurt for some explanation. "Go ahead and open it," Kurt said.

Inside the pouch was an eagle-bone choker, identical to the one Jesse was wearing.

"Soon you will be making a long journey to another land, but I want you to always remember that you once roamed these mountains," Jesse said, gently tying the choker around Hunter's neck. "You are Weminuche Ute, the Blue Sky People. Your name is Echohawk. Go and make a sound that rings forever."

Kurt looked over at Meg and Lennon, spooned together, watching the ceremony with a reverent awe.

Jesse Nighthawk dug his fingers into the earth and scooped out a handful of dirt. "This is your mother," he said, showing Hunter the dark soil. He lifted the boy's T-shirt and rubbed the dirt over his bare chest. "Carry her with you all the rest of your days."

With this blessing Kurt's heart lifted and he felt himself letting go.

Acknowledgments

MY SINCERE GRATITUDE to the writers whose books and articles have shed light on various aspects of this work, especially David Helvarg, John D. Leshy, Oliver Houck, Carl Deal, Rudolph C. Rÿser, Nancy Wood, and Wilson Rockwell. Thanks to Don Stuber for introducing important material, to Doug Hattersley and Ben Ryberg for answering my questions, and to Holt Williamson for filling my mailbox with background information. And a great big *abrazo* to Paul Foreman, the last Renaissance man, who can speak with authority about hardrock mining and Pliny the Elder in the same sentence.

I also extend my appreciation to Esther Newberg, who has believed in Kurt from the beginning, and to Susan Kamil, who pushes me to make it better.